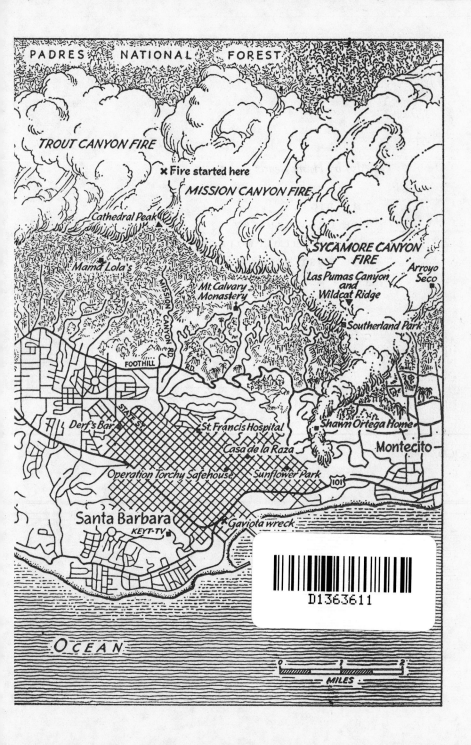

HANK SEARLS

Firewind

DOUBLEDAY & COMPANY, INC.
GARDEN CITY, NEW YORK
1981

Library of Congress Cataloging in Publication Data

Searls, Henry.
  Firewind.

  I. Title.
PS3569.E18F57   813'.54

ISBN: 0-385-17084-X
Library of Congress Catalog Card Number 80-648
Copyright © 1981 by Hank Searls
All Rights Reserved
Printed in the United States of America
First Edition

For Shawn and Brink, Crissy and Nicole, and even Armando Castillo. And for Bunny, who allowed them and the other beings in this book, all fictional, to live with us so long.

When I am dead let fire destroy the world;
it matters not to me, for I am safe.

Anonymous
Greek Anthology
Book IX
Fragment 430

ONE

Firebugs

One

She had been working the Kentucky Fried Chicken counter alone since the evening rush began at six. Now it was 9 P.M. and the place was empty. It was time, thank God, to close. She was seven weeks pregnant and her bladder was bursting.

She had white California teeth and a surfer's tan. In the summer she stayed slim for the beach, but by this first week of December she had thickened from sneaking too many chicken thighs and from munching carrot cakes when she grew bored.

She heard the Colonel's lighted bucket rattling on the roof. Another Santa Ana wind was beginning. She hated them. They whipped sand along the beach, doubled the breakers against themselves, and killed the surf for days. She felt irritated and hassled by fate. Last winter it had been rain and flood from February on. This winter it was wind. Pregnant or not, it would be a drag to have to quit surfing now, during the Christmas semester break.

She was about to lock up and break for the john when she saw someone at the door. It was the fat young Chicano mechanic from the corner gas station. He blew in on a warm gust that kept the entrance open behind him. He muscled it closed. Smiling bravely, she jigged in distress while he tried to decide between Ribs and the Thrift.

He decided Thrift, so she punched a button and let the computer disgorge the tab. He was a dollar short. "Bring it tomorrow," she said, and waited for the inside girl to hand his box through the window. Then she passed it to the Chicano, who fumbled it and dropped it on the counter. It spilled and she tried to grin over her discomfort as they repacked it together.

"Santa Ana," he apologized. "You know?"

She understood. The winds transformed her Marine Biology lab partner at UCSB into a ten-thumbed klutz. Plus driving her room-mate, father of her unborn child, up the wall. She'd heard that the dry, howling gales drove up the suicide rate and knew that they raised the price of marijuana on the streets of Isla Vista.

When the Chicano left she quickly flicked a switch to darken and stop the Colonel's bucket rotating on the roof, then she turned out the lights on a plastic Christmas tree and locked the door. As instructed, she left fourteen dollars in the open register to placate a hypothetical burglar. But the rest of the day's receipts—$824.68—were in the locked safe before she whisked through the swinging panels to the kitchen.

The inside girl, a lovely blond cretin who seemed to gobble chicken by the ton without gaining a pound or an inch, was standing over the stove, drumstick in hand, grease rolling down her classic chin. Silently, she offered a portion.

"No," mumbled the counter girl, in agony. "Got to go, got to go, got to go. Lock up when you leave." She swung through the fire doors to a corridor.

The Flake's apron hung outside the biffy by the exit, so she assumed he had split. Desperately, she tugged at the toilet door. It resisted, then snapped open in a cloud of smoke. She stared at the Flake, sitting on the john.

"Sorry," she coughed, face flaming, and slammed the door.

In shock, she punched out and stumbled from the employees' entrance to the parking lot. *Sorry?* Hell, it hadn't been her fault. And, my God, couldn't he have waited to get home, or wherever?

She'd make it to the john in the gas station, or somewhere, before it was too late.

She'd known he was freaky. But she'd seen a more human expression on the face of a bull bass, guarding its hole, when she was diving for abalone off the Goleta rocks.

A bearded, stoop-shouldered bass, in a fry cook's hat, askew, mouth gaping, with his thing in hand, big as a moray eel . . .

And the smoke? He didn't smoke cigarettes, as far as she knew. It hadn't smelled like tobacco anyway, or pot. More like plain paper.

Burning *paper* in the sink, while he masturbated? Why?

Nothing behind those eyes, nothing.

She was through here, forever. She'd quit tomorrow. By phone.

It was a wonder she hadn't wet her pants.

Two

Lieutenant Shawn Ortega, of Santa Barbara County Sheriff's Homicide, watched the white-cowled Franciscan Sister probing for the vein in Brink's arm.

"When he leaves, Sister," Brink stage-whispered from the pillow, "when the pig goes, come back, and you and me, we'll get it on, right?"

The nun was forty, with owl eyeglasses, and apparently not too long from Ireland. She glanced up at Shawn. "Now, what's he mean by that, Leftenant?"

Shawn shook his head. The sight of Brink's wasted arm, once the size of another man's calf, had brought him suddenly to the edge of tears. His throat caught and he turned, a little too quickly, to gaze out the hospital window. Six foot three, one ninety-eight, square-jawed, and ordinarily police-taciturn, he envisioned himself sniffling before them both.

"What does he mean?" the nurse persisted.

"Nothing, probably."

"I'm sure," she scoffed. "Ah!"

In the window glass, he saw her bend closer to the bed. She must have found the vein. Every night it seemed to get smaller. A month ago it would have been standing out like a steel cable from the bronzed forearm. He heard Brink grunt: "*Shit!* That stuff's useless as balls on the Pope—And look, darlin', could ye be practicin' on an orange or somethin', before the next—?" He began to cough and Shawn felt his own muscles tense.

"Next time," the nun warned, gathering her tray, "I'll be askin' Doctor what you meant!"

"Means . . . under those robes," Brink managed, "there's . . . the body . . . of a woman full of passion . . . and desire."

The nun snorted and left. Brink continued to hack. With every explosion, Shawn felt himself tense. He wanted to fluff the pillow, raise Brink's head, somehow stop the agony, but he knew it was useless and would only reveal the tears in his eyes.

Unbelievable. He hadn't cried since his parents' funeral. Probably the new Santa Ana, hot with the breath of the distant Mojave, frying his brain. God help the watch commander. The phone must be ringing already, for the crazies would be feeling it, too.

Trying to ignore Brink's coughing, he gazed at the city below. The air was desert-clear. A green running light on a northbound freighter seemed near enough to touch, though the ship was fifteen miles from where he stood, plowing the Santa Barbara Channel between the mainland and the island of Santa Cruz.

A quick gust from San Marcos Pass ripped seaward. The pane shivered and the crystal lights in the marina bounced.

Santa Ana wind, Santana, Diablo, Devil Wind, Witch's Wind. A Santa Ana in 1836 had blown Richard Henry Dana, anchored below in the shelter of Goleta Point, halfway to Hawaii. The wind was an evil of his own life since infancy.

Viento de fuego—"firewind"—his grandfather called the hot, dry gales. Sipping Coors last night at sunset on the patio, Irish eyes watering, el Viejito had wrinkled his great Spanish nose at some canyon breeze nobody else had noticed.

"Another one. That's the curse of our lands, *hijo.*"

Not *our* lands, Shawn had thought. No, Don Miguel Ortega y Riordan, poet, ranchero, genius *manqué*. Not your lands for very long, never mine at all, some of them Brink's lands today, probably, if ever we bothered to check. The last of them gone fifty years ago, even if you care to forget it. Anyway, Anglo land now, from the surf to the mountains of Santa Ynez.

Face it, Viejo. We have always lived on treacherous earth, but the curse on our lands was not wind, drought, quake, flood, fire, or Yankee. It was us.

Brink's coughing peaked in a strangling paroxysm. He spit into a Kleenex and lay back. Somewhere the wind was howling through an elevator shaft, or a window not quite shut. Brink cocked his head. "Another one?" he panted. "They set Red Flag Alert?"

"Not when I left the station." Anyway, his own voice had steadied.

"They better, this wind."

"They will."

But Red Flag Alert or not, more fires would come. If not from one firebug or another, then from the exhaust of a passing Diesel, a butt tossed from a car, or a beam of sunlight through a Coke bottle. And if not this Santa Ana, the next.

For, time and again, all during late summer and into the fall and winter, the hot winds had blown, diminished, begun again, and still no storm in sight at sea. Three years ago fires had swept the country, stripping it of the brush that held mountain soil in rains; then the cloudbursts and floods of '80 had scoured the canyons but seeded them with growing fuel. Now drought had baked it to tinder, and it was far past the normal fire season.

The chaparral in Los Padres National Forest, embracing city and harbor, was like kindling. Manzanita bushes had been squealing in the winds all summer and fall. Toyon clumps and greasewood rattled like ticking bombs. The canyon streets of Montecito crackled in the breeze. The shingles on the hill homes were brittle as hot toast.

Towering stands of eucalyptus shading the foothill dwellings, deceptively cool, were heavy with oil, waiting to explode when the chaparral set them off.

And as usual when the dry winds blew, there were assholes setting fires, a dozen sets in two weeks.

But this year, hopefully, setting them only at the risk of arrest.

"They stake people out tonight?" yawned Brink.

"I think so." The Great Arson Stakeout—officially Operation Torchy, unofficially the Poison Oak Crawl, Chaparral Shuffle, or Barranca Ballbuster—was so secret that Shawn had discussed it with no other civilians, not even his own wife. But Brink was safely out of the stream of Santa Barbara gossip, and he'd told him about it days ago. "Patrol's supposed to have half a dozen guys up the canyons right now, plainclothes. San Antonio Road, Painted Cave Road, Sycamore Canyon. In campers and dune buggies."

"Hoping some bug'll ask them for a match," Brink muttered. "Lots of luck."

"You know Martinez? Stubby? Wears a goatee?"

Brink shrugged. "All you greaseballs look alike."

"Anyway, he's up by Ronald Reagan's ranch every night on a Yamaha with a sleeping bag. And my old female patrol partner."

"Porky Lousy-lay? He ought to get overtime, double." Brink punched his pillow and lay back again. "They got anybody up by my place?"

Brink's home was perched magnificently on the rim of Las Pumas Canyon, like a California condor waiting to take flight. The main house was a sprawling manor of tinted glass, oaken beams, and massive redwood timbers. The roofs were wood-shake, without a single red tile in sight. The home was the antithesis of Santa Barbara Spanish. Every dwelling for miles around was Casa this or Rancho that: Brink, who had built and named so many of them, had called his own place Wildcat Ridge.

The home, on five acres of oak-studded lawn, looked down on Brink's final—and crowning—residential development, Las Pumas Estates. The Estates were all properly Santa Bareño stucco and whitewashed adobe, with roof tiles, as Brink said, the color a newborn baby's ass. They had started at half a million dollars each, before the building freeze.

Down-canyon from the Estates lay the Southerland Botanical Park, on land he'd been forced, under protest, to cede the city to get permits to build the rest. Far below Wildcat Ridge, beneath Estates and Park, Santa Barbara gleamed, distantly hugging the plate-glass sea.

"*Somebody's* up Pumas," Shawn assured him. "Maybe city detectives or Forest Service."

"The DA himself?" Brink suggested. "Hey, Kelso's up there himself, handing out leftover campaign fliers on Las Pumas Drive!"

Kelso, the DA, was titular head of Operation Torchy and, quite properly, he was scared to death of the recent rash of fire-sets and the current Fire Danger Index. He apparently had everybody but the CIA up one canyon or another; the hills were alive with detectives and special agents, drawn from U. S. Forest Service, California Division of Forestry, even from the Air Force at Vandenberg and ONI from Point Mugu. Kelso had run on the strength of dissatisfaction over the previous DA's arson investigations, and had yet to indict his first firebug.

The city would bust his butt if Southerland Park got burned. He had sucked on foothill wealth in his campaign, too: Las Pumas Estates property owners would hang him if the next fire started there. "Relax," Shawn said. "Your buddies down the hill will see you're covered."

"They'd eat him alive if anybody set one in the Estates," agreed Brink. "Pricks . . ."

Brink, having made four and a half million unneeded dollars peopling the canyon below him with fellow millionaires, detested them all, like any builder once the tract was sold and the complaints came pouring in. And, of course, the higher you lived on Santa Barbara's slopes, the further you looked down on your neighbors.

Brink was tiring. Shawn moved to the bed and squeezed his shoulder. "Okay, junkie. She gave you your fix . . ."

Brink shook his head. "Stick around. Where was I when that penguin started pecking my arm?"

"Come on, guy. It's late."

"You can say that again," Brink muttered. "And it won't get earlier." He moved impatiently. "Where was I?"

Brink's single-minded recital of his unofficial will, through coughing, pain, and drugs, was probably motivated as much by hatred of the tax collector as by love for wife and son. But it was an awesome fight against sleep and pain and confusion. And fear—there must be fear, although Shawn saw, so far, only rage.

Shawn capitulated. "You had Nicole stuffing gold in the vault in your barbecue pit."

Brink looked vague. "Gold? Oh, yeah. Well, make sure she picks it up and does that. None of this *après demain* crap. *Tomorrow.* OK? Because, man, the IRS will seal those safe-deposit boxes before they close my fucking eyes. We got three drawers. Tell her she's got the keys: they're in her vanity case. Tell her to take out the treasury notes, too, and the Orange County municipals. They're unregistered: I don't want the IRS to even know she's got them. *Or* the executor, either." He held up three fingers. They looked gnarled, like Shawn's grandfather's. "Gold, treasury notes, municipals. OK?"

"I'll wait outside the bank," offered Shawn, "and follow her home." He didn't want to embarrass her by seeing how much there was, but he didn't want her ripped off en route, either.

"No. There's a shitpot-full in there. Ingots, fifty-pesos, Kruger-rands. Heavy. Go in and help her. OK?" The eyes closed for a moment, snapped open. "*OK?*"

"Of course. Look, you're on your can. Let's finish this tomorrow."

"I might not know my name by tomorrow. OK, when I check out, the IRS will inventory the house. So, before that, quick as you can, have a garage sale. Sell my bikes, and my tools and the . . ." His voice trailed off, he fought a yawn, and recovered. "OK?"

"The bikes, you'll have to sign the pink slips."

"Nicole will bring them down. Get seven-fifty for the Kawasaki. The Suzukis ought to go for nine. No checks. Cash."

Estate taxes. Every bit liquidated under the table would help. "Gotcha," Shawn promised. His voice was steady enough now, but he could still not trust himself to look into the blazing eyes.

"Sell everything you can. That pinball machine I was fixing. And, hey, the hang glider! And remember the VW engine, for if we built the gyrocopter? It's fuck-Uncle-Sam week. All cash."

They'd been going to start building the gyrocopter last summer. Then Shawn himself had postponed the project, because his wife wanted him to plant ceanothus in the back yard. Ceanothus! Which of course had died of thirst. Christ!

"Cash," Shawn affirmed. "OK." Again grief gripped his throat and tears misted his eyes, so he turned back to the window. "What'll I ask for the Honda?"

The Honda was Brink's big, 1,000 cc Gold Wing, water-cooled, shaft-driven, maroon, bought last month. Five thousand dollars worth of bike, polished, admired, and hardly used. Shit, shit, shit . . .

There was no answer. He turned.

Around Brink's left bicep hung the gold chronograph Nicole had given him for his thirty-eighth birthday. On the shrunken arm it looked like an alarm clock. Brink had slid it up there when his weight dropped below 120. "Hey, look: King Tut," he'd told everyone.

Now, with immense concentration, he was untaping the i.v. tube beneath the watchband. He was always trying to screw up his treatment. Shawn took a step toward him. The sapphire eyes swung on him. "OK." Brink shrugged. "Sorry."

"The Honda?" Shawn swallowed. "What'll I ask?"

"Merry Christmas," said Brink. "Ride it in good health."

"Come on!"

"It's all yours."

"What'd you do?" Shawn choked. "Bend the forks?"

"Never did run right."

He couldn't accept it. "Look, give it to Val."

"It's too heavy. He'd kill himself, our road. It's yours." Brink flashed a death's head grin. "Plane, too."

"*What?* No way!"

"Look, you fly it better than anybody else—"

"Glad . . ." He was choking up again. "Glad you're finally admitting it—"

"Except me," continued Brink. "Anyway, it's yours."

Shawn fought mightily to keep the tears inside, where they belonged. "No. Bike, thanks. Plane, no. Couldn't afford to—" He cleared his throat: Jesus, what was wrong with him? "Couldn't afford to keep it up. Fucking toy."

"Already done, in writing. A codicil to the will." Brink coughed and Shawn caught a flash of agony. "Hey, Shawn?"

Shawn? In seven years, since their first meeting in near battle at the bottom of Arroyo Seco, they'd called each other Shawn or Brink not half a dozen times. Spud, Buddy, Sarge—later, Lieut—Ace, Slugger, Asshole . . . These were their sobriquets, or: Bean, Wetback, Cholo, Gringo, Paddy, Yankee, Honkey . . . Almost never Brink, very seldom Shawn.

"Shawn?" Brink said again.

"Yo?"

"I been thinking. That goddamn contribution? The sheriff won't dump on *you*, will he?"

Shawn looked him dead in the eye. "No," he lied.

"Good. Hate to split, thinking I screwed things up for you. I mean, *twice.* Hate to split *anyway,* you want to know." He seemed to gather himself. "Speaking of that . . ."

"Shoot," Shawn said reluctantly. He foresaw a confrontation he wasn't ready for.

Brink regarded him steadily. He tapped his sunken chest. "Kind of heavy trip, you know? Like drowning for a month. If it gets much worse . . . Well, the bike, and the plane? You may end up earning 'em."

Shawn chilled. He had sensed it coming all week, with the rising pain. He had read it night after night in the angry eyes, and a certain speculative tilt of the head when Brink thought he was not watching.

He didn't know if he had the guts to somehow pull the plug if asked, or if he would know how to do it, even, but at least he wouldn't pretend not to understand.

"Jesus," he murmured finally. "I don't know if I could . . ."

The bright blue eyes studied him. Brink could talk you into anything. "Don't *mean* right now . . . Haven't signed the deal for the Hammond acreage . . . and I got to brief Nickie on the estate . . ." His eyelids dropped, and Shawn thought he had drifted into sleep. Then they popped open. "*Later*, though? Look, would *I* do it for you?"

No question: without a tremor. "Yes."

"Well?"

"Not for a while, Ace," Shawn muttered. "OK?"

Brink lay back. Suddenly he grinned, wildly. "Hey, tomorrow, sneak in a pack of cigarettes?"

"No."

"Low tar?"

"Night, Asshole," said Shawn, and turned out the light.

He was passing the owlish nun standing at the night desk. The radio was playing behind her: *God rest ye, merry gentlemen! let nothing you dismay.* He heard Brink's shout resound down the corridor. "Viceroys? Thinking man's filter?"

Outside, he climbed into his car and leaned his head on the steering wheel. Finally he could weep, and he did, like an angry child. When it was over, he started the engine and headed home.

Tomorrow he faced the sheriff. He needed all the sleep he could get.

Three

A bolt of fear had torn through Zimmer the fry cook, alias Jake Klinger, when the counter girl slammed the toilet door. She had seen it, seen it all.

His erection died. He doused the flames of his little paper houses in the sink and let the ashes swirl down the drain. In the mirror he noticed that his pocked forehead was red beneath the cookhat. His skin, under a thick black beard, shimmered with sweat; his shirt was soaked with it and his massive forearms slick. His eyes were hot, as they had been for weeks in the dry, nervous gales, and his heart was hammering.

Rage seared away his fear. He'd locked the door, the best he could. She had no call to fucking near tear it down. Horny, filthy college snatch. Cockteaser, like the blonde, the ass-swishing, leg-flashing blonde, who tormented him from noon until ten, jiggling her tits, stooping at the stove, brushing his leg. Either one would probably spread on the chopping block tonight for anybody that grabbed her butt.

He zipped up his pants and stood shaking with anger, his hand on the doorknob, trying to think.

The blonde had walked in on him once, same scene, but backed off giggling, before she'd seen anything, too stupid anyway to know what was coming down. This one, though, was a college cunt, studying what? Biology, he thought. Or psychology? Jesus, *Psychiatry?*

Not stupid, anyway. And now they had a reward out, whether

she knew it or not, to anyone who finked on an arsonist—which he wasn't anymore, but he couldn't prove that. Suppose she'd gone back to the kitchen, suppose they were talking now, about this. He knew they were always talking about him, when they thought he wasn't listening.

Hurriedly, he yanked open the door and swung through the fire panels. The blonde was digging into the basket of unsold legs, as she always did at quitting time. Alone . . .

"Hey," she complained. "Little salty, you know?"

"Tell the Colonel, not me." All ass, tits, and legs. He'd like to fry her up some day.

Anyway, she hadn't been told. So only the other one knew, on all the coast of California, from Dago to Paso Robles. North of Paso Robles he didn't care; he'd never go up there again.

Or to Lompoc, Atascadero, or Patton State Hospital, either. *"You make it on the street, you hear? Don't want to see you back."*

He hung his chef's hat above his apron next to the toilet, pulled on his leather jacket, and headed across the gusty parking lot to his chopped black Harley.

She drove a red VW. He knew she lived in Isla Vista, close to the university. She'd have to take the freeway. With only a two-minute start, he'd catch her on 101 and tail her home. Even if she noticed him in her rearview, with his helmet and black-tinted wind mask, there was no way she could recognize him.

He mounted the bike. He was rumbling past the greaser's gas station when he spotted her bug, stopped outside the women's crapper. The old Mexican who ran the place and the fat young Chicano who repaired cars for him were locking up. The big orange 76 outside went dark, casting the VW into shadow. As he glided past, he saw the two men close the station door and climb into their triple-A tow truck. Their engine started and their lights went on.

He braked, cut his own headlight, hit the kill switch, and rolled into the blackness behind the station. He dropped his kickstand, moved to the VW, tried its door. It was locked.

He heard a toilet flush and stepped back into the shadows. The girl came out, closing the door behind her.

He became very conscious of his power, but cautious. She might be stronger than she seemed. He remembered her talking of surfing, diving, volleyball. Years ago in Oceanside, at a Marine beer bust, he

2

had grabbed a girl from behind and she had spun and kneed him in the groin. The platoon had stood around and laughed, and he had damn near had to strangle her to shut the mothers up.

So he'd watch out for a knee, a kick, or a scream. But he had hands of steel from clutch, brake, and throttle, and great forearms from dirt-riding, and he would go directly for her throat.

His heart began to hammer. He had seen a patient choked to death at Atascadero, by another inmate, on the lawn near the Administration Building, while guards flailed and shouted and a half-dozen loonies cheered.

He hadn't cheered, himself. Maybe the Voice of the Shrink had warned him to cool it; he couldn't remember. But he had watched, fascinated, as the victim finally quivered and died.

The killing itself would be easy. But the body?

All at once he was scared again. Even though the howling winds had been prodding him, he hadn't set a brush fire since he'd been back on the street. Or burned a building, except for his own little paper houses, and they couldn't bust you for that.

But others had been torching the hills, goddamn maniacs; there'd been fires around for almost a month, all over. If he let her fink, they'd try to burn him for half the sets in Southern California.

So he had no choice, really. Afterward, he'd roast her fucking body in the bug. Even if they managed to find the car, they wouldn't know who she was, if he did it right. His mouth went dry and his hands turned moist.

The girl reached her VW, began jingling through her keys. He waited for her to open the door. *Now?*

A voice called out of the night, pressing him into the shadow. "Hey, lady?"

She whirled. "Yes?"

The fat young Chicano appeared, crossing from the truck.

"I got your dollar."

She thanked him, climbed into her car, and bumped onto the lighted street.

He stood sweating in the hot wind. He could still tail her home, find out where she lived, torch the place if he wanted. Everything in Isla Vista was crackerbox, wood and drywall. He could hang around and watch it go up. He felt a stirring in his groin.

But if she survived, she might put it all together.

The fire in his body went out.

She hadn't told the blonde. And she hadn't called the cops.

Maybe she thought he'd been blowing a joint.

He'd see how she acted tomorrow, at work.

Shawn Ortega slowed, crossing Sycamore Canyon Road. He observed that the Santa Ana had turned locally into a sundowner, reversing, to whip landward up the arroyo rather than down. It had backed in the same way in the Romero Saddle fire of 1971, killing four Forest Service Caterpillar drivers and, again, in the Sycamore Canyon fire of '77, belching 260 gold-plated hillside homes into rosy skies.

Now he turned left onto his own street, Eucalyptus Hill Road. Their house was a twenty-year-old white frame, with green shutters, on the lower end of the drive at Cedar Lane. He had discovered it for sale, a jewel still grimy from the nearby flames, during the usual post-fire panic the week after Coyote Canyon, which had taken 230 homes within a half mile of the front door.

The instant he had seen it, spared by some vagary of wind and flame, he had known it was saved for him. Set back on the winding road, lush with purple bougainvillea, it seemed a South Sea fantasy from Melville, transported in a dream. From the bedroom window you could glimpse the ocean, far below, and Anacapa Island.

He had argued every inch of the way with Crissy, who was terrified of fire. At first, on the day he had brought her to see it, she'd hated even to talk of it.

They had stood on the sidewalk under the eucalyptus tree. The walk was deep in week-old cinders. The home's haunches lay on the canyon rim, the smell of burned brush had been heavy on the air, and they could hear the clatter of the first dozers clearing rubble only one arroyo away.

"It may be our last chance," he had warned. "Prices will go up again."

"This *house* will go up. In flames."

He reminded her that nothing on this side of the canyon had been touched. She told him it was due next time, then: there wasn't an arroyo south of Mountain Drive that hadn't been burned in the last fifty years, ask his grandfather.

"We have to live somewhere, Cris!"

"We *live* somewhere."

"Between a Taco Bell and a laundry!"

"We can't afford *this*. Thirty thousand dollars! If we sweat out the payments, we'll never make the insurance!"

He swore he'd make lieutenant, reminded her that there was a county raise coming up, promised to moonlight on weekends, flying advertising banners for Skytow, pointed out that they couldn't afford *not* to buy it. The den could be her studio, north light; there weren't any hillside lots left, it *had* to appreciate, good construction, new stuff was crap . . .

"And of course," she murmured, "there's the real reason. It's a long way from Pueblo Viejo. Straight up. Right?"

What was wrong with that? "You're damn right. Seven hundred feet up, three miles as the crow flies."

"But a long way *down* from the house at Rancho Rojo," she'd murmured.

He'd stared at her, feeling his cheeks go warm. "I never even *saw* the house at Rancho Rojo, it's been gone fifty years."

"Just don't forget that, OK?" And with the madonna smile he loved and sometimes hated: "Or *how* it went."

It had perished in flames, actual flames and financial ones, too, so he wasn't too sure which she meant, and he ignored it as he often did her little enigmas. "I'll cut back that brush. I'll fireproof the shingles. I'll put Rainbird sprinklers on the roof." And then, his ace: "Damn it, it's Mary Lou. I don't want her brought up in a barrio."

She shrugged. "'S'not so bad, man. Din' hurt me none."

"No, you OK girl, for Chicana, y'know?"

"I mean, really, you act like PV was East LA. Anyway, it'll never get better if everybody bails out."

"I don't care if it gets better or not. I *want* out. Crissy?"

Softly, resignedly: "Yes?"

"This *is* out."

"Period?"

"Period."

She had looked up at him for a long moment, clear amber eyes in a perfect oval face. The bulldozers snorted in the still canyon air. Finally she bowed and murmured: "Sí, esposo mío. Sí, Don Shawn."

And had given him, again, the faint madonna smile: "I'm sure you're right. Pardon the *hell* out of me."

Now, turning into his driveway, Shawn could see in the sweep of his headlights that the eucalyptus, which had prospered through drought-proof Australian genes, was stripped of leaves by the wind and whipping like a giant metronome over their sidewalk. If it toppled tonight, it would fall across the parched yellow corpse of what they laughingly still called their "lawn." Their upstairs bedroom would take the upper limbs. But there was nothing he could do about that. If he got out his chain saw and beat the wind to felling it, the city would cite him for destroying public property.

He aimed the garage door opener and pressed the button. Nothing happened. "Zap," he pleaded. "*Zap,* you mother!"

The door opened halfway, caught a gust, shuddered, and slammed shut again before he could move. He got out, leaving the Chevy to be sandblasted by the wind or crushed by the tree, whatever. If the Santa Ana destroyed his home, which seemed possible any moment, he might as well let it take the automobile, too. Behind the house, a limb crashed from a canyon oak.

He started across the deceased grass, stumbling on a sprinkler they hadn't legally been allowed to use since spring.

Too little water, for too many new mouths, sprinklers, car washes, bathtubs. And still people flowed from the frozen East, the mountain states, the northern counties, Mexico. Too many people, too many cars jamming the stations, too many motor homes, too many boats cramming the harbor, too many planes circling the airport, too many new hippies in the canyons, new Birchers in the hills, braceros in the flats.

There was no way, anymore, during traffic hours, to plow through town on 101 from west to east without risking ulcers or a rear-end collision. And despite gas shortages, and smog, more people, incredibly, came every week.

Tierra adorada . . .

The influx had made the house worth a fortune on paper. Ninety thousand dollars, he'd been told. If not for Proposition 13, three years ago, he'd have had to sell it by now, for taxes.

Sell it, and live . . . where?

Seventy thousand people, and no more land in the county. When it happened to rats, they ate their young.

Yankee, go home.

He opened the door. His grandfather, silhouetted in the light from the den, stood in pajama pants and a UCLA T-shirt, squinting over a seven-and-a-half-inch single-action Colt cavalry .44.

"Jesus, Pops!" Shawn screamed.

The gun, reputedly a relic of some great-uncle's service in the Spanish–American War, went down. "I heard somebody fooling with the garage door."

"Me," swallowed Shawn.

"Well, there's somebody behind the house."

"The wind. Hey, you don't keep that thing loaded?"

The old man shook his head, opened the loading gate, and jabbed at the ejector rod. A blackened cartridge bounced on the rug.

"Beautiful," breathed Shawn.

"Madre de Dios!" whispered Don Miguel.

Shawn unloaded the other five rounds. He saw that the shock remained in the old man's eyes. He hugged the bony shoulders. "Hey, come on. You weren't going to pull the trigger! Beer?"

The old man shook his head. He sagged to the torn leather chair he favored, a relic of Carrillo Street and, for all Shawn knew, of Rancho Rojo before that. For a moment his grandfather inspected his shaking, twisted fingers, then seemed to get hold of himself.

"And Brink?" Don Miguel asked. "How is our friend Brink?"

"Don Miguel, you don't care."

"I asked."

"He's just fine. Dying, of course."

The old man shrugged. "Yes. Well, so am I. So are you." Another limb split in the barranca, and Don Miguel hoisted himself to his feet, wandered to the french windows, and looked out at a beckoning shape on the rim of the canyon. "So is that oak, from the instant it fell as an acorn."

Viejo, pleaded Shawn silently, go back to bed. I can't handle it tonight. "So?" he asked wearily.

The old man turned. "You don't find that consoling?"

"No. The goddamn oak's a hundred years old, you're eighty-three. Brink," he said savagely, "is thirty-nine."

"Your father was thirty-four. And your mother wasn't yet thirty."

And, Shawn added silently, I could have got wasted tonight, at thirty-eight, if I hadn't yelled in time.

"Proving what, Don Miguel? Somebody's up there laughing?"

"Do not blaspheme! Not in my presence."

"Sorry."

Don Miguel had met Brink only once, years ago, when Shawn had dragged Crissy and him to the dedication of Southerland Botanical Gardens. From Brink, unusual courtliness; from Don Miguel, uncharacteristic coolness. Winding home down the canyon road, the old man had murmured from the rear seat:

> "The laws of God, the laws of man
> He may keep that will and can.
> Not I: let God and man decree
> Laws for themselves and not for me . . ."

From childhood, Shawn had been taught at least to try. "Henley?"

"A. E. Housman."

"OK." He knew the reason, but asked anyway. "¿Por qué?"

A long silence. "He has the scent of danger, your friend. I thought you were through with that, after the Navy. I do not like the smell."

And still didn't. "You don't give a damn about Brink." Shawn shrugged now. "Neither does Crissy." He looked at their ship's clock, a present from Brink. Eleven-ten. "Where the hell *is* she, anyway?"

"Pueblo Viejo. Why not? You sit with a sick friend, she teaches 'art' to braceros." The old man started for the den. Elaborately, he said: "Me and Mary Lou? We can watch reruns of *All in the Family*."

So that was it. Shawn hid a smile. "OK, Pops. A week, two weeks, it'll all be over. We'll watch *All in the Family* together."

The emerald eyes flared. "Don't speak to me like that! I'm not a child." At the window, he paused. "You hear the oak?"

It was screeching. A shame to lose it. "Yes."

"It fights to live, you hear?"

"OK," murmured Shawn, puzzled. "I'll buy that."

"All his life, your friend has been trying to kill himself—"

"Bullshit!"

"Trying to kill himself. And take you with him, if he could. So do not blame God now if He laughs a little. Or your wife if she doesn't cry. Or your grandfather, either."

Shawn watched him close the door. He hid the gun in the hall-
way closet, went to the refrigerator and cracked a beer, then sat
sipping it slowly, listening to the wind. When the oak went, in a
mighty crash, he crushed the can, hurled it into the garbage, and
climbed the stairs to bed.

Quietly, so as not to awaken her lover, the girl slipped from her
candy-striped working uniform in the darkened upstairs bedroom of
the Isla Vista duplex. She sniffed the armpits of the dress, and then
remembered that she need not wash it tonight: she was quitting, tomorrow, by phone. She wondered if they'd want it back.

Wearing bra and panties, she scampered down the hall to the
communal bathroom. She was still unused to the risk of meeting
their fellow lodgers en route, but ashamed to admit it by wearing a
robe.

She made it safely, and after she had brushed her teeth, she
climbed onto the toilet seat to see in the mirror if her belly showed
the baby.

There was no discernible bulge; wouldn't be for months, for all
she knew. The Colonel's thighs were doing her figure more harm
than the child. But she had better damn well make her mind up
about whether to keep it, before too long, and about other things.

She skittered back to her room. If her dad and mother in Denver
had seen the cluttered duplex, with four couples living in space for
two, they'd probably have tried to remove her bodily.

But they hadn't seen it, and it was her senior year: she was a big
girl now. This time she wouldn't even be home for Christmas.

She began to fold back the sheets on her side of the bed.

He was on his back, the bedclothes pulled aside in the hot, dry
air. His golden body lay in shadow, except when a gust moved the
curtain and unveiled him to the light of a streetlamp below.

A siren wailed distantly. Another fire in the hills? She hoped not,
with such a wind. For some reason she flashed on Jake the Flake, all
zits and hair and blank dead eyes.

She never expected to see him again.

But now she froze in thought, one knee on the bed. If she did
quit her job, she'd have no excuse not to go home for Christmas, not
with the new air fares. In fact, she'd *have* to go home. She'd have no

way financially to hang in until the next semester; no way, without bread coming in, to last on her own.

But if she left for a month, she might return to find her lover sleeping with somebody else.

She shivered, strangely chilled, as she traced a finger lightly down his tanned, hairless chest.

"You back?" he asked suddenly. He always awakened awake.

"Not me. The Colonel's got ribs. I'm down there selling them."

"*You've* got ribs. Get 'em over here."

She hesitated: "Rick?"

"Um?"

"I might go back to Denver tomorrow? For Christmas?"

Silently, she begged him to protest.

"Hey, that'll be nice."

So much for that. She gave up and slithered close. If Santa Anas drove him up the wall, they also made him horny. She hoped they kept on forever.

She guessed she'd better hang on to the dumb job, after all.

Four

In 5 A.M. darkness, Jerry Castle, of the U. S. National Forest Service, rolled his Ford slowly into the slot reserved for Assistant Supervisor (Fire), at Headquarters, Los Padres National Forest, near Santa Barbara Municipal Airport, in industrial Goleta.

The building was stark in the fading moonlight, stranded desolately on a dead-end street. In an hour, with the sunrise, it would dance with blowing scrap paper and dust swirls, but in the predawn shine it seemed fresh and scrubbed.

Absently, he switched off his lights and emergency radio and opened the door. He was immediately aware of the forest essences borne by the Santa Ana wind, across freeway, suburbs, and concrete, all the way from San Marcos Pass five miles northeast. A gust almost ripped the door from his grasp. He got out and closed it, sniffing for the acrid smoke of chaparral.

Not yet, but he had a very bad feeling about this particular wind.

The feeling had awakened him all night, sporadically, and he was not often wrong.

He was a grayhaired, mild man, slightly built, of medium height. He thought of himself in terms of gray, a good color for the Forest Service, which rewarded the low-keyed and punished flamboyance. General Patton, with whom he'd served as an aerial spotter and artillery observer, wouldn't have lasted a week.

The headquarters reception room was unmanned until eight, except for a beefy female guard at the desk and a jolly fake-carving of

Smokey the Bear, wearing blue Levis and surveying the area with
stunned eyes. Jerry nodded at the woman, who seemed shocked to
see him at this hour, and he trudged up the stairs, not sure exactly
why he was here.

He stepped into the semi-deserted dispatch office, heart of an empire so vast that it still frightened him.

Into this command center flowed all of the inputs he needed to
calculate Burning Index and Danger Index for the Danger Board:
wind, humidity, fuel moisture, temperature. The board was an impressive green, orange, and red affair, with magnetic bugs on it to in-
dicate the volatility of a half-dozen selected areas in the Los Padres
National Forest. Most of the bugs rested on the red column indicat-
ing "extreme fire danger." The night duty dispatcher had just placed
the last one, and turned to him, bleary-eyed.

"My God, Jerry! You know what time it is?"

Jerry nodded, poured a cup of coffee, and flopped to a chair in one
of an empty line of open-faced phone cubicles which would be
manned, in time of fire, by command post officers communicating
with their counterparts in the field.

"Couldn't sleep. Anything from BIFSY?"

The dispatcher shook his head. Boise Inter-Agency Fire Service
was keeping a special watch on the mass weather picture, which
might at least tell him when and if the Santa Ana would stop. No
news was good news, he imagined; hell, he could have phoned in, or
stayed in bed. He was getting to be an old woman when the wind
blew.

Another tossing, turning night like the last would bring back the
visions of North Africa that hot desert gales always evoked. Finally,
at four-thirty, he had given up trying to sleep and come to work instead.

The largest of the four big radio consoles in the center of the
room burst into life with a dry cackle: "Goleta Control?"

He almost spilled his coffee. He lurched for the mike, beating the
dispatcher. "Goleta here! Go ahead!"

"Hey, Stan, you got a nine-letter word for 'reasonable'?"

He glared at the dispatcher. The man turned red.

Jerry felt his blood pressure rise. *He* was sweating out a potential
Burning Index of 100, or more, and someone in a lookout station,
somewhere, was doing crossword puzzles?

"Jerry Castle here," he barked, into the mike. "Try 'plausible.' Then put away the goddamn newspaper and watch for smoke, OK?"

He was no hardnose, everybody knew that. And he loved the Forest Service and those who manned its outposts.

But sometimes he almost wished he was back in the Army.

Almost.

Where was the word from Boise?

Robert Wendell Holmes, Topographical Wind Section-Head at the National Weather Service liaison office in Boise Inter-Agency Fire Service, shrugged out of his sheepskin parka and hung it in his cubicle.

It was barely 8 A.M. Mountain Standard Time. The center was almost deserted, but the Idaho local forecaster was already hogging the IBM 3278 that Holmes wanted to use. Holmes poured a cup of coffee, his one transgression against the Church of the LDS, and wandered over to stand behind him.

"Snow," murmured the forecaster, scanning the dancing green lines on his CRT screen. "Here, anyway. Hubcap-deep by noon." He began to punch up temperature gradients.

Snow, good news and bad. Holmes had last night met a female air cadet who was home on Christmas leave, leafing through a ski magazine in a drugstore. He had her phone number and a room in a Ketchum condo, and wanted to take her skiing at Sun Valley. A fresh dusting of snow on the hills would be bait.

But conversely, another storm in Colorado meant winds in California, a new siege of nerves on the Coast, and a call from Santa Barbara that would have him flying South to LA in an hour. If the Santa Anas continued to blow, his duties would keep him off the slopes for a week. Or a month, if the coastal forests started to burn.

"Let me know when you're through," he hinted to the local man. He strolled with his coffee to the huge relief map on the wall of the center. All during autumn, arctic gales had swirled in from the northern Pacific, marching past the Queen Charlotte Islands and Vancouver, churning over the Canadian Rockies, and sending icy fingers south along the Great Plains. It all had to do, he was sure, with the warming trend of recent years, which some of the long-range boys heralded, paradoxically, as the beginning of the new ice age. Whatever it was, it was making the Bering Sea and the Gulf of Alaska spew storms as never before.

But he was not concerned with the storms themselves, except to wish they would flow further south, with moisture for the parched forests on the Coast.

His concern, and the nervousness of those who depended on him, was with the icy lakes of dry air that the storms left, squeezed of moisture by passage over the coastal ranges. The air masses lay trapped in a great sink. The basin was bounded on the west by the Sierra Nevadas, the east by the Rockies, and the southeast by the Wasatch Range, the Virgin Mountains, and the Black Mountain Range south of Las Vegas.

He traced a finger along the boundaries, struck by something. He had done his thesis on drainage winds, taught part time at Idaho State, had published on chubascos, Tehuantepecers, boras, chinooks, and föhns. He liked to think of himself as a world authority on Santa Anas.

But not until this moment had he ever noticed that the basin in which the Santa Ana gestated was not a basin at all.

It was a huge womb, in profile exactly like a woman's, a thousand miles long on its western side, from Seattle to Santa Barbara; and eight hundred on its eastern, from Salt Lake City to Los Angeles. Its vagina was the Mojave, its labium the coastal plain from Santa Barbara across the smog-ridden flat of the Los Angeles River to the Santa Ana Basin, from which the name of the winds derived. When the winds were born, the mountains burned.

A concept to keep the boys and girls at University Extension awake next lecture.

He moved to a plastic-covered weather map twenty feet long and ten feet high, dominating the eastern end of the center. Yesterday's storm system from the Gulf of Alaska was moving toward British Columbia. What was worse, another low pressure area was forming south of the Pribilof Islands in the Bering Sea. He assumed that both would dump their moisture uselessly in the Pacific Northwest, and then replenish the lake of heavy dry air which had spilled from the canyons of Southern California last night.

When the local forecaster left the computer terminal empty, Holmes took his place and punched out upper-air temperatures, jet stream flow, temperature–dew point spread, and winds aloft, from two dozen stations all the way from Seattle to Santa Barbara. He added the Large Scale Guidance Package winds from the National Meteorological Center in Camp Springs, Maryland. When he was through he had filled the womb he envisioned with a soaring new mount of frigid, stagnant air. It had only one way to escape, downhill, warming as air from a bicycle pump warmed, by compression, as it flowed southwest. The deserts would act as stream beds, ever narrowing, channeling the hot, dry residue from the Salt Lake Desert to the Escalante, to Devil's Playground, to the Lucerne Valley, along the Smoke Creek Desert, to the Carson Sink, and Big Smoky Valley, then along Death Valley to the Mojave. Finally, all of the millions of tons of superheated air must pass through the mouth of the vagina between Santa Barbara and the Los Angeles Basin.

Picking up, all the time, the strange load of positive electrical ions which, as they did in the föhn winds of the Alps, could drive men half insane. Drainage winds were infinite in character, barely predictable. Which made them fascinating to him in maps and in books, and in the memory of the computer. No one knew why the ions they carried wreaked havoc on the circuitry of the brain. He was as sensitive to the damage as anyone. And the fires they brought terrified him.

In the field, he hated the winds he had studied all his life.

When he was through at the computer, he'd compiled a wind forecast that would jolt hell out of Santa Barbara County and the Los Padres National Forest: hot dry gales out of the canyon mouths, increasing in velocity for the next ten days.

Reluctantly, he typed it into the keyboard for Forest Service Headquarters in Washington and Jerry Castle's shop in Santa Barbara.

Local fire-weather forecasters out of Redding and LA would refine and massage his prediction. And could handle the field situation better, he was sure. But he'd been oversold to everyone as the weather genius of the Marble Cone fire of '78, through no virtue of his own, just luck. And Santa Barbara would demand him on the scene. The burden of the successful academic was apparently a heavy one.

There was no use crying about it. He might as well go back to his pad and pack.

Sorry, Ms. Cadet.

Five

Alone, in running shoes and a faded gray sweat shirt, Shawn Ortega pounded along Mountain Drive in slanted morning light. The sun was dragging itself from the ocean below as if to dry in the desert air. His feet flopped at the blacktop—nine-minute mile—160 slaps a minute—the sound like rifle shots echoing from the stone walls and brick escarpments of the grassy estates he was passing.

To the northeast, far past Ventura, a ribbon of gold over the Los Angeles Basin—Chumash Indian Valley of the Smokes—promised that, later, hot winds already moving the morning smog would sear the coast again. But the Santa Ana, thank God, had died momentarily. Though the calm had him sweating heavily from the long, shuffling run up Coyote Road, he preferred the sweat to the maddening wind.

These weeks he was seldom happy, running.

He wondered, really, why he was here. He still ran Mondays, Wednesdays, and Fridays, from three to five miles a day, enough to earn thirty-five Aerobic points a week. When he and Brink had started, three years ago, they had run every morning, each reluctant to ease the pace and ending, usually, in a neck-and-neck race around Westmont College track.

It went much slower alone.

He heard the high-pitched whine of a two-stroke motorcycle behind him, and hugged the right shoulder. A bright red Kawasaki screamed by. He glimpsed the rider as a black shadow with an afro, tearing toward work or school along streets on which a black was, even now, almost never seen. The sound of the engine receded, and finally faded in the dawn.

All at once he was back six—no, seven—years, staked out not far from here, on East Mountain Drive, high above Montecito, listening for just such a sound. He was sitting alone at dawn in the department's best Ford squad car, new sergeant's stripes bright on his olive shirt. He'd hoped that morning, after a week of half-ass failures by his men, to catch the Sunrise Kid, whoever he was, Mad Motorcyclist of Montecito.

Every dawn for weeks, his morning watch had been hellish. The phantom rider was blasting the silent streets, howling past the mossy estates, striking fury into the wealthy heart and lighting up the switchboard at headquarters.

Sure of his own driving, Shawn had deserted his desk to stake himself out by the Dalton Sykes estate, for Sykes was chief complainer of them all. Shawn had hidden in a parking niche in Sykes's ivied wall. And at sunrise, on schedule, he'd heard the unholy yowl of a two-stroke bike, building and fading as it passed the mouths of the cold canyons further down the hill, apparently heading toward him.

He reached for the mike to call for a Highway Patrol backup, then changed his mind. He had the department's finest car, with a 350 V8 and hardened shocks. In his youth he'd rocketed around these same stonewalled roads for years. If he couldn't tag him single-handed, the Sunrise Kid had earned the right to wake the world until he killed himself, unhindered by law and order.

So he simply started the engine and waited. Much sooner than he expected, an orange sprint bike screamed by in a blaring crescendo of noise. He caught a flash of chrome and a glimpse of the bare-headed rider, yellow hair flying, prone along his tank, and then he was off on what should have been the last hot pursuit of his life.

He peeled out Code Three, so that his siren would tell the homeowners that their calls had not gone unheeded, and his flashing red light would alert oncoming motorists. The bike had passed him so quickly that he almost lost it before the first screeching turn.

The motorcyclist teased him down East Mountain Road, heading, Shawn hoped, toward Summerland on the coast. He reached again

for the mike, intending to cut him off with CHP. Again, he drew
back his hand. Somehow, it seemed like cheating. Summerland?

Or Romero Canyon Road?

Christ, he hoped not, not Romero. Romero was motorcycle country, convoluted as a worm in heat. He flashed on his daughter Mary
Lou, intent, beyond her six years, on a serve he'd lobbed her, wield-
ing a racket as big as herself. *Don't worry, baby; if he turns up
Romero, I'll let him go scot-free.*

But in the end, he had not let him go, could not. The bike slowed
at Romero, turned sedately inland, giving him plenty of time. He
even saw the rider's bare arm, beckoning him onward. Like a rookie,
he accepted, knowing that if he met someone coming down he'd kill
them both, that no bust was worth this, that tragedy lurked on the
switchbacks ahead, that if Sheriff McCrae could see him now, he'd
fire him cold.

But he was constitutionally unable to turn and go home.

The Ford hung in on the curves as if on tracks. He very nearly
caught the bike somewhere between Camino Cielo and Blue Canyon. He identified it as a Moto Guzzi, rare enough in itself, and
even caught the last two digits of the plate. God, if he had his *own*
bike now, what a race it would be . . .

He screamed after the flashing Guzzi through turn after turn,
glimpsing him when the road straightened, losing him on every
horseshoe, dreading oncoming traffic, catching now and again the
blare of the Guzzi's engine, losing it when his own siren rose.

He skidded, fishtailed, corrected with power, and straightened. He
braked as a deer flashed across the road before him, swerved to the
shoulder, regained control.

He was two thirds up Romero Canyon, and gaining again, when
he crested a rise to find a yellow road grader, parked overnight, too
far onto the road. He clipped it with a rear fender, lost control, and
was suddenly hurtled off the shoulder, airborne, and over the bot-
tomless void of Arroyo Seco.

So this was how it would end. He glimpsed Mary Lou again, and
was shocked with guilt, and Crissy at her easel, and of course
Nicole, who might not know until she read it in the papers . . .

A mighty jolt, black nothingness, and then the sound of a mourn-
ing dove and metal creaking as the engine cooled. He opened his

eyes. The sun was blazing through a shattered windshield. The car was on its left side, absolutely immobile, and the smell of gasoline was everywhere. He had to get out of his safety belt, quick . . .

He couldn't move a finger.

Drip, drip, drip . . .

Oh, Christ, why couldn't he move?

He tried again. No pain. Blood from a cut on his hand, and he felt his nose bleeding, but no pain. Also, no motion.

"Hey!" he croaked. "Help!"

Nothing.

He managed to turn his head. OK, his neck wasn't broken. If he could just get his hands to *move*.

Now he found that he could, slowly. He reached first to turn off the ignition switch, discovered he already had, automatically, apparently on becoming airborne; a jet fighter reaction that just might have saved his life. But the engine was hot, and the gas still dripping, and he wanted out, out, out . . .

Jesus, he was tired. But only stunned, right? Back OK, thank Christ, arms, legs, neck . . . all OK, and coming back fast. He worked his feet free of the steering column: his pants were torn. He stood on the driver's door, pushed up the passenger's. It wouldn't budge.

He heard rocks falling. An avalanche? Or somebody throwing boulders on the car? He felt for his gun. It had fallen from his holster and he couldn't find it. He wasn't going to dig around for a gun now, not in this mess, not with gasoline reeking everywhere.

Suddenly he heard the chortle of a motorcycle engine, and a report like a .45. Firing at him? He ducked, painfully, feeling at his feet for the gun. Nowhere. Another shot? No, a backfire. Carefully, he stuck his head through the open passenger window.

Above him, slithering, sliding, slaloming down the face of the arroyo, came the Guzzi. The rider, eyes intent on the ground, was standing high on the pegs. Shawn couldn't believe it. No one could come down the face of that canyon with a vehicle and not end up in a pile of junk. But this rider, making it, finally finished with a squirt of power and a neat half-turn. He dismounted and approached on the run.

Shawn, standing with his head out the passenger window, peered out in surprise. Not a kid, as he'd assumed, but an adult, thirty years old, easily. And very concerned. "You OK?"

Shawn didn't answer. Angrily, he shoved up again on the door. Then he hooked his elbows over the window frame and tried to pull himself out. He was weak as a child. The stench of gasoline was stifling.

The cyclist hoisted himself from the ground to the hood, scrambled easily to the upturned side, and stood over the window, squinting down at Shawn in the golden morning sun. He loomed immensely from this angle, a tall man with startling blue eyes and polished, even teeth. "Lose a lot of cars, this road?"

He'd been magnificent slaloming down the slope, but the only reason he could have risked coming back would be that he assumed Shawn hadn't got close enough to identify the bike. He would try to pass himself off as an innocent witness. Shawn mustn't scare him off.

"Chasing some asshole," Shawn muttered. "Another biker."

The tall man squatted, grinning. He had a spectacular grin, and laser eyes. No man to try to bullshit. "That's interesting," he murmured. "Because the 'biker' was me. As you damn well know." He drew a pack of cigarettes from his shirt pocket. While Shawn stared, he knocked one loose, stuck it between his lips. "Cigarette?"

"Christ!" exclaimed Shawn. "Don't light that!"

"Hey, it's not fire season." The rider smiled. He produced a gold cigarette lighter, flicked open the top, hesitated significantly. "You going to write me for speeding?"

Shawn looked into the face, half-shadowed by the early sun. The man was bluffing: he wouldn't dare flick the lighter: he'd be blown up himself. But you never knew: anyone who rode a bike like that was crazy. Common sense screamed for discretion, but there was no way he was going to crawl.

"You're fucking *right* I'm going to write you! Now, put that thing away and get my ass out of here!"

The man laughed, suddenly pocketed the lighter, grabbed Shawn by the armpits, and heaved. Shawn weighed almost two hundred pounds, but he felt himself drawn from the window like a loose cork from a bottle. He scrambled after the rider to the ground, weak-kneed and close to fainting.

The man was regarding the crumpled hood. "Needs paint."

"Let me see your license, please?" Shawn asked. His voice sounded tremulous. His knees were shaking. Despite the smell of gasoline, he had to lean against the hood of the car so that the trembling wouldn't show.

"What? Pilot, marriage, contractor's, driver's?" The man was grinning.

"Driver's, sir," grated Shawn. "*Now!*"

He sounded better. He was coming back.

The man only studied him.

"I don't think," he speculated, "you got close enough to see my plate."

"Don't count on it." It sounded like trouble coming. Shawn wished he'd looked further for his gun. "Where's that driver's license?"

The man glanced back at his bike and murmured: "And you can't see it from here . . ."

"Goddamn it, I asked for your license!" If he didn't find some place to sit down he was going to drop.

"Suppose, instead of that," proposed the man reasonably, "I knocked you on your ass—"

"You want to try, buster?" flared Shawn. He measured the distance between them. If he could close fast enough, get an armlock . . .

"Or just let you fold, like you're going to, and then ride that mother back up the hill?"

Shawn left the support of the car and lurched at the man. He stumbled and fell. The man pulled him to his feet, laughing, guided him to a boulder, studied him for a moment, and shook his head helplessly. "You're a stubborn bastard, you know?" From a thin pigskin wallet he drew his driver's license. Shawn's vision was blurry, he felt faint, but he could read the name.

Southerland . . . Southerland? *Brinkley* Southerland? He almost groaned aloud. Shit! Inevitable, sooner or later, in a city so small, but why now? And here?

He exploded: "You out of your mind, Southerland? What are you, some kind of kid? Screaming around these roads, six o'clock in the morning, waking people up? Running them off the roads?" He found that he was shouting. *"Who the fuck do you think you are?"*

"If you're going to write me," Brink said mildly, "then *write* me. I got an appointment at nine."

"Well," Shawn mumbled, studying the license for a moment, then handing it back. "I can't."

Brink's eyes widened. "What, you lose your tickets?"

"Your wife would kill me . . . I used to know Nicole."

The blue eyes grew wide. "Jesus Christ," Brink cried, "it's Jesus Christ! Ortega? *Shawn* Ortega?"

Shawn nodded, Brink arose, stuck out his hand. Shawn shook it. It felt more like a house framer's than a millionaire developer's. Brink moved suddenly to his bike, started it, whipped it back to Shawn. "You're one hell of a driver, Sarge. Well, almost. And I hear you're a great stud and the world's hottest pilot. Let's see how you are on the back of a bike."

The trip up the hill on the Guzzi was only a little less exciting than the trip in the Ford coming down. Back on the turns of Romero Canyon Road, Shawn had almost begged to be let off, but of course hadn't, and the next week he'd got even, wringing out Brink in the Stearman from Skytow, which he'd afterward taught him to fly and which Brink had later bought.

Their friendship had teetered on a knife-edge of competition over the years. "Like two children on the high board, daring each other," Crissy said. They'd bounced over bike trails and mountain slopes that neither would have ridden alone, they'd sky dived, floated hanggliders over the coastal cliffs, strained the ancient Stearman's wings in aerobatics. They'd spent a week rafting the Colorado with Nicole —and without Crissy, who couldn't leave Mary Lou—and another flying a Cessna down to Mexico, where Brink had fallen in love with the cross-eyed six-year-old daughter of a Mexican aviation mechanic and sent her to Los Angeles for eye surgery.

Brink often acted on emotion. It turned out that he had been blasting the Montecito neighborhood at dawn as a private protest against wealthy No-Growthers who were trying to stop his building permit for Las Pumas Estates.

Wrecking the squad car in Arroyo Seco, with no citation to show for it, had earned Shawn a year on the Coroner's Unit for unprofessional conduct, but the game that had started here in the foothills had changed his life.

For better or for worse? He still didn't know: all the dice were not yet cast.

But now Brink was leaving, and if Shawn kept jogging, he faced an eternity of pounding along alone.

He heard the sudden slap of shoes behind him, driving fast. A muscular young man drew abreast. He had a drooping guardsman's moustache, bulbous biceps, knotted shoulders, and a wrestler's neck.

"Morning," panted Shawn.

"Have a nice one." The young man leaped ahead with a bounce that Shawn had grown to hate in anyone under thirty. For a moment Shawn tried to keep up. The agony lessened if you used another runner as a pacer.

Shawn could no more stay with him than with Bill Rogers in a marathon. In a few minutes he was back to a jog, feet flopping more slowly even than before.

When he reached the Westmont College track, the sun was a flattened orange, hurting his eyes. And the band of gold over the basin had spread. The Santa Ana was coming back, bearing desert dust.

He forced four laps around the track—one mile. He did not even bother to time it, he was so slow today.

It was simply no fun running alone.

He headed downhill toward home, cutting through Westmont Canyon on a fire trail he had found with Brink, hoping to cool off under the trees, but only feeling the wild grass slashing at his calves.

He climbed a dry creek bed, hit a stone, twisted his ankle.

An awful run: lousy.

And this morning, again because of Brink, he had to face another sheriff, this one an ogre.

He hobbled down the fire trail toward the house on Eucalyptus Hill.

Showered, shaved, dressed in slacks and a sober sport shirt for Sheriff Castillo, Shawn brought his All-Bran from the kitchen. The sun, slanting through the french doors from the patio, crowned Crissy with a halo of burnished copper. She was reading the *News-*

Press at the breakfast table. There was a time, before her first paintings had sold, when she would have arisen to serve him, but what the hell: he guessed he was happier without her waiting on him hand and foot. He dumped two slices of health bread into the toaster, poured low-fat milk on the cereal, and sat down.

Now he should be feeling a runner's high, or at least the satisfaction of having done what he could for heart, lungs, and legs.

He felt no high, no satisfaction. He hadn't since Brink had quit.

"El Viejo up?" he asked.

"Long gone."

He glanced at her quickly. Flat voice, tired eyes. Migraine, from the Santa Ana. Which meant that the wind would return today: she was more sensitive than the barometer on the patio.

Her headache could last for weeks. He wanted to comfort her, but she didn't like to be reminded that it showed.

"He tell you about last night?" he asked carefully.

"He said you were at the hospital." She looked up from the paper. "How's Brink?"

He searched for concern in her eyes but found only her own pain. The migraines drew her into herself like an affronted turtle.

"He's going," he said flatly. "Won't be long."

"It's rough. You need him."

"*I* need *him?*"

She nodded. Her lovely eyes went soft. "I know you think I don't like him. OK, I don't. He steals you. But I *am* sorry." She winced, suddenly.

He reached across the table and touched her temple. "*I'm* sorry. Headache?"

"No." She was lying. "So what happened last night, with Granddad?"

He had been going to tell her about the horse pistol, but now he didn't feel like it. If the old man hadn't mentioned it, he'd forgotten, or was ashamed, which was understandable. Anyway, why scare her? Shawn shifted his ground. "He was pissed nobody was home."

A mistake.

"Mary Lou was home," she flared. "My God, what am I supposed to do? Grandpa-sit? Quit teaching?"

"Of course not."

"And look, he forgot about the license thing again. He wanted to use my car this morning. To drive to Sunflower Park. Shawn, what am I supposed to do?"

His grandfather had let his license expire, probably afraid he'd forget the answers to the written exam, or flunk on his eyesight. Nearsighted, reluctant to wear glasses except to read, with his peripheral vision fading and reactions like molasses, he was a menace to traffic from the moment he turned the key.

Shawn thought for a moment and shrugged. "Next time, let him *use* your car."

"Great!"

"Just the once. I'll ask one of the city motor officers to wait at the foot of Alameda Padre Serra. He gets pulled over, that'll cool him."

She said that if he'd forgotten he didn't have a license, he'd forget the warning too, and added that it all seemed a little too *mucho macho* that they had to spare the old man's feelings no matter what.

"Hey, *mucho macho*," Shawn muttered. "Is that Casa de la Raza? Or women's lib?"

She returned to her paper. "Anyway, he's walking, if you want to pick him up."

He did want to, and finished his coffee.

Instead of cutting west toward headquarters on the far side of town, he drove seaward down Eucalyptus to Salinas Street. He spotted Don Miguel striding under the sidewalk shade trees. Tall, straight, moving with princely gait, he'd have looked great in a sombrero, sash, and jingling spurs. Born a hundred years too late.

Shawn picked him up and took him the rest of the way to Sunflower Park. There he would sit on a bench in the sun until noon, revered by the other ancients, bored, but politely declining checkers or chess.

"Have a nice day, Pops," Shawn said, as he opened the door to let him out.

Don Miguel grinned. "I think so. I am meeting Alberto for lunch."

Shawn stared. "Alberto?"

Don Miguel nodded. "Alberto García. *If* he is able. He's been ill."

Shawn looked into the smiling green eyes. All at once they watered and shifted. The old man had suddenly remembered.

Shawn had nothing to say, so he closed the door gently. Turning onto Milpas Street, he almost clipped a cyclist in the bike lane.

Alberto García had been dead for fifteen years.

Cristina Ortega sat listening to the wind moan up the canyon. She had sat so since Shawn left, fascinated by the misery of this particular migraine, trying to ease its hostility by giving it the respect it deserved.

Some said the migraines came from the Santa Ana winds screwing around with ions, whatever they were. Some doctors—and her reading on the subject was extensive—said it was sexual frustration, others that it was an elitist pain denied all but the intelligent or talented. Cervantes had had them, and Tolstoy, too. Morons never did. She was in beautiful company.

If all of these theories were true, fate had this time achieved a combination unknown in her experience. The winds had blown on and off for weeks, Shawn had hardly touched her in bed since Brink had been stricken, and she was painting better than ever.

The headache had begun days ago, with the first sighing breaths of the Santa Ana. The usual aura of off-kilter vision, sensitivity to light, and a sharp, insistent pain between the left eye and the bridge of her nose had warned her that the next few weeks would be bitches.

She had usually one of three types of migraines: a Diesel locomotive model, in which the pain would come pounding out of the sleepless night, clackety-clackety, air horn rising and falling as it peaked and diminished; the spike variety, in which a spindly silver nail was driven sideways through her skull; and the steel band, into which her head was inserted while some zesty phantom screwed it tight.

This time, all three had been presented her consecutively. The spike had been withdrawn sometime last night, and now she sat with her head in the great invisible vise in the sky.

For years she had successfully hidden her less excruciating migraines from Shawn, remembering how her mother had tortured them all with her own. But there was no way she was going to keep this particular one secret, she had realized that from the beginning. And so she had simply been moving with it, through a haze of half-heard conversations, half-experienced irritations, immersed in her private sea of pain.

This time she had the granddaddy of them all.

Somewhere up the canyon, a dog, excited by the wind, began to bark. She glided to the window so as not to jar her head, shut it. "Shut up!" she whispered to the dog, the groaning oaks, the creaking house. "Shut up, shut up, shut up!"

She felt better. She cleared the table, leaving the dishes for Mary Lou to do after tennis. Now she had the major chore of her housekeeping to worry about, and it could not be sluffed off on Mary Lou, for it was her secret and el Viejito's.

She moved to the den and opened the door tentatively.

Thank God. The air was musty, but that was simply the smell of the old; she was used to that, it was nothing, *nada* . . .

But once or twice in the last few months, Don Miguel had fouled himself after awakening. Unable to make it to the bathroom, always doing his pitiful best to clean up, hide the evidence, somehow make it all right again, he always failed.

His eyes had told her that *he* knew *she* knew: after all, she daily made up the room, washed the sheets, did his laundry. One part of her cried for his macho shame: she wanted to pat his cheek, tell him it was all right, not his fault, that never would she tell Shawn.

The other part, the devil-part, longed to drive him from the den, which was to have been hers, to force him from the house, which was to have been theirs, to tell Shawn, yank his attention from his dying friend to his grandfather, dying only a little less swiftly.

But today, thank God, no problem. She drew open the blinds and the room flooded with light. Now, for eight hours, or nine, until Don Miguel returned, it was her studio again.

Swiftly, she drew the sheets and blankets from the hideaway couch, turned it into a settee, hung up his pajamas and his robe in the closet.

Only then did she permit herself to study the canvas on her easel. Absently, she reached for a palette knife on the stand beside it. She looked down. He had somehow kicked the stand over. The pallet had landed wet side down. Her paint and knives were scattered far and wide.

Her head began to pound so madly that she ran to the bathroom and was sick. Then she returned, picked up the mess, rubbed ineffectually with thinner at the oil stain on the rug, and went to work.

After a while she was conscious only of the private window on the world she opened with her brush.

Six

Sheriff-Coroner Headquarters, Santa Barbara County, lay on Sanitary Fill Road, just outside the western city limits. Despite the unappetizing address, the grounds were green and open. The building itself was sparkling new, heavy-duty Spanish like everything else the county owned.

Across uncrowded parking lots lay the fine new jail and, in its basement, the fire and police Emergency Communications Center. The jail was edged by lawns. Near its entrance, from a towering pole, huge U.S. and California Bear Republic flags whipped in the rising wind.

Shawn Ortega glanced at the flags, which collapsed, flopped again, and flowed out like breaking surf. Plenty of wind already, and still early in the morning. He tried to remember if a Santa Ana had ever lasted the whole winter through.

He walked up the path to headquarters. In the lobby he nodded to Bernice, the sheriff's receptionist. He passed the rogue's gallery of Santa Barbara politician-sheriffs, from the 1870s on. His grandfather had known most of them. Studying the photos, Don Miguel had claimed that *bandido* sombreros would have been more appropriate for nine out of ten of them, and that their venality had only increased when their western hats changed to visored caps.

Well, the previous sheriff, Alan McCrae, had been honest enough, and a real pro, besides. The present one, Armando Castillo, was a lateral transfer years ago from the LA Sheriff's Department. He had always since had some job in Administration, kissing ass.

Today, Shawn was afraid, he'd learn more about him than he really wanted to know.

He stopped at the coffee machine in the corridor. He found no change in his pocket, and so moved into the squad room empty-handed. Inside, at a fake-oak table, a uniformed deputy sat on one of the chrome-and-orange chairs, reading the paper as he waited for roll call. Shawn didn't know his name.

The old headquarters had been grimy and noisy and Shawn had bitched as loudly as anyone. But at least you poured your own coffee into your own cup and they trusted you to feed the kitty for it, and you seemed to know everybody you saw.

He moved past neat pigeonholes stuffed with forms: arrest reports and property reports, booking forms, accident forms, coroner-reportable death forms, traffic forms, forms that he seemed to have spent two thirds of his adult life filling out. He groped into his own cubbyhole: "DETECTIVE BUREAU: Homicide: Lt. S. Ortega." Only a note in Bernice's rigid handwriting, to see the sheriff at nine. Thank you, Bernice.

He drifted to the morning report tacked by the night watch commander to the bulletin board. Nothing specifically for Homicide. For the Detective Bureau, two follow-ups. A Seven-Eleven grocery on Hollister had got itself hit by an armed robber, at midnight, silent alarm set off by the proprietor. Cal Trumbell, a sour little deputy on the edge of retirement, had responded. He'd apparently rolled Code Three, full living color, siren screaming and red light flashing. He'd scared off the bandit, which was what he doubtless intended but which would send the patrol division commander straight up the nearest wall.

And a potential stat-rape at 1 A.M. in the back of a Dodge van near Community Christian School. The girl, Juanita Arguello, was fourteen. Her old man, armed with a .45, had been searching for her and her boyfriend, found them, had miraculously chosen a citizen's arrest over murder, and brought him in. The boy was nineteen, and presumably now in a holding tank across the parking lot.

In today's cold light the old man would probably change his mind on the stat-rape. Family honor, don't make waves. The boy, one Paul

Baker, would probably never know how close he'd come to a .45 slug in the ass.

Good for you, Father Arguello, whoever you are, for thinking twice and going the Anglo route. With Brink dying in the hospital, Shawn needed a homicide this week like he needed a hole in the head.

He tacked up an ad for Brink's motorcycles, ignoring the rule against using the bulletin board for commerce.

Captain James Perkapek, of Crimes Against Persons, wandered in. He was a tall, pale officer with squinting green eyes set too close together, a holdover from the bad days in the early sixties. He had been disliked by McCrae, but was a sailing companion and favorite of the present sheriff. Icy-cold, he felt his pockets for a dime when Shawn hit him for a cup of coffee, then decided that he had no change.

They weren't the best of friends: Perkapek saw a revolutionary in every university student busted for a lid, and a rerun of the Isla Vista trashings of '70 every time the Save the Whales Society held a street meeting.

Obviously, he knew of Shawn's appointment with the Man, and was getting all the distance he could between them.

A chime sounded discreetly, and the room began to fill with more apolitical friends from the morning watch.

Plenty of coffee change now, but time to see the sheriff. With no coffee. Unhappily, he headed down the hall.

The counter girl parked her red VW in a slot as far from the kitchen entrance as was possible, to leave space for customers, in accordance with an edict from the manager.

She looked at her watch. Five minutes to nine. The Flake would be inside already, having arrived at eight-thirty, to set up the kitchen and start the cooker.

She did not want to be alone with him. She had no way of knowing if the inside girl had beat her to work. The blonde was borne on random currents, like some beautiful single-celled undersea creature, sometimes arriving with her mother, sometimes deposited by a boyfriend, sometimes arriving by bus. Apparently no one trusted her to drive a car.

The manager would not show up until eleven, to pick up yesterday's receipts and inventory the stock. Perhaps, if the Flake had ordered it, he would drop off a bag of the Colonel's Super-Secret formula, which he purchased from the LA distributor and apparently kept at home for fear of compromising the whole Kentucky Fried Chicken empire.

None of the high school girls who came in to handle the heavy traffic would arrive until 5 P.M.

She waited until the last possible moment, hoping that if the blonde was not already inside, she would turn up before nine. But the time clock was ticking inexorably. She only earned $3.25 an hour, and could not afford to lose any portion of it. Reluctantly, she got out, locked the car, and started across the lot.

A hot gust whipped her candy-striped skirt to her thighs. She caught at it. The Santa Ana was coming up again.

She punched in and checked her makeup in the bathroom mirror. She thought she could still detect, twelve hours after, the smell of burning paper from whatever rite the Flake had been performing the night before. She winced, still perplexed, and stepped through the fire doors to the kitchen.

The Flake had started his stove and was standing by the oven, meditatively dipping chicken parts into batter he had poured. He swung his eyes at her. They were muddy and yellow, the color of the estuary behind the Marine Biology Lab. She felt her cheeks grow hot.

"Good morning," she mumbled.

He nodded, never taking his eyes from her face. Jesus, this was going to be impossible. Where was the inside girl? Had *she* quit? If so, she couldn't be blamed, working so close to the Flake all day. At least her own station kept a wall and a serving window between them.

She moved to the giant reefer. Ordinarily graceful, she seemed to have gone spastic, and she stumbled. She shot him a glance. He was still staring at her, splashing chicken backs into the goo.

Anyway, if she stayed, her problem with calories would end. She wanted nothing the Flake touched, not thighs, not spareribs, not slaw. She'd live on the carrot cakes, brought in from outside.

She opened the reefer, slid out a tray of coleslaw containers. She was backing through the swinging doors to the front when the cups began to slide.

"No!" she yelled as they hit the floor.

Shoveling the mess into a garbage bag, she sneaked another look at the cook.

He seemed to be studying her, still dunking the chicken, as if trying to read her thoughts.

"Santa Ana," she mumbled. Why apologize? Everybody dropped things, sometimes.

He smiled sarcastically and nodded, as if he didn't believe her at all. Jerk, creep, what was she *doing* here?

The fire doors swung, and the inside girl swished in. "Bus was late," she announced, heading for the refrigerator. "I'm starved." She noticed the mess. "Hey, I'll get that, go open up."

The counter girl had envied the blonde her looks, trim figure, and even her vacuous smile.

But she had never really liked her before. Suddenly she did, very much, just for coming to work.

She unlocked the front entrance, switched on the Colonel's bucket on the roof, and started the business day.

Seven

Shawn Ortega stared down at the sheriff. "Would you run that by *again*?"

Sheriff Armando Castillo smiled and leaned back in a squawking 1880 swivel chair. The chair suffered under his weight and clashed with his pastel office, but tradition demanded that he keep it.

He had always had a great smile; Shawn had noticed over the last three years that power was making it dazzling. He had a high-domed head, tanned from his sailboat, and soft brown eyes, still young and twinkling at fifty-five.

"I said, 'Shawn, we're pulling you off Homicide.'"

"Why?"

The sheriff didn't answer. He stood, moved to the window, gazed for a moment across the parking lot at the county jail. "How's your friend? Brinkley Southerland the Third?" he asked suddenly.

Surprised, Shawn answered: "He's not going to hack it. He's dying."

Castillo turned back to the room. To his credit, he faked no regret. "Did you know about that contribution? *Before* he made it?"

Brink, without telling Shawn, had given $2,500 to ex-Sheriff McCrae's current campaign fund. The *News-Press* had picked it up. "No," he said hopelessly. Castillo wouldn't believe him anyway.

"If you *had* known, say? How would you have advised him?"

Shawn saw a plaintive invitation to get off the hook and simply join Castillo's clique. But it was a hell of a question, like how a man

had voted, a question McCrae would never ask, none of his goddamn business.

He wasn't going to lie about it. "Sorry. I'd have told him to do
just what he did. You *know* I support McCrae."

"Yes. But why?"

"Because you're an administrator! Mac was in the field! He was a
good sheriff. Brink knew that anyway."

Castillo's eyes were cold. He leaned on the edge of the desk.
"Rodríguez, Gómez, Rojas, Álvärez—*they* support me! I'm *Castillo!*
You're *Ortega!* What about a little sense of *la raza?*"

Shawn couldn't believe it. He sounded like Crissy. "That's
bullshit! This department runs on merit! Or it won't run!"

"Well, it's had some crappy Anglo sheriffs."

"Not McCrae. And it's had some crappy Spanish ones, too."

"I keep forgetting"—Castillo smiled tightly—"you *are* half
Anglo."

"A quarter," Shawn snapped. "And Ortegas have lost more to
Anglos around here in the last hundred and fifty years than . . ."

His voice trailed off. He was in too deep. Castillo relaxed and
grinned.

"Go on."

"Skip it."

Castillo shook his head: " ' . . . lost more to Anglos than us wetback *cholos* ever saw'? Right?"

"No, sir," Shawn said stiffly. "I'm from the unlucky side of the
family. And I don't ordinarily say 'wetback.' Or 'cholo.' "

"But since *I've* said it, am I right? *Right,* compadre?"

Shawn shrugged. "No, but you've answered my question about
Homicide. Thanks."

"Oh, no. Not that at all. We've just been discussing politics, *that's*
reorganization." The sheriff sat down, never taking his eyes from
Shawn's face. He began to drum a pencil on his desk. "No. It's because you're *wasted* in Homicide."

"Wasted?"

"That's what people say." Castillo smiled. He lifted a sheaf of
papers. "I've been reading your file. I agree."

Shawn suddenly realized that he was dealing with a very cautious
and complicated man. "I wonder why 'people' say I'm 'wasted'?" he

murmured. "Until I took over Homicide, this department hadn't cleared a murder in eighteen months."

"Right!" Castillo grinned. "Regular Kojak, for a while. Jeez, you got a better local press than poor old McCrae himself. Maybe *you* should have run." He leafed through the file. "Montoya case, cleared. Rickles murder, cleared. The Solvang Slasher—hey, you invent that name?"

"No."

"Solvang Slasher, indicted . . ." He looked up. "You worked yourself out of a job, is all. Hell, we're all caught up."

They weren't, and never would be. There were twenty-seven open murders in the files from 1970 on, but the sheriff knew that as well as he. "So who handles homicides?" asked Shawn. "Just in case we ever have another one?"

"Perkapek. Crimes Against Persons Unit, like they used to. Before we got delusions of grandeur around here."

"And what do 'people' have in mind for me?" His anger was rising. "Coroner's Unit?"

"Now, now . . ."

"Why not? That's tradition, isn't it? You guess wrong, they stick you in the morgue. Happened to me *once* already!"

"You were being punished, I heard." Castillo beamed.

"Well, McCrae was right," Shawn admitted.

"Anyway"—Castillo shrugged—"this time, you haven't done anything."

And besides, added Shawn silently, Coroner's Unit is a sergeant's job, you can't put a lieutenant on the Ghoul Squad. You might get hit with a Board of Rights hearing, or the Peace Officers' League, or sued. Thank God he'd made some rank under McCrae. If he were still a sergeant, Castillo would have him back scraping stiffs off the woodwork.

"OK. Where *won't* a man of my peculiar talents be wasted?" he asked carefully.

"We've been giving that some thought, Administration and me." Castillo murmured. "We *could* make you Public Information Officer. You're certainly good with the press. On the other hand, it's hard to justify a lieutenant's salary for just feeding the media, Proposition 13 and all. Juvey Court Bailiff? You might be soft on kids. Besides, it only calls for a deputy. What do we *do* with an ex-Homicide lieutenant? Make him Spanish Community Liaison Officer? No, that fag-Castilian you speak scares the hell out of braceros. Give him the Narc Squad, or maybe the Civil Addict Program?" He studied his fingernails. "Thought of that, but frankly . . . Well, Brink Southerland, those hill people, Mamá Lola, Las Pumas Canyon, Wildcat Ridge, pretty rich for the blood. God knows what-all they're snorting up there."

"Look," flared Shawn, "you think that's a problem, you better *charge* somebody. And try to back it up."

Castillo spread his hands. "I can't. So what *do* we do with you?"

The sheriff was having a ball. Shawn had a wild inclination to slap his badge on the desk and head for the *News-Press.*

But a gray specter of Christmas bills, house payments, finance charges, Mary Lou's tennis lessons, Crissy's dental work, and, perhaps, not far in the future, Don Miguel in some rest home, restrained him. Besides, his badge was exactly what Castillo wanted.

The chair screeched in agony as Castillo rose. "So, something new." He moved to a wall and motioned Shawn to a new table of organization, all beautifully done in color for the next meeting of the County Supervisors: red for Patrol, green for Investigation, yellow for Administrative Services, purple for Detention-Corrections, orange for Court Services. Penciled alongside each box was the proposed budget.

"It was time to reorganize again," explained Castillo. "Now, murder's fun, people like to read about it, but it's not statistically important. And burglary, ADW, rape . . . They're all problems, kind of, even here in Mr. Clean-land. But what's the real nitty-gritty in this county? What scares people the worst?"

"Political corruption," Shawn suggested. "No offense."

Castillo's eyes blazed. "The shine's stayed on *my* badge, just see it stays on yours!"

"Yes, sir. Not to cut this discussion short, but—"

"You're an arrogant bastard, you know?"

"No, sir. Where's *my* slot?"

"What scares people the most," Castillo continued, squatting to search the organization table, "is brush fires, firebugs. Come here, you kind of have to stoop a little . . . which may be good for you. Here!"

He whipped out a pencil and wrote Shawn's name into a tiny square.

Shawn squinted.

"Arson and Explosives? Where'd *that* come from?"

"LA County." Castillo grinned, straightening. "Good enough for them, good enough for us."

"In *this* county," Shawn said bleakly, "County Fire does arson."

"Yeah. You'll work with their arson guy . . . the fat Jap?"

"Hash Ono. Look, I don't *know* anything about arson investigation!"

"*He* does."

Shawn peered down at the slot. "I don't see any personnel."

"Just you." Castillo jabbed his arm companionably. "And you'll be our liaison with Operation Torchy, you've heard of that. Hey, you'll get to know the DA: he don't like Latinos much, but *you* got that touch of class. He's revving up for re-election—"

"Aren't you all?" Shawn murmured.

"What? Oh . . . Well, he'll point at *us* on this arson thing, and I want him to know we're trying. Maybe you can draw some men from Patrol or Detective Bureau, for stakeouts in the hills." He smiled again. "If they'll give them to you."

It was very clear. In a week he'd have every captain and inspector in the department as a sworn enemy, and without a directive, get no men anyway. Without sufficient personnel, he could only piss off the DA. And *explosives?*

"I don't know TNT from owlshit!"

"That's bad," admitted Castillo. "I guess you better learn."

Christ, he'd be better off in the Coroner's Unit. The job sounded like the kiss of death for his career. He moved to the window, looked out.

Behind the vehicle entrance to the county jail he saw the prisoner transfer van from Lompoc Substation. It was unloading. As a deputy opened the van door, a long-haired, cadaverous youth, stoned or drunk, stumbled out and fell to his hands and knees. His hair hung to the dirt. The emerging prisoners laughed at him, but the deputy stooped, massaged his neck, helped him up, and guided him to the booking entrance.

There were departments in the state, Shawn knew, where the cop would have booted him while he was down, for giggles.

He had twelve years in. He was damned if the sheriff was going to run him off. But if he didn't get out of the office in a hurry, he'd knock the pudgy prick on his can. He started for the door.

"Lieutenant!"

Shawn turned. "Yes, sir?"

"The firebugs are out. Unless it rains, the hills will burn. With or without our fucking 'Arson Detail.' But the DA asked for it, he's got it. You're liaison. Liaison means somebody for him to hang. Just remember that, OK?"

"When does this sentence start?" His voice was hoarse with anger.

"'Transfer,' son." Castillo smiled. "It started just then, when I wrote in your name."

"And when do you figure I'll get Homicide back?"

Castillo sat down at his desk, grinning. The chair screamed wildly. "Let's see. I got ten years in here. I plan to go out on twenty." He jabbed his desk calculator. He looked up. "How about 1992?"

"How about next election?" Shawn smiled. "Before you wreck that chair?"

"*Vete a la chingada*," Castillo said softly. "And you got a briefing at noon; Operation Torchy. Get your ass in gear."

Shawn parked and waited outside Montecito Savings and Loan, a small establishment of weathered, diagonally planked knotty pine with cool dark-tinted windows and a fountain outside. Brink had been a founder.

Brink's silver Porsche slammed into the space beside him, and he glimpsed Nicole's swirling hair, golden in the bright sunlight, as she slithered from behind the wheel.

She was thirty-six and had a fifteen-year-old son. But she still moved like a teen-ager, with the long-gaited coltishness that had plucked at his throat when she was twenty. It was a loose-limbed, honest stride, and it fooled you every time.

That she could be as phony as a TV commercial, you couldn't see at first.

He had loved her very much.

He got out of his car, shifting his stubby .38 so that it would ride under his sport shirt. He felt strangely guilty, as always when going armed into a bank. Nicole squeezed his hand, kissed his cheek, and gave him two empty attaché cases from the car.

"Well," a voice croaked, as he shouldered through the door, "Shawn Ortega! This a heist, Lieutenant?"

He turned and faced Sleepy Doyle, a retired deputy he hadn't seen in years. He could see from the old man's spangled cheeks and bloodshot eyes that he still lived out of a bottle. His gray misfitted uniform meant that Montecito S&L had been misguided enough to hire him as a guard. His hand, on the butt of his revolver, showed that, at sixty, he was still a child playing cops and robbers. Shawn would have thought he'd eaten the gun by now.

He nodded at Sleepy and followed Nicole and the vault girl through a heavy steel gate. The room was banked with rows of locked metal drawers. Shawn, never having accumulated anything he'd put in a safe-deposit box, watched curiously as the girl, using the bank's key, turned the bottom lock on all three drawers, then, with Nicole's keys, turned the top ones too.

Shawn carried the three drawers into an adjoining counting room. He was amazed at the weight of two of them. The girl left the vault and he and Nicole were alone at the counting room table.

She opened the light drawer first. It was full of envelopes and little jewel boxes. She found the Orange County municipals and the treasury notes. Shawn had no idea of the denominations or how many there were, and no desire to find out.

She packed the securities in one of the briefcases and began to open the jewel boxes, looking for something. Finally, out of a jumble of rings, bracelets, and charms, in a battered cardboard box, she drew a gold football on a tiny wrist-chain. Her smoky gray eyes seemed only amused, but after sixteen years, they could still make him feel like a horny oaf. She dangled the football between them.

"It's stupid for me to have this," she murmured. "Take it back."

"What'll I do with it?" His voice sounded hoarse.

"Well"—she grinned—"you could fumble it away before you got hit . . . like you did before . . ."

She laid the gold football on the counter next to the drawer, began to toy with the baubles in the cardboard box. She commenced to hum softly, and for a moment he did not catch the tune, and when he did, he felt the blood rush to his face. "La Paloma" . . .

"Knock it off, Nicks," he growled, a little too quickly. He hadn't called her "Nicks" for sixteen years, and didn't want to now.

She glanced at him narrowly. She was very sensitive to voice, on the screen or off, and the timbre of his must somehow have jarred her. "Damn," she murmured, studying him. "*I* think . . . Hey, it had something to *do* with 'La Paloma'? Right? Why didn't you tell me? Why don't you tell me *now?*"

Jesus, what a time to bring it up! Incredible. "Don't know what you're talking about," he muttered.

"Bullshit." She shrugged. "All right, I don't care."

She lowered her head, counting diamonds, or emeralds, or whatever the hell she had in the box. Her back was stiff and her face was rigid. He had a crazy impulse to tell her for once and for all what had really happened, but knew he couldn't, now or ever, it was too late now, it had been too late then.

They'd met two weeks before Fiesta. The Navy had just accepted his resignation: his grandmother had died and he had to take care of el Viejito. Lyndon Johnson was President; Nam was hot; he had been lucky to get out. A glorious summer of freedom and beautiful girls: Crissy, at eighteen, was to be Fiesta queen. He was enrolled at Santa Barbara City College, teaching flying on the side.

Nicole, on location for a TV commercial at Santa Barbara Municipal, had wandered, between takes, into the hangar and into his life. She wanted, or said she wanted, flight lessons. There was an Amelia Earhart script she'd auditioned for. She thought if she got the part, she'd grasp it better if she flew. All, of course, b.s. . . .

He'd been overwhelmed by her offhand beauty and the easy, graceful stride, turned on by her careless humor. He'd given her flying lessons, at the going rate. Later, after he'd discovered that she didn't want to learn to fly at all, the lessons had turned free.

There'd been thrashing wild nights in her cottage at the Miramar; she was Cleopatra, he was Anthony, in a bedsheet toga; the asp was something else. There was a sunset sail on a sloop borrowed from an account executive: Shawn was Captain Blood, and she a captured trollop. She was always writing little dramas in her mind. And a horseback ride up Cathedral Peak: he was Zorro, and she was Ramona the Indian maid.

One night at his favorite bar, El Casito, high on wine at a table in back, he'd borrowed a Spanish guitar from the empty bandstand.

He'd sung her the songs his mother had sung to him: "La Golondrina" and "Perfidia" and "La Paloma"—which was forever to be theirs—and her eyes had widened. He was *professional*, should be *auditioning, fantastic, incredible,* he *must* have had *training* . . .

He had left El Casito in love.

One afternoon, while she was on location at the Polo Field, he'd stretched on the beach near her cottage. Wonderously, dunes he knew so well from childhood had turned to gold, because of her; the surf beat its fists in joy at his happiness on the hot throbbing sand. And finally he had gone, sandy, to her cabin to shower. He'd been drying when the phone rang, and heard her enter, and answer it.

"Hi, Brian . . ."

Her gay agent. Shawn loved Brian, though he hadn't met him, because Brian was a part of her; Shawn loved her mother, an MGM script editor he hadn't met either, and each of her three stepfathers, none of whom he'd seen, loved them all simply because they were hers.

He continued quietly to dry himself. She was the only girl he'd ever met whose voice gave him an erection.

"No. I won't *be* at the fucking screening. I'm staying here another week . . ."

A rush of joy. Jesus, what he'd do when she *did* leave, he didn't know. A flight instructor couldn't earn a living in Hollywood. Well, you couldn't here, either. He'd already applied for the Santa Barbara Sheriff's Department, maybe he ought to try for Los Angeles instead.

"Yes, darling, *again!* You handle the career, I'll handle the love life, OK?"

She didn't know he was there. He slowed his toweling. The voice had a cutting edge he hadn't heard before. He really ought to declare himself. He hung up the towel and had his hand on the doorknob when he hesitated.

"Part Spanish, got a granddaddy, you know, right out of a B Western. The whole *Californio* schmear . . ."

A fair enough evaluation, but suddenly he didn't want to hear any more. He started to call to her, found himself inexplicably waiting.

"About nine feet tall, all muscle, football, airplane driver, good IQ . . ."

Thanks, kid, I try . . .

"Terrible singer, tin ear, doesn't know it. No drive, no future. Full of all that old-California-fallen-on-evil-times, 'La Paloma' crap. But, Brian? Hey, you'd *love* him in the sack."

He still blushed to think of himself strumming to her misty eyes; he hadn't touched a guitar since. Though, of course, the guitar and "La Paloma" had nothing to do with it, and the bullshit everything . . .

Face frozen, he'd simply stepped back into the shower, eased on the water, and feigned surprise when she'd stepped in. Vestigial Hispanic pride had kept him from telling her *why*, thank God—for she'd only have conned him again. He'd simply dressed and given an excuse and headed back for Pueblo Viejo.

> Cock the gun that is not loaded,
> Cook the frozen dynamite,
> But oh, beware my country,
> When my country grows polite . . .

Six months later he was married to Crissy, Queen of the May.
Whom he loved, very dearly, as he loved Mary Lou.
Saved his ass, that shower.
And almost broke his heart.

"You know," Nicole murmured now, shoving the jewels aside and casting up the enormous gray eyes, "for months I couldn't decide whether to change my toothpaste or my douche? So, where *did* our song come in?"

"It didn't, Nicks." *Nicks*, again. "Look, we going to pack this stuff or not?"

She picked up the golden football again, swung it. He'd given it to her at an ad agency cocktail party sometime during the crazy two weeks: even then, when he was twenty-two, it had seemed juvenile.

"I *don't* want it, Nickie," he insisted. *Nickie.* Better.

"Then give it to Mary Lou."

"She has better taste than that already."

"*I* wore it, and I was *twenty*."

She had, too; laughing at it, probably, all the time.

Oh, hell, why not? Brusquely, he held out his hand and she let it drop into his palm.

She opened the other two drawers. One was packed with case-sized golden ingots, three inches by two inches by perhaps a quarter inch thick. They had a phony brassy glitter under the fluorescent lights. The other drawer was stuffed with little translucent plastic cubes, through which he could see stacked gold coins.

He stared at the drawers. Before him, he was sure, lay only a microscopic portion of Brink's wealth, but more than Shawn would make in all his working days.

He dropped the football into his pocket and began to help her stow the gold in the briefcases.

Eight

Zimmer, the fry cook—alias Jake Klinger—stood at the stove, studying the backs and thighs and legs bubbling in the boiling hydrogenized oil over the singing blue flames. Occasionally he would prod a piece of chicken with a long-handled fork. He'd learned from a bullet-headed jig, murder one, in the inmate kitchen at Lompoc, that regardless of what they told you, you had to keep moving the parts.

He liked to watch the flesh turn brown, especially the Colonel's Crispy. He poked at a fine young Arkansas breast still untouched by the oil in the cooker, and forced his mind back to his problem.

So the counter girl hadn't missed a thing in the crapper last night. He should have known from the shock on her face. She was still so shook this morning she'd spilled the goddamn slaw.

She suspected that he was pyro. But she hadn't finked yet, or he'd be down with the sheriff answering questions. With his record, they'd try to frame him for the fires he hadn't set.

Or turn him loose with a tail.

He already had a tail: the Shrink. The last thing he wanted was another.

At dawn he'd awakened in the stolen trailer he kept in a Mexican's back yard, near the SP tracks in Goleta. The Voice of the Shrink had come to him on the clatter of a passing freight: *"Don't, unless . . . Don't, unless . . . Don't, unless . . ."*

Unless *what?* Unless she was going to the cops? How could *he* know that, if the Shrink didn't?

When the freight had passed, he'd ramped the Harley onto the bed of his pickup and bundled it under a tarp. The pickup and bike were outside now, in the parking lot.

Just in case he needed them.

He had a plan: stash the bike in the hills at noon, use it to get back down tonight.

Almost five years since he'd driven San Marcos Pass.

But: *Don't, unless . . .*

He'd been trying to study the girl all morning: she'd been staying up front.

He rubbed his eyes, thinking it through. He began again to prod the chicken.

Near the center of the enormous frying basket rose the Arkansas breast, shimmering but not yet scarred on top. He touched it with the fork. OK, he would overturn it: if the underside was simply caked with batter, "regular" by the Colonel's standards, the girl did not intend to talk. If it was crispy already, she was going to blow the whistle.

He waited for an instant, heart hammering. Then he flipped the breast.

It was crispy. More than crispy, scorched. "OK," he told the Shrink, aloud. "See?"

"What?" The blonde had been mopping the floor, just fast enough to finish the job by the time the manager arrived. With every swish, her ass shimmied and quivered in the tight little candy-striped dress.

"Didn't say nothing."

He wished there were some way tonight he could handle the blonde, too. But, like they said, two was company, three was a crowd.

It took all of Shawn's skills to keep his Chevy on Nicole's tail as she squealed up switchbacks, around blind turns, and over the little stone bridges of Las Pumas Canyon Drive.

She had, he estimated, $750,000 in bullion and coins in the brief-cases beside her; if she met another speeder coming down, Las Pumas Canyon would become another Mother Lode.

She whipped the silver Porsche between the towering flagstone gates of Wildcat Ridge. He followed her past Ruben's gatehouse, sped under oaks down a shadowed driveway, twisting through manicured lawns. Shawn caught a glimpse of Ruben gaping from a power mower, as he rocketed past, then turned under a massive portico and parked behind her at the front door.

Wet with sweat, he stepped to her passenger window. "Jesus, Nickie!"

Her smoky gray eyes were innocent. "You said you had a meeting. Go on back down. Ruben's here."

He clasped his head. "Ruben's going to help you? Put three quarters of a million in a *barbecue* pit? In gold?"

"You can trust Ruben."

"Oh, God," he moaned. "I don't trust *me!* Unlock the door!"

She did, and he jerked the briefcases from the seat. He staggered under eighty pounds of gold, following her through the cool timbered grandeur of the living room, out past the patio and the swimming pool, and along a cobbled path to the little glen where he and Brink had built the barbecue.

It was a colossal affair of brick, and he and Brink had bedded a safe in concrete inside an oven under one of its sweeping arms, good standard practice in fire country, where the home itself could melt before your eyes, and looters would poke through the ashes.

When he had the vault stowed and locked, they started back to the house. "Shawn?"

"Yeah?"

"See Val again, before you go?"

He'd already tried to get the kid to visit his father more often, and failed. "It didn't do any good."

"Try again?"

He nodded. He went to Val's room and knocked. Inside, he could hear stereo, full blast. No answer. He knocked louder.

"Yeah?"

"Shawn, OK?" He opened the door.

The room was dominated by a photo-mural of Brink's biplane, caught landing years ago by Shawn, with Brink's camera. Val, at twelve, had been flying from the front cockpit, helmeted and goggled, shoulders tense and scarf whipping in the slipstream. Brink sat in the rear, grinning at the lens, goggles up, hands ostentatiously raised to show that Val had the controls.

Not a bad shot, Shawn had always thought, a little stagy, but what the hell.

Val rose from the bed under the mural. He turned off the TV and the stereo, which had been playing simultaneously. He was almost sixteen now, broad-shouldered, slim-hipped, with bleached surfer's hair and Brink's blue eyes. Like his dad, he used them as bludgeons. He stuck out his hand, reversed, black-power, football-style. They shook.

"Saw you lugging the family jewels, or whatever," he said. "Heavy?"

Interesting. He could have offered to help. Well, the velvet glove hadn't worked. Today he'd try the fist. "Thanks, spud," Shawn said acidly. "Wouldn't want you to strain your gut. Not before the Santa Paula game."

Val looked shocked.

"Sorry, nobody asked."

"I'm asking something now. I want you to see your dad more."

It wasn't the approach Nicole had in mind, he was sure, but at least it was clear. The blue eyes were jolted again, but never left his own. "I saw him Tuesday, after practice."

"See him today."

"Late practice, no time." Val got up, moved to the window, stared across the sweeping lawn. "I better check the pool pump, you know? There's *got* to be a fire."

"See him tomorrow, then."

Val whirled. His eyes were frigid. "You think he can slot me in?"

"Quit your goddamn bleeding!"

"I'm not bleeding, Shawn. Just wondering. Can he maybe work me in between you and Mom? Or his lawyer and the accountant? Or Tinkerbell and . . . what's the fucking redhead's name?"

Shawn moved closer and looked down at him. The blue eyes were already very nearly level with his own: he'd be six-four someday, taller than his dad. He felt like slapping his face, belting him in the gut, anything to break the ice in the angry eyes. Instead, he spoke quietly: "Val, I'm warning you! When he's gone, unless you see him more—"

"Did he ask?"

That, he didn't want to answer. He continued: "*My* folks died together, same night. They couldn't get me there, so it wasn't even my fault." His throat grew tight. "That was twenty-five years ago, and I *still* feel guilty!"

"You told me all that. *Did he ask?*"

To lie would be stupid. Val knew that Brink would ask no one to visit him, not Nicole, not another woman, not Val. People had been fighting for his attention all his life. For all Shawn knew, Brink didn't care how often Val saw him before the end. Shawn was thinking of Val, not Brink.

"You *know* he won't ask." He jabbed a thumb toward the mural. "Remember that day?"

Suddenly Val was fighting tears. He nodded.

"Did he have to *ask* you to land it?" asked Shawn.

Val shook his head.

"What'd he say? 'You got it?'" Shawn demanded.

Val nodded.

"So you landed it. OK, buddy. I won't ask you this again, either. But you got it."

He started for the door.

"No!"

He turned. Val's face was working, holding back the sobs. "That landing was shit! To get the fucking picture, to show his friends, maybe, I don't know, I never could get inside his head." He began to tremble. "That landing was *four years ago!* How many times did he take me up since? Two, no, three! In four years? Hell, I got more time in his fucking bird with *you!*"

"Val, he was building the Estates—"

Val's eyes flared. "I forgot: the Estates. Well, we were millionaires *before* the Estates. I'll be the richest kid in Las Pumas Canyon."

"Santa Barbara."

"Fantastic!" Val's face was working again. "You know, if you guys . . . If I just could have worked on the barbecue pit, or that half-assed chopper you wanted to build . . . Or gone skydiving with you . . ." Now he was crying, for sure. Shawn moved to him, tried to hug his shoulders. Val threw him off roughly. "Oh, fuck it! Could you book *out* of here?"

Shawn nodded and headed again for the door.

"Hey?" Val called. His voice seemed strangled.

"Yeah?"

"Could you *ask* him to ask?"

"We won't have to twist his arm," promised Shawn.

He hoped.

Nicole walked back to his car with him.

"I'm going down to the hospital," she said, "for that so-called lunch they feed him. And he damn well *will* ask to see Val, or I'll beat his brains out!"

"Good."

"Shawn?"

"Yeah?"

"I'd be there all the time. I *want* to be near him. And I *want* to learn how to handle things. But I can't keep my mind on what he's telling me. And I *bore* him."

"*Bore* him?" He studied her quizzically. The one thing she'd never done was bore anyone.

"I can't talk municipal yields, I can't tune a motorcycle, I don't like airplanes, I don't know the women he's been screwing. He's more relaxed with you."

He told her that she was wrong: it was simply the coughing, and the pain. "He can't hold it back, sometimes. And he doesn't want you watching."

"That's the stupidest thing I ever heard! As if *I* cared!"

"*He* cares." He reminded her that Brink wanted no one feeling sorry for him, that he was hurting ten times worse than he showed, that he wouldn't yell for help, so even the nurses didn't know.

She accepted that, but seemed reluctant to let him go. And he could not bring himself to drive off. She was looking away, over the ranges, her profile etched on a windswept sky. The Santa Ana momentarily died. It was very warm. She blew a strand of hair from her forehead. "I wish the goddamn wind would quit. Brink worries about fire." She glanced at the house. "If it burns, it burns! Just so we get the horses."

Her hand lay on the window. He covered it briefly, sensing that she honestly wanted him out of the car, folding her into his arms for comfort, nothing erotic, but a pat on the hand would not do.

He left his hand but sat impassively. He'd survived her once, and didn't care to risk it again.

The Santa Ana rose once more, hissing through the oaks. A horse whinnied nervously. She glanced at the stables, barn-red with white trim. "Water, he wants," she murmured. "Don't let me keep you." She squeezed his hand and turned away.

Pulling out through the gates, he looked into his rearview mirror. The wind was molding her blouse to her breasts, her hair was streaming in it, her skirt whipping wildly. She was heading for the stables, moving with the long, loose stride.

He clenched his hands on the wheel. It was bullshit, all bullshit, the walk toward the stable. She didn't water the stock: Ruben took care of that.

She was simply an actress, he told himself, using the only stage she had. And she knew how she looked in the wind.

Nine

Five miles north of Santa Barbara, climbing San Marcos Pass, the fry cook downshifted his pickup.

He knew the road—California Scenic 154—very well. Five years ago, before Lompoc and Atascadero, he'd set seven fires in these hills, playing tag with the Forest Service. He'd almost got caught when he'd tried one too many, too far up Painted Cave Road, and been spotted from the air.

He wouldn't take chances again: the Shrink didn't want him back. Tonight would be different: necessary, right?

"She's going to the cops," he reminded the Shrink.

No answer.

Screw him.

Despite his familiarity with the highway and the power of his full-blown engine, he drove carefully. Not much traffic here at noon, but he didn't want to attract attention to the pickup. And he didn't want a speeding bust today.

He passed San Antonio Creek Road and noticed a camper parked at the intersection. The driver was sitting at the wheel. He had his ears up: two CB antennas projecting from either side of the cab. Two? Like a big Diesel, but he wasn't a Diesel, just an RV with a beach mural on the side. He slowed and continued to Painted Cave Road, thrilling to the remembered chase five years before. There was a van parked there today, also with rabbit ears.

Campers? Sightseers? Somebody up for a quickie, during lunch?

Bullshit. The fuckers were staked out all over the hills. For a moment he wavered. Then the situation tickled his throat.

He hadn't made the first set, and already they were busting their asses looking for him. He gave the second van a hidden finger. He began to laugh, roaring up the barren, brush-dry highway, yodeling like a cowboy. He flicked on his AM radio.

"Torn between two lovers,
Feeling like a fool . . ."

He spotted the turnoff he was looking for, squealed left off the highway and jounced down Trout Canyon Road. In three minutes he had the bike down, off the truck, and hidden in the chaparral.

He was climbing back into the truck when a hot gust of wind whipped a dust devil into the cab. He hesitated.

Sitting all afternoon in a Santa Ana could foul the Harley's points. And he might need a fast start tonight.

He grabbed the tarp, returned to the brush, draped the bike, and drove the pickup back to work.

Shawn found the Operation Torchy safe-house easily in the Pueblo Viejo district of old Santa Barbara. He drove past the secret headquarters, staring at it incredulously, and had to park two blocks away. To a child of the barrio the safe-house was as obtrusive as Ronald Reagan at a Chicano barbecue.

He was twelve minutes late for the noontime briefing, set around a long table in the dining room of an old wooden residence. An assistant DA glared at him from the head of the table. Everyone else craned, like schoolkids glad someone else was late.

"Shawn Ortega," offered Shawn, slipping into the last empty seat. "Sheriff's Department. Sorry."

The assistant DA, a pudgy young man with slate-gray eyes, checked him off a list. "Lieutenant Shawn Ortega, Arson and Explosives. Know everybody?"

He saw Hash Ono, the County Fire Department's arson investigator, chuckling at the new title. Everyone was of course in civvies, but he assumed that most of the people at the table were gold-badge fire types, city and county, or Montecito and Carpinteria fire and police.

He recognized Jerry Castle, a mild, weathered little man with sincere, crinkling eyes. Shawn had seen him on a local TV talk show. He was head firefighter and an assistant supervisor of the Los Padres National Forest, which stretched in two vast separate timberlands from the Los Angeles County line to Monterey, three hundred miles to the north. Under Jerry lay two million acres of tinder-dry forest. It was not surprising that he'd decided to come to the half-assed briefing in person.

Shawn knew almost nobody else by name, but he nodded nevertheless, to save introductions. "Morning, gentlemen."

"*Afternoon,*" muttered the ADA, glancing at the clock. "OK, let's see. Where are we?"

Where you *are,* Shawn told him silently, is in the wrong place. You are one block from my grandfather's old frame shack, smack in the middle of my childhood neighborhood, which is *un barrio muy malo* and quite sensitive to foreign bodies in its bloodstream. The computer you installed in the parlor did not escape local comment, I'm sure. There is an aerial sticking out the roof the likes of which nobody in PV has ever seen.

And you have crammed the street with so many plainclothes cars, vans, and phony campers that you undoubtedly blew your cover ten minutes before your first meeting. Low rent, granted. But why rent a safe-house at all if you're going to make it stick out like a sore thumb?

The folklore on firebugs was that unless they were arsonists-for-profit, they were crying to be caught and cured. The trouble was, they never seemed to co-operate with those hired to touch them in the game of tag they played. Pyros were not stupid, he'd heard. If this was true, any pyromaniac who lived within a square mile of the Operation Torchy safe-house should have copied the license numbers of the stakeout vehicles parked outside, long ago.

That's where you are, Fatass, he thought. He tried to concentrate on the business of the day.

A Santa Barbara police inspector was crying for supplementary funds from the DA's office for his stakeout teams in the hills. Standard. And boring. He caught Hash Ono's eye.

Shawn hadn't seen him since his worst day on the Ghoul Squad, when they'd picked up four dead Caterpillar drivers in the Romero Canyon fire. Hash seemed as solid as ever, with the deep chest of a

diver and the quick, watchful eyes of an athlete, but he was potbellied now. In college, he'd been a favorite of South Coast
sportswriters: "The Flying Buddha," "Orient Express," "Kamikaze
Kid."

Shawn had first met him twenty years ago, the hard way, in a
Santa Barbara College–Ventura football game. Shawn, leaping for
a pass, had tried to ignore Hash's footsteps thundering from the blind
side. Everything had turned black. He'd dropped the ball, of course,
and awakened on the grass with a sprained knee and a psychic scar
that made him drop footballs the rest of his college career.

Now Hash winked, shook his watch, and sighed audibly.

The pudgy young man droned on: Dr. Herbert Dubois, of Atascadero State Hospital for the Criminally Insane, author of *Profiles of
Adult Firesetters*, would be on Channel 3 at 6 P.M. Wednesday;
anyone who'd missed his briefing last week should tune in.

Three small brush fires in the county since the last meeting: all
determined to be accidental. But one possible set in Los Padres. Jerry
Castle's special agents were investigating. Eight suspicious vehicles
on foothill roads last night, reported by teams Delta and Foxtrot; license plates noted, no arrests; the computer showed no previous records of the same vehicles in the hills. One pedestrian, reported to
police and questioned: he'd turned out to be a local resident.

The ADA explained the function of the computer terminal in the
next room: license numbers radioed in by stakeout teams would be
digested by the terminal at the State Bureau of Investigation in
Sacramento: vehicles appearing consistently in fire-danger areas
would be sorted out and pinpointed and their registered owners in-
terrogated. Any questions?

"Yeah!" Hash spoke up. "What about setting Red Flag Alert? And
keeping the frigging cars *out*?"

"I told you last week," the ADA said uncomfortably, "we want to
stay with the stakeout teams and wait."

He enumerated the reasons. Those he gave were budgetary: if the
Red Flag Alert were set too soon and continued too long, it would
guarantee fiscal disaster. The plan was a quarter-inch-thick recipe for
overtime that depended on closing the hills. Roads would be
blocked, to all but residents, by the Sheriff's Department, the city
police, the Santa Barbara City and County Fire Departments, Mon-

tecito and Carpinteria-Summerland Fire Departments, and the U. S. Forest Service.

Everyone at the table had apparently memorized the plan except Shawn. He leafed through his copy now. He was appalled. Last year had been complicated enough, but this year's scheme was massive. Police patrol schedules and routes had to be altered to give fire-hazardous areas extra coverage, checkpoints on mountain roads had to be manned, passing vehicles registered, fire closure invoked on all private and public land in designated areas.

Red flags were hoisted, vehicles engaged in enforcement were placarded. Signs were posted, field report forms distributed to deputies, city policemen, and even private residents, so that all eyes were alert for strangers.

Volunteer mobile communications units were to be alerted and the volunteers fed. Key local residents were instructed to make citizens' arrests.

The treatment grew more drastic every year, as arsonists-for-kicks grew harder to convict in court. How could you prove felony, when the suspect had no motive? Every fire season the bugs seemed to be reborn in the county's bloodstream, rekindled by the fever in the winds. The medication—Red Flag Alert—grew more expensive. The dosage was doubled. The bugs grew smarter, like germs immune to antibiotics.

The official DA's line was that, this year, the prescription might be worse than the disease. The DA was delaying medication, crying budget. That was crap. The real reason was that a former DA had convicted two firebugs, through luck, hard work, a reward, and a fink. Ordinarily, you had to catch them redhanded or your case fell down in court.

The new DA, Kelso, needed solid arrests, and soon. When Red Flag Alert went on, there would be so many private citizens and amateurs legally in the fire areas no one could make a bust that would stick, and Operation Torchy's stakeout teams would wither and die on the vine.

Red Flag Alerts were hell on convictions.

On the other hand, with hundreds of additional eyes watching night and day, you felt better when you went to bed.

As a cop, Shawn dreaded a Red Flag Alert; as a canyon homeowner, he could hardly wait for them to set it.

"Look," Hash exploded. "Let's skip the budget crap, OK?"

Chubby-cheeks flushed angrily, but Hash went on: "All you guys in law enforcement *really* want to do is hog the hills in plainclothes all by yourselves so you can apprehend. But you might as well spend the money and set Red Flag and show up in force and try to scare them away. Because Operation Torchy sucks, gentlemen. There's no way you're gonna catch bugs in the act, or convict them if you don't." He stood up, gathering his papers. "Every fire we had this season, I been knee-deep in hot ashes trying to find you evidence. I gave you three suspects. They're bugs, all right, you can bet your sweet butts. But what can you do with them?"

"Nothing, Hash," said the ADA. "You know that. We can't indict unless they admit something, let alone convict."

"I agree. So let's knock off the horseshit. If you keep trying to use the county for bait, you're going to get us burned." He announced that he was recommending a General Red Flag Alert to his chief tomorrow, *Extreme* Red Flag Alert if the winds kept up.

"The winds," Jerry Castle assured him, "will *increase*." He was closing Los Padres National Forest tomorrow. "I punched up the Fire Weather Forecast from BIFSY. The Burning Index is eighty *already!* That's enough for me: I got the guy who invented this kind of weather flying in from Boise right now."

The young man from the DA gave up. He had done all he could with firemen. Over cops, he had authority, or thought he had. He turned to Shawn. "You ready to put men on Ono's suspects?"

"Men?" Shawn asked blankly. "I'm all the men I got."

"Shall I tell the boss you're working on your personnel problems, then?"

"Tell him anything you want."

The young man turned icy. "A pleasure," he said, and adjourned the meeting.

Ono got up, chuckling. "'Arson and Explosives,'" he said to Shawn. "You still get blindsided in the flat. Was it politics? How come you never learn?"

"For an oriental type of guy, you aren't the soul of tact yourself."

They moved through what had been the parlor. Now it was a hive of bureaucratic inactivity, dominated by the computer console. They stepped into bright sunlight and breasted the scurrying wind. Shawn asked Hash for his suspect file.

"You can't give me surveillance, though?" mused Hash.

"I wasn't kidding, I got no men."

"Then you won't need the files. Anyway, it's easy: one is a nine-year-old posing as a retard, IQ about a hundred and thirty, emotions like a sea snake. He'll admit anything and offer you his little sister. Claims he set Coyote Canyon, and he wasn't even born yet. He sets fires, all right, he probably set half the fires this year, but if you tried to tail him, he'd tie you in knots. And give you the finger. Mommy says prove it. Daddy's long gone. You think we'll ever indict *him?*"

Two was Sparky, an amateur photographer, always on the scene snapping pictures when the trucks rolled up, probably got off on them at home. But there was nothing on him, not a damn thing. And for some reason, he seemed reluctant to volunteer his guilt.

"The last one's a jogger—"

"I run. Maybe it's me."

"Stranger things have happened." This one was male, Caucasian, name and address unknown. "Age around twenty-five, five-eight to six-two, a hundred and thirty pounds to one-seventy."

Hash went on: blond, unless dark-haired or bald. Clean-shaven, or else moustached with a curly beard. Red trunks, unless they were yellow, and a UCSB T-shirt unless it was Boston Marathon.

"The only thing he isn't is black, and the only thing he doesn't wear is bloomers. Observed before the Arroyo Seco fire and two others. Nothing since. If you're a jogger, tail *him.*"

Hash stopped at a battered green scout car that looked as if it had just lost the Baja 500. He climbed in and glanced up at Shawn.

"This isn't Homicide, friend," he added. "In Arson, you're on your own. You're the first help *I* ever got, and you probably don't know doodly-squat."

"I don't. But I still get paid. So what *can* I do?"

Hash started the engine, drummed his fingers on the battered wheel, and muttered: "No surveillance, no men?" He thought for a moment. "OK. One, don't come until I holler—"

"*Will* you holler?"

"I doubt it."

"Then, man, I'll have to come anyway. Or the sheriff will have my ass."

"OK. Then, Rule Number Two is, when you do come, don't step on anything. Three . . . oh hell, that's stupid."

"What's three?"

"If I ever get a hot one, bust him." He smiled tightly. "Just don't hold your breath."

He wheeled out, hung a U, and rocketed toward the hills.

Shawn walked to his car. It seemed that the sheriff had retired him with pay.

Well, with the things he'd promised to do for Brink, he could use the time off. And with the Burning Index where it was, he ought to go home and trim the brush.

Instead, he went to the hangar at Santa Barbara Municipal. He took his leather helmet and goggles from the locker he shared with Brink. He stalked to Brink's jaunty yellow Stearman biplane—apparently his own, now, in all but name. Suddenly sick at heart, he nonetheless cast off the tie-down lines and taxied to the runway. The tower must have thought he was insane, to fly a biplane on so gusty a day. They warned him not once, but twice, of crosswinds from the east.

He sat with the engine ticking, then checked the mags, felt a mighty shove from the wind, and almost scrubbed the flight. But Brink would not have scrubbed it, though he had nowhere near Shawn's time in the air. And Brink was very much in the empty forward cockpit.

Shawn cleared with the tower and roared into the afternoon sun, fighting for control as he wove down the runway, finally wobbling into the air and banking toward the sea.

He told himself that Brink would have wanted him to be elated and happy on this flight: Shawn's dream since flight training had been to own just such a grand old relic. He caressed the stick, snuggled into the seat, patted the fuselage in the howling slipstream. His, all his?

Not all. Though the plane had known him long before it had felt Brink's hands on the throttle, it seemed as angry and bitter as Brink himself, and almost unmanageable in the hot, violent air.

The Santa Ana carried him halfway to Santa Cruz Island. For twenty minutes he wrung himself out at 5,000 feet: slow rolls, Immelmanns, split S, snap roll after snap roll above the golden haze.

He and Brink had shared this hour often, at sunset, in just this place. Usually, if they didn't make themselves airsick, they'd get high from it all.

This time the aerobatics failed the test.

He banked back toward the coast and flew home. The Stearman plopped to the runway like a weary bumblebee, into raging winds that almost stopped it cold.

He tied it down and decided to go see Brink.

Ten

Herb Dubois, M.D., staff psychiatrist at the Atascadero State Hospital for the Criminally Insane, shifted in his wheelchair and tried to concentrate on the yawning young slob across the circle of bland-eyed inmates. "OK, Mike. So what did you decide?"

Outside, on the lawn, a power mower started: visiting day tomorrow. A sleepy sound. He could feel his eyes glazing over. He swallowed. In medical school he had learned that the well-timed swallow could keep him awake. Here, in Group Session 9A—or Show and Tell, as the inmates called it—the trick was to swallow just often enough to stay awake but not enough to excite suspicion. He was sick of it all.

The slob had killed an elderly cabby three years ago for eight dollars. After a year of group therapy, doctor and patient were still worrying the motive like a pair of kittens with a ball of wool.

"I think, man, you know . . ." mumbled the slob, "I think I was, you know, 'acting out.'"

"Acting out." Dubois nodded. "OK. Fair enough. Any comments?"

"Hey, Mike," spat a light-tan sexual psychopath with muddy amber eyes, "I think you fulla shidaya eyeballs."

Shidaya? Shidaya . . . Oh, *shidaya!* Full of shit to your eyeballs. OK. "Judgmental, Perry," Dubois warned. "No value judgments, OK?"

Perry ignored him. "Fulla shidaya eyeballs," he insisted, arising to tower over the murderer. "You wanted the *bread,* man! Sheeyut! 'Acting out'!"

Dubois stifled another yawn. They were both wrong. The slob had killed because he had a gun and a helpless victim. They would peel that onion, he and Mike, with comments from the rest, for the next three or four years and find nothing. Then the slob, to whom they'd taught the proper buzz words, would repeat them back and be released to test his new ego with the first gun and cabby he could find.

"Sit down, Perry!" he ordered the black.

"Sheeyut." Perry glowered, but did.

Lion tamer in a wheelchair. He had to pee. He'd set his Seiko wristwatch to beep at the session's end, because to glance at a watch in this group of lacerated psyches was to invite disaster. Just the same, the goddamn hour was stretching interminably. Maybe the battery had died.

Julian, his classic firebug, was groping for attention like a schoolkid, his hand pumping excitedly.

"Yeah, Jule."

"Jule" . . . Freudian slip for jewel . . . He treasured Julian as Liz Taylor might treasure the Hope Diamond. Julian was the perfect, pristine firebug, the only one he had ever had unflawed by clouded symptoms. All the rest—and there were 163 in his files—were marred by some sort of hyphenated complexity: firebug-sadists, firebug-rapists, firebug-murderers. One, a psychopathic short-order cook named Zimmer, was probably all these things. Zimmer had been paroled against Dubois' advice. Now he had jumped parole and was out on the street. God knew where. He had seemed easily capable of murder and could haunt the early morning hours, when Dubois lay in bed cursing his infirmity, his profession, and the futility of psychotherapy in the state penal system.

He beckoned his mind back to the group session.

"Herb, does *Mike* have enuresis?" Julian was asking.

No, Julian, thought Dubois. That's *you*, baby. "Ask him."

"Mike? You wet the bed?"

"You mothuh!"

The slob was halfway across the circle, going for Julian, when Perry grabbed him. He wrestled him back to his seat, laughing. "Hey, Julian, cool it! This dude's a killer, not a *enuretic*. Sheeyut!"

There was a time, thought Dubois, when the little rumble would have shaken him into buzzing for a guard. Now his heart had hardly raced. "That answers your question, Julian. Now, are *you* staying dry at night?"

A sudden fear came into Julian's eyes. Dubois had grown to expect it. Julian's father, a civilian firefighter at Vandenberg Air Force Base, had shot the family puppy for wetting their mobile home rug. In front of Julian, five years old. Julian had not cried, even when it was explained to him that *that* was what happened to bed wetters, too.

What happened to Julian was that he began to light fires. The little ones he sometimes tried to put out by urinating on them. The bigger ones were allowed to burn. He lit brush fires and house fires, grass fires and forest fires. He burned half an empty school and a Navy warehouse. He torched a truck and a camper. At eleven, he burned a mobile home and a beachside hot dog stand. He was inept, but lucky, until he was fifteen.

The day after his fifteenth birthday he tried to burn the Vandenberg fire station. He was caught, and confessed to half the fires in the county over the preceding ten years. He went to the California Youth Authority for a year, was released, and torched an old motel.

Two persons, to Julian's apparent distress, died in the motel fire. Julian returned to CYA camp, where he burned a dorm, and from CYA to Atascadero, where Dubois, who had begun to doubt Freud's symptomatic firebug triad—enuresis, theft, and fire setting—was finishing his first study on pyromania.

It appeared that only theft was missing from Julian's history. But when the two had completed the preliminary psychiatric interview, Dubois had noticed that the pen was gone from his desk set.

God bless Julian and his daddy. Sigmund would have loved them both.

"I asked you, Julian? Dry this week?"

"Yes, sir!"

"Bullshit, he pees his sack every night," said someone. "Fucking fag."

"Unfair, no value judgments." Julian grinned.

"Anyway"—Dubois smiled—"no fires, I know that."

"No matches." Perry chuckled. "They don't let him have no *matches!*"

Julian threw back his head and laughed. "Hey, Perry, you're right. Sheeyut!"

The Seiko beeped. Dubois wheeled himself out the door.

He was going to be on Santa Barbara TV Wednesday. Maybe he'd take Julian along on a pass. The viewers might as well meet the real thing.

The manager's enormous face appeared at the serving window while the counter girl was ringing up a sale. "Honey, when you have time?"

She was glad to see him, even though she'd have to report that she'd destroyed five pints of coleslaw. The vibes with the fry cook had stayed wrong all morning.

She finished serving two linemen from Southern California Edison and stepped into the kitchen. He was doing the books, as usual overwhelming his tiny desk next to the door of the storage closet. He looked like an aging sea lion on a tidal rock.

On the desk, neatly stacked, lay yesterday's receipts. "Dollar short, honey."

Honey. Ordinarily, she disliked endearments from strangers. But today the Flake had her so nervous with his strange little looks that "honey" from the older man sounded good, middle-America, avuncular. She felt comforted, as if her father had just squeezed her close, watching TV on a chilly Denver night.

"Let *me*," she said, quickly flipping through the bills and counting the change. He was right: short one buck. She could not understand it. Her first reaction was to glance at the Flake, working at the stove. The Flake seemed to sense it, meeting her eyes.

She was ashamed. He might be kinky, but it didn't mean he was a thief. Who'd steal a dollar, anyway? Even the blonde made three dollars an hour, and was just as likely as he to have ripped it off. Probably nobody had stolen it, she'd simply made too much change for somebody. Maybe the wind was getting to *her*.

"Sorry. I dropped five pints of coleslaw, too. Take it out of my check."

"Don't be silly." The manager shrugged. "Just watch it, is all."

She passed the Flake at the stove. There was an odd smile on his face. She shivered. He was making her physically cold.

Tomorrow was payday. She *would* quit.

Eleven

Shawn sat in the easy chair by the hospital window and squinted at Brink as the owlish nun changed the i.v. bottle. In Shawn's shirt pocket, hidden in the hope that Brink had forgotten, sat a pack of Viceroys.

Brink looked stronger. Despite Shawn's resolutions not to wish for the impossible, he felt a surge of hope. He told Brink his color was better.

"Prayer." Brink patted the nun's rump. She jumped away, almost dropping the bottle. "Thank Sister Margaret. Regular saint."

He flashed the famous grin. Now it was cadaverous, flesh too pale, dimples too deep, veins at his temples like roots around the State Street fig tree. Two months ago the grin, properly timed, might have sold a half-million-dollar home or shaken a woman's marriage. It still melted the nun's granite eyes.

"A saint," Brink sighed again. "But goosey. Jumps around. Got to get her out of the habit."

"*Habit,*" groaned the woman. "Saints preserve us!"

She left, smiling. She'd come a long way from last night.

He studied Brink. Hell, he wasn't better, just ripped on something. For a moment he hoped that Stewart, the oncologist who was treating him, had relented. "Mustn't build a tolerance—there'll be nowhere to go at the end if we do," he'd told Shawn when he'd asked why they hadn't started morphine. No, not that prick, he decided, no way. Booze, probably, sneaked in by Nicole.

"Whatever you're drinking—" began Shawn.

"Snorting. Want a toot?"

"No, but it's doing you good."

"Support your local pusher."

"Mavis?" guessed Shawn. Mavis was the wife of a wealthy plumbing contractor who had won a bid on the Estates, and virtually lost his wife.

"Not Mavis." Brink turned over on his side. He groped in his bedside table, shook coke from a small plastic bag onto a shaving mirror, and sniffed it. He lay back. "Not Mavis," he repeated. "Tinkerbell."

Tinkerbell was another face of the legend of Brink Southerland. She was a control tower operator at Santa Barbara Municipal. Last year Brink, low on gas after a prohibited scuba-diving sortie to the Navy's San Nicolas Island, had landed the Stearman on a taxiway, downwind, against her frantic red light. It had taken every bit of charm he had to keep her from getting his license lifted. And by the time he was through grinning she was in love.

Like all the rest.

Including Nicole, still?

Probably . . .

"Coke's a little high for Tinker's salary, isn't it?"

"But she's going to cure me. Or Mavis is. One or the other."

Mavis, it seemed, was into holistic health. "You visualize little animals, squirrels, whatever, eating away at the cells. Pretty soon, no more cells."

"Whatever works."

"Some of Mamá Lola's Mary Johanna cookies would work fine," Brink said pointedly. "You got time to go up there?"

"I'll find time," promised Shawn. When, he didn't know. He'd sold the motorcycles, instantly, via the notice posted on the morning watch bulletin board at Sheriff's headquarters; that, at least, was out of the way.

And they were staying off the subject of the cigarettes: he'd rather see him snorting than smoking. And off the subject of pulling the plug. And he *did* look better, coke, squirrels, or whatever. Jesus, you heard of remissions all the time. Breakthroughs like interferon were supposed to be close in the future. Brink had a constitution like a Sherman tank, why couldn't he hang on until they found the drug to beat it?

Maybe, with the nun's prayer? As a kid, Shawn had prayed rather well, when pushed into a corner.

No, not prayer. The night his parents had died, he'd learned that God was blind and deaf to prayer: a Helen Keller God.

He was restless and jumpy: the wind, again. He was supposed to wait for Nicole, who still had the pink slips for the motorcycles.

He was about to tell him about tomorrow's Red Flag Alert, to ease his mind, when Brink began to cough. It was a bad spell. Finally, strangled, he managed: "Coming down . . . hard."

"OK, buddy," said Shawn, and pressed his hand.

It was thin and bony now, but still calloused from dirt bike handlebars, and stronger than he'd expected.

It occurred to him that over all the years they'd never gripped hands before, except when Brink had pulled him from the car at the bottom of Arroyo Seco off Romero Canyon Road.

Twelve

By the time the counter girl locked up, the Colonel's bucket on the roof was rattling harder in the wind than it had the night before. She had turned off its motor at dusk, afraid that if the bucket blew down, its wire would short out. The last thing anyone needed in the searing gale was a shower of sparks.

She deposited the receipts in the safe, wrote down the exact change—$12.87—that she was leaving in the open cash box, and stuffed the paper into her worn leather pocketbook.

All day she had puzzled over the one-dollar shortage, and despite herself, suspected the Flake. She hoped it didn't show. During the last twenty-four hours he had changed in her mind from a blob to an object of fear.

She locked the front door, passed through the kitchen, discovered that the blonde and the Flake had both left, and carefully secured the kitchen entrance.

She crossed the parking lot to her little red bug. It squatted forlornly in the furthest reaches of the area, near the Flake's pickup. She wondered why he had chosen to drive it instead of his motorcycle. The wind, perhaps. She glanced into the cab, wondering where he was. In the service station john, lighting toilet paper, probably.

Creep. She fumbled in her pocketbook for her car keys. She couldn't find them in the spot where she usually kept them. She moved under the light from the Union 76. She poked around in the pocketbook, and finally caught the glitter of her keys in the main compartment of her purse. Strange: she must have jammed them there in a hurry. Disorganized today. She saw the Chicano and his boss hosing down the concrete between the pumps. She suddenly flashed on the missing dollar. The Chicano had returned it at her car the night before. She'd simply forgotten to replace it in the register this morning. That, she could catch tomorrow, before she quit.

She unlocked her door and slid behind the wheel. She was conscious of armpit odor in the car. She grimaced. She hadn't washed her uniform last night; letting everything go to hell.

She put her key in the ignition. All at once she knew, and froze: someone was in the back seat. Paralyzed, she sat up, afraid to look, even afraid to scream.

When she felt the steel hands around her throat, she broke through icy immobility long enough to try the horn. It beeped once, and she was torn roughly away and slammed across the passenger seat. The grip never slackened. She saw the Chicano glance from the pumps, give a cheerful wave, bend back to his work.

She clutched backwards at hairy arms. They were solid as concrete. She arched, half twisted, groping again for the horn. She was suddenly jammed against the armrest, nose ground into the upholstery.

Her diver's lungs were the equal of most of the men she swam with, and she struggled to fill them; she knew certainly that she was fighting the Flake, and that she could scare him off if only she could get the one breath she needed.

Her vision dimmed. She was all at once in an underwater tunnel she knew at Anacapa Island, diving with her lover for lobsters. His diving light was beckoning her onward, but suddenly there was no more air in her tank. She thrashed toward the tiny gleam receding in the void ahead.

And after that, there was nothing.

Zimmer waited for a long time for the girl to quiver, as he had seen the victim do at Atascadero. But before she did, the Shrink said: "That's enough, man, split!"

So he released his grip. She remained slumped across the front seat, probably dead.

His heart had been hammering until she stepped into the car, but somehow during the brief struggle he had turned calm, and now he felt fine. He squeezed himself out of the left-hand door, and looked around, stretching innocently and yawning like anyone too long cramped.

The Mexicans had closed their station and were driving away in their tow truck. There was no one else in sight. He walked to his pickup. From the cab he took five emergency road flares. He carried them to the VW, raised the front hood to expose the luggage compartment, and laid the flares inside. He slammed the hood, pulled the girl's body as erect as he could on the passenger side, got behind the wheel, slid back the seat, and started the engine.

He stayed north of the freeway, fearing the lights and traffic along 101. He took Cathedral Oaks Road eastward, toward the city, then turned north on 154 toward San Marcos at Foothill Road.

He drove up San Marcos Pass in the darkness, even more slowly than he had driven his pickup at noon. The winds were fiercer now, buffeting the little car from side to side. A big Diesel semi labored up the grade behind him, blasting with an air horn. He gave the driver a finger and made him swerve to the oncoming lane to get by.

He noted that the van he had seen parked at San Antonio Creek Road had been replaced by the camper he had seen at Painted Cave. Or had it been the other way around? He was becoming excited again and he couldn't remember.

He didn't give a shit if they had a stakeout at every turn: they'd never get her number, because he'd ripped her plates off with vise-grips in the parking lot and dumped them.

He began to look for the turnoff to Trout Canyon Road. He slowed the VW further, squinting. He glimpsed a warning sign at the entrance to Los Padres National Forest: Smokey the Bear, nine feet high, holding up a wooden sign: "Fire Danger: Very High."

The sign amused him, but told him he had missed Trout Canyon. He hung a screaming U, retraced his route a half mile, and recognized the spot he was looking for. He pulled to the shoulder and parked in the turnaround area with the front wheels on the rim of the cliff. He left the lights and engine on.

The girl had toppled sideways. He opened his door and was pulling her into the driver's seat when he heard her groan. Startled, he peered into her face in the bright moonlight. Her eyes were still closed. He touched her forehead. Still warm. Alive!

He felt his mouth go dry. Quickly, he hauled her behind the wheel, reached in, pulled her feet across the car, even fastened her safety belt, brushing her firm fine tits.

He felt flames rising in his body, and an urge to rape, but he had tried to rape once, years ago. He knew it to be beyond him, a mauling, frustrating embarrassment, so he slugged her for kicks, splintering her jaw. He rolled up her window and slammed the door.

He crossed the highway and skirted the shoulder under the glaring moon. He found a half-buried rock of perhaps ten pounds. He took it back to the VW, raised the front hood.

He had worked occasionally on VWs in a filling station, before Atascadero. VW gas tanks were in the luggage compartment under the front bonnet. He lifted the boulder high and smashed at the tank's plastic cover until gasoline dripped from its forward end. He glanced through the windshield. She was moving, restlessly, restrained by the safety belt.

He scratched one of the flares into life, and tossed it on the others in the open luggage compartment. It ignited the gas with a whoosh that singed his eyebrows as he scrambled to the rear. With a grunt he shoved the car over the canyon face.

So long, baby . . . He moved to the edge of the cliff and watched.

Like a toy hurled in anger, the VW bounced end over end down the side of the canyon, streaming flame. The headlights arced suddenly and went out. A finger of fire flicked back up the chaparral on the face of the cliff, almost catching him. There was a mighty crunch as the car struck the canyon bottom, and a puff and a roar of flame as the gas tank went.

He found himself running down the highway, then short-cutting, sliding down the hillside through brush to the Trout Canyon Road. He quickly found his bike in the clump of bushes, yanked off the tarp, and trundled it out. He headed it up the road and started the engine. He looked back.

At the foot of the canyon an orange glare was growing. He should get his ass out and onto the highway, before he got trapped by the flames or a patrol.

"Hey, man, *go!*" commanded the Shrink.

"Fuck you!" He powered the bike around in a shower of moonlit dust and rocketed toward the flames.

The Volks had struck on a dry creek bed and was hidden by a hillock. He left the road, rose on the foot pegs, cranked on throttle, and crested the little ridge.

The car was right side up, hood gone, flames licking at its paint. The canyon face above it was an inferno already. He could see the girl very plainly in the moonlight, behind the shattered glass. It seemed to him—oh, Christ, yes—she was alive, arching her back, Christ, screaming . . .

He dismounted. Dancing from foot to foot, craning to see into the car, he inched closer and closer to the conflagration. Once, he thought he saw her hand clutching at the window. He moaned in ecstasy, ignoring the blast-furnace heat. The remaining flares went off in a violet flash, lighting the hillsides.

For a long while he watched, until she was still and his skin seemed ready to blister and he feared for the Harley's paint.

Then, drained, he roared up the dirt road and onto San Marcos Highway, heading for the carpet of lights below. Above him, he heard a distant siren begin to wail from the top of San Marcos Pass.

He had told the Shrink to screw himself.

For the first time in months he felt peace.

Thirteen

Shawn listened to Brink and Nicole argue, looking out over the city from the hospital window.

"I'm going to tell Val," Nicole informed Brink, "that you asked him to come down more often."

He heard Brink shift on his pillow. "I shouldn't *have* to ask him."

"But you *do* have to. He thinks you don't give a damn."

"*He's* the one that doesn't seem to give—"

"Look," Shawn cut in, "you sound like a two-year-old. He wants to be *asked*, OK?"

Brink smiled. "OK. I'm asking. Pink slips?"

While Nicole handed Brink the motorcycle slips to sign, Shawn set down his drink. The Santa Ana had washed the sky, and the sinking moon shivered as gusts played with the windowpane. Shawn suddenly tensed. Rising from the western ridges was an orange glow that no Santa Barbareño could ever mistake. There was no use trying to keep the news from Brink.

"Guys?" he breathed. "There's one on San Marcos Pass!"

"That figures," said Brink. He took the remote control from his bedside table and pressed it. The TV set suspended from the hospital wall snapped on to KEYT.

Gene Forsell, Shawn's favorite local newscaster, had interrupted the "Mork and Mindy Show" to announce that Trout Canyon was ablaze and taking off. Gale winds, fire uncontrollable, Trout Club residents being ordered from the upper end of the canyon. The fire was less than an hour old, but already very bad. Sightseers were asked to stay out of the foothills: San Marcos Pass was closed. A camera crew was en route to the fire lines, updates later.

Standard Santa Barbara TV nightmare on a warm December night. Again.

Nicole joined him at the window, tense with anger. "Crazy, cowardly sons of *bitches* . . ."

Shawn shrugged. She was assuming, as most natives did from experience, that the source of the fire was a set. She was probably right. As the world's newest arson investigator, he had a great desire to find out; he supposed that, for the record, he'd have to visit the scene, but from the sound of the newscast, the last thing Hash would want on the pass tonight was an amateur in the way. He'd wait until things cooled down.

"Long way from the city," he reassured Nicole. "And it's ten miles from Wildcat Ridge. No sweat."

"Give them time to set some more," she said bitterly. "This *wind!* Shawn, what *drives* them?"

"How would I know?" He might be on the way to finding out, but he hadn't told Brink about his new detail, or the scene with the sheriff, and didn't intend to now. "*Supposed* to be sexual."

"I don't believe that," she muttered.

"They used to tell us: 'Pick up the guy that's watching the hardest, if you can.' That's the Police Academy poop. 'Check his drawers for semen.' Setting fires is the only way they can get off, some of them."

"*Lack* of sex," Brink said hollowly.

They turned. With great intensity, Brink was striking a match. As they stared, he picked a Christmas card from the stack on his bedside table and lit it. Shawn jumped across the room, snatched the card, and stamped it out.

"I think," murmured Nicole, "I get the message."

"Good night, you horny fuckers," Shawn said, forcing a smile. "Watch those i.v. tubes."

Striding too quickly down the hall, he searched for the source of an ache in his throat. He should be happy: he'd got away without leaving Brink the cigarettes and without mention of pulling the plug. Coke or not, Brink had seemed palpably stronger, strong enough to get it on, apparently.

Then why his own ache? Over another man's wife? After so many years?

Stupid. He glanced at his watch. He had to pick up Mary Lou. Jesus, it was almost ten. Unless someone else had brought her home, she was still on the courts, and the lights went out in five minutes.

A few years ago, before the Great Influx began, it wouldn't have bothered him. Now it scared him to death.

He ended up jogging to his car.

Jerry Castle glowered at the huge situation map covering the western wall of Goleta Command Center, Los Padres National Forest Headquarters. Of all possible places for the inevitable fire to start, Trout Canyon off San Marcos Pass Highway was worst.

County Highway 154 wound through San Marcos Pass. It was the traditional highway, from stagecoach days, between coastal city and inland valley, and the only one besides the coastline route, which took you far out of your way if you were heading north. Highway 154 swept grandly up to the pass, on modern curves, from sea and city, and left the old stage route on the mountainous inland grade to curve gently down to the interior valley. It was a four-lane, active artery, pulsing with traffic by daylight, and not entirely deserted by night.

To close it to fight fire was a major operation in itself.

And the walls of Trout Canyon, and all the other arroyos, barrancas, and dry washes which radiated from the highway like legs from a centipede, were deep in tinder-dry brush.

Shit.

Two out of the three dispatchers in the command post were smokers, and already the place was reeking. Well, he wouldn't be here long, unless somehow the fire was contained. Very quickly, once the command post was operating properly, he'd move to a mobile one, near the line.

He left the map. The row of tiny phone-desk cubicles stood ready to be manned. He hoped that most would remain empty, but if the fire spread, as he feared it would, more and more specialists and functionaries—supply, intelligence, press relations, equipment management—would be added to the command center.

Last night, so that he could at least get some sleep, he had ordered

Joe Culligan, the head dispatcher, to triple the night watch here, and the hell with overtime. Now, with the three dispatch men already working, he was glad he had. The tapes which monitored his operation would be reviewed someday in Washington. When they were, response time, with three men transmitting from the very first, should be excellent.

From the cluster of four big radio consoles in the center of the room, the Los Padres Area set crackled into life. No crossword puzzles tonight: "Goleta, this is San Marcos Pass, Truck Number One. I'm on the scene. It's still Class C. County's got two engines working it down the Trout Canyon Road. Wind gusting to thirty. We're going to want an airdrop."

He recognized Luke Tallman's voice. Tallman was his Santa Barbara District Ranger, a squat, chunky Navajo from Albuquerque. They'd worked Marble Cone together, before Jerry had become fire boss. Luke was solid, reliable, conservative. He wouldn't ask for an airdrop unless things looked bad.

"Tell him ten-four," he told one of the dispatchers, "and call in my airboss."

He moved to a huge map of California dominating the eastern wall of the center. On it were shown local aviation navigational aids. At each aviation VOR beacon, a little magnetic marker-bug rested over a hole. Nothing fancy, nothing electronic, not a computer in sight.

The magnetic bugs were on strings, and behind the map hung counterweights. Nothing that couldn't have been built in 1850, if they'd had aircraft, or aircraft beacons. When you pulled the bug from the hole and laid it on the location of a fire, you automatically had a bearing from the aviation VOR station to the blaze. As for distance, you measured it with a mileage ruler hanging from a string.

Crude, but very little downtime: you could repair the whole setup with scotch tape and a paper clip.

The pilot, even if on instruments in smoke, could find the fire by flying the bearings from the VOR. Theoretically. For there were pilots, and there were aces. Forest Service contract work attracted few of the latter.

Castle moved to the map, pulled the magnetic bug from the Santa Barbara VOR, laid it on the head of the fire at Trout Canyon. He measured the distance, stepped back to the console, and called San

Marcos Pass Heliport. He ordered the chopper to make a Phos-chek drop for Tallman.

Choppers didn't carry much retardant, and if the gusts increased, he couldn't use them long. But there was no way he was going to get anything bigger up those canyons at night.

The chopper at San Marcos was a chartered one, got overtime at night, and the drop would cost a fortune. But an airdrop now could prevent a hundred airdrops later.

Dollars, dollars, dollars.

He envied the Navajo on the line, making life-and-death decisions instead of fiscal ones, and promised himself that if the fire kept up, he would join him soon.

Shawn Ortega parked near the Holly Park tennis courts, which were hidden from the street by a wall of rustling bushes. He could see through the foliage that the bright night-lights were still on, thank God. Over the sound of the Santa Ana, he heard the *tchung* of a racket against a ball.

He cut through the bushes and stopped, staring with relief and anger.

His daughter stood behind the base line in the dazzle of footlights, tall, slim, serving to an empty court.

Alone.

Her racket moved in a swift arc. The ball smoked over the net, ticked the service line, and slammed the fence. Incredible power. He opened the gate softly and crept toward her from behind.

She tossed up the next ball. It wobbled in a sudden gust. She lowered her racket and caught it. She was setting herself again when, treading silently, he put his arms around her from the rear.

"Daddy, you dirty old man," she said quietly, "let me go."

Not the slightest fear. She should not be let out after dark.

Roughly, he turned her around. Her crinkly brown eyes narrowed as she sensed his mood.

He found himself shaking: "What the *hell* are you doing here by yourself?"

She brushed back the ringlets of her short, curly hair. "Well, everybody went home. Rodge had to have his car in by ten." God, she was getting beautiful. "There *was* a couple on the other court, Daddy!"

"But they aren't there *now*, are they?" he demanded as he followed her to the other side of the net and began to help her stuff mangy practice balls into a plastic shopping bag. "It's the last damn time you do this," he swore, "and when I see Rodge-baby, I'll kick his butt!"

"He *had* to go." Her voice reverted to a childish whine.

He remembered the bulletin board and told her there'd been a rape last night, not adding that it was statutory. "Jesus, *I'm* nervous out here and *I'm* packing a gun."

"Nobody's raping *my* Daddy," she promised him. They moved toward the car. She asked him to play with her Saturday, and promised to spot him three games a set. He told her that he'd planned to deliver Brink's motorcycles Saturday, to the new owners. Her face went blank. He broke the news that he was no longer homicide honcho, but the Department's first arson expert; and that there was a fire on San Marcos Pass, and until he knew what he was supposed to do about it, he couldn't make weekend plans anyway. As usual, two excuses sounded weaker than one. She'd withdrawn inside herself.

He took a deep breath, estimating costs. If he drank beer instead of scotch for a few weeks . . . not a bad idea anyway . . .

"How about we get you Mike? For a few hours during vacation?"

Her instructor cost fifteen dollars an hour, on special. Awful, but she needed to stay sharp to be seeded for the Juniors, and there were no women and few men from Ventura to Paso Robles who could lay a racket on her serve. Certainly not her father.

"I don't want to *rent* anybody. Besides, he has group lessons all Christmas." They climbed into the car. "Daddy?"

He started the engine. Something was coming, to make him pay for his Saturday's rejection. "Yes?"

"The job at Big Mac? Rodge says it's still open."

She'd be working nights, and he didn't like it.

"That's silly!" he protested. "Three bucks an hour? To screw up your whole vacation?"

"Three-ten. I already said I might. Rodge goes, 'If you don't grab it, ding-dong, somebody else will,' and I go, 'What's it pay?' and he goes, 'Three-ten,' and I go, 'Sure,' and so—"

"You're under sixteen."

"You just *tell* them you're sixteen, and get a social security card. How'll they know?"

That was against the law, he pointed out: how would it be if a lieutenant on the local gendarmerie condoned such a fraud? She asked him how it would be if his grandfather knew he had a stash of Kona gold in his dresser drawer.

"What were *you* doing in there?"

"Putting your socks away."

"You'll notice that stash doesn't go down very fast."

"Don't preach."

At least, he consoled himself, she didn't know Kona from Mamá Lola's homegrown grass. She just wanted him to think she did.

He reached over, squeezed her hand, and grinned at her. "You're a funny type kid, ML. You make my every day."

"I got a funny type father. How about the job?"

"I don't know."

"We'll see, though?" She moved closer, crinkling her eyes. "We'll see?"

"We'll see," he said morosely.

She'd won that one already, and they both knew it. She would crinkle her eyes until "We'll see" turned out to be "yes."

At home, in the den, they found Crissy and Don Miguel watching a news flash from KEYT.

The news crew had finally got to the fire camp on San Marcos Pass. On the tube Shawn could see the usual orange mushroom, and then, further down Trout Canyon near the apparent source, a wall of flame chewing stubbornly at a fire line near San Antonio Creek Road.

He stepped to the patio to search the western sky for the same show, live. He found it: the orange glow he had first seen from the hospital window. It pulsed, growing larger, then diminishing, then growing again as its own winds arose within it. He could smell nothing: the fire was across-wind, and too far away. He watched for a while and went in.

"The Santa Barbara Fire Department reports arson investigators already on the scene," said KEYT. Investigators? Plural? Delusions

of grandeur, or a statement calculated to scare away potential
firebugs, with visions of trained men sifting ashes? BS, anyway.

Despite Hash Ono's request that he stay out of the way, he'd better get up there himself, however useless he might be. Not until
dawn, he decided: he'd set the alarm for five, take his bike, and run
by Mamá Lola's, too.

He hadn't told Crissy about his demotion yet, just Mary Lou. He
told her, now. She seemed relieved and said she'd rather have him
tracking firebugs than murderers anyway.

She was strangely unangered by Castillo. "I could have *told* you
that, Shawn. Supporting the Anglo. I mean, from his point of
view . . ."

"His point of view," he said coldly, "is wrong. I'm sorry it's yours."

"It *isn't* mine! I just *understand* it."

"Good," said Shawn, and went to bed.

Crissy sat awash in pain, watching flickering images of a fire she
feared, as she feared them all, but couldn't concentrate on. It was too
early to worry, anyway; they'd had fires closer than San Marcos Pass
almost every season; you learned to ignore them, or you moved.

She dreaded the next commercial. She seemed to have, with her
migraine, a sort of ESP early-warning system, and she sensed that
Don Miguel was lying in wait for the end of the program, that he'd
followed, for once, her argument with Shawn about Castillo, and
hadn't liked it at all.

When the news was over, she arose swiftly, wincing as the motion
hit her eyeballs. "Buenas noches, Don Mi—"

"Shawn was right not to support Castillo," he growled. "Castillo is
nothing. I knew his uncle. You shouldn't side with him."

"I'm not," she sighed. "I said I was sorry."

Reverence for Don Miguel was bred into her bones. Her father, a
barrio pharmacist, had set the pattern, bowing and scraping, though
he could probably have bought out the old man at any time within
the past half century. And her mother, while chuckling at her husband's fawning, had gone along, too.

Well, Don Miguel, no adulation tonight. If you don't get off my
case, with the migraine squeezing my brain to jelly, I won't be responsible.

And if you hit me with one of your goddamn quotations, I'll hit *you* with an ashtray.

"Shawn is under strain," Don Miguel grumbled. "His friend is dying. You must not be 'a wife who lectures in her gown and preaches in her nightdress.'"

She wasn't. "I lecture in my painting and, nowadays," she added bitterly, "I seem to *sleep* in my nightdress. Nothing more."

"¿Qué?" he asked sharply. "What's that?"

He heard Shawn very well and Mary Lou perfectly. To her own voice he often seemed deaf. She didn't care anymore.

"Nada." She kissed him lightly. "No importa. Good night, señor."

He smiled. The older he got, the younger grew his smile. Obviously he wasn't sleepy, and didn't want her to go. "'Man's best possession is a sympathetic wife,'" he said. "Don't forget."

"Man's *'possession'*?" She stared at him, incredulously.

"Euripides," he announced. "In *Antigone*."

"I thought it was Bobby Riggs."

"Pardon?" He leaned forward, tilting his head. "Again?"

She shook her head and left.

He'd probably heard, but not understood. Nothing that had happened in the last two thousand years seemed to have escaped him, except everything in the last fifty.

She glided up to bed on her private stairway of agony, her head throbbing, with a station of the cross at every step.

Fourteen

Hash Ono awakened at dawn, stretched on the seat of his Land Rover. Above him, through the windshield, he could see a dull green Forest Service chopper thrashing down from the pass.

He eased himself from under the steering wheel, massaging his neck. His eyes were gritty with the blowing ash and dust of the night before. He yawned loudly, startling a jay on the face of the road cut.

He had penetrated the billowing smoke at midnight, to a point on the highway that the San Marcos hotshot crew was laughingly calling the Primary Control Line. Luke Tallman, the line boss, had taken time to lead him to the rim of the canyon. There they had gazed into hell, stretching a half mile up the arroyo. Luke had defined the general area on the floor of the canyon as the source of the fire. He suggested that if Hash wanted to check it tonight, he'd better leave a farewell note to his wife and the keys to his car.

Obviously, he should have gone home to wait, but by this time he had been hooked. B platoon, County, with rigs from Hollister Avenue Station, Los Carneros, Mission Canyon, and University, had arrived. He could hear sirens of trucks from stations in Sisquoc, Los Alamos, Buellton, Santa Ynez, and New Cuyama splitting the night from the other side of Trout Canyon. In the rosy pulse of a rotating beacon on a big La France pumper from Mission Canyon, he had donned spare equipment, then slithered down the slope like a blue-card smokechaser. Under a squad boss from San Marcos Pass Fire

Station, he spent the night with the Feds, in a line of Chicanos from Lompoc, laying hose. All the time he was scared to death of a breakover whipping back up the canyon on the breath of a sundowner and catching them on the face of the cliff.

When the slopover inevitably came, he had been the first to escape up the narrow fire trail. He scrambled finally to the highway, panting, filthy, bathed in sweat, eyes stinging in the darkness.

Never again. He was forty-one. Well, psychologists had been studying firemen for years without success.

He had driven a half mile back down from the hubbub, lain down on the seat, and gone to sleep, to await tomorrow.

Now the rising sun was tinting the smoke-veiled canyon. The whole vista was jaundiced, as if observed through a yellow camera filter. The Santa Ana wind was taking its morning snooze. Nothing directly below the highway had been burned, which meant that Tallman had stopped it last night and was chasing the fire up-canyon this morning, while he had the chance. The burned-out source was probably clear of flames. He'd better drive back up and go to work.

A Dodge camper-truck, heading inland, pulled to the shoulder, fifty yards from where he'd parked. A bearded young man in Levis climbed down from the cab, waved, and wandered up the road.

"Hi," said the young man.

Hash nodded. "Morning." If the kid had got through the CHP roadblock on the Santa Barbara grade, he was probably an Operation Torchy stakeout, but you never knew. "Come up to see the fire?" asked Hash.

"Nah. You?"

"Yeah," said Hash.

The two smiled at each other. The young man had a nice smile, phony, but nice. If a stakeout, he was probably remembering Pearl Harbor, no, too young for Pearl. The movie, then, *Tora! Tora! Tora!*

"Road blocked to Santa Barbara?" asked Hash.

"I don't know," said the young man. "I been up here camping since yesterday. You?"

"Came up last night. From the valley side," lied Hash. He was waiting to see if the young man tried to spot his license plate. Maybe he already had. As for the license on the camper, it was too far away; his frigging eyes. But he'd have to get it, somehow, before either left.

If Hash showed his ID and the kid was a pyro, he'd have blown his own cover and the scout car's, for the future. Too many weirdos knew him already. And, of course, if the kid was a city or county detective, he'd be equally slow to flash his own badge.

There were antennas on all Operation Torchy vehicles and on the camper, too. But that meant nothing: everybody had CB. He tried to see if the kid was carrying a gun: cops were attached to their firearms with bonds of desperation: on duty like this, they wore sport shirts to hide their shoulder holsters. The kid had a T-shirt. But he could be a Forest Service special agent: they went unarmed. And a batch of them had come up from Angeles National Forest a week ago.

He studied the man. *Male, Caucasian, five-ten, 170, brown eyes, red beard and red hair, medium build, around twenty-five. Scar on chin, no arm tattoos or gang tattoos on the webs of his fingers. Earth shoes.* Remember all that.

"Nice-looking camper," said Hash, moving toward it.

The kid gave him a sidelong glance and asked him if *he'd* seen much of the fire. Hash said yes, he'd seen it on TV in a Santa Ynez bar, hopped in the scout car to get a closer look before they closed 154 at Lake Cachuma.

The kid nodded casually, introduced himself as one Chip Bolton, from Goleta, and asked where Hash lived. Midwest accent. Probably Forest Service, but you couldn't be sure.

Hash bowed slightly. "George Yamamoto, Santa Ynez," he said. He glanced at the camper. *License TPI 475, white cabin, Dodge '78 body, one small ding on the right rear fender.* Done . . . if he could remember it all.

"Jesus, it was burning last night," the kid grinned.

"Still is, further up, I guess," volunteered Hash.

"Wait for that afternoon wind! Hey, you look like you might have been *in* it," suggested the kid.

"Changed a tire," said Hash.

The kid's eyes held his. "You like fires?"

"I'm here, right?"

"Yeah."

"Ever set one?" asked Hash idly. Sometimes bugs like company. Of course, if he got a pyro to make a move, the DA would throw it out anyway. Entrapment.

"Not yet. I'd be scared. You?"

"Not yet, anyway."

Hash was almost certain that the whole conversation was getting on tape. They'd probably meet again, more formally, coughed up when their license numbers crossed in the innards of Operation Torchy's computer. When they did, he'd buy the kid a drink.

In the meantime, they'd wasted fifty bucks of the taxpayers' time and generated almost enough bullshit to bust one another. Not quite, all very soft, but almost.

So much for fun and games. He'd better get down to the floor of the canyon and try to develop something hard.

He nodded good-by, climbed into the scout car and flicked on his radio, switching to Operation Torchy's restricted channel.

". . . male, oriental, six-foot, two hundred pounds, age around fifty—"

"Forty-one, asshole!" he barked into his mike.

He hung it up and headed for Fire Camp One.

Shawn Ortega nosed his Yamaha down the dappled trail, gliding from smoky early sunlight into canyon shadow. He was used to Mamá Lola's road, and kept his forearms stiff to bear his weight on the handlebars, favoring his rear brake to keep control on the dusty, rock-strewn surface. Along this cowpath, Mamá Lola, at seventy-one, somehow drove her jeep each Saturday, bringing home her groceries, an occasional social security check, and whatever agricultural inputs she needed for her marijuana farm.

He shot across a little wooden bridge at the bottom of the dry arroyo, slammed up the opposite slope, and crested a rise into her shady glen. He stopped and blasted the silence with a roar from the engine, because she loved the sound.

Her half-mastiff Perro, lying on the rickety porch, awakened. He stared at Shawn in disbelief, then rose, shouting of murder and rapine. He collapsed when Shawn raised a finger like a pistol. As Shawn dismounted, he lay sulking, mumbling of dirty pool.

"Mamá Lola!" called Shawn. "Where are you, mi corazón?"

"My God, it's the fuzz." Her voice, clear and youthful, floated
from the outhouse near her shack. "Hold your water, lover." In an
instant she emerged, kicking the leather-hinged door closed behind
her, cinching up her Levis.

She seemed to grow tubbier and sturdier with every passing
month. She glanced at the sun, which was just clearing the notch in
her hills. "What are you doing up so early?"

He pulled off his gloves and stuffed them into his jacket. He
hugged her solid body. Her cheeks were like leather, but her eyes
were bright. She grinned up at him. She'd lost another tooth.
"Christ, Mamá, you look like a pumpkin! Get that fixed!"

"For who? Perro?" Her eyes darkened. "How's Brink?"

"Hurting."

She kicked at a rock. "That beautiful body! It makes me so mad I
could spit," she said, spitting. "You think of all the *old* fuckers
around, better off dead. Like your granddaddy . . ." Her gaze grew
distant with years, and then she came back. "How is the old fart?"

"Sends you his best," lied Shawn.

"I bet," she chuckled. "He'd shit broomsticks if he ate sawdust. I
should have married him when Rosa died, *I'd* a kept him young."

"Why didn't you?" He thought of Don Miguel, tied to this bouncing bundle, quoting Aristotle as he harvested her grass.

"He didn't ask me. When I asked *him,* he almost drove off Palo
Rojo Road."

She'd inherited from some long-dead husband the ranch neighbor-
ing Don Miguel's. Before Shawn's father was born, the two had
fallen into the normal property-line disputes of *Californianos,* in and
out of the courts. But they'd both been burned out in the fire of
1931, making all their litigation useless after they'd enriched a generation of Anglo lawyers. All of whom now, she liked to point out,
were thrashing around in hell.

"I'd have brought *you* up better," she grinned, "if we *had* got married."

"You would?"

"You wouldn't be a frigging cop."

They climbed to the creaking porch. She brought out a jug of
homemade wine: he knew that it was her breakfast, and pretended
to sip, but turned down her offer of a joint of Arroyo Burro gold.

"How's the crop?"

She scowled at the wind. "Santa Ana won't help."

"It's blowing a fire up Trout Canyon," he warned her. She refused to have a radio, TV, or telephone on the place. "And coming over San Marcos grade."

"I smelled it, first thing this morning." She yawned. "Maybe I better harvest, quick. Comes over Cieneguitas Ridge, I'll be asshole-deep in stoned firemen."

He told her that he had a vested interest in fires now, and that he was no longer Homicide. Her eyes flashed. "Castillo did *that?* That no-class, *cholo,* sonofabitch!"

"He almost made me the local narc."

Her face softened. "And you turned it down, because you wouldn't bust Mamá Lola."

"Not really. But who would? And go out of town on a rail?"

"They warned me again," she said, took a long drag from her joint, closed her eyes, and basked in the morning sun. "Hammond."

"Not to worry." Sergeant Hammond, sheriff's narcotic investigator assigned to these hills, recognized Mamá Lola's value to the community. She touched nothing hard, welcomed college kids from Isla Vista but let no high school children near the place. She undersold the Mexican Mafia from LA. "You'll never go to jail."

"Good. I *need* those Isla Vista kids." She smiled faintly. "Who'd I talk to? Perro? I mean, hell, Shawnito . . . Even *you,* you didn't come up here for sex."

"Don't be too sure."

"*Or* to talk." She peered into his eyes. He had never seen her wear glasses. "What can I do for you?"

"Cookies. For Brink. Load them good."

"I'll bake 'em tonight, and bring them down tomorrow, they'll blow his mind." She continued to search his face. The two had always been tuned closely. "And?"

"I don't know . . ." His throat caught, and he cleared it. He took a deep, shuddering breath, and found himself blurting what he could not have told Crissy, or Nicole, or another human soul. He listened to himself with amazement. "He's . . . Well, he's going to want out, pretty soon."

Her face stayed blank. "Sounds like him. Suicide, you mean?"

"Well, yes. No, maybe not exactly. . . ."

She arose, moved to the railing, gazed over her canyon. She

played with a rawhide thong on an ancient saddle rotting on the
rail. Her last horse had died fifteen years ago. "*You're* elected?" she
muttered finally. She turned. "*You?*"

He nodded, afraid to speak with his throat so tight.

"That bastard!" she spat.

Startled, he raised his hand. "Now, wait a minute—"

"Why not the doctor? Some nurse? There's got to be a way! Why
not himself?"

There were all kinds of reasons why not. The main one was an
insurance policy for half a million, thought now to be necessary to
keep Nicole and Wildcat Ridge going when the estate was tied in
probate. The policy had been taken out just nine months ago, before
Brink had had the slightest hint of cancer, and was cancelable during the first two years, by suicide. No need to go into all that. He
said simply: "He's got to die naturally, or it's got to look that way."

"Why *you?*" she demanded. "You aren't ready for this!"

"I'm his best friend," he said tersely. "And the local homicide-
hero. If I can't handle it, who can?"

"I think you came up to ask my advice, Shawn, and—"

"I didn't," he said quietly. "Just cookies."

"Shawn," she begged, "don't listen to him. ¿Querido?"

"Just cookies, Mamá Lola," he repeated. "No folk wisdom. OK?"

He drew on his gloves and climbed onto the bike. At the top of
the jeep trail he stopped. He looked down on the tiny shack far
below, the tall cannabis plants climbing the slopes behind. She was
on the porch, where he had left her. He lifted a hand and waved.

She brushed off the wave with a toss of the head and went inside.
Angrily, he spun onto Arroyo Burro Road in a cloud of dust, spewing rocks.

Now, however trusted, there was an *a priori* witness.

He'd been stupid to come up at all.

In early gray light, Zimmer the fry cook climbed to the bed of his
pickup truck, parked behind his trailer near the SP tracks. The
Harley had spent the night on the pickup, under a sheet from his
bunk inside, because he'd left the tarp on Trout Canyon Road. He
pulled off the sheet and ramped the bike to the ground.

It had been past midnight by the time he'd roared back down the pass, returned to the darkened Colonel's, loaded the bike back into the pickup, and driven home. Then he'd sat in the trailer trying to get a decent picture of the fire on his black-and-white TV set. He'd rip off a color TV the first window he saw open. The picture was crappy, so finally he'd lain down on his bed. All night he'd imagined the girl in the VW, arching her back and clawing at the window. He didn't think he'd slept at all.

But now he felt good. The sun was coming up, as if from behind a yellow curtain. The curtain was smoke, drifting over the whole fucking town, and he had done it all himself, he and the girl. Hot date.

Another fire truck thundered past on Highway 101, moving down from the north. All night long he'd heard them. So the fire was doing fine, and the wind would pick up soon. The siren excited him. He felt like riding, but there was no way he was going to get back up San Marcos Pass to see the excitement, because they'd set Red Flag Alert, he knew that from the early morning news. So, not San Marcos Pass.

He re-entered the trailer and got a bag of doughnuts and a jar of mustard. He ate the doughnuts outside, smeared mustard on his license plate and drew on his hard hat. Then he lowered the black visor, mounted the bike, and rumbled from the shadows of his trailer into the yellow dawn.

He'd been cruising the west side hills for weeks. The Shrink had always stopped him from making a set. Now the Shrink was quiet, sulking, ego hurt, maybe didn't give a damn. So screw him.

He'd see if he couldn't set another one before he went to work.

Ahead of Shawn Ortega's motorcycle, a Ventura County fire truck crawled through choking smoke up the San Marcos grade. Shawn was afraid to pass, for fear of running into something coming down in the murk.

On the way up, he'd been stopped at roadblocks twice, once by a young highway patrolman and the second time by an aging reserve deputy. If indeed the fire was arson, the stable was well locked, now that the horse was gone.

He found the fire camp, overflowing a tourist-view turnoff area on a wide shoulder projecting over Trout Canyon. Far below, a river of

dark-gray smoke moved seaward down the arroyo on the first whisper of today's Santa Ana. Under the smoke he glimpsed the burned-
out floor of the canyon. The fire was further up, isolating the San
Marcos Lookout Station and helicopter pad.

He moved through a mass of fire trucks, command trailers, and
field kitchens, avoiding the bodies of fire fighters resting for the battle they would face when the wind picked up. He located the line
boss, a preoccupied Navajo with a totem face and running eyes.

"Ono?" the Indian repeated. He waved a hand over the valley.
"Down there, somewhere, I don't know."

"How do I get down?"

"You don't, Lieutenant."

"I'm Sheriff's Arson Investigation, I'm afraid I *got* to."

"*Sheriff's* Arson? Jesus, does Hash know you're in the act?"

"Since yesterday."

"Lots of luck. He won't let *us* go down until he's finished."

Hell, he didn't *want* to go, he simply had to be able to tell the
sheriff he'd been. But it sounded too stupid to say. "So I get down,
how?"

"Hash climbed over the side." The Indian jerked his thumb at the
edge of the cliff. "But *you* better backtrack, and walk along Trout
Canyon Road."

The hell with that. He was in better shape than Hash, and probably younger. He moved to the rim of the canyon.

"Jesus," he breathed. It was virtually straight down.

If he tried it, he'd probably finish off the football knee that Hash
had started twenty years ago.

He returned to his bike, wheeled around, and drove to Trout
Canyon Road.

Fifteen

At the bottom of the canyon, Hash Ono sat coughing in the smoke. He should never have descended the face of the wash. There was an easier way, which was to walk along Trout Canyon Road from the highway.

But he'd been afraid of hot spots remaining along the road. Besides, he'd wanted to check the face of the canyon for signs of wind shifts that would be significant further down.

On the way down the cliff he'd twice grabbed roots of manzanita that were too hot for his hands. He would have put a crew to cold-trailing the slope until it was safe for him, but the smoke eaters, reaching the bottom before him, would inevitably have destroyed any evidence there was.

So, in the end, he'd been unable to look for signs on the canyon face after all, having fallen halfway, worn out the seat of his canvas pants, and dropped the last ten feet, straight down, into a blackened clump of poison oak.

Anyway, he was here, and uninjured. He shrugged out from under his orange backpack. He set it on the charred stump of an ancient oak, destroyed in another fire, perhaps a hundred years before.

He noticed that the flap of the backpack had come open. He laid out his arson kit to see if he'd lost anything.

A half-dozen rolls of linen, to flag the source and sector it off, a measuring tape, two dozen one-foot wooden stakes and a boy scout axe to pound them. A magnet for metal debris, which he'd coated with plastic to make it easier to clean, wire cutters . . .

His Nikon camera, bought at his own expense after years of useless battle with the Fire Department Purchasing Agent, a sketch pad, pencils, compass, an acrylic spray can to harden charred matches and cigarette ashes, and Tupperware containers to put them in. Tweezers, a sieve, magnifying glass, walkie-talkie . . .

A canteen, from which he took a slug of water for breakfast, swirling it around in his mouth. Up above, inmate crews had begun feeding, twenty-four hours a day, but he'd been too eager to begin work.

He was always enthusiastic at the start. Disillusionment came later, sometimes in the ashes, sometimes in the courtroom.

He wet a handkerchief and tied it over his mouth. He repacked his gear, took his bearings through the smoke, gazing across a jackstraw jumble of blackened chamise, manzanita, sugar-bush, and toyon, all creaking in the pale brown sun.

A ground squirrel popped from its hole a yard from his feet. It had failed to make it out before the fire, miraculously survived suffocation, and now it decided to go for broke. Dodging and darting, it scurried up the hill.

Acres and acres of moonscape. All his, now. But temporary moonscape, only.

For, like the squirrel, the burned chaparral would survive. Fire was its mother. After a conflagration like this, only charred, dead branches remained to the eye, but deep in the soil lay ancient seeds of a new generation. They had slept there for years, protected by diamond-hard shells, waiting for last night.

Sometime during darkness, while he'd been humping hose or sleeping in the scout car, the heat from the fire had cracked the seed coats. With the first winter rains, the seeds would germinate. With dead shade removed, sunshine could reach soil shadowed by old chaparral for years. And the seeds would sprout.

With the parasitic chaparral burned off, there would be water for new sproutings with stronger, younger roots. If the rains were early, as in '80, the ravine would be a sea of mud, but in a normal springtime the greening canyon would be a haven for returning squirrels, gophers, weasels, and snakes. By March or April the arroyo would be lush.

He'd once tried to explain the life cycle of chaparral to his old man, likening it to the Nisei condition after Pearl. With ancestral shade burned off in relocation camps, his own generation had sprouted, right? His father, who had thought Hash wanted his abalone packing plant, had smiled and offered him a match.

No communication, never had been. And he'd made a good decision to cut loose from the family fortunes: abalone, today, were practically extinct. Fires were here forever. Despite Red Flag Alerts, lookout stations, Phos-Chek airdrops, and arson investigators, the canyons here would be blazing for the next ten thousand years.

Chaparral required fire, and the ground required chaparral, or the land would wash into the sea.

Lightning and desert winds were a part of the cycle.

And maybe, if you took the long view, sets by firebugs, too.

But not so close to the city, OK?

The line boss and Forest Service lookout who'd first spotted the fire had agreed that the source seemed to be at the bottom of one of the small dry creek beds on the canyon floor. They'd had no time to triangulate before the whole canyon turned into a furnace. This left him with 100 acres of blackened canyon bottom to sift for the burned butt of a cigarette or the remains of a book of matches.

There were, of course, tricks he could use to focus the search.

He struggled into his backpack and began.

Leaning the Harley into the turns of the Old San Marcos Road, Zimmer the fry cook could see a plume of yellow smoke between La Cumbre Peak and the new San Marcos Pass Highway. To his disappointment, he noticed that it was rising straight up. Morning had killed the Santa Ana.

He slowed, trying to remember if there was a Red Flag checkpoint over the next crest, at Twin Ridge Road. He'd cruised this pass in the last Alert, but couldn't remember. He awaited the warning Voice of the Shrink. Nothing.

Deciding not to take the chance, he pulled to the shoulder, under a sign tacked to a pine tree: "Extreme Fire Danger: Non-residents Proceed No Further."

If he continued up Old San Marcos Road, he'd be risking contact not only with a potential roadblock, but with any resident he met.

With a $5,000 reward out for anyone found setting brush fires, the safe thing to do was to turn down the creek.

He spotted a trail sign at the side of the road, with the letters burned into a rustic plank: "Maria Ygnacia Creek Equestrian Trail." "Equestrian," he thought, meant horseback rider. Bikes were illegal off the road, but he was pretty sure that he could get the Harley anywhere a horse could go.

He left it to the breeze. If he felt a gust, he'd turn down the path: if not, he'd continue on the road and take his chances with a check-point.

He was about to blast forward when he heard it rising in the tangled creek-canyon below: the swishing, creaking sound of chaparral, squeaking under the rush of wind.

He turned down the trail, rising on his pegs and concentrating on the path. He drove for half a mile. The Harley was no trail bike, but his skill compensated for the lack of maneuverability.

He heard the distant drone of a plane and pulled off the trail to watch from under a tree. The plane was a little one, circling the smoke from his last night's fire. Cameramen in it, maybe, or forest rangers. It was too far away to see him.

The base of the smoke cloud, maybe two miles off, began to glow suddenly with an orange hue. And the column of smoke was beginning to sway toward the city. Wind, wind, wind . . . Trout Canyon would go all day, no sweat, and the evening Santa Anas would fan it higher. San Marcos Pass must be a frigging circus; equipment tangled every whichway on the curves, men yelling, radios yakking. A hot, acrid gust hit him. He lifted his black visor. The orange base of the plume turned red, exciting him further. Shaking with tension, he fumbled in his saddlebag, drew out a six-foot length of coiled quarter-inch plastic hose. He took the gas cap off his tank, inserted the hose, and sucked.

He had not done this in years, and he gagged when the gasoline hit his lips. But when he spat it out, he had a siphon going. He squatted and began to squirt the gas on the chaparral around him.

When he had siphoned out half the gas in his tank, he quit. He recapped the bike, wheeled it carefully some fifty feet back up the trail; then he returned quickly, lit a match, and tossed it into the brush. Nothing happened. He moved a little closer, tossed another, fleeing while it was still in the air.

At his bike, he heard the roar. He whirled, looking back. Half the hillside seemed afire already.

He jumped on the bike, flicked the ignition, and pressed the starter button. Nothing happened. He pressed it again. The starter whined, but the engine coughed and died.

He felt furnace-heat on his back. For a wild instant, he almost abandoned the bike. No way. He dropped the foot-starter, rose on it, and kicked with all of his weight. The engine fired, and then he was charging up the trail, spewing dust, burning rubber, high on his foot pegs, high in his mind.

At Old San Marcos Road he looked back. The ravine behind him was a wall of flame. He could hear shouting from over the crest: there'd been a roadblock there, sure as hell, and they'd already spotted the fire.

He swept back down the curves to the coastal plain. He'd still get the kitchen open on time. He felt empty inside, but good.

"Idiot!" yelled the Shrink, suddenly.

He ignored him. He didn't need the goddamn Shrink.

But it was good to know somebody cared.

Button Berger, California Division of Forestry engineer of Engine 8411, glimpsed the sign flashing past her right cab window, but her cabman had his nose buried in a map and missed the turnoff.

"Old San Marcos Road!" she shouted angrily, standing on the brake of the big CDF No. 9 Ford pumper. "Come *on*, Mac! What good's the map if we miss the road signs!"

"Sorry." The big, sandy-haired fireman twisted in his seat. "Hey, I wouldn't stop here!"

She wouldn't have, either, in normal circumstances, *shouldn't* have with traffic screaming past at sixty miles per hour, but the fire was brand-new and it looked as if they'd be early on the scene. She'd never made it first to a working fire, and she was damned if she was going to let it get away.

"Report San Marcos . . . *Old* San Marcos Road," she ordered. She heard the rest of her crew pounding on the top of the rear cab, terrified of oncoming traffic.

All right, all right, she breathed silently, angry at herself for giv-

ing them more "woman driver" ammunition. She eased the rig into
reverse, steering with the side mirrors. She winced as an overtaking
passenger vehicle, oblivious to her red beacon and backing light,
skimmed by, horn wailing like a passing locomotive's. When she had
the turning radius she needed, she slammed the rig into drive, wrestled the wheel and started up the Old San Marcos Road.

She was exhausted already, and they hadn't sniffed the first breath
of smoke. She had been driving three solid hours, rolling from Lake
Joshua Station at dawn, heading for the Trout Canyon fire. But
somewhere south of Montecito, as they screamed gloriously up 101,
the U. S. Forest Service dispatcher at Goleta had diverted them to a
brand-new blaze on Maria Ygnacia Creek.

She had considered turning over the wheel to Mac at that point.
It was a power trip to tool the big pump truck happily along the
highway, but a drag, when you weighed 125 pounds, to try to muscle it through twisting residential roads, Code Three, with two tons
of water sloshing in the tanks.

She should indeed have let Mac take it, rolling, arching her body
so that he could slide beneath her, as they had practiced too damn
much. But there was still too much going on between them, most of
it bad, and she couldn't risk even that contact, and a foothold on
command, from a man who seemed to turn her body into jelly at a
touch. So she'd hogged the wheel until too late. And now, on the
snaky streets of the western suburbs, they'd have to stop if she asked
him to change.

OK. To change was what he wanted, in more ways than one. But
it was her wheel, her truck, her crew, in the hills of home or here in
the coastal canyons, and he might as well discover it now.

She scanned the road ahead. "There'll be a Red Flag checkpoint
at a road called Twin Ridges," she told Mac. "If we go past that,
we've missed the creek."

Out of the corner of her eye she could see him glance at her, surprised that she'd know where roadblocks would be set, so far from
home. If he'd bothered to read the South Coast Red Flag Alert Plan,
he'd have known, too. Which was the reason she was engineer and
he was cabman. Don't tell him that, bite your tongue, Button. She
told him anyway, gently.

"*One* reason," he said. "Yeah."

She braked, then eased on the power, and somehow negotiated a turn which would have paralyzed her in a passenger vehicle before her divorce. Now she didn't seem to care.

"*One* reason?" She shot her eyes at him angrily. She knew they thought she was at best a token, at worst that she'd earned her rank on her back. "What's *that* supposed to mean?"

He ignored that and pointed ahead. She felt her body tense.

A dirty yellow fountain of smoke was vomiting into the morning sky. Vermillion flames licked at its base. She wouldn't need the checkpoint at Twin Ridge Road to find this one. She would be lucky if it didn't find *her* before she got set up.

She reported to Goleta that she was 10-97, on scene: "Fifty acres, heavy brush, winds gusting to thirty, steep terrain, rocky, no power lines, no dwellings, safe for an airdrop."

She told them that she was commencing First Attack, and that she wanted two more trucks, a tanker, helijumpers, and a hotshot crew.

From the sound of the radio, things were not going well at the main Trout Canyon Fire. She knew she was straining Goleta's capabilities, but she had a genuine ripper and didn't want to be left out in the cold.

She decided to use Old San Marcos Road as a fire line. The cab of the truck would be her fire camp. She looked out the window, and saw that Mac and the others were making a simple hose-lay.

She ordered a progressive lay, so that they could get started on the edge of the fire sooner. They moved to comply; not as fast as if Mac had ordered it, maybe, but fast enough.

It was time to get out of the cab and to set up the panel. She hesitated. If she didn't ask Goleta for a forester now, she might end up as fire boss for hours to come. She reached for the mike, and then changed her mind.

She jammed her visored hard hat on her head, pulled her goggles over her eyes, and climbed stiffly from the cab. In her bulky yellow fire jacket, with hotshot shoes and goggles on, she looked like any other smoke eater on the line.

They paid her $1,450 a month to be an engineer. With only her rig on the scene, that meant fire boss until someone better arrived.

Mac, Hal, and Mitch were hooking hose toward a clump of manzanita overhanging the road. Mac turned from the nozzle to look at

her, and signaled, bringing his stiffened arm, palm out, in a sweeping arc to the side from his knee to above his head.

She cracked valve number one, the one-and-a-half-inch line
stiffened like an eager phallus, the quarter-inch nozzle jerked in Big
Mac's hand, and a forty-foot stream almost tore down the bush.

She wouldn't holler for relief, not until she was hurt.

Sixteen

Steamboat Haley of Haley Air Service, Cachuma Municipal Airport, left his lady snarling at a creditor on the telephone and overpowered a minor windstorm to open the door of his hangar office. He was panting by the time he got outside.

The gale was nerve-racking, generated jointly by the rising Santa Ana and one of his lineboys turning up their ancient Beech Bonanza. But he preferred the howl of the wind and the roar of their engine to the screech of her voice inside.

He almost lost his ten-gallon hat as he fought his way through swirling dust, whiffing the smoke from the fire they hoped would save them. He reached his sole tanker, a World War II B-17. With a grunt, he hoisted himself up a scaffold at the wing and joined the old mechanic at the number three engine. There he teetered in the morning gale on his cowboy heels, breath heaving, clinging to the pitot tube. Beer, booze, and too many years . . .

"How long?" he demanded when he caught his breath.

"Who wants to know?" growled the mech, without looking up. "You or Suzy?"

Steamboat groaned inwardly. From his tone, she'd done it again, as if A&P mechanics grew on trees. If he told the mech it was Suzy, he'd never get an answer.

"The Forest Service will! Me, too, goddamn it! Fire won't last forever."

"It'll last," the mechanic murmured. "This *bird*, that's another question. I don't know how long. Or *if*."

The mechanic straightened, easing his back. He was even older than Steamboat, but wiry, a relic of bush pilot days in the mountain states. Which made a bond between them, probably the reason the mechanic was still putting up with them, for she was screwing up again, as she'd done in Denver, Tonopah, Reno, and Jackson, Wyoming. He'd nurse an operation off the ground, everybody's buddy, and whammo! She'd piss off every A&P engine butcher for forty miles, and flight students, charter customers, bankers, and creditors, too.

"It don't much matter," muttered Steamboat. It didn't, either. This was their last shot. The good times were almost lost to memory. "Smiling Jack" Haley had long before turned into "Steamboat," and the Girl of a Thousand Laughs into a growling bitch. It would be social security, next, for him: God knew what *she* would do. His Alaskan pipeline money was gone, his flight physicals grew yearly more lengthy as his arteries hardened, his left ear, ruined from radio ranges long abandoned, grew worse; he was too old and fat for the dope run to Baja.

If he couldn't get the tanker airborne for the rising fire, Cachuma Trust would own it in a week—and the Bonanza, one battered Cessna, and the office typewriter, too.

The only thing they wouldn't want was Suzy, his mistress. Mistress? He had a "mistress" like a dog had one. But he was damned if he'd see the poor old mech sit up and beg her for his dough.

"Old-timer?"

"Yeah?" The old man's shirt flapped on his scrawny chest.

"We're about to go belly-up, you know." Suzy would scream at him for warning the poor bastard, who'd slap a mechanic's lien on the tanker and really foul their plugs. But better him than the bank.

The red, windshot eyes swung toward him. "Thanks, but I ain't filing a lien. She'd kill me."

"You know, you're right? Take off, I'll try to finish—"

"*I'll* finish," the mechanic said irascibly, unscrewing a Zeus fastener on the cowling. "I been fucked for my wages before." He froze. "I mean fucked *out* of 'em, I didn't mean—"

Steamboat restrained a smile. Both he and the mechanic knew

that, twenty years ago, she'd have let him take it out in trade. Every airstrip from Fargo to Vegas had known it. Snaproll Suzy, Suzy Hotpants, Suzy the Flying Callgirl . . .

Unfair. She'd quit when they met, except when they were pressed.

Which was frequently, of course, but the half truths had angered him then. Now, nobody wanted her.

"You got a good memory," Steamboat remarked.

"I told you, I didn't *mean* that. Christ, I'm damn near seventy, and she must be fifty. Look, you want this done or not?"

Steamboat squinted toward the southeast. Far past Lake Cachuma, the soaring plume of smoke was bending seaward and flattening. The fire, which had turned inland during the night, was doubling back toward Santa Barbara. He was more and more convinced that, despite the Forest Service's dim opinion of his partner, Los Padres would have to call them in. It was their last chance for solvency in a bankers' world of avarice and overdrawn accounts.

"Let's both do it." He found another screwdriver in the tool box. "Keep 'em flying."

For Snaproll Suzy, Girl of a Thousand Laughs.

Hash Ono moved more and more slowly as the charred ravine whispered clues to guide him to the source of the Trout Canyon fire.

He had learned as a child to concentrate on the tiny. In *Gakuen* —Japanese school-after-regular school—squinting with *fude* brush in hand at useless *oshuji* ideographs on a ricepaper sheet—he had seethed, angry to be there while his paler classmates played baseball. But the ideographs had taught him to reduce his frame of attention from 100 acres to ten square feet to a square inch, as wind signs and char patterns led him closer to the birthplace of a fire.

Thank you, Honorable Father. The county thanks you, too.

He had little formal schooling in arson investigation, nothing like that of the Quantico-trained Forest Service Special Agents who would have been doing this job if the fire had started on federal land another mile up the canyon.

But he'd learned what he could over the years, from professional papers and the Special Agents themselves and Forest Service manuals. Now he'd accumulated more experience than his mentors, at least in the brush. He traveled very, very slowly, always by his own rules, always alone.

Last night, when he'd succumbed to firehouse instincts and joined the firemen on the line, there had been a period when the Bessemer-heat from the giant canyon-furnace, inhaling surrounding air to feed its invisible chimney—one mile around and jet stream high—had reversed the seaward-bound Santa Ana. It was that sudden change that had almost trapped him, scaring him back to his scout car for the night.

The sudden reversal explained a good deal that he was noticing now.

In order to find the source, he must of course backtrack the fire.

Fire burned outward from its origin. If there was no wind, on level ground, with equally volatile brush in all directions, it would burn in a perfect circle from its source. When you introduced wind, it burned downwind, making the circle egg-shaped. When you introduced a hill, it raced upslope, forming an ellipse up the grade. But there was another factor, which he thought of as the "total heat." And that heat caused a wind of its own.

At the very start of this conflagration, when it had burned only at the source he was looking for, the fire would have been nervous. It would waltz aside at every puff, explore the slopes of every hummock. It would lick at a limb of dry toyon, avoid a branch of moist manzanita. It was selective, leaving unburned material around until it was too late to return and consume it.

The Forest Service, with its federal need to categorize, called this phase the "circle of confusion." Hash thought of it as a kind of pre-coital stage.

As more and more brush was consumed, the internal heat arose.

Now the fire, like a woman teased to passion, left portions of the original circle forever unburned, and took a direction all its own. Now it would only be guided by the wind as long as the wind was strong; only follow a slope uphill if the grade was steep and long.

Finally, when its excitement grew strong enough, it would suck even the strongest surface gale into itself, and then it would burn as fast against prevailing winds as with them, eat level land and hillside indiscriminately. Now it would form a circle again, this time consuming everything on the circumference, burning from the outside in.

But even in its most passionate moments the fire left clues through which you could retrace the flames to their source. You could tell the direction from which it had been burning at any given moment. An untouched stem of grass falling backward into an already burned area might remain unburned and green in its blackened grave, after the fire was past. A stem of grass next to it, falling forward into unburned ground, would be consumed with the brush around it as the flame passed through. And the same was true of anything felled by the flames: limbs, fence posts, and sometimes even trees.

He turned and looked back up-canyon. Near the source when the heat had not yet peaked, the fire would have charred only that side of the vegetation facing its approach. So, because ash was light-colored, and unburned ground cover dark, the earth looked paler when facing away from the source than toward it. It was paler up-canyon, so he turned and continued down.

He spotted the body of a full-grown deer, caught last night by the momentary backfire. It lay stifflegged and bloated, but its rump was charred black and its chest still had fur. It had obviously been running from the fire when overcome. Since it had fallen just as it had run, the source must have been to its rear.

He found a fallen limb and checked it. The windward side of a branch, exposed to the most oxygen, would burn the deepest while the other side, protected in the lee, showed less charring. He continued in the direction of the deepest charring.

A few yards further, in the blowing smoke, he came upon a barbed wire fence. It had been destroyed long ago, except for a few rough posts. The barbs were of an antique design he had never seen before, probably shipped around the Horn in a clipper, by Boston merchants in exchange for cattle hides.

To a collector of antique wire, the barbs were valuable. His interest was in the strands between. He ran a finger delicately along a length between two barbs. Soot was deposited along one side, the side that had faced the flames. And the fence posts were alligatored, charred in scales that told him that the fire had approached from the side of the post.

The alligatoring told him something else. The scales were not as deep as they might have been, or as black, or as shiny. The fire here had not been as hot as further up the canyon: younger, not yet impassioned.

He was approaching the source. Further up the barranca, small stems and leaves had bent in the wind and frozen in their positions: a sign of tremendous heat. But they were erect; so they had never been as hot as those he had just passed, which must have burned later. Rocks he had been passing five minutes before had been stained with vaporized oils from a raging blaze. But here the rocks were clean: they'd been cooler in comparison.

He found a dry manzanita twig unburned. At eye level on a dry creek bank, a clump of chaparral was not even touched. The fire, very young here, had hit, missed, climbed a bank in one spot, skipped another.

He was in the circle of confusion, near the source.

His heart began to pound. He froze, looking about. Every step he took now could destroy evidence.

First, campfire? No evidence of that that he could see, and besides, this had been no place to camp. Dry creek, full of towering chaparral twelve hours ago, a searing, dusty wind racing down the canyon: not even a spaced-out hippy would have dared to light a campfire here.

Cigarette from the highway? No way. The highway was up there, all right, above the drifting smoke, but a cigarette would have had to breast a forty-knot gale last night to have landed so far away.

So he was looking for an arson device, maybe as small as a matchstick, as unobtrusive as a length of cigarette ash, maybe as obvious as a shattered Coke bottle smelling of gasoline.

Selecting every footstep in advance, he began to move through the ashes. He set his knapsack on the bank of the dry creek. In slow motion, he began to cordon off the area from firemen who'd be cold-trailing soon; he needed at least eight hours of daylight, undisturbed, and God help anybody who stepped into his domain.

He laid out parallel strips of tape between stakes, a yard apart, six inches high, making a gridiron. With a straight piece of chaparral held at right angles to his path, he'd inch along the gridiron, sliding the stick as a guide to make sure he missed nothing on the ground between the strips. And tomorrow, if he found nothing today, he'd be back to start again.

When he was through constructing his gridiron, he arose. There was something wrong. He sniffed, then removed his wet handkerchief. His nose was desensitized from the smoke, but he sensed an anomaly, something outside the odor of burned-out chaparral, distinct from the smoke drifting down from the departed fire.

It was hard to evaluate. Hot metal? Engine oil? Gasoline? From the camp above?

No. He was a long way from the fire camp. But the bottom of the canyon smelled like a freeway traffic jam.

Vehicle fire?

Jesus!

Still moving cautiously, he began to crawl through the smoke to the crest of a hillock on the lip of the ditch. He used the blackened limbs of a manzanita for a handhold; this one was cool to the touch; the fire had left here long ago.

On the crest of the hillock he stiffened. Through the drifting haze he saw it, first as a shape, then, as the smoke momentarily cleared, for what it was: the blackened hulk of a small sedan—a Volkswagen —right side up at the foot of the canyon face.

He relaxed. The car must have been here for years, one of the ancient wrecks that you ran into in the brush, abandoned as too expensive to salvage, sometimes invisible under chaparral for decades. Incinerated long after its crash, in this fire or some other.

Nothing to do with his own investigation.

But he smelled gasoline. And gas was volatile; the odor didn't last a month in the open air.

He moved closer, heart sinking. The smell grew, that and another odor he knew too well and didn't want to define.

He stumbled to the car and looked in.

"Holy jumping Jesus Christ!"

In the Box Canyon fire, in which two of A platoon's men had been trapped and incinerated under their engine by a breakover, he thought he'd seen everything that heat could do to the human body.

He apparently hadn't.

He lurched back up the hillock, away from the smell, yanked his walkie-talkie from his pack and called the line boss. He asked for the California Highway Patrol to come and get the car, and the Sheriff's Coroner Unit to come and get the body.

"*Body?*" Luke's voice crackled back incredulously. "No shit, a *body?*"

"Body!"

The line boss had news for him, too. Maria Ygnacia Canyon was blazing—Class C now—from the equestrian trail south, and there was no way *that* was a vehicle fire, right?

Hash agreed, relieved by the excuse to leave. His job was arson investigation, not traffic, and his task here was virtually done. Any man-made fire was actionable. The county, state, and even the U. S. Government—now that the fire was spreading into the National Forest—would go after the driver's estate.

He could already testify that the dead driver's car had started the fire.

The Highway Patrol would try to guess whether brakes or steering had failed, or if another car had run him off the road, or if he'd gone to sleep. The Sheriff's Coroner's Unit would probably try to determine if he'd been drunk or on drugs, and take pictures.

All, of course, a charade. None of their findings would make a damn to the burned-out corpse in the car.

And whatever happened, no liability policy in the world would come through with more than a drop toward filling this particular million-dollar bucket. As usual, the taxpayer would pay the bill.

He noticed that the license plates were missing. He looked for them at the foot of the grade, unenthusiastically: probably torn off somewhere on the face of the canyon. Let the CHP go for that one, or identify the car from the motor number.

Suddenly he was exhausted. And he had the other fire to check, on Maria Ygnacia Creek. He sat down to wait for the CHP or the coroner. But somebody was moving below, thrashing through brush along the smoky canyon bottom. Too close to his gridiron, not that it mattered now. A voice called out: "Hash? Hey, Hash?"

Shawn Ortega? Jesus, he didn't want a dialog: he wanted to start on Maria Ygnacia Creek.

But, support your local fuzz. "Up here, buster."

Ortega materialized from the smoke. He looked as if he'd crawled to the canyon floor through a factory smokestack. His eyes were red; he'd apparently not thought to put a damp handkerchief over his mouth. One of Hash's gridiron tapes was trailing from his ankle, but he still had an air of authority. Cops . . .

Ortega picked off the tape, apologizing. He stared at the car. "What have we *here*, pray tell?"

"Not a set, anyway," said Hash. Which was lucky, he added silently, because if there'd been a device, you'd have buried it six inches deep with your size-twelve ripple soles. He had a flash of inspiration. "Hey, weren't you on that Ghoul Squad once?"

"Once," admitted Shawn. He paled. "My God, there's no *body* in there?"

"Well, there kind of is." Hash moved down the slope and began to yank up his pickets.

"What are *you* doing?" asked Ortega.

"Pulling up my stakes, to steal gently away." He stowed everything in his backpack and drew it on. "Traffic accident, right? For the CHP and Coroner's Unit? Well, they're on the way."

"But we can't *leave* the poor bastard!" Ortega cried.

"*You* can't," agreed Hash. He asked Ortega if the sheriff wasn't county coroner. And thus all deputies, deputy coroners, whether assigned to Coroner's Unit or not? Ortega admitted they were. Hash smiled. "OK, I'm booking out now." He mentioned the new fire up Maria Ygnacia Creek.

"I'm supposed to be Arson, like you," Shawn complained, but he started toward the vehicle.

"Sayonara, Shawn." Hash smiled. "You just got blindsided, one more time."

A little help wasn't all that bad, in the right place at the right time.

Skirting the eastern flank of the Trout Canyon fire, Bull Durham, California Department of Forestry supervisor of Inmate Crew ⚭3, La Mirada Rehabilitation Center, had been pretending to doze in the front of the crew bus as it jounced along Red Rock Canyon Road.

He had learned long ago, in dealing with prisoners, to hide his considerable intelligence, and to veil his perfectly normal hearing. He was his own spy, as a matter of self-preservation. No management technique he had discovered at the CDF camp, nestled under the prison's accordion-wired fences, had been as valuable as pretended ignorance.

He was a big redheaded man with the belly of a small-town county sheriff, flat twinkling eyes, and widely spaced yellowing teeth. The tiny silver trumpets of a fireman on his shirt collar were tarnished with age and he was wise in the ways of brush fires and the misfits who fought them.

The brakes shussed, the bus slowed, and a sudden silence fell over the sixteen-man crew. The quiet told him that Cubehead Rankin, his wild-eyed driver-mechanic, had reached the junction with Rattlesnake Road, and intended to turn up it, contrary to orders. With Bull apparently asleep, Cubehead could get the crew to the crest line on wheels, though Bull had told him to stop at the bottom. This would earn Cubehead a dozen status points with the assorted thieves, strongarm men, and "N"-number addicts that Bull, unarmed and alone, must somehow con, cajole, and inspire to bust their asses for the illusion of freedom and seventy-five cents an hour, as long as the fire survived.

For reasons connected with wind, brush height, and their physical safety, Bull wanted them cutting firebreak uphill, not down. But to explain the reasons would turn the forestry bus into a caucus of shouting jailhouse lawyers: it was the last thing he intended to do.

Through lowered lids, he studied the black, bronze, yellow, and shaggy white faces in the curved rearview mirror he used as a window on the moods of his charges. Dumptruck Jergins, his drag shovel man, began to speak in his grating, alcoholic whine, and Mother, the ebony lead-hook who was the star in Bull's troupe of experts, glared him into silence.

Bull knew why. When the Man was asleep, you let him lie. Especially now, when Cubehead's scam might get them up the first hill on wheels instead of afoot. Once safely on the ridge, everyone would swear they'd heard Bull tell Cubehead to unload at the top.

Bull waited until Cubehead jockeyed the big International around the turn, then stretched and yawned. "OK, Cube, they walk from here."

The wild, acid-blurred eyes flashed to him, and Bull saw the Cube's brow furrow. Had the Man been toying with them or not? Cube would never know.

Bull hoisted himself to his feet. He beckoned his swamper, Juan Cortez, a slit-eyed Chicano reputed to be high in the Mexican mafia. The foreman padded down the aisle to his side.

"Nomex suits," Bull decided. "Jackets *and* pants." Everyone groaned: the fire-resistant yellow material didn't breathe, and was stifling. But it gave you an extra ten seconds when a blowup sent fireballs hurtling everywhere, and Bull did not trust the dust devils he now saw dancing up the canyon. Juan accepted the order impassively: he'd run lines with Bull from San Diego to the Ventana Wilderness. He either trusted the forester, or distrusted the wind as much as his boss. Bull didn't care which.

"Four brush hooks," Bull continued, stretching. "And I want four McClouds, four Pulaskis, four shovels." If you balanced cutting and clearing tools, you couldn't go wrong. He glanced out the window of the bus, at the north side of the canyons, where the brush grew thickest. Bad. Three years of rain, no fires, and now this. Asshole high to Mother, who stood six-six.

You were supposed to cut firebreaks to a width one and a half times the highest brush; Bull cut double, to make sure, allowing those of the prisoners who knew the official formula to simply figure he was too stupid to argue with.

"I want a six-foot-wide line," he announced.

"Shit!" someone exploded.

Bull pretended not to hear, and the crew, filing out and rounding the bus to pick up its gear, grew quiet, having expected nothing less anyway: one of the virtues of consistency in leadership. Only Juan nodded, imperceptibly, in agreement. Under a towering pack, he'd lead the line of men up the hill, picking the right contours, with Mother slashing his razor brush hook next, and Booster McClain, the second hook, gnawing at Mother's heels. The crew would cut eighty yards an hour, through smoke, ashes, soaring heat, and swooping wind.

Behind Booster would trudge the two other hooks, and then the McClouds, which were half blade, half rake; then the Pulaskis, half hoe, half axe, finally the shovels. Dumptruck Jergins, the drag shovel, would bring up the rear, complaining of the pace, and of the "staubs" left by the others, which he'd have to clean out. Placing Dumptruck last had given Bull a litmus to test the rest of the crew's effectiveness: as long as he could hear Dumptruck bitching, he knew they were leaving clean trail. It was when Dumptruck was silent that Bull knew he was out of breath from tidying up.

Bull strolled to the rear of the truck. The crew was suiting up, hefting tools, eyeing the dirty brown smoke plumes drifting over the ridges. It was a big one, and everyone knew it by now, even Booster, who'd come onto the crew so recently he was still trying to look good for Bull's monthly reports, and Mother, who was Murder One and couldn't have cared less.

Mother, dressed in yellow Nomex now, towered hugely. Sweat was already pouring from his anvil jaws. Something was bugging him, Bull knew. Bull's role was that of an observer, when crew tensions rose, not that of an umpire or participant. He tried to look duller.

Mother swung his brush hook delicately, as if to test its edge, against a trunk of rock-hard mesquite six inches thick. The bush collapsed with a whoosh. Mother's eyes swung to Booster.

"Keep the dime, hear?" he said softly.

The "dime" was the ten-foot distance between men, inviolate as their souls.

"Just keep movin'." Booster shrugged, unimpressed. "And then you got it. Hear?"

Trouble, but competition at the head of the line kept the column moving faster. Bull watched them file into the brush. He yelled after them: "Your crank'll be hot at the top."

He kept hot coffee ahead of the crew, for bait.

Though ordinarily he traveled afoot, close to his troops, never turning his back on them or the fire, he had decided to ride for a while. He was nearly fifty, the fire was a half mile away, and he had better save himself for later. He climbed back into the bus with Cubehead, who started inching up the road.

"'Crank,'" Cubehead mused, testing him. "Wonder where we came up with *that*, for coffee."

"Crank," on the street, was meth. Cubehead, who had shot, sniffed, dropped, smoked, and popped every drug known to man, knew that as well as he.

No way, Cube.

You learned a lot more if the natives thought you didn't know the language.

Cube had the bus barely crawling, hardly keeping abreast of the hooks in the brush glinting in the auburn sunlight. If the bus lagged, you got stragglers: sprains, blisters, heat exhaustion. When the truck stayed ahead, the stragglers had to cut brush to get to it. "Let's go, Cubehead," Bull sighed. "OK?"

Reluctantly, Cubehead stepped on the gas.

"Trying to save the shocks," he mumbled.

In life, son, there was no *way* to save the shocks.

He wondered what Cubehead would think if he said it aloud.

He guessed he never could.

Even with the trip up Maria Ygnacia Creek, Zimmer the fry cook had been only twenty minutes late punching in, and he'd opened up the kitchen practically on time. But the manager had come in right after, and the old fart hadn't shut up since he'd seen his time card, and now he was asking questions about the counter girl. The wind was rising outside. The cook wished he'd called in sick: he could have had half the county burning by dark.

"You mean," demanded the manager, "she didn't say she'd be late today, or she'd called in, or *something?*"

He shook his head, salting the batter. The manager looked irritated. "You *don't* season the Colonel's mix," he said, just to bitch, "so knock off the salt, OK?"

The cook turned from the stove. Slowly, he took off his chef's hat and held it out to the old fucker.

"Oh, come *on!*" the manager said. "Just do your job!" He was nibbling his lip. Nobody seemed to know whether to shit or go blind without the counter girl there. Well, they better find another one.

"She never taught me the register," complained the blonde.

"I'll handle the register," said the manager. "Her paycheck! She must have said something," he insisted to the cook.

"Well, yeah," he lied. "She said, 'Don't forget to lock up.'"

The old man looked at him. "You mean *she* left before you did?"

He nodded.

"That isn't what the time cards say." The manager frowned.

He'd have to be more careful. "I forgot. I left first. But it was after quitting time."

The old bastard said that wasn't the point, all he wanted to know was what time she'd be in today, the least she could have done was to call in if she wasn't coming, so he could have got one of the noon-time kids in early.

"Whyn't you call *her?*" asked the blonde.

The cook tensed. None of the blonde's fucking business. He jabbed at a thigh, pressed it into the hot grease. He began to wonder if he shouldn't split, when he got his paycheck, before the heat came down. Well, he'd dumped her license plates. He had plenty of time to decide.

"I *did* call," the manager said. "Line stays busy."

"She lives in Isla Vista with about a dozen other kids," the blonde volunteered. "She told me once."

A fire truck screamed past up Fairview Avenue, air horn croaking, heading for the hills. On the kitchen radio, the cook had heard that both the Trout Canyon and Maria Ygnacia fires were out of control. And heard a prediction of high afternoon winds. Jesus, he'd like to be out there. He stirred the chicken thighs. "Maybe she got, you know, held up by the fires?"

"There's no fire between here and Isla Vista," said the manager.

"Hey," exclaimed the blonde. "You ought to ask that fat kid works the pumps! They were talking at the gas station when I left."

The cook couldn't believe it. The stupid broad had seen the greaser returning the girl some money *two* nights before, and thought it was yesterday.

"Yeah," he said, smiling inside. "I saw that."

"I'll call her again," said the manager, moving toward his desk. "Now, damn it, watch the salt!"

The cook relaxed. He might not have to leave at all.

He'd hate to be the fat Chicano, if they ever identified the body in the fire.

The counter girl's roommate trimmed his golden beard, angrily, in the bedroom mirror. She hadn't even said good-by. He heard one of the girls—Deedee or Charlie's new lady or the kook from Stanford —calling her name. "Phone!"

Let 'em call. She'd left no note, no nothing. He'd awakened to an empty bed, and horny, too. He'd thought after two, three months, there was more between them than sharing the rent.

Deep inside, he knew he'd played it too cool. *"Denver? That'll be nice."* As if he didn't care. Well, he cared, or he wouldn't be pissed. In his shorts, he walked to the landing.

"Phone! For your lady."

Deedee was sitting on the floor below, cradling the phone. Her stud, a black premed student, must have gone home on vacation. She wore a skimpy nightie. She looked like a milk-chocolate *Playboy* centerfold. Jesus, the *bod*: long tawny legs, boobs you couldn't believe, and a trim, flat stomach.

He smiled down at her. "She drove home for Christmas, I guess. Tell them that."

The great almond eyes widened. "You *guess*? Well, this dude says she's due at work; he has her paycheck."

That was odd, to leave her check. She'd been cutting it close financially. Damn, he'd have to come up with the rent, alone. Maybe she'd found somebody at the last minute to share driving expenses, and figured she couldn't wait.

"She'll be back after Christmas, tell them to hold the check."

When she hung up, he continued to grin down at her. Somewhere a siren cried distantly. She gave him a long, hard look, crawled to the stereo, searched for a tape, put it on, smiled up mischievously.

"I'm dreaming of a white Christmas . . ."

"Yeah . . ." he breathed. "All *right!*"

"Why not?" She drifted up the stairs.

He led her through his bedroom door.

Why not, indeed?

Seventeen

Shawn Ortega inched back down the canyon face after an unsuccessful hunt for the VW's missing plates. He circled the car. The blackened shape—grinning, as so many burned corpses did—sat far from the wheel, as if it had recoiled and braced for the impact. Shawn sensed an inconsistency in the scene but couldn't define it.

He'd made a cursory inspection of the whole area. He saw no reason to open the door until the Ghoul Squad actually arrived. In fact, he intended to become an innocent bystander then, knowing from experience what faced the poor bastards who had to handle this particular burned and twisted body.

But when Sergeant Curt Blossom of the Coroner's Unit actually showed, with his deputy Phelps, on foot and staggering under their equipment, he found himself reluctant to leave.

He'd made some observations while waiting. He gave them to Blossom. The sergeant, a cherubic ball of energy who'd been a Navy corpsman, took notes of his own. Curt's assistant, Phelps, was a lanky black with an acid smile, reputedly sentenced to the Coroner's Unit for driving with a defective siren and totaling a squad car on a Code Three response.

Shawn had known from his first glance through the windshield that the corpse itself would be little help in its own identification. The vehicle would be the key to early notification of the next of kin.

He should be used to it now, but he found himself, as always, shaken in the presence of an unidentified corpse, knowing how survivors felt when they learned, too long after the fact, of their loss.

He'd been batting a stupid baseball around in the park, while, in the hospital, his father lay dead and his mother dying from a Coast Highway crash. And he had not been told in time to reach her, though he'd prayed all the way from the park.

The thought of this victim's loved ones going happily through the day, unaware, drove him up the wall, for he knew that the few false hours of surcease would haunt them forever.

With both plates missing, it was very possible that he was dealing with a stolen car, though most thieves would have replaced them with stolen plates as well.

So, though it was rightly the job of the CHP, he'd found the Vehicle Identification Number on the jumbled engine block and rubbed soot off it with his handkerchief. The first two digits were worn smooth by friction against a radiator hose, but he'd done his best to decipher them. Now he gave them to Curt Blossom.

"Thank you, Shawn," said Blossom, looking at the hulk distastefully. "Christ!"

Phelps was already shooting pictures with a Polaroid. Under the loom of the canyon wall, the bug looked tiny. Shawn wondered what color it had been; there was simply no way to tell.

Time for him to shove off, try to track Hash down at the fire up Maria Ygnacia Creek, welcome or not. He wanted to learn his new job, or at least keep away from the sheriff's flak. But something held him to the spot, something wrong in what he saw before him.

Absently, he circled the bug again. It had obviously tumbled end over end during its fall. Its headlights were smashed and its windows broken into crazy mosaics, probably by the ensuing fire. He went closer.

He saw no way the CHP would ever assign blame to the brakes: tangled hydraulic lines, heat-twisted drums, and a battered master cylinder would stymie them from the start. No way to check out the steering either: frame bent, tie bar bowed; tires consumed in the fire.

Forward, in the open luggage compartment, the gas tank had ruptured. A pile of white ash, like what you'd find on the highway near an accident, told him that the driver had carried warning flares, and perhaps told him something about the driver himself: careful enough to carry flares, but careless enough, through fatigue, drink, or last night's wind, to leave a paved dry highway and hurtle to his death.

Failed headlights? Run off by another car? Unless the CHP found skid marks near the fire camp above, they'd never know.

He caught a sudden retching odor of burned hair and flesh, exactly like overcooked pork. Curt Blossom, on the other side of the car, had opened the door. Phelps was standing beside him, clipboard ready for notes, Polaroid hanging loosely.

"A kid?" muttered Phelps, peering at the body.

Curt Blossom ignored him. His voice, muffled, reached Shawn. "No documents, no baggage, no pocketbooks, all ashes. Engine in neutral. Body restrained by remnants of safety belt," he dictated, in a slow, flat monotone that seemed to make Phelps impatient.

Gearshift neutral didn't mean much. The driver's knee could have kicked it out of gear. But safety belt fastened? Another sign of caution. Flares, safety belt; it didn't sound like your average flatland tourist on a mountain road. Or like a drunk or a suicide either.

"Brain," continued Curt profoundly, "boiled and apparently exploded late in fire due to intense interior temperature . . ."

"Ugh," grunted Phelps, as if through a stuffed nose. Shawn noticed that he was breathing through his mouth himself.

"Brain tissue," Curt droned, "splattered widely through interior. Overhead, dashboard, remnants of dome light . . . Phelps-baby? You got all that?"

"I *got* it! Come on, Curt! Let's get him in the bag!"

"Her."

Shawn winced. "Her?"

A chopper wobbled up the canyon, engorged with Phos-Chek, heading north toward the blaze. He heard a distant fire truck.

Curt pulled his head out and reappeared over the hood. "Take a look. It's either a woman or a guy with his pecker burned off."

"I'll take your word." Now he really felt sick. Curt was his best friend on the force. "Christ, Curt, you talk like one of the Choir Boys."

"People have told me that," Curt said sadly. "Actually, I'm a very sensitive guy. I don't beat my wife, and I like little kids. It's just that I got a high horror threshold." He looked at Shawn and delivered his thrust. "At least, *I'm* still hanging in."

Shawn had screamed for a year at his own sentence to purgatory on the Coroner's Unit and finally got off. Curt seemed to serve forever, like a lifer. And he'd never done anything to deserve it, as far as Shawn knew.

"You're a credit to the department," conceded Shawn.

"Thank you, Lieutenant. We've missed you in the pits." He turned to his deputy. "Am *I* going to shoot her, or you?"

The deputy fumbled with his strobe, took a deep breath, and ducked his head into the car.

Curt was looking at Shawn curiously, probably trying to decide why he was here. "A question I didn't want to ask, but . . ." He nodded at the car. "*Homicide?*"

Curt obviously hadn't heard yet of his exile to Arson. Actually, he should walk away from the case, as Hash had. Instead, he shrugged and cut Curt in on the story: "Homicide, arson, who knows? Hell of a fire, anyway. First, we got to identify her."

The county had no morgue, so the Coroner's Unit simply delivered unclaimed bodies to private mortuaries, rotating monthly to keep the locals happy. Fine for storing traffic accidents for relatives. But to find this woman's next of kin without a license plate, they might need more than a look at her bridgework. "What's the Morgue-of-the-Month?"

"Dinsmore's Memorial Garden."

"They can't give us X-rays," Shawn pointed out.

"X-rays?" Curt was staring at him. "Look, she rolled down a three-hundred-foot cliff! Her skull's popped and her clavicle looks like a stick of kindling and she's got a heat-fractured tibia and maybe her femurs too. *X-rays?*"

Heat fractures, which he'd seen in the Box Canyon fire, occurred when the muscles burned so fast that the bones simply cracked. The VW must have a hit a thousand degrees inside. Shawn tried not to think of it.

"And, hey," continued Curt, "I'm just talking about *gross* trauma! Inside, she's got to look like you ran over a box of spaghetti with a Mack truck! What are *X-rays* going to tell us?"

"*Old* fractures. For ID."

"We can't throw that kind of bucks around anymore!"

"I want X-rays," Shawn insisted, as if he owned the department. "Look, *both* plates are missing. Something stinks!"

"What's wrong with her VIN number?"

"Well, it's obscured, take a look. You can't really read the first two—"

"Somebody will file a Missing Person on her," Curt insisted. "She's not much for looks, but *somebody'll* miss her."

Shawn's mind raced. Something was bugging him, beyond the missing plates. Two years before, he'd broken the "Solvang Slasher" murders. For weeks he'd puzzled over a clue: the suspect took a longer drive to work than was necessary. Shawn had discovered that a witness to the murder lived on the direct route: the suspect had simply been trying to avoid him. The same sort of hidden clue tugged at his subconscious here, something discordant in the setup, accident or not.

He *should* back off. If she was an arson victim, she was a murder victim also, and he no longer had a right to the case. If it was a simple highway accident, if the plates had been torn off in the descent, then he was off it too.

He didn't care. "County General," he demanded. "For X-rays. And tox scan, carbon monoxide, the works."

Curt looked stricken. So did Phelps. The morgue at County General was out of a Vincent Price horror movie: marble slab, lead sinks, 1880 Bunsen burners, formaldehyde, and ether.

"You want an *autopsy?*" demanded Curt, who would have to assist.

"Yep!" Shawn nodded. "Get Atherton."

He didn't like Atherton, but he was the best forensic pathologist in town.

"Not on *my* budget," Curt warned. "So, you got a Master Charge, or what?"

High above him, from the rim of the canyon, Shawn became conscious of radio transmissions from the fire equipment. Like bees in a heated hive, they sounded excited. The wind began to rise, gusting down the canyon, then slacking, then returning with hot, replenished force. Each gust deepened the gloom and added to his depression. Curt Blossom glanced uncomfortably at the charred canyon slopes towering over them. None of them had masks. Shawn got a cinder the size of a dime in his eye and Phelps began to sneeze as the yellow clouds drifted down on them.

"Invoice Homicide," Shawn told Curt recklessly. That, he'd take up with Castillo if the crap hit the fan. "Now, let's get our asses out of here."

He helped Curt and Phelps remove the body, which immediately assumed the classic pugilistic stance of the roasted corpse, nauseating him further. He helped them bag it and guide it up the hill while the Los Padres Search and Rescue Team winched. From Curt's van, he called Emergency Communications Center and checked for Missing Person Reports. None. So he helped Los Padres SAR hunt for the plates on the canyon slope: no luck. But there was no sign of a front plate-holder and the VW's rear one had been torn off, not simply unscrewed. A puzzle.

On Scenic Highway, he searched for skid marks with a young highway patrolman until late afternoon. They found none.

Finally he climbed back on his Yamaha, picked up his car at home, and headed for the Operation Torchy computer. All the way down he wondered why he'd put his head in the noose, instead of simply backing off the case.

He didn't know. Anyway, whether arson, accident, or murder, he wanted the girl identified, for the sake of whomever she'd left, and soon.

Eighteen

Jerry Castle, fire boss of the Los Padres National Forest, squinted at the new fire on the map. Maria Ygnacia? There was something flammable in the name itself. Maria Ygnacia Creek seemed, from the steep contours to be a narrow, twisting dry gorge. He visualized wall-to-wall chaparral, now turned to a holocaust. Nothing in size compared to the Trout Canyon fire, which was a fast-growing red-ringed cancer gnawing at the edge of his forest. But still, he was sure, by now Maria Ygnacia was a vertical hell of flame.

He wanted to establish his headquarters—"Incident Command Post" nowadays—on the San Marcos fire line itself. You couldn't fight a fire from a downtown office; you had to be slashing away at the front, with the smell of sweat and the snarl of radios, and feel the shifts of wind on the hairs of your nose. From here in the city you were tempted like any rear echelon general to underestimate the enemy and sometimes to risk the lives of your troops. Out there, you were more careful.

Besides, his presence here was making the dispatch people indecisive, unwilling to commit, too eager to pass the buck.

But before he left, he had some decisions to make. If they were wrong, he could cost the Forest Service hundreds of thousands, perhaps millions of dollars.

Washington subscribed to the Economic Theory of fire fighting; the cost of prevention plus suppression plus damage must be kept to a minimum. Loving the forest, he subscribed to the more emotional

Minimum Damage Theory: save the wildlands, and damn the expense. Washington ruled, ultimately, but there was plenty of rope to hang himself before Washington tallied the score.

It was up to him to decide how quickly and extravagantly, or slowly and cheaply, his headquarters and troops in the field would grow. If he cried wolf too soon, it could cost a million to control a hundred-thousand-dollar fire, and he would find his whole career in shambles.

Conversely . . .

He didn't like to think of conversely. Conversely, you ended up with a half-million acres of blackened wildland, and money left in the budget. You couldn't buy back the trees.

He'd been conservative all day, declared the fire Class D, as if only a hundred acres or so were at risk. There were only seven hundred men on the line, under Tallman. Nevertheless, even so limited a mobilization had had impressive results here in the dispatch room.

Manning telephone cubicles were a half-dozen foresters brought in from the Santa Barbara District Ranger's Headquarters. Sitting in the cubicles, empty fifty weeks out of the year, he had a skeleton staff: service chief, finance chief, safety officer, air service officer. The service chief was tracking down equipment they would need, calling Boise or "Firescope" at Riverside every two minutes or so, landline. The finance chief was starting a running account of expenses and obligations incurred during the fire.

The air service officer was rounding up contract aerial tankers, chartering helicopters, already transporting crews to and from the line. Under him, if the fire grew, would be a helicopter manager, a tanker manager, and a general operations officer called, simply, the aerial manager.

Already, sweating in the computerized communications vans at the San Marcos Fire Camp, were counterparts of the chiefs here, manning the fire camp ends of the lines.

The question now, before he left to join them, was whether to call it a Class E fire, which meant over three hundred acres and called for a Class One team of nine hundred men, or to hope they could contain it by tomorrow with the Class Two team they had, and potentially save a fortune.

"Jerry," called the dispatcher. "County Fire called in. The source of Trout Canyon was a highway accident: some asshole woman went over the edge."

He heard cheers around the room. You could live with a one-shot, random highway incident: a pyro was something else. Still, why Maria Ygnacia Creek so soon after? Not another vehicular fire, up there. No lightning around today. Therefore, man-made. Power line down in the wind?

No power lines, there.

Campfire? Hunter?

Doubtful, during Red Flag Alert.

A firebug, triggered perhaps by Trout Canyon on TV?

Suppose the rising Santa Ana wedded the two conflagrations tonight, bringing pyros, like moths to a candle, from the whole of Southern California, as the big blazes always did. As no one publicly could *admit* they did, for fear of fanning the madness.

The implications of that, in the rushing wind, were too horrible to contemplate. He moved to his dispatcher's side. "Where's Holmes? That wind guy from Boise?"

"Fire Camp One. LA's sent him two forecasters and a mobile weather station," called the service chief.

Castle told the dispatcher he was heading for the camp, too. The dispatcher winced at his leaving but managed to dodge one last decision.

"That CDF broad, Jerry? With the Lake Joshua crew? I think we ought to relieve her with a forester."

"Did she ask?"

"No *way!*" But, he said, she'd been given six airdrops and had three trucks under her now, up a narrow road. She wanted more engines. The dispatcher was afraid she was going to get trapped.

It did sound like trouble. But would they take the fire from her if she'd been a man?

At Marble Cone in '77, one out of ten smokechasers on the fire line had been a woman. He'd seen them in blackface, hacking with Pulaskis and raking with McClouds, humping hose, jumping with hotshot crews. He'd seen them sprinting for safety and sobbing in aid stations. He'd seen some of them fold. But men quit too, and the lady on Maria Ygnacia Creek hadn't, apparently, yet.

His own ex-wife, whom he still loved very much, was a civil

rights lawyer in Houston. Her life was threatened regularly, but she'd never quit either.

First to the fire became fire boss, that was the rule. By now, the girl on Maria Ygnacia would have felt the fire's muscle, learned its whims, studied the terrain.

He'd never take a fire away from Luke Tallman, just because he seemed to be getting boxed in.

"Get her the rigs. From Luke Tallman, or Paso Robles, or Salinas, I don't care. But it's her damn fire till she hollers."

He decided to stay small, with a Class D for one more night, and to stay with a Class Two team. If half San Marcos Pass burned up, at least no one could say he hadn't heard the voice of the taxpayer.

Just the same, he and the little lady on Maria Ygnacia had better corral their fires, or they'd both end up a creek together.

He went to his office to suit up for camp.

Shawn stood behind the computer operator in the shabby parlor of Operation Torchy's safe-house. As she turned on her CRT screen, he imagined the place without the cop at the door, the file cabinets, the computer console dominating the room.

What was left he furnished in his mind with polished, old-fashioned pieces. Then he had a close approximation of his childhood home, Don Miguel's, and the homes of half his childhood friends. He felt uncomfortable in the parlor, as if in church. For the sitting room, with its cheap wallpaper, creaky waxed floors, and cracked plaster ceiling, was for funerals and the priest. You didn't live in such a room, but in the dining room, or on the back porch, or in the flowering yard.

Such buildings as these were flexible survivors of earthquake, gale, flood, and fire. The quake of 1925 had leveled the less stubbornly built of them almost two decades before he was born, and pulverized the eighteenth-century adobes of the Old Town. It had been downhill for Pueblo Viejo ever since. But this place, like Don Miguel's a block away, would sway with the times and last forever.

Unless some firebug with a sense of humor lit it off.

The woman turned from the keyboard. She'd recognized him, greeted him by name. She was a Chicana, around forty, named María González, probably the older sister of one of the hordes of

González kids he had played and warred with twenty-five years ago. He saw in her eyes that he was still half hero, half enemy in the barrio: Ortega was a princely name, lieutenant a regal rank. She had obviously made it partway up herself.

"So, Lieutenant, you want . . . What?"

"Stakeout reports from the San Marcos Pass. I'm looking for the license number on a VW."

Her fingers danced, and he saw, on the screen in front of her: "TORCHY. SAN MARCOS PASS." She paused, and words flashed on: "DATE? TIME? VEHICLE MAKE? TYPE? YEAR?"

"Last night," he told her. "Between ten and eleven. VW sedan. Around a '68, '69?"

She was very fast, and so was the computer.

"NORTHBOUND? SOUTHBOUND? EITHER?" asked the screen.

"Either way," said Shawn.

"LICENSE PLATE: STATE AND NUMBER?" demanded the computer.

"We don't know, *estúpido*, that's what we *want*," muttered the woman, and typed in: "UNKNOWN."

The computer stayed blank.

"He gets mad when I say that," explained María. "He's picking up Spanish." She typed in: "NOT OBSERVED."

No answer.

"Come on, Torchy," she warned. "La policía . . ." She turned. "Did it have a plate at *all*?"

A good question. "It should have had, going up. Don't we all?"

"Not around here, you forgot, hey?" She whirled and typed: "NONE."

The computer thought it over. Suddenly the green letters began to ripple from left to right across the screen:

TEAM CHARLIE

1018 PM LOCATION SAN MARCOS PASS HGWY—SAN ANTONIO CREEK
   ROAD

RED VW SEDAN

NO PLATES

NORTHBOUND MODERATE SPEED

NUMBER OCCUPANTS NOT OBSERVED

REMARKS: NO PLATES NO PLATES NO PLATES NO PLATES

WHY NOTED: REPEAT NO PLATES NO PLATES NO PLATES.

"Jesus," breathed Shawn. "*Why* no plates?"

"He can't tell you that," said María. "Anything else?"

He wrote her a shopping list. When they finished, he had the names and local phone number of the two Forest Service special agents who were Team Charlie, and Torchy's assurance that the VW minus the plates had indeed never got as far as Team Delta, on the other side of San Marcos Pass. He had the license numbers of eight cars, two vans, and a truck which had climbed the grade north-bound between 10 P.M. and eleven. He also had the license numbers of twelve southbound vehicles descending.

Torchy had discovered that the Department of Motor Vehicles in Sacramento, to whom Torchy talked, had no record of a VW with the engine number he'd rubbed clean. He'd been practically guessing at the first two digits, anyway. So they asked Torchy about that. If you substituted possible numbers from one to ten for each, Torchy assured you, then you had narrowed the search to only some 14,000 red VWs. Assuming the VW was a California car.

He drove to Headquarters, where he ran through the day's Missing Person Reports. One eight-year-old male, chronic runaway. One senile millionaire, from the Santa Barbara Biltmore—they'd probably hear about that on the news. No females at all.

He telephoned Team Charlie. He roused them in their motel room: they were unhappy at being awakened, and due on the pass again tonight, and no, they hadn't heard that the VW they'd spotted had started the fire, and didn't much care. They couldn't tell if the VW driver was alone, male, or female. A semi had passed it while they watched, blinding them. They'd got the semi's plates and passed them on to Torchy. That was standard, right, so why'd he called the room?

"Sorry, gentlemen." He checked out the semi with the DMV in Sacramento, using the sheriff's computer terminal in the front office. It was slower than Torchy but laboriously gave him a print-out. The semi was registered to a Fresno trucker named Lopes, apparently an independent. Shawn called Fresno information, got his number, and found no one home.

The fastest way he could think of to find a rolling truck in California was to ask help from highway weigh stations, manned by CHP patrolmen. He had the computer clerk type the request into an APB. Now he could only wait.

He stepped into the Coroner's Unit office, off the main entrance. Phelps was sorting through his pictures of the VW, writing a preliminary incident report. Curt Blossom was still at the morgue, in County General, assisting the pathologist. Shawn called County, got the morgue, and spoke to him.

The tox scan showed no drugs or alcohol. The deceased had 40 per cent carbon monoxide in her blood. So she'd either had a leaky exhaust pipe, which could have put her to sleep on the highway—

"Come on, Curt! No way! The engine's in back! And the windows were closed."

"Hey, you know, you're right? So she was still breathing when she hit the bottom."

Shawn winced. "But unconscious, check?"

"Beats me. Anyway, you hit it, buddy. The CO must be from smoke after the fire, not exhaust."

He sounded so elated that he made Shawn suspicious. "What's so good about that?"

"We were about to dissect her trachea."

They should: if her trachea showed signs of soot, she'd been alive when she burned. It made no real difference. Still . . .

"And now you figure you don't have to go for the trachea?" demanded Shawn. "Do it anyway."

"It's a two-hour job!"

"Do it."

Curt objected. It was five o'clock. He lived on Mountain Drive: there was a fire and rising wind: he'd like to cut some brush around the house. Shawn got hard-nosed, and Curt finally agreed, then gave the victim's description: height about five-five, pre-fire: estimated weight alive, 125. Race was indeterminate, all wisdom teeth were intact. No old fractures, plenty of new ones.

"Oh, hey!" Curt added: "Age twelve to fifty."

"Magic!" Shawn said caustically. "How'd you ever pin it down?"

"Pregnant."

Shawn felt sick. "Oh, no . . ."

"Just two or three months. Nothing serious."

Jesus, Curt was getting worse every day. "Curt, you've been on that detail too long."

"Hey, don't use *your* pull to get me off, OK?"

So he'd heard about Shawn's demotion.

Shawn hung up. Now, so far as he could see, he was stymied until someone filed missing on a woman. He still had to find the trucker who had passed the VW. What he expected to learn from him he had no idea.

He called the Department's public information officer and gave him what little description they had of the VW and the woman, asked him to try to get it on the evening news.

He wandered back to the Detective Bureau. For a long while he stood staring at the bulletin board, blindly, thinking, while a bunco detective across the room dictated a fraud report. Someone, probably a Gypsy, was promising to flame-proof roofs, pocketing the down payments, and splitting. Ten years ago, they'd have made him after the first two scams, from the description alone.

With 70,000 people in the city now, and close to 300,000 in the county, the Gypsy would probably retire rich before he was collared.

He moved back to his desk. On it was his plaque: "LT. SHAWN ORTEGA, Homicide." Someone had penciled in "Ex" in front of the "Homicide." He dropped the plaque in a drawer, wondering if it wouldn't be ex-*lieutenant*, when the sheriff found out about the autopsy.

While he was driving home, he heard on the radio that Trout Canyon and the Ygnacia fires had joined.

High winds tonight, again, they said, gusting below the canyons.

Three units from the city fire department were trying to control a new blaze, a small brush fire on Cold Springs Road and Sycamore Canyon.

He groaned. Not half a dozen blocks from home.

"Cause of the new fire is unknown. Elsewhere—"

He turned off the radio. Cause unknown? Bullshit! A *bug*.

He tramped on the throttle. They'd be crawling from the woodwork, east and west, from here on in. He wished he'd trimmed the brush behind his home.

Nineteen

Derf's Saloon was jammed with fire fighters, as always. The young man with the cavalryman's moustache and bulging muscles moved gracefully through the crowd on the gusty patio, smiling at acquaintances, and into the saloon itself. He was known here as a county fireman: actually, he was an unemployed carpenter who'd failed to make the squad.

He eased to a barstool close to the TV, putting an elbow on the bar to check his bicep in the mirror. The arm was getting better definition all the time, but tomorrow he'd add fifty more reps with the ten-pound bells. Good enough, though, to jangle the gonads of the girl behind the counter swabbing suds. Cynthia? Cindy.

"Hi," she said, remembering him. "Coors, right?"

"On my tab, OK?" He sipped at the beer, rippling his deltoid, so she'd hang close. She did, ignoring the outstretched glass of a yellow-coated captain in a County Fire hard hat.

"Rough on the line?" she wanted to know.

"Semi." He shrugged. Probably was rough. He hadn't been on a fire line since last summer, when he'd trained two weeks for a state blue card and finally got to work hourly, as a smoke eater on a blaze he'd set himself, in Arroyo Seco.

"You on Trout Canyon? Or the other?" She wiped at nothing on the spotless mahogany. "Hey, you county or city? I forgot."

"County," he lied. "Mission Canyon Station. B platoon."

"That's right, I remember. You're Ned, right? Chimp and Ira just left. They said it was awful."

He'd been watching it on TV half the morning, since he'd returned from the unemployment office. It wasn't "awful," it was wonderful, and if she waited awhile, she'd see the one he'd started up Sycamore Canyon that might put the others on the back burner for good.

"Cindy," called the yellow coat, "get your pretty ass down here!"

She gave the captain a scathing glance, but went to fill his glass. The young man smiled at yellow coat in the mirror. He'd seen him here before. Probably got on the fire department when all you had to do was read, write, and let them count your arms and legs.

Well, he'd be on it too, in not too long a time. He'd passed agility, strength, and come in eighty-three out of four hundred on the last written exam. You had to be a college frigging genius to come in first, and then they wouldn't take you until somebody died or quit. Prop 13.

He was working on that, and they better damn well put on some help, or their city just might burn down. Somebody turned up the TV behind the bar and the noise in the place dropped. His heart jumped. Flames soared from the screen: his own fire, at Sycamore and Cold Springs. His beer mug began to tremble in his hand. He sat it on the bar, startled and thrilled, as always, at what a book of matches around a burning cigarette could do.

Flames engulfed the screen above him, but he suddenly tensed. A city engine was knocking them down. Damn, damn, damn!

"Fire department spokesmen declared the Sycamore Canyon fire contained. But west of Santa Barbara, the Trout Canyon and Maria Ygnacia fires, now joined, rage unabated . . ."

He sagged. He'd picked Sycamore Canyon to spread out the troops, to give whatever nut was trying to burn the west side a little help, to strain the department further. It was his third set this year, and it had fizzled.

OK. Scratch one. There were plenty of other nearby canyons, chock full of dried-out brush. And plenty of wind, tonight, besides.

He'd go home, put on his shoes, and take a little jog up Mission Canyon Road. Some exercise would do him good.

And the County Fire Department, too.

"Chaos," breathed Shawn, surveying his family from the head of the dinner table. "Norman Rockwell could have painted it. End of the American Dream."

"Sorry," said Crissy, intent on her sketchpad. Mary Lou, reading *World Tennis* while she dug at her frozen-food pizza, did not look up. Neither did Don Miguel, who had years ago given up the fight for a nuclear family and rolled a small black-and-white TV set permanently in from the kitchen.

Crissy glanced up. "Look, I *am* sorry. I promised it to the class by tomorrow night. And it has to be *up* there by Fiesta." She touched her sketch with the side of her charcoal pencil, shading, then held the pad up to Shawn. "What do you think?"

It was a rough drawing which would in a few months become one of the blazing murals her Chicano students were spreading on walls, construction fences, and highway abutments.

From a riot of writhing bodies and outstretched hands in the background, a careworn Mexican madonna gazed angrily. The hint of a halo hung over her head. In her arms was a newborn infant and on her face were furrows of work and pain. The child was a laughing, healthy boy.

Shawn had seen the sketch take life, but for the first time he noticed that the child's eyes had turned crafty, and that on the webbing between the tiny fingers were gang tattoos.

"Jesus," murmured Shawn. "On city property? They won't let you paint that!"

"Let's see!" demanded Mary Lou. She raised her eyebrows. "Mom! Come *on!* On an overpass? For Fiesta Week? In Montecito?"

"Beats spray cans," stated Crissy.

Don Miguel reached over, turned the pad, and glared at the sketch. "No! It does not! It is not a mural! It's a political cartoon!"

Without a word the old man stood and marched stiff-backed from the room.

"Gracias!" blazed Crissy. "Gracias, señor!"

Shawn poked at his plate, pushed it away. Christ, he should have eaten in the hospital room, with Brink. "If you think *El Viejo's* pissed," he reminded Crissy, "wait until the city fathers see it."

"They won't, until it's up. In acrylic paints. Let 'em sandblast. They *wanted* atmosphere."

"They'll think you're, you know, a bunch of commies," begged Mary Lou.

"They already do," Crissy said serenely.

"So much for the Santa Barbara Tennis Club," moaned Mary Lou.

"We'll never afford it anyway," Crissy offered, "unless they make you pro."

His daughter was seldom serious, but she was in dead earnest now, couldn't Crissy see that? To get Mary Lou away from the table, he asked her to make him some coffee. When she was gone, he said: "Crissy, she means it!"

Crissy looked up slowly from the sketch and began to speak softly and intensely. Did Shawn want her to drop the class, the baby in the mural, or its finger tattoos? So that their daughter could flail a path to her rightful place in society with a tennis racket? "I'll do what you want, Shawn. I mean, I'm not Diego Rivera, just another Chicana artist. Nobody'll notice anyway."

She was a mistress of mental karate, always seeming to give in and never giving in at all. But Mary Lou had a right to her own aspirations, crass or not, and had the wit to see that she was in the one city in California where the sins of the mother would visit the daughter, and the sense to try to forestall it. Where did he go from here?

Crissy winced suddenly. He'd forgotten her migraine. His irritation with her disappeared. He leaned across the table. "Headache worse?"

"Better," she said fiercely. She was no hypochondriac.

"You paint what you want," he decided. "This is stupid. Just take her seriously, is all." He reached for the sketch and grinned. "You're a hell of an artist, you know? For a lady?"

"You're not a bad critic." She grinned. "For a cop."

He tried to make up for his disloyalty to Mary Lou by taking her for a walk up the street to see where the Sycamore fire had been stopped. There was a city crew waiting over the embers of the dead fire, in case the wind fanned undiscovered coals. Hash Ono was there, interviewing a fire fighter who had been early on the blaze. Hash suspected a set, but had found nothing to prove it. He told Shawn that a new blaze had erupted behind Santa Barbara Mission, off Mission Canyon Road, but rejected Shawn's offer to go up and help him scout the area.

On the way home, Shawn and Mary Lou talked about fire sets.

"People say it's kids," said Mary Lou. "For kicks."

"Not your kind of kids."

"I don't know," she bragged. "I know some pretty freaky dudes."

"I bet." He smiled. "Keep your ears open, five-grand reward."

"*Me* fink?"

He began to wonder if there was anything behind her remark, or if, as usual, she was simply trying to bug him. Policeman's paranoia, but . . . "You *haven't* heard anything, have you?" he asked carefully. Kids were always bragging to each other.

There was a long silence. He couldn't stand it. "Well, *have* you?"

"Five thousand?" she muttered. She looked up at him furtively, nibbled a fingernail. "Well . . . No, I better not."

"Mary Lou?" he warned. "Don't put me on."

"There's one guy . . ."

He stopped under a streetlight, inspecting her face. She seemed solemn as a choirgirl. She whispered a name he didn't catch. He bent closer. He still couldn't hear, and stooped more. Suddenly she nipped his earlobe and whirled, racing for home.

He slapped at her tail as she went, but missed. There was no way he could catch her anymore, so he didn't even try.

Twenty

Shawn turned off the 11 P.M. Channel 3 News. The new Mission Canyon fire had made it to the LA TV stations already, and locally, KEYT had a team on the scene. Though Mission Canyon was reasonably scary, he'd been sated with the coverage of Trout Canyon and Ygnacia in the last twenty-four hours and he couldn't stand the sight of one more crying homeowner on the tube.

"Leave it on," Crissy said. "We're sitting ducks!"

"No," he said flatly. "It's just psyching us out. Mission Canyon's six miles away and—"

"But *upwind,* right? Upwind?"

"I'm going to bed," Mary Lou said loyally. "If Daddy's not worried, I'm not either." She strode to the door, and turned. "He's the *head* of the whole Arson Detail!"

She played it straight, and Shawn supposed he would never know if she was putting him on again or not. Doubting his own judgment on the fire, he pretended to head for the john but stepped to the patio instead.

He saw no glow nearer than the permanent radiance from the Trout Canyon–Maria Ygnacia–San Marcos Pass fire. Even the scent of the smoke, heavy on the wind, was really nothing to worry about.

He reported his findings to Crissy. "We got a lot of Santa Barbara between us and the new one. You can't even see it, so no sweat."

She reminded him of the Malibu-Agoura fire of '78, where Steve McQueen and half the stars on the beach thought they had the

Santa Monica Mountains between them and the fire, and an hour later were burying their Monets in the sand. "And we haven't had a fire drill since the week after we moved in."

"Paintings first, in the big car," Shawn recited. "Mary Lou with me and Don Miguel with you. Ammo and my shotgun with me, household accounts and your jewelry with you. Your mother's pictures with you, licenses, passports, and Mary Lou's tennis rackets with me. Insurance policy—"

Crissy was ignoring him, starting up the stairs. Suddenly she turned. "Speaking of cars, mine's in the driveway. I couldn't get the garage door open."

He didn't mind leaving his own car out, but the paint on Crissy's little Datsun was still mint-perfect, and the payments almost killed them every month. He didn't want the body sandblasted, or even dusted with ashes if the wind shifted. He managed to overpower the garage door, climbed into the Datsun, slid back the seat, and parked the car inside.

He moved the seat back to her driving position, and sat for a moment in thought, something plucking at his subconscious. When he couldn't dredge it up, he closed the garage door and went upstairs.

Stripping down for bed, he suddenly froze.

Where had the VW seat been locked when they eased out the body? The woman was only five feet five. Had the seat been forward? Or back?

That was stupid. There was no way to tell where it had been *before* the crash. Anything could have happened in the wild flight down the canyon.

Still, they should have checked for slack in the seat belt and damage to the locking mechanism.

His mind all at once swam with inconsistencies. License plates torn off, before the crash. The car in neutral. After driving up the pass? Knocked there, by the woman's knee? Possible.

No air conditioning, but windows rolled up, in a car traditionally so tight it floated when sealed? Closed up in hot desert winds? Maybe, against the blowing dust . . .

Seat *back*, though? Or not?

He found one pant leg on, the other off. He decided to get dressed, changed his mind, stripped.

Suppose the woman hadn't driven to San Marcos Pass, herself.

Had *been* driven? She was pregnant. A panicked boyfriend? Not likely in today's climate: abortion was too easy. Suicide? No, suicide was inconsistent with the fastened safety belt.

He had to get hold of the truck driver who'd passed the VW; he'd try again tomorrow. And check with Curt Blossom and Phelps, to see if they'd moved the seat before they removed the body.

He called the night watch commander. "Any MPRs since five?"

He heard him rustling Missing Person Reports.

"No, Shawn. You find somebody?"

"Just looking," Shawn said, and hung up.

He moved to the window and searched the northwest, checking the Mission Canyon fire. Still no glow. He took the flashlight from his bedside table and flashed it at a pine tree on the canyon rim.

The limbs were still, the wind had died, he could sleep.

He crawled into bed. In the bright moonlight he could see Crissy stirring lightly. Her glossy hair spilled from the pillow like a black torrent washing a boulder in a stream. He studied her profile, as he would never have done if she had been awake, for it embarrassed her.

Crissy was truly beautiful: straight nose, full lips, sturdy little chin; cameo-perfect Spanish. Goya.

He felt a rising urge to take her in his arms. No. Migraine.

Sometimes, when he looked at Crissy this way, Nicole would take her place, filling him with guilt, but turning him on. He'd noticed on the Colorado rafting trip that Nickie still liked to be studied.

All at once a vision intruded, and it was not Nicole. He heard the distant braying of a fire truck crawling up a canyon road, and he thought of the grinning woman behind the wheel at the base of San Marcos Pass.

That turned him off, for good.

He'd be up there by dawn tomorrow, checking the VW's seat.

He turned over, punched the pillow, and tried to go to sleep.

TWO

Firewind

One

Within half an hour after arriving by helicopter from Goleta Headquarters, Jerry Castle had overruled Luke Tallman and moved the fire camp forward. Like an army counterattacking, it had groaned and growled and whined its way from the original site on the shoulder of the highway to a point three miles closer to the fire line, settling on the crest of San Marcos Pass, astraddle the Santa Ynez Range.

Now, just before dawn, Castle stood in moonlight at the foot of his command center van and saw the last of the units being backed into place. If the sea breeze held, this was a better place to fight.

The Trout Canyon Fire, combined with Ygnacia, had retreated up the pass and over the ridge. He would have liked to think that Luke Tallman had won a victory, routing the fire and chasing it inland, but he knew they owed the triumph to the light breeze from the sea, which had filled the vacuum when the Santa Ana died for the night.

The fire had long passed Class D proportions, would already justify a Class One team, or several of them, of nine hundred men each. But he was still reluctant—until he had today's fire-weather forecast—to disjoint the whole Forest Service by hitting the panic switch.

Here, at least, he had all his wagons drawn into a circle: communications van, weather van, air ops, aid station, kitchens. They were all parked now before the San Marcos Pass Fire Station, where radio communications seemed, so far, nearly perfect. From here he could look down on the sea of orange flames crawling northwest, away from the sea and city, slithering through Los Padres National Forest, toward Lake Cachuma, the Valley of Santa Ynez, and his San Rafael Wilderness Area.

The sea breeze had temporarily eased the pressure on the foothill suburbs, but increased the danger to his own domain.

The most valuable resources of his two-million-acre empire were not the 6,500 head of privately owned cattle grazing its slopes or the billion board feet of lumber on it, or the 25,000 deer which ranged it. Neither black bear, wild turkey, and pig, nor pigeons fluttering through its forests, nor even the last fifty California condors at Sisquoc, ten miles from where he stood, were truly significant.

His most valuable resource was future water, and the fire below him threatened the watershed of the whole of the Santa Barbara coast.

If he saved the forests, the rains in the coming three months would race down the ranges through predictable streams and waterways, and the lakes and reservoirs would fill.

But if he failed, the rivers would go wild and the hillsides flood.

The first two horsemen of the California apocalypse—wind and fire—were in full gallop. Unless he saved the forests, the next two—flood and drought—would scour and then sear the mountains and the valleys he loved. If he lost the trees and roots which chained the slopes, the water would drain to the sea, and Lake Cachuma and all the other catchments in the country would go without.

The fires of '79 had caused the floods and slides of '80, and the new drought which sat on the land.

If the sea breeze fought off tomorrow's Santa Ana, he would deploy his troops to fight in the valley before him and on the slopes of the Santa Ynez Range, until the fire crossed the valley and attacked the San Rafael Wilderness Area. Then it would be out of his hands: you did not fight fire in a wilderness area, you let nature take its course. That decision had been made in Washington years before, in the National Forest Service Headquarters, and in the Congress. You let the wilderness burn, deaf to the screams of landowners whose ranches bordered federal forests, just as it would have burned two hundred years ago when dons and padres ruled the land.

His problem now, with the Santa Ana slumbering and the fire riding inland toward the valleys and forests, was serious enough, in terms of watershed. But the danger to the inland acreage was nothing compared to the risks his career would face when the Santa Ana awakened to drive the flames back up the northern slopes and down again into the coastal plains. Then his responsibility, as fire boss—"Incident Commander," they wanted you to say now—would shift to even more sensitive acreage, and to homes, and human lives.

He moved to the weather van to speak to the young man from Boise who, he believed, knew more about Santa Ana winds than God Almighty.

If the Battle of the Bulge was approaching, he needed all the advice he could get.

Shawn Ortega trudged for the second time along Trout Canyon Road, heading back to the site of the VW crash. The way was still impassable to vehicles.

The Trout Canyon-Ygnacia fire, as it was being called, had been channeled over the ranges to the inland valleys, at least temporarily. The yellow veil of smoke had parted along the canyon bed and he could see again the battleground devastation on the brush along the draw.

Mopping-up crews—inmates from California Department of Corrections prison camps as far as Mount Bullion in Mariposa County—were cold-trailing the shambles, checking branches and limbs by hand for hot spots, like savages searching for living survivors of a battle.

Blackened, twisted oaks framed the cliffs. The road itself was deep in ash. There was a pungent, rotten smell of dead brush and trees and, probably, dead game.

He had always liked the canyons and barrancas of the coastal ranges. He had hunted ground squirrels in this one with his father, when he was small. The main buildings of Rancho Rojo had been on the slopes of La Cumbre Peak, only three miles away. He was walking on part of the land, probably, that had been granted Don Miguel's grandfather by the Kind of Spain in 1820; earth that might have been his today had his ancestors been wiser or luckier.

He had walked Trout Canyon happily, once. Today it was a ruin, and he hated it.

He had been dreading the sight of the VW, but as he approached the hillock which hid it, he heard the chomping of a helicopter and suspected that he had arrived too late. He broke into a trot. Rounding a bend in the dry canyon bottom, he spotted a Jolly Green Giant Sikorsky treading air over the place where Hash had found the car. A cable dangled from its belly. He scrambled up the rise just in time to see the Volkswagen yanked, like a beetle on a hook, from its resting place. As he watched, a door dropped, spun in yellow sunlight, and landed with a clang fifty feet away.

The young state patrolman with whom he'd searched the highway for skid marks approached, clipboard in hand. Shawn asked him if he'd noticed the seat position: a mistake.

"It was all the way back," said the young man, suddenly alert. "Hey! How tall *was* that broad?"

Shawn shrugged. It was a county case, and there was no use cutting the CHP in on his suspicions: with the county's track record on homicide, he needed all the head start he could get. "Five feet five, but *I'll* look into it."

"I mean, you think somebody *else* drove that thing up here?"

Shawn suggested that they may have moved the seat getting her out, or that it may have broken loose coming down. He jerked a thumb toward the VW, fast disappearing into the pall of smoke, heading for Santa Barbara. "Impound area?"

"Yeah. I'll shoot over and check the seat track, OK?"

"I *said* I'd handle it."

So he'd wasted an hour. Now he had to walk back down Trout Canyon Road, climb the switchbacks to the Scenic Highway, and then drive to the CHP impound area in the Goleta boondocks. The prospect didn't please him, nor did the presence of the patrolman, who tagged along as far as the highway, yakking, now that his Sherlockian instincts had been aroused, about the seat position, the missing plates, the gearshift status, and in general disturbing Shawn's thoughts.

On the way down the Valley of Death he noticed that two smoke eaters, cold-trailing, had tugged a charred tarpaulin from a tangle of burned gorse, to check for hot spots under it. It lay now like a shroud at the side of the highway, reminding him of the unknown woman on the slab at County General and depressing him further.

Thirty-six hours, she'd been dead. No, thirty-seven.

And they didn't even know her name.

Robert Wendell Holmes, Ph.D., sat in the weather van on San Marcos Pass, conscious of the hubbub outside and growing more and more worried as the computer print-out spat the fire maps to the counter beneath it.

He wished that he were back in Boise, snowstorm or not. Or skiing with the female cadet at Sun Valley. Or on a field trip to Arlberg Pass in Austria, where he had done his basic work on alpine föhn winds, and where mountains did not burn. Almost anywhere but sitting atop what might turn into a funeral pyre.

For the maps spewing from the print-out slot were the crystal balls of fire-weather forecasting. The primary data on them were born in isolated, unmanned weather stations, strategically placed in the national forests of the West, on Sierra peaks and in tiny clearings of the Rockies and the Buttes and the Wasatch Range, from the Canadian border to the Rio Grande.

There were hundreds of these stations. They grew like metal trees, from heights above the timberline and in gulches tangled with brush. Most of them could not be reached except by helicopter.

Each was a latticed steel structure fifty feet high. At its top was a small propeller and a whirling array of cupped vanes to read wind speed. At the base of each tower, behind the chain link fence which protected it from human and animal predators, was apparatus for reading temperature, humidity, and precipitation.

Twenty-two thousand miles over the United States hovered a LANDSAT. Signals from the lonely little weather stations were transmitted to the satellite, which relayed their voices to Wallops Island, Virginia, across the continent from their source.

Airborne infrared sensors sniffing for minor fires and major areas of fire danger, flown in Forest Service aircraft and riding orbiters, contributed more data.

At Wallops Island, these meteorological facts were integrated with other information derived previously from the land itself: fuel type, age of timber stand, and density of wooded areas.

There were many outputs from the computer. But the most important output, once a fire had started, was the series of maps he was receiving now. They were models of what the fire would do. Given the wind, humidity, fuel type, age of stand, density of brush, slope of ground, and the wind prediction, Wallops Island could draw a prediction.

In the computer's vast and intricate memory, all data were compared with previous fires. With enough information, the system could be induced to produce a map showing the fire as it would be one hour in the future, two hours, three hours, twelve, twenty-four. You could even send back to Wallops Island your various game plans for fighting it and judge the result of your future efforts, usually minuscule and sometimes even harmful, on the spread of the fire.

The bottom map on the counter was the computer's forecast of the perimeters of the Trout Canyon fire an hour from now, at 8 A.M. The blaze was spotting, launching outriders of flame in advance on the wind, starting scores of fires on La Cumbre Peak. Holmes saw no danger to human life on the map there, only a Federal Aviation Agency repeater station, which he assumed was unmanned.

It was not the 8 A.M. model that disturbed him. The nine o'clock model hinted that the Santa Ana would return; by ten it would have whipped the Trout Canyon-Ignacia fire due south toward Cathedral Peak. By noon it would be racing back toward the Lauro Canyon Dam on the northwest Santa Barbara city limits, gobbling two hundred acres of brush per hour and surging forward at twenty feet per minute. The 4 P.M. map showed the fire charging up Cieneguitas Creek, having described an almost perfect crescent around their position on San Marcos Pass. Winds by that time would be gusting to fifty miles per hour.

By 6 P.M. dwellings in the northwest foothills overlooking Santa Barbara would be threatened. By tomorrow, the Mission Canyon fire would join forces with the main column of advance.

"Jesus," he breathed. He sensed someone standing behind him, turned in his swivel chair, and found Jerry Castle reading over his shoulder.

Jerry was white-faced. "You think that's *valid?*" he asked hoarsely.

"Give or take ten per cent of the acreage per hour, and maybe five per cent forward movement," Holmes said. His voice sounded tinny in his own ears. "Look at the six P.M. wind!"

Castle seemed hardly to hear him. "I'm late, late, *late* . . ." He spun and bolted out the door.

Holmes forced himself to be calm. He took another look at the 6 P.M. map. It was such an awful forecast that he checked it manually, punching up raw data from the CRT display in front of him to develop his own synoptic wind picture. The massive lake of cold air in the womb of the mountain states, root of all their troubles, had filled the Great Basin and was ready to spill again.

He had a sudden vision of the city behind him burning: freeways choked, sirens screaming, the cradling hills afire. He'd seen pictures of cities hit by wartime fire storms: Santa Barbara, in its natural furnace of foothills, could be Dresden and Tokyo and Hamburg wrapped into one.

Ridiculous. Between the fire and chaos lay the resources of the National Forest Service, the California Department of Forestry, the brush-wise county and city fire fighters, drawn all the way from the Mexican border halfway to Canada. Some were here already, more were speeding in. Aerial tankers and modern chemicals, satellite communications and infrared detectors, all were on call to help.

It hadn't happened in '55, '64, '71, '77, or '79. It wouldn't happen now.

But he felt suddenly confined in the weather van. He shut down his terminal, awakened one of the forecasters from the LA station, and told him to read the models and weep. He picked his way through a battlefield scene of sleeping bodies and resting engines to the portable kitchen outside the ranger station, where he stood at the end of a breakfast line of California Department of Forestry fire fighters. Suddenly he realized that the smoke eater in front of him was a woman. Across the shoulders of her bright yellow CDF jacket was stenciled: "BUTTON BERGER."

"I've had Big Macs," he murmured to her. "I never had a button-berger."

She turned and regarded him without emotion. "Don't feel bad," she sighed. "You're not alone." She had round smudged cheeks and white even teeth; the minute spacing between the top two saved her from a plastic Hollywood type of beauty. Her lips were chapped and there was a scratch across her forehead. Her eyes were green, bloodshot, but very cool.

A black inmate cook, spooning scrambled eggs, noticed her. Without missing a dip with his ladle, he began to tell the man serving sausages next to him, as loudly as possible, an ageless firehouse story, setting it in Marble Cone.

"Crew I fed once, mixed, you know? Chicks and guys. Big backfire they set in Carmel Valley, don't work, so they got to fight it. Line boss musters 'em at the truck. Movin' out, he says. Broad named Kolaski and fucker named Schuler— Eggs, lady?"

She nodded wearily and he flipped a blob onto her tray.

"Kolaski and Schuler, they ain't *there*, you know? Line boss finds 'em behind a big yellow cat. She's *blowin'* him— Eggs, man?" he asked Holmes.

Holmes nodded, trying to glare the black into silence. The cook grinned widely, smacking his tray with a glob. "Line boss says, 'Whadafuck, Kolaski, we're movin' *out*, what's goin' *on*?' She says, 'Schuler had a heart attack . . .' Eggs?"

The fireman behind Holmes said, "Yeah, asshole, look—"

The cook splattered a spoonful onto his tray. "Line boss says, 'Hey, Kolaski, that's mouth-to-*mouth* you s'posed to give, not—'"

"And she says," yawned Button Berger, "'*That's* how it all began'? Let me have some sausage?"

"Button Berger," said Holmes softly, catching up with her as she left the chow line, "I don't know what a nice girl like you is doing in a place like this—"

"That's sweet," she yawned. "You're spilling coffee down my boot."

"But I think I'd like to take you to lunch. I think," he added softly, "I want to take you to dinner, too."

"Don't count on it," she said. "I'll be gone in an hour." Wordlessly, he took her tray and followed her to an engine. He guessed, somehow, by the deference with which one of the firemen made a place for them to sit on the running board, that she was in charge of the rig.

As she gazed blearily at the great gray-black pall of smoke over the inland valley, he explained to her the lake of cold air that was causing it all, and the forces they were about to face.

When she made no comment, he glanced at her. She had fallen

asleep. A wisp of blond hair from under her hard hat was blowing in the morning breeze. He envisioned the rest of it, washed and golden, fluttering on a ski slope.

He had an impulse to brush the strand back. He felt the hard gray eyes of her cabman on him, so instead, he carried her plate to a trash can and dumped it.

He wished some meteorological miracle would change the coming flow of wind.

It wouldn't.

He wished they'd send that particular crew back toward the coast instead of back into battle on the front line.

They wouldn't do that either.

He went back to his ivory tower in the van.

TWO

By nine-thirty, Shawn Ortega had inspected the burned carcass of the VW at the CHP impound area. He discovered no signs that the seat-locking ratchet had given way during the ride down the canyon face. He put a "hold for SBSD" on the car and returned to Sheriff's Department headquarters.

He checked with Communications for a Missing Person Report. Nothing yet, despite last night's newscast. But the Fresno trucker named Lopes, now southbound with a load for LA, had just been picked up at the Santa Maria weigh station. "Put him on," Shawn demanded.

Yes, Lopes said, in a pleasant Chicano drawl, he'd been on the road, northbound and south, for the last three days. And yes, he'd used San Marcos Pass just before the fire. He thought he was being accused of tossing a butt from his cab. "Look, I don't even smoke, man."

Shawn reassured him, and then hit him with the Volks. Lopes thought he remembered; guy forced him to pass, gave him the finger . . .

"Guy?" blurted Shawn. His heart began to race.

"Girl, maybe, I don't know."

"You see a passenger?"

"You got to be kidding! I pass fifty VWs a day!"

And of the car, Lopes remembered nothing more: not color, plate, or whether it was driven erratically. He'd be two hours more to Santa Barbara: Shawn asked him to stop at headquarters. "Park your rig in the sheriff's lot."

Lopes groaned. "I told you everything I remember, man!"

Maybe, maybe not, thought Shawn. Neither he nor Lopes really knew.

"By three P.M., latest? If you forget," warned Shawn, "they'll remind you at Camarillo weigh station, and you'll just have to come back."

He hung up and called the Santa Barbara Psychological Center. He spoke to a clinical psychologist named Harry Asp, whom he'd hired in the Solvang Slasher case. "You up for more magic, Harry?"

"I am at the service of the community." Asp was a certified horse's ass, but effective, and anyway the only hypnotist Shawn knew. "At sixty bucks an hour."

"Three o'clock in your star chamber? Sharp?"

He didn't know how he'd pay for that, either, but it was too late to worry now. He went to the Coroner's Unit office, where he found Phelps scanning the autopsy report on the woman. Phelps looked up. "Hey, is there an 'h' in trachea?"

Shawn nodded. "Was there soot in hers?"

"Yes, sir."

Which meant that she'd been breathing—possibly conscious—as the flames devoured her. He felt sick. He studied the pictures, learning nothing, and when Curt Blossom came in, managed to con him into sending Phelps to the impound yard to photograph the undamaged seat mechanism for evidence.

When Phelps had gone, Curt lit a cigarette. "Why are you trying to make Murder One out of this? I mean, even if it's homicide, it isn't your case anyway."

" 'We are born to inquire after truth . . .' Montaigne."

"How *is* your granddaddy?"

"I don't think he gets laid much."

"Who does?" Blossom studied the tip of his cigarette. "To get back to the fiscal operations of this Flatfoot Factory . . . You talk to the sheriff about costing out the autopsy?"

"Don't push me, Curt," Shawn muttered. "If it's homicide, he'll be glad we didn't miss it."

"'*We*'?" Blossom smiled. "I hear what you're saying, but *I* didn't want to autopsy her. Hey, suppose you drop dead on the way home tonight? Where's my authority?"

"Just hang on to the invoice, is all. Until I see what we got."

"There's that 'we' again." Blossom sighed, watching the smoke curling from his cigarette. "Your charisma cracks me up. But OK, I'll hold it twenty-four hours."

In twenty-four hours, Shawn reflected, they might all be digging out of the ashes if the fire reports were accurate, so he put the budgetary problem from his mind and returned to his desk in the Detective Bureau.

The light on his phone was flashing. It was Neil Hart of KEYT's "Today in Santa Barbara." He was doing a five-minute special on pyros. He would have a psychiatrist from Atascadero and a firebug-patient on, live, at six, and wondered if the new head of the Arson Squad would appear.

"No way, Neil! Every firebug in town would make me."

But he added that the woman found in the car was still unidentified, and Hart would be doing a public service if he worked her description into his spiel.

"Was *that* arson?" Hart asked quickly. "Or an auto accident?"

Shawn winced. Careful . . . "Just went off the road, as far as we know so far . . . Anyway, red VW, woman's age unknown, height five-five. Pregnant. Weight estimated at a hundred and twenty-five."

Hart promised to work it in. Within moments Shawn was called to the sheriff's office. He faced Castillo, framed behind his desk in the smoky morning sunlight. "KEYT called," said the sheriff. "*Be* there."

Shawn squinted. The sheriff turned back to his work, silhouetted, a shaft of light glancing off his bald dome. It was difficult to argue with a man whose eyes you couldn't read, as they both knew from interrogations.

"And blow what cover I got?" protested Shawn.

Castillo sat back and his chair screeched. "Cover? You busted the Solvang Slasher, you *been* in the papers. Everybody knows you already."

"But why *again*?"

"Because there's *pyros* out there. People are scared. I want to brag a little, let 'em see who I got working on it."

No, Castillo wanted him to fall flat on his face. Shawn's stupid threat to help unseat him in the election had scared him. Castillo was throwing him, ignorant of subject and TV technique, to the masses.

It was impossible to tell, into the sunlight, if the sheriff was laughing at him. "You *know*," Shawn warned him, "I don't know a damn thing about arson."

"Make something up." The chair screamed again and the sheriff bent over his paperwork. When Shawn didn't move, he looked up. "You got a question?"

Actually, he did: *Fatlip, why don't you go into politics full time, instead of posing as a cop?*

But he thought again of his own twelve years on the department, and decided not to ask.

"No, sir," he said, and left.

Jerry Castle turned from the command console in the van and took the updated fire forecast model from Robert Wendell Holmes. He left his seat, moved the length of the vehicle, and compared the model forecast with the cancerous crescent on the wall map, chewing at the inland base of the San Marcos grade. He noticed that Luke Tallman's district ranger station at Los Prietos, near the foot of Sage Hill, was in the path of the fire-head.

The computer forecast showed that Los Prietos would be engulfed in flames by 8 P.M. He called to his communications chief at the other end of the van and told him to radio Tallman at the Baptist spike camp. Luke's wife, Mary, and daughter Tina were presumably still at home, and sometime today would have to be evacuated.

He turned to problems of wider range. From his first look at Holmes's computerized projections at dawn, he had been trying to make up for his optimism of the night before.

If the computer models were right, he had not moved quickly enough. If they were wrong he'd overreacted and was spending the Service blind, and would probably end up in Alaska shuffling papers.

For at 9 A.M. he had finally pushed the panic button, classified the fire Class E, and demanded not *one* Class One team or five, but *ten*. Now, a torrent of overhead personnel—crew leaders, fire bosses, line bosses, plans chiefs, camp chiefs—would be pouring into Santa Barbara Municipal Airport on Forest Service aircraft and commercial airliners.

By the time his demands winged north to Boise, east to Washington, and south to Riverside, he had spent two million dollars. Restlessly, he checked his mobilization status with his plans chief, sitting at a radiotelephone behind him.

From the breadth of the United States, from the Eastern, Rocky Mountain, Northern, Southwestern, Intermountain, Pacific Northwestern, and Southern Forest Service regions, foresters were winging in. Each was a specialist, coded to slot into a fire job when he arrived. Most of the California Region foresters had been dumped on the airfield already, and were awaiting their crews. Forest Service personnel from Alaska and Puerto Rico were not due until tomorrow.

Of the 20,000 full-time National Forest employees, two thousand were en route or had already arrived. His call had virtually stripped the Service of operational leaders.

En route to join the supervisory personnel, local blue-card hourly smoke eaters, and inmate crews already on the line, additional hard-hatted volunteers from state and county prison camps were rumbling in under guard on National Guard trucks. Called up through the Riverside "Firescope" Operations Center, from camps as far as Morena in San Diego and the Calaveras in the Sierra foothills, all were fire-ready.

The inmate crews were often heroic—sometimes reckless. In the short run, they were dependable enough, swinging rakes and axes with outlaw courage in the face of crackling flames, though inclined to escape or lay down their arms if the fire lasted too long.

Volunteer search and rescue teams, with their own amateur mountaineers and paramedics, fire-trained and self-equipped, were bouncing in from the desert and mountains, to set up medical stations on the fire lines and in the fire camps.

He had Indian crews swooping in from Region Three, out of Arizona and New Mexico.

There were scores of locally trained Mexican farm labor crews, eager for the four-dollar-an-hour wages, waiting for leaders and orders in Fire Camp Two, on the Santa Barbara Mission grounds.

At Boise Inter-Agency Fire Council Facility in Idaho, from cavernous warehouses, they would be trundling emergency foodpacks, cots, tents, vehicles, portable aid stations. Additional command vans like the one he was in, more communications centers and weather vans, field kitchens and aid stations, were sliding into Hercules aircraft for the flight southwest.

The Santa Barbara foothills and Los Padres National Forest were crawling with green Forest Service engines from his own district ranger stations in Santa Barbara, Santa Lucia, Ojai, and Mount Pinos, as well as every California Department of Forestry truck the CDF could spare. Speeding down the coast from the Ventana Wilderness Area in the Monterey District were fire-hardened engine crews from the Marble Cone fire of '77. Of them, he knew every man by name.

Marble Cone had burned 90 per cent of the Ventana. Despite 7,500 men on the fire line, it had lasted twenty-one days and scared hell out of the coastal town of Carmel.

If this one lasted half as long, with the winds that Holmes and the Wallops Island computer predicted, then the city behind him, its back to the sea, would perish with the trees of his mountains.

The fire status officer moved between Jerry and the map, sketching a new perimeter, using data he'd just received from Luke Tallman and the other line bosses in the valley. The fire was doubling back as predicted, spotting wildly ahead of itself before rising winds, slowed only by areas it had burned during the night.

Trout Canyon-Ignacia was performing in accordance with Holmes's script. As Jerry studied the new battle line, he felt his palms go damp. He was all at once frightened, not of the fire, which could be seen and smelled and sometimes tricked into devouring itself, but of the invulnerable lake of air which commanded the rivers of wind.

Like General Arnim and his panzers . . .

No time, he told himself, for North Africa. Not now, not today . . .

He began suddenly to shiver, on another pass, a desert pass, at Wadi Akarit . . .

After Médenine, but before Quairwan . . .

Wadi Akarit, about which he must not think. Better to remember Médenine than Wadi Akarit, better the pass at Fondouk—blackened, boulder-strewn foothills, gasoline, cordite, howling wind, sand, panzers as far as his dusty scope could see—better Fondouk than Wadi Akarit . . . Not Wadi Akarit, not today . . .

"Jerry? Hey, you OK?"

He found himself clinging to a map rack on the wall of the van, mouth dry, heart pounding. He straightened and turned, and nodded to his air service officer, who reported that he'd found an additional eighteen contract air tankers available for the fire, thirteen flyable now, the other five within twelve hours.

"Not enough, Corp—"

Jesus, he'd better get hold of himself. Not 'Corporal,' or Quairwan, Fondouk Pass, or Wadi Akarit. San Marcos Pass, in peaceful Santa Barbara County. And the lake of air could somehow be fought and beaten.

The air boss was looking at him strangely.

"Not enough planes, Mike," Jerry repeated. "Alert the 146th."

Mike Kane, the air boss, a towering, slender forester from the Redwood National Forest, groaned. They'd worked Marble Cone together. "Oh, Gawd, not that one again!"

"That one," Jerry said sharply.

Mike looked shocked. It was too early for nerves, which could spread in a fire camp like Hong Kong flu.

"The contract aircraft," Mike complained, "will scream!"

"Just *alert* the 146th, is all. If the contract aircraft *can* handle it, they never need to know we did it."

They'd been through it all before, together. The Forest Service was supposed to use civilian air tanker services. The civilian contract planes were a ragtag fleet of surplus B-17s and DC-6s and 7s, cranky and feeble in capacity, always slow to respond despite the almost $1,000-per-hour airtime charge for using them.

They were spotted all the way up the Washington and Oregon coasts, and into the mountain states. They squatted through the lean fireless months like vultures, waiting for just such conflagrations as Trout Canyon-Ignacia.

It took twenty-four hours completely to mobilize the contractors: the 146th Air National Guard out of Van Nuys, California, could be over the fire with three Hercules tankers in ninety minutes, and five more within hours.

But the civilian segment had banded together in an Air Tankers Association and extracted a written memo from the Forest Service agreeing not to call in the Air National Guard until the contractors themselves yelled for help.

Which would be, thought Jerry, about the time the state of California burned to the ground below their battered wings.

Nobody had had the guts—or time—to call the 146th for the Malibu-Agoura fire of '78, and 25,000 acres of brush had blown to sea in smoke while two hundred homeowners watched their dreams go up in flames.

"Look, Jerry," protested Mike, "the 146th—"

"I want them alerted." He might end up before a congressional committee, but he wasn't going to lose his forest to a scrap of paper he'd never signed.

"We can't! We'd have to go through BIFSY now," insisted Mike, "and Riverside, I think, and the Sixth Army in San Francisco, and then the Pentagon and the National Guard Bureau. Now, you *know* somebody'll bring up that memo!"

"Call the squadron commander at Van Nuys," insisted Jerry. "Direct."

"Jere!" Mike was aghast.

"You want it in *writing?*" Castle asked brutally.

Mike's gentle brown eyes looked hurt. "Of course not."

"Then just goddamn *do* it, OK?"

A sudden gust rocked the van. Some line boss on a distant radio pleaded for a chopper, somewhere. The wind raised its voice an octave. If it increased much more, there would be no more choppers for anyone, no matter what the problem.

"Yes, Jerry, I will," Mike said softly, and left.

Jerry Castle went back to his console. He felt awful. He had sounded like a cavalry sergeant with a recruit. He and Mike were old friends; they'd been through Marble Cone without a quiver of distrust.

OK. So be it.

He wished that he could play it, as Mike did, by the book. But he had a thousand men on a dozen fire lines, with more coming in every hour, and the wind was rising fast.

San Marcos Pass was not Wadi Akarit, but no one could say he hadn't learned.

Shawn sat yawning next to Harry Asp's desk in the psychologist's darkened office. On Asp's big velour couch lay Nando Lopes, a wiry little truck driver with a face like a crumpled shopping bag. He had been reluctant, a little scared of hypnosis, but now, after five minutes, Asp had him comatose as an overturned lizard with a tickled belly. Now Asp approached his subject quietly, peered down at his twitching eyelids.

"You are drifting, Nando, down, down, down. Your left hand is growing light, light, lighter . . . Lifting up, like a balloon . . . Up, up, up . . ."

Slowly, Nando's left arm began to tremble, and his hand to rise, and when it was raised, Asp had him lower it. Asp nodded at Shawn, who started his tape recorder.

The psychologist dropped his voice: "You're going back, Nando, to the night before last. You're in the cab of your truck, climbing San Marcos Pass . . ." His voice was resonant, vibrant, admitting no question. Nando lay like death. Asp dropped his pitch even further.

"It's dark, dark, dark on the grade, Nando, and you can hear your engine, and see the road ahead. And you're in what gear, Nando? What gear are you in?"

"Third," mumbled Nando. "Goin' down to second . . ."

"Because?"

"Bug, VW, too slow . . . Wind?"

"He's going too slow because it's windy?"

"Don't wanna downshift," mumbled Nando. "Get over, will ya?" He moved restlessly.

"You are in a deep, deep trance, Nando," Asp reminded him. "On the San Marcos grade."

"Yeah . . . Move it over, man!"

"What color is the bug?"

"Red."

"What's the license number?"

"None, no plates, fucker's got no plates!"

Shawn's mind had been drifting. Now he came alert. He checked the recorder. Red light on: recording; everything OK.

"And who's driving it? Man or a woman?"

"Man's driving, yeah. Woman's asleep."

"Where's she asleep?" murmured Asp. He had a deep baritone, soothing and full.

"Passenger seat, she's asleep. Goin' to pass him now, got to pass him . . . Horn, lights . . . he's givin' me the finger, screw you too, buddy . . ."

Shawn felt himself drifting, again. Asp was breaking his case, he should be excited, but he didn't really care, euphoric, relaxed . . .

He fought to stay alert. Someone was calling him: "——else? Anything else, Shawn?"

"Hm?"

"Shawn! Snap out of it! Anything else?"

He sat up swiftly. "Description of the driver?"

"He's been telling you, all he could see was the back of his head. Black hair, beard."

"Passenger?"

"Like he says, brown hair, that's all. It's on your tape."

Asp gave his subject a posthypnotic suggestion to remember the Volks in court, if ever asked to testify, and brought the truck driver back with a snap of his fingers. Nando sat up, grinning.

"Hey, you know? I was, like, *there!*"

"Yes," Asp said, amused. "And you almost had a passenger yourself."

He punched a stopwatch, briskly raised the blinds, and wrote the department a bill for seventy-five dollars, which he gave Shawn then and there, expressing a hope, having dealt with the county before, that Shawn could process it quickly.

Shawn dropped Lopes at his rig and went home to get ready for KEYT-TV.

Three

Shawn checked his best blue suit in the bedroom mirror. The pants were wrinkled. OK for the show, since he'd be sitting down, but he'd better get them pressed before Brink's funeral.

God . . . Brink not dead, and he was planning his wardrobe for the wake. Hang on, buddy, until I get my pants pressed. An awful thought, though Brink would probably find it funny.

He was knotting his tie when Mary Lou came in. She frowned at the color. "Not *that* one!"

She must think he was Johnny Carson. He found a newer one, circa 1970. He hated ties. She remembered hearing that you couldn't wear white on TV, and went to his bureau to find a light-blue shirt to match. She emerged with the shirt, dangling his gold football. "Hey, cool! I haven't seen this!"

"It's older than you are."

"Can I wear it?"

"That's what it's for." He fastened the chain around her wrist and kissed the top of her head. Her hair smelled young and clean. She flopped on the bed with the phone. "I've been passing the word about the TV show. I called Rodge, and Joan, they're going to watch. I told them I'd ask questions tomorrow." She nibbled her lip, counting on her fingers. "Flick, Debbie, Ian, Nancy. Who else?"

She was alerting half the teen-agers in Santa Barbara, and by extension, their parents. His Nielsen would be breathtaking. "ML," he said, intent on the knot, "I wish you wouldn't call all those people."

"When your dad's the coolest cop in town," she explained, rising to straighten his tie, "you flaunt it."

Flattering, but not quite up-front. "Lieutenant" Ortega would sound good to her on TV, but he wondered if she'd be doing the advance publicity if he'd still been, for instance, a sergeant.

He'd always been saddened by what seemed, behind her beauty, brain, and grace, a fragile ego. A zit on her cheek could plunge her into hell. Anything was fine as long as it was perfect.

She was insecure because she carried a Spanish name, and the fact that it was the oldest in town didn't compensate for the ease she'd feel if it were Smith or Jones or Brown.

The tennis circles she was exploring were not biased against certain Latinos. Since her name was Ortega, she was potentially acceptable. There were plenty of Ortegas in private tennis clubs: a distant cousin who'd made federal judge and a surgeon Shawn had never even met. And other Santa Barbareño Spanish names were golden, too: a Covarrubias rancher and a state assemblyman from the Alvarado family; several De la Guerras who had somehow regenerated their wealth. Any Carrillo was welcomed by Anglos anywhere on the strength of the late actor Leo.

Mary Lou was directly descended from the Spanish officer who, after discovering the Golden Gate for Portolá, had returned with the explorer to build Santa Barbara Presidio and design the mission. Theoretically, she had it made.

The problem was, he had to admit, not her name but Shawn himself. Sergeant or lieutenant, captain or inspector, he was a policeman. Seen from the Hill, a cop was a cop was a cop. So she'd owe any acceptance she got to her forehand, not his rank.

"I haven't had time for much homework," he said softly. "I hope I don't blow it for you."

Her eyes flashed alarm, but she answered bravely. "When in doubt, go to the net."

He nodded.

He just hoped nobody lobbed one over his head.

Dr. Herb Dubois, M.D., slowed the Ford with his paraplegic brake control, easing to the side of the freeway past the Lompoc off-ramp. He had been quietly observing his frightened prisoner-patient all the way down the coast from Atascadero.

Julian's forehead seemed damp, despite the dry northeast wind, and his knees were jiggling. Perhaps the Santa Ana was disturbing him, as it did more balanced personalities; more likely it was stage fright, acute.

Whatever it was, he'd never get Julian on camera unless he somehow calmed him. He decided on therapeutic grounds that a display of trust would be useful.

"Got a driver's license, Julian?"

Julian nodded, and Dubois asked him to drive. Just out of his teens, he seemed touched by this demonstration to the point of tears, but had doubts about the paraplegic controls.

"They're extra," explained Dubois. "Just use the regular brake and gas pedals."

"Man, I haven't driven anything but those damn lawnmowers for two years," warned Julian. "You sure?"

"You'll do fine." He jerked himself over, changing places, and Julian entered the flow of freeway traffic. They talked for a while about Julian's chances on the street, and about his coming parole hearing. "The TV thing will look good," promised Dubois. "You'll get Brownie points for trying to help."

Julian pointed out that it might look good to the parole board, but if his father saw him on the tube, Julian wouldn't want parole, he'd rather hide at 'Tasky.

"He can't hurt you, Julian, you're a big boy now," Dubois said, irritated. He reminded him testily that, anyway, the station had promised to shoot him from behind, distort his voice, use an alias. Nobody would know him, not even his father.

"That son of a bitch would know me," Julian said flatly, "if they shot me in the dark talking sign language and called me Jesus Christ."

Julian's nervousness bothered Dubois. He'd been fighting his own guilt for bringing him, not sure it wouldn't undo his treatment, unsure his own motivation wasn't an ego trip. Silently, he marshaled his arguments: parents hearing Julian's history might be warned, and more careful of how they punished children; the taxpayer, having supported an archetypical pyromaniac's therapy for two years, was entitled for once to see the successful results. And the clincher, as presented in the Chief of Psychiatry's office: Atascadero, squirming under Prop 13, needed all the coverage it could get.

Now he began to wish he'd never suggested it. Julian, at ease in group therapy, was one thing: from the look of him now in the car, he'd do the Atascadero group therapy class more harm than good on the tube.

"Relax, Jule," he said now.

"No sweat," Julian smiled, his voice high with tension.

Dubois sat back and closed his eyes, creating a curtain. It was too late to back out now, for him or Julian.

He was sick of damaged psyches, battered ids, paranoids whining in his ear. A mistake to choose psychiatry. He'd been interning in pediatrics when he'd pulverized his fifth lumbar, skiing Squaw Valley. He'd decided in traction that kids in a doctor's office would be scared enough without a half-man on wheels peering down their throats. A shrink in a wheelchair didn't seem as sad.

He knew now he'd been wrong. At least a pediatrician knew if he'd hurt a patient or helped him. He should have switched to pathology and learned to talk to slides.

"Jesus!" he heard Julian murmur.

He opened his eyes. They had crested Gaviota Pass and were winding down the seaward side of the mountains. Between two parched golden hills, as if caught in a gunsight, rose a dark brown column of smoke. Its base was dull orange. From here, it looked as if the plume was rising from precisely the center of Santa Barbara, fifteen miles away.

A trick of perspective. The fire was in the hills behind the city. But from what he'd heard on the radio, it might not stay in the hills for long.

"Jule?" he asked swiftly. "What are your feelings? Right *now!*"

"Sheeyut," Julian snorted impassively. "I don't feel *anything.*"

"*Nothing?*"

Julian glanced at him, his eyes blank. "Naw. Piss on it."

Piss on it?

His heart sank. Pure Freud, all the way, was Julian.

"I'm *cured,*" said Julian. He thought for a moment. "Am I going to have to talk about . . . ? You know. Enuresis?"

His voice trembled.

"Why do you ask?"

"It don't seem right, you know, on TV. It's not like Show and Tell."

"If you feel that way, don't mention it."

For, he promised Julian silently, your dread secret is safe with me. Admit to burned schools and warehouses, charred trucks and campers, homeless persons shivering in the night. Tell of the blazing mobile home and the burned hot dog stand and God knew what else. Confess and commiserate with us over the ashes of the motel and the two old people roasted in their room.

But don't for God's sake mention that you wet the bed: you'll give pyromania a bad name.

He wished he could get Julian's father in front of the TV camera. Or in front of a firing squad.

Cured, my ass.

But he didn't really care.

High on a hill above the city, in front of the television studio, Shawn Ortega paused for a moment in the parking lot, watching the camera crew from KEYT-TV. The director was staring at the smoke plume over San Marcos Pass, morosely, though it was placed as conveniently for Neil Hart's teaser as if a set designer had planned it.

The director seemed drawn and weary. Shawn remembered that he lived high above the northern foothills on Painted Cove Road. His home was built near an ancient Chumash Indian cave site, on a ridge. The crest bore a colony of artists, writers, and alternative-life-style executives like the director, who commuted to the city below on a winding road better for jeeps than automobiles.

How in hell anyone had slept up there in the last two nights, with the fire raging through the canyons below, Shawn couldn't imagine. No wonder he looked tired.

And worried. The wind was rising again. Shawn's tie was whipping and the column of smoke was arching seaward, already shadowing the island of Santa Cruz, almost thirty miles south.

Neil Hart, a portly presence with a trim gray beard, appeared from the studio entrance. He crossed the lot, hoarding his smile for the camera. He shook hands with Shawn and thanked him for being here.

"You and the sheriff," Shawn said, "didn't give me any choice." Hart shrugged and positioned himself in front of the lens, with

the smoke in the background. He smoothed his lapels and nodded at
the director.

"Rolling," the director yawned. "Go, man."

Hart turned on a grin to light the world. "Tonight in our studio,
you'll meet three timely guests. Timely, because we'll talk of one of
the causes for Santa Barbara's recurring fires: the pyromaniac. Not
the original cause, apparently, of this one"—he paused to let the
camera cut to the smoke—"No, Trout Canyon was apparently
ignited when a still unidentified and apparently pregnant woman
hurtled into the arroyo from the highway in her red VW sedan.
But arson without motive has been the certain source of many other
fires in recent years, and recent weeks."

He promised that in the studio the viewer would meet two men
who understood, if anyone did, the strange impulses that moved
pyromaniacs to set fires. "One is a psychiatrist at the State Hospital
for the Criminally Insane, Atascadero. The other is the law enforcement officer of Santa Barbara County charged with bringing the
firebug to justice. And, perhaps *more* importantly, you'll meet a
young man who may or may not understand the fire-setting syn-
drome. For our last guest is one of the doctor's patients, a youth we'll
call just . . . 'Dave.' "

He drew a forefinger across his throat. The director muttered:
"Cut, wrap the intro."

The crew began to straggle toward the studio entrance. A hatchback Ford glided across the parking lot and slid into the "Handi-
capped" parking space next to the station manager's.

Hart opened the passenger door for a lean, iron-faced man of perhaps thirty-five with gray specks in his hair. The driver was a youth
with a face like an angel, long lashes, and trusting brown eyes.
Presumably, he was the firebug, and the first that Shawn had ever
met.

The prisoner lifted a folded wheelchair from the hatchback and
set it up, helping the doctor ease into it. Neil Hart introduced them
to Shawn and led his three victims inside.

In the living room in the Isla Vista duplex, the blond, bearded
young man took a last hit and passed the Thai stick to his new love,

the girl with the milk-chocolate skin. He flashed, in the fading light, on her eyes, ebony saunas into which he could slip at will.

They had had the duplex to themselves for the past thirty hours. Everyone else had left for Christmas, at home or skiing. He'd long got over his anger at his lady leaving without a good-by; had almost forgotten her face in a swirl of other images he'd never quite forget.

For the last night and day would live in his memory forever.

Now he picked the thump of the bass viol from the rumbling stereo, then the tinkling chime of a xylophone, the sinuous rhythms of a Moog synthesizer. He focused on Deedee, feeling a great love for all the earth. She was nude, dancing, by herself, hands moving hypnotically.

He was absolutely zonked, wasted, and pigged-out on sex. They'd done it every way there was, every place there was. He'd been blown in the john and under the kitchen table. They'd thrashed his bed to a tangled mess and beaten hers to a morass. They'd screwed in the tub and torn down the curtain and got it on under the shower. He'd escaped to the haven of Kona-grown grass for a while this morning, for an indefinite rest, but raised the standard of his race for another go after a hearty lunch of Cold Duck.

They had done it horizontally, vertically, sidewise. He had a cloudy recollection of somehow doing it, a minute or an hour ago, just after dark while he hung from the porch railing by his knees.

Unreal, gross, outrageous. The room dissolved. New scene. Now she was curled in front of the TV, still nude, still leading the stereo with her hands, but watching a bearded man speaking. Hours later, or minutes? Far in the background, on the TV screen, rose a mighty brown phallus of smoke. Like his own, it was tired, supine, leaning flaccidly toward the ocean. He giggled, pointing it out silently, and she nodded. He could hear the man on TV, talking. Russian? Chinese? Whale? Whales talked. He told her this in ESP.

The black limpid eyes drew close. *She* was talking. "What?" he asked.

"Wagvoksen?" she said, from miles away.

He began to laugh, doubled up in mirth. " 'Wagvoksen'?"

"Volkswagen, goddammit! I said Volkswagen!"

"You said . . . You said . . ." He was strangling with laughter. "You said 'vogwasken.'"

Now she was yelling at him, black eyes suddenly hard, whites enormous, what the hell, bad trip? On *pot?*

"Honkey!" she shrieked. She slapped his face, hard. "Honkey bastard!"

"What's going down?" he demanded, hurt.

The enormous eyes were full of tears. "What was she driving? To Denver?"

"Who?"

"Your *lady!* Lynn! Rick, come *on!*"

He came down with a crash. "VW, red VW, you've seen it around, what's . . . ?"

She stared at him. A tear slid down her cheek.

"Oh, God," she whispered. "Oh-fucking-God, the fire! It was *her!*"

He dimly recalled a news story on TV.

"No!" he bellowed. "No, it wasn't! No, no, no!"

She went to call the cops.

Four

Shawn sat at a coffee table facing the cameras, between Neil Hart and the psychiatrist; Julian sat opposite, his back to the lenses so that he could appear in limbo. Julian had been introduced, his face unseen, as "Dave," a rehabilitated fire setter due for parole, reciting his ghastly childhood under gentle prodding from Dubois.

Julian didn't know, or wouldn't tell, why he set fires. There was pathos in his story, and injustice: his father should have done his time, not him. But that didn't mean the boy was cured, or that he wouldn't kill again.

Neil Hart was leading them from Julian's life to the present fires, and then to the Red Flag Alert. Shawn shifted uncomfortably.

He wished they gave a course on TV at the Academy. He was trained, instead, for the witness stand, where you sat mute as a statue until questioned, addressed the judge, answered precisely, expanding on nothing.

Where, on TV, did you keep your eyes? On lens, host, or the person talking? How long should you speak at a crack? How did it look if you broke in? Hart was claiming that the hills were impenetrable now, with roadblocks: suppose Shawn interrupted, to puncture the euphoria, and the camera ignored him?

"So, Lieutenant," Hart asked importantly, "what can *we* do to help? Me? And the viewer?"

He was on: "Law enforcement's powerless, Neil, without the citizen's help." Using Hart's first name was phony, but everybody on

TV did it, didn't they? *Marvelous chap, Neil: my very dearest friend.* "Apprehension of suspects is difficult, at best." Too stiff: it sounded as if he were reading a manual. "We're spread awfully thin." A kick at Prop 13, but trite. "Suspicious persons must be reported, anyone seen around a fire, before or after." Really? No shit! "And that's why we've posted the five-thousand-dollar reward."

Jesus, awful. His face had turned to cement. You couldn't hide ignorance from the big glass eye. Or could you?

Politicians did it with platitudes. He searched his mind. He knew one basic fact about arson, a truism he'd checked this afternoon in a quick session over the department's skimpy file and last year's FBI statistics. The penalty for arson was a slap on the wrist: tell them that. The kid's innocent eyes made him uneasy, but he got it out: "Lastly, we can insist that our legislators vote stiffer arson penalties."

The youth looked as if he'd been slapped across the face with a wet condom; the doctor tensed in his wheelchair. Neil Hart, sensing conflict, grabbed at it. "Doctor, how do *you* feel about that?"

"He's entirely misinformed." The doctor's face grew on the monitor, while Shawn sat dreading the reappearance of the red light on the camera facing him. His hands, he found, were clenching and unclenching. He forced them to lie still. Cameras loved to zoom in on nervous hands.

". . . the lieutenant's solution would be tougher sentencing," the doctor was saying. "That's punitive, and Band-Aid. It's a primarily psychiatric problem, unless you're talking about arson-for-profit, which isn't Santa Barbara's trouble. To start with, in the genital phase of a child's development . . ."

Whatever Shawn said, he clearly wasn't going to upstage Dubois, who had medical degree, wheelchair, and advance publicity all going for him, and obviously spent most of his waking hours spewing similar jargon.

". . . regression to the urethral-phallic phase occurs either because masturbation is prohibited or it is associated with considerable castration anxiety. It's *that* basic. I'm afraid that a stiffer sentence for psychologically motivated fire setting isn't the answer to *that.*"

The red light on Shawn's camera began to glow expectantly. Jesus, he hadn't been following Dubois' arguments at all. He hated the classic policeman's reply to the liberal, but used it: "At least it would keep them off the street," he pointed out. "You can't start a brush fire in Santa Barbara if you're doing time at Lompoc." He warmed to his argument. "It's rare enough to find a suspect. If the courts don't put him away for a reasonable time when we *do*—"

"Lieutenant," Dubois cut in, "if you confine yourself to apprehension of fire setters, fine. That's *your* field of expertise, but—"

Christ, if Dubois asked him how many firebugs he'd arrested, the show would turn into comedy hour. Swiftly, he cut the doctor off: "Arson wasn't even a Part One felony until 1978. Out of every hundred suspicious fires, only nine suspects are arrested!" Thank God he was a quick study. "Only two are tried! Only *one* is convicted! And half the time, *he* gets probation, if it's his first offense!"

He pointed out that the situation was so critical that the International Police Chiefs Association had opposed classifying arson as a major crime, because it would make their conviction rates look bad.

"Now, they were dead wrong," Shawn explained, "and it *was* reclassified finally." He felt suddenly at home with the camera. He stared into its lens. "We pay an arm and a leg for arson. Thirty per cent of our insurance bill's because of firebugs, whether we live in a shack in Pueblo Viejo or a ranch house in the foothills."

His knowledge of the subject exhausted, but confident now, he fired his last shot. "A convicted fire setter is a criminal. He has to be taken out of circulation long enough to make his conviction worthwhile. Arsonists have killed ten people in Santa Barbara in the last fifteen years. I think we should push for mandatory sentencing."

He sat back. That should give the shrink something to chew on. He felt better. His argument was on firm ground, and his whole pitch would shake hell out of Castillo, who'd probably see it as a hint that he'd grabbed a platform and would someday run for office, splitting the Spanish vote.

Sorry, Sheriff, you made me do it, I didn't even want to come.

"That's the typical view of law enforcement," protested Dubois. "The problem's psychiatric! The patient who sets a brush fire should be paroled when he's *cured!* He's disturbed, he's not some kind of murderous psychotic—"

"*One's* a psychotic," Julian said suddenly. "*He's* out. Remember Eric?"

The psychiatrist gaped at his patient, his eyes growing hard. He looked ready to murder him.

"Who's Eric?" demanded Neil Hart.

Julian shrugged. "A paranoid schiz—"

"An *ex*-inmate," Dubois cut in, his voice like steel. "From our therapy group. Who's *making* it outside." His jaw was clenched and a muscle jumped in his temple. "As far as we know, he's *making* it. Right? '*Dave*'?"

"Well, Herb"—the youth grinned—"he did jump parole."

There was a long silence. The youth's smile faded. The tension between doctor and patient was tight as the string on a guitar. Neil Hart plucked it with a few smooth phrases, ending with a caution to his viewers against prematurely wetting down roofs in the foothills and wasting water pressure, and a plea that non-residents stay out of fire areas. The camera light went out. Robert Conrad appeared on the monitor in full macho, daring the viewer to knock a battery from his shoulder, and the doctor spun his wheelchair out and away, heading for the exit. The kid looked after him, shocked and seemingly ready to cry. "What'd *I* do?" he mumbled to himself.

"I don't know," said Shawn, rising. "Hey, is this 'Eric' local talent? Somebody I ought to know?"

The innocent brown eyes looked up at him. "Sure, pig," he snarled. "You probably got a lot in common. You like to beat up women? Set fire to dog pounds? Torch filling stations? Give a little head?"

"Yeah, Julian," Shawn sighed, "you're ready for the street, all right. Eric who?"

"Kiss my fucking ass."

So Shawn caught up with Dubois in the parking lot and helped him into his car. "You seem a little sensitive about 'Eric,' Doctor. Who is he?"

The psychiatrist studied him for a moment. "Not one of our screaming successes."

Eric, he said, was one Eric Zimmer, ex-Marine, habitat coastal California: ADW, burglary, arson three counts, sentenced to two years. Eric was a time bomb with legs, and the whole therapy group had sensed it.

But the doctor had, he thought, got through to Eric, who'd somehow cooled it under treatment at 'Tasky, become a model patient. There was no way to keep him forever, anyway, so they'd cut him loose early. Dubois, who said he'd had doubts from the start, winced as he admitted that Eric had jumped parole, proving he'd conned the shrinks.

Assuming Eric hadn't simply wasted himself anonymously somewhere on his motorcycle, he'd apparently, so far, made it, or Dubois would have heard differently. "Because," he said grimly, "if he *really* blows it, they'll have our tails." He looked up at Shawn. "Listen, Lieutenant, *you* know firebugs—"

"I've seen a lot of their work. But no, I don't, really."

"*Now* you tell me." Dubois smiled wryly. "Between you and Julian, you blow me out of the water, and—" He lit a cigar. "Ah, screw it. Where is that schmuck?"

Julian arrived at the car. "Can I still drive, Herb?"

"Start any fires in the studio?"

"No."

"Then, be my guest." He struggled across to the passenger seat. "Good night, Lieutenant." He waved. "About that sentencing, you know, you may be right."

Shawn watched them drive from the parking lot and glanced at his watch. He'd have time to visit Brink. He moved to his plainclothes car, stopped, staring. A matchbook blazed on the hood.

"You little son of a bitch!" he howled after the retreating tail lights. He began to whisk at the burning book. When he'd knocked it to the pavement, he inspected the damage with a flashlight. It would cost the county fifty bucks. He unlocked the door, dove inside, started the engine, picked up the mike to cut Julian off with a squad car at Loma Alta Drive. Then he put it slowly back.

He couldn't prove anything but malicious mischief, if that. The kid was already a felon. It would cost the county more than it was worth to cage him tonight on a misdemeanor, and screw up the doctor's whole trip, besides.

He'd call Dubois tomorrow and leave it up to him.

The psychiatrist might be a world authority on the care and feeding of firebugs, but it seemed as if he had a lot to learn.

Eric Zimmer, fry cook, worked swiftly in his trailer near the SP tracks, ignoring the newscast which followed the Neil Hart show.

Within moments of Julian's finking, he had field-stripped his Marine .45 automatic. Now he had it reassembled. He slapped in a clip and slammed the first round into the chamber. He locked the safety and dropped a second clip into the pocket of his leather jacket.

He plucked a matchbox from his rusty stove, then looked around to see if he'd forgotten anything. His new color TV was still on. He'd spotted the set in an unoccupied Goleta bungalow, cruising this afternoon in his pickup for just that item. He'd pried open a rear bedroom window and burgled it unhesitatingly. Then he'd paused, thinking of lighting the place off, for kicks. He'd decided not to torch it, because it lay only two blocks from his own trailer, upwind: in this weather, he'd have been risking his own pad.

Through his inner argument about lighting it off, the Shrink had remained silent.

In his trailer, he'd plugged in the set and was flipping the channels when he'd frozen, incredulous. The Shrink and Julian had popped onto the screen. He'd watched the whole show, astonished. When the shock was over, he began to chuckle. The Shrink and Julian, the cop and the TV guy, laughing at *him?*

"Who's Eric?" "He's a paranoid schiz—"

Sure, Julie. Sure, Shrink. The Shrink seemed proud of Julian, had become his big daddy on wheels . . . They'd called it, what? In Show and Tell at 'Tasky? *Transference.* The Shrink was going to parole Julian, or thought he was, was probably fag by now and all over Julie lately, sweet Julie, ass like an apple, lips like wine . . .

Well, Julian would have to be back in his ward by midnight tonight. They'd be starting up now. Two ways to Atascadero: San Marcos Highway, shorter, but nobody could drive San Marcos tonight, not even a fire engine. So they had to take Coastal 101, through Gaviota.

They had a head start already, but the Harley could do 130, would eat them alive. If he didn't catch them, it meant they'd stopped to eat, and he'd wait on Gaviota Pass.

He turned off the TV, rechecked everything: piece, ammo, matchbox, helmet, gloves. He went outside.

He was weaving through traffic up 101, past El Capitan State Beach, when he spotted the Shrink's car ahead, a special Pinto hatchback that Dubois had driven for years. He wiped at his visor with his sleeve, flicked up his headlight to check. He could see the folded wheelchair through the rear window. He had the impression that Julian was driving. Good.

He dropped back. Too many cars, here. Gaviota Pass, on the crest of the coastal foothills, would be better.

Loafing far behind the tail lights, he could feel the hot winds blow. He smelled sage and the desert a hundred miles away. At the mouth of every canyon, cooler, harder gusts would try to slam him from his seat. He clenched his knees on the Harley's tank, became one with the machine, and grew a hard-on like a telephone pole.

He wished Julian could feel it.

> "Torn between two lovers,
> Feeling like a fool . . ."

See you, Fink.
See you, Shrink.

Five

Shawn hated hospitals. Arrogant interns and starched, swishing nurses, smell of ether and sound of muted paging in the corridors, all brought him back to the night his parents had died and his world had dissolved.

Now he stepped from the elevator on Brink's floor and stood suddenly face to face with Nicole and Val. Her eyes were reddened and Val's were moist with rage, but typically, she gushed: "*God,* you're wonderful on the tube! You should run for Congress."

"Yeah," he said tersely. "How is he?"

"They're letting him lie there and *hurt,*" Val squeaked. "He doesn't want it to show, so he practically kicked us out!"

His voice had chosen this month to break: it was hard to take him seriously when he soared into falsetto. He knew it, and it fueled his anger.

"OK, buddy. I'll try to twist some arms."

He got them into the elevator and moved down the corridor. A deep bellow, seemingly torn from the depths of hell, resounded suddenly down the hall. Heart pounding, he moved swiftly toward Brink's room.

The owl-faced nun was backing out the door, drawing a medicine cart. She seemed very tired: she'd aged years in a day.

"He's tryin' to be a man of iron, your friend. And can't, of course."

"Can't you give him morphine?" asked Shawn.

"I've called the bloody Scots doctor." But even morphine, she feared, was too late: heroin, standard medication in hers or any other civilized country, was indicated but of course illegal here.

For this she blamed American police in general, confusing those who enforced the law with those who made it. "You've brainwashed your people too long, Leftenant. He's sufferin' for it now."

Eyes locked, the two stood for a moment. From inside the room, a rumbling groan began, rose and became the howl of a timber wolf caught in a trap. Shivers swept up his forearms. Suddenly, behind the door, he heard a siren wail, then shots, and the blare of a cop show theme. He saw tears start into her eyes, enormous behind the thick glasses.

"He turns it on," she quavered, "to drown himself out."

She trundled the cart away, and he stepped into the cacophony inside the room.

Brink was half sitting in bed, twisted oddly to relieve some bone-deep pain that Shawn couldn't imagine. His face was distorted, and he was moaning. He looked at Shawn blankly, then lay back. Weakly, he flicked off the TV.

"Mamá Lola came," he murmured. "Cookies . . . Have one."

He waved toward a box on his bedside table.

"No. They're for you."

"Don't help, much. Told her that . . ." He sighed. "Thought you'd never come." He closed his eyes. "You bring my cigarettes?"

"You know," muttered Shawn, "I forgot?"

"'S all right. Think I'll . . . quit."

Shawn sat down on the side of the bed to wait for Dr. Stewart. "That'd be nice."

"They just might . . . you know . . . cut my wind?"

Julian was speeding up the Gaviota grade on the rim of Nojoqui Canyon. Dubois glanced at the speedometer. It hovered at seventy.

"Cool it, Jule."

"Hey, you're a poet!"

"Slow down, OK?"

Julian eased off. "You pissed about Eric?"

He wasn't pissed, just tired of Julian and the whole scene. "Forget it."

"Look, *you* were talking, the pig was talking, the TV guy was talking. I was, you know, just sitting there. I had to say something!"

It was no use reminding him that he'd probably torpedoed the Group Therapy program for the next fiscal year; he'd blame it on his basic insecurity and Oedipus and his father's dominance, and they'd be talking about it for the next interminable hour, and by the time Julian was through he'd have convinced both of them that he was guiltless as a baby seal.

Show and Tell might not teach them to live in the real world, but it sure as hell taught them to talk their way back into it.

"Jule-baby," he warned again, "the speedometer?"

Julian slowed, then tensed, glancing into the rearview mirror. "Oh shit . . ."

Dubois twisted in his seat. A single headlight gleamed in their wake. *That* would do it, Julian's getting pinched. He had got a prisoner out on pass, got the hospital's release program questioned on TV, and then let the kid get busted for speeding. Sorry, Chief . . .

"Herb," Julian confessed suddenly, "they took my license, when I went up."

"Great . . . Just frigging *great*." He was deputized himself, as a correctional officer. Maybe he could talk their way out of it. "Well, pull over."

Julian shook his head, watching the mirror. "No red on that light . . . Hey, that hog's *chopped*! It's not a cop, just a *biker* . . ."

Dubois sat back. "Keep it down, anyway." He closed his eyes again, but opened them when he heard the drone of the bike drawing closer. He was strangely uncomfortable, vulnerable in his paralysis, very sensitive to the danger of an accident. He wished that the idiot would drop back, or pass: instead, he hung like a wingman in close echelon off the Pinto's left rear fender. In this wind, if car or motorcycle swerved, they could collide.

He was about to tell Julian to slow again when the cyclist made his move in a thundering roar.

He drew abreast, and Dubois was suddenly staring at a faceless dark visor only feet beyond Julian's nose. The black helmet, having drawn even, stayed implacably where it was. As he watched, the head turned. In the light of their own dashboard he had the sense that, behind the plastic mask, the motorcyclist was laughing. Then he saw a gun, gleaming darkly, immense, trained on Julian's head.

He tried to kick at the brake, to disrupt the aim, forgetting his life-less legs.

"Jule!" he screamed.

He was groping at the paraplegic brake lever on the steering col-umn when Julian's head exploded in a roar of orange light. He grabbed too late at the wheel, as the car skewed left over the double line. He heard a blast of power as the cyclist rocketed clear.

Then a pair of headlights leaped at him from the highway ahead, brighter and brighter, higher and higher. He fought to regain the lane, hearing the rising blast of an approaching horn, the shriek of brakes, and a mighty rending of metal.

The impact was immense, and nothing. He had the sense of drift-ing, cut loose from infirmity, free of words sewed patchwork over ig-norance. He sensed moonlight, a darkened highway strewn with bodies, and someone with his own voice moaning softly. He heard the bubbling sound of the motorcycle gliding back. Then there was no more.

Shawn watched Dr. Malcolm Den Stewart examine Brink. The doctor's considerable beam stretched his tight Levis. On his feet were work boots. He had been riding the ridges or shoveling horseshit or whatever horsemen did in the sunset hours, and every flabby fiber of his being radiated distaste: he had not liked being called at all.

And Brink, of course, had turned stoic the moment he arrived. The doctor glanced at Shawn. "I'll see you in the chart room," he snapped, and left.

Brink's eyes, a little dulled by pain, followed Stewart to the door. "Well, I didn't ask for the son of a bitch."

"Sister Margaret did," Shawn told him. "She was right. Look, you don't have to John Wayne it!" He looked into Brink's eyes. "Ace? I don't like this guy. Neither does Nicole. Neither do you." The time had come to try to drum Stewart off the case. "Let's get a second opinion."

"A second—" Brink began to cough, hacked up sputum, motioned for a Kleenex, jerked it away when Shawn tried to wipe his mouth, did it himself. "Second opinion? On what? For what?" He snorted, lay back. "Hey, maybe it's nothing but flu? They read the wrong bi-opsy?"

"For *relief*," Shawn said quietly, "not diagnosis."

"So I make some other turkey rich? To come in and hold my hand? In a pig's ass!"

Shawn told him that he wasn't thinking of sympathy, just stronger drugs. Brink managed a caricature of his old grin. "But I don't have to worry about that! When I *do* holler, you're putting me under, right?"

Shawn chilled. "I don't want you to *have* to holler!"

Brink ignored that. "Right?" he demanded.

"If I can." His heart was pounding.

"You can. All set up."

Shawn looked down at him. The blue eyes were expressionless. "What's *that* mean?"

Brink began to cough again, hacking and spitting. Finally he caught his breath, nodded toward a slim pigskin briefcase on a table in the corner. "Briefcase . . ." He fumbled in his bedside table, found a key, handed it to Shawn, and again jerked his head at the case. Shawn opened it. It was full of contracts, liens, and soil reports; he had no idea what he was looking for, but Brink managed, "Bottle," half strangling, and he found a brown-wrapped package, tied in string. He opened it and discovered a small brown bottle full of liquid, and a syringe. He turned. "What—"

"OK, you know where it is, put it back."

"I don't know *what* it is!" His voice trembled.

" 'Di . . . Dilaudid', something . . . Put it back."

Shawn rewrapped the package, put it back under the papers. "Where the hell—?"

"Doesn't matter, does it?"

"It does to me!"

"Mamá Lola." Brink struggled. "She bought it . . . Isla Vista . . . Medical students . . . shooting it . . . for kicks. Experimental . . . cancer pain. Stronger than morphine. Enough there . . . to put out my lights."

"She deals pot. How would she *know*?"

"She *got* it . . . which is more'n you did, right?"

It wasn't his fault, he almost blurted. He'd been swamped.

Or evading the job? He didn't really know. "You're right. I'm sorry."

"OK, Ace. So . . . Let's just figure . . . she knows what she's talking about . . . OK?" He moved painfully, seeking a better position. "She says *she'll* do it . . . Don't want that."

Shawn studied his own hands. They were trembling. But Brink was right. If *he* did the job, and anything went wrong, at least he was experienced in the ways of investigating officers, who'd be city and hard-nosed, not county and flexible. Mamá Lola, for whom the DA had long been gunning anyway, might be a sitting duck, if only because she didn't care.

He could tell when Brink's eyes flickered that a fresh pain was building somewhere. He watched him fight it and heard him mutter: "OK. Anyway, for now . . . I got a land deal to sign . . . Until it's signed . . . Got to keep my smarts . . . Even if it hurts a little."

"Then it looks," Shawn said bitterly, "like you got the right doctor."

"Point is—" Brink winced. "Point is, have I got the right *friend?*"

"I'll do it, Ace," Shawn promised softly. He looked deeply into the blazing eyes. "All you got to do is ask."

Walking down the corridor to the chart room he heard the TV in Brink's room go on, and froze, waiting for another bellow of agony. But he heard nothing else, and went on.

Stewart was sitting on a stool at a counter, studying Brink's chart. He looked up balefully: "You and I better have a little talk."

In essence, stated the doctor, there was going to be more pain. More pain than Brink could imagine. He could ease it now with morphine, but, as he'd told the patient, once they let it start, it was irreversible. Without heavy drugs now, he was going to end up animalistic, howling. But Brink was refusing even a Brompton Cocktail—cocaine, alcohol, syrup, and morphine—wanting his head clear for business things he had to handle. "Lieutenant, I suggest you change his mind."

"I can't change it, he doesn't scare."

Stewart smiled coldly. "We'll see. Only then, it'll be too late."

Shawn felt dread in the pit of his stomach. "*Give* him something, then, anyway. *He* doesn't know what you're shooting him with!"

"Against his wishes?" Stewart pointed out that Brink wasn't a cop leaving a widow's pension, or even a doctor with three hundred grand in a Keogh Plan. "He's working on something big, some land, ten million, twenty million dollars? And *I* fog him up? And Nickie sues me after he's dead?" He shook his head. "Get yourself another boy."

I wish he'd let us, Shawn thought, God, how I wish he'd let us.

Stewart moved to a little window in the chart room and looked out over the city. Past him, Shawn saw the glow in the northwest sky. "Christ," murmured the doctor, "it must be all the way to Lauro Reservoir." He turned suddenly, and his pale eyes fastened on Shawn's. "*Nobody* turns down that last lifeboat. What's he got in mind?"

Shawn stiffened. "What's that supposed to mean?"

"I've been treating terminal thoracics for thirty years. I've had Christian Scientists, holistic nuts, I even had a Buddhist monk. *Nobody* refuses morphine, when it starts, not after I explain what's ahead, not past the point of no return." He sat down on the stool, drumming his fingers on the counter. "He's planning on suicide. Or somebody putting him under, when he gives the word. Who? Not me, that's for sure. Not that nurse. Nicole's too soft. Val? That's monstrous. No. *You.*"

"Bullshit," Shawn said. His voice sounded tinny.

"You're bringing him coke, already. I can tell by his mucus."

"The hell I am."

"Somebody is." He moved back to the window, probably worried about his horses. "And nobody's kidding me with those cookies, I smelled them. OK, but just don't let him talk you into bringing him anything more *drastic*." He turned. "I better tell you something, Ortega, that may save you a lot of grief." When Shawn didn't answer, the doctor went on: "You're riding high in this town. I saw you on TV. Someday you could be sheriff: your family's been here long enough."

Longer than yours, Lard-butt. "So what?"

"So remember this. You think you know your way around, but he's *my* patient, I'm on the staff of this hospital, I sign his death certificate, I'm a practicing Catholic, I believe in God's will." His jowls began to quiver. "If I have suspicions, I'll get him autopsied, I guarantee it, and if it turns out somebody screwed around, then all his bucks, and your whole damn Sheriff's Department, aren't going to do you a goddamn bit of good. So—"

"I don't have to take this crap!" Shawn towered over him, fighting the urge to belt him, hard.

Stewart looked scared, but got it out: "So when he dies, it better be of cancer!"

"Meaning," Shawn murmured, "he goes out screaming?"

"His choice." Stewart's eyes, pale blue and bulbous, held his own. "I don't make the law, Ortega. Neither do you."

"You," said Shawn softly, "are one *sick* son of a bitch."

He slammed from the room and stalked toward the elevator.

From Brink's closed door he could hear the faint sound of moaning, over canned laughter, turned high. He seemed to be hearing it all the way home, where he had a message to contact the watch commander.

They'd had a call from Isla Vista: some woman thought she knew who the girl in the red VW had been: the watch officer had Deputy Trumbell down checking it out, but was Shawn still interested?

Shawn got the Isla Vista address and took off. Anyone who knew the victim was a suspect, and he wanted first crack at them all.

Besides, anything was better than sitting home, imagining Brink's pain.

Six

Steamboat Haley shifted in the pilot seat, trimmed the B-17's nose, and tried to peer through the left-hand window into a pitch-black void. The Fortress rattled and whined with a hundred woes, moaning dirges through chinks in her fuselage.

He was on a low-frequency instrument approach to Santa Barbara Municipal, and though he was riding his pattern in from eight miles at sea, the smoke was so thick at thirty-five hundred feet that he could smell it in the cockpit.

In the copilot seat, Snaproll Suzy, Girl of a Thousand Laughs, knocked her microphone on her knee to jolt it into life. He heard her call Santa Barbara Approach Control, inbound for runway seven.

His heart was pounding from the exertion of getting the ancient Fortress airborne in the first place, and his head ached from the strain of having unexpectedly to change his flight plan, on this clear and cloudless night, from visual to instrument, when they'd encountered the pall of smoke.

The cockpit lights flickered suddenly and went out, leaving him helpless in darkness. He heard Snaproll kicking at the panel. The lights returned, went out, came on again, and stayed. Beautiful. He settled back.

"Report Halibut Intersection," he yelled. The intercom switch didn't work.

She gave him a thumbs-up in the faint blue light. "Approach

Control!" she bawled. "One-seven-two Tango, Halibut Intersection at zero-eight, thirty-five hundred, descending . . ."

The controller rogered and told them to report at the Naples Fan Marker. The voice was female. He cringed, anticipating grief. There had been a day when the only woman you heard on aircraft frequencies was Snaproll. She hated female voices competing with her own.

Steamboat eased back his throttles. One of them resisted, and for a moment the number two prop went out of synch, setting up a new dissonance in the surrounding racket, and troubling a tooth with a loose filling. He pounded the throttle lightly with the heel of his hand. The sound diminished.

He was nervous and jumpy. He had worked all afternoon on the flight line at Cachuma, with the ancient mechanic, longing only for nightfall and the fifth of Old Taylor that Snaproll hid in the office safe. But at dusk, when they had finished, she was standing below their scaffold in her leather flight jacket.

Forest Service Headquarters at Goleta, the TV news had said, was crying for every tanker it could get. To Snaproll it meant that they were scraping the bottom of the barrel so that they could legally bring in the 146th Tactical Wing from Van Nuys. This last infuriated Snaproll, though it was all right with Steamboat, who had his mind on the Old Taylor and would have loved to let the soldiers handle the fire till dawn.

But: "Let's go, Steamboat," she'd yelled. "Santa-frigging Barbara, baby!"

"*We* ain't invited. Not yet."

"We will be tomorrow," she said grimly. "I want to load slurry tonight."

"Jesus, let's wait till they—"

"The Old Taylor's locked in the safe," she warned, over the whistling wind. "I'll take it along, but if you want a drink, you got to fly."

Bitch . . . He could never remember the safe's combination, for she seemed to change it every day.

He'd scowled down from the scaffold, ready to refuse, but she'd only grinned.

The wind had been whipping her hair. In the fading light he couldn't see the white roots under the dye, so the blond waves had seemed as rich to him and lustrous as ever. Her gleaming teeth were cheap dentures, now, and her dimples lay buried in lines, but her hazel eyes, laughing or furious, could still send his blood pressure soaring.

Well, his own eyesight was dimming faster than her looks—maybe nature's way of keeping them wing to wing in the sunset years—and when she climbed the scaffold to help them button up the cowling, and pressed close, the old warmth worked on him again.

Besides, if he'd refused to go, she'd probably have tried to fly it over solo, and buttered herself all over Condor Peak.

So here he was at 3,500 feet, IFR, where he had no wish to be, blind as a bat in the flickering light, in an aircraft which had already, according to its horrifying log, gone through two combat crews by the time it got over Omaha Beach. There, it had lost an engine and its last pilot to an ME 109 and been barely saved by its wounded copilot. He'd found it in a line of similar relics at Litchfield Park, Arizona, plumbed its tanks, and bid on it on the strength of the gasoline still aboard. Its Air Corps name, *Marvin's Mistress*, had been nearly sandblasted clean by the desert wind. He should have sold the gas and junked the plane, and he knew it more surely with every passing year.

Poor Marvin. Poor Haley Air Service.

Poor plane: *Marvin's Mistress*, as battered by life as his own mistress had been, was probably wondering why it was thrashing through billowing smoke, thirty-five years after Normandy. But that, he really didn't know himself.

He heard the woman's voice from Santa Barbara through the one good earphone on his one good ear. "One-seven-two Tango? Did you *miss* Naples Fan Marker?"

He hadn't really missed it, the indicator on his panel just hadn't worked. Snaproll cut in: "No, Santa Barbara," she snarled. "You just missed our transmission, is all. Listen up!"

He groaned and sank more deeply into the shabby leather seat. She'd got him three letters of admonition in his FAA file already; if the fire lasted long enough, she'd get him another one here. Some day she'd get his ticket lifted, for sure.

He glared at her in the dim blue light. "Can't you be nice? Just once?"

She reached over and squeezed his leg. "No little airport bitch goin' to say old *Steamboat* missed a fan marker! Right?"

"Drop the gear," he said tiredly, "and finish the check-off list."

He listened to the wheels grind down, tensed when they hesitated, and sagged in relief when they locked, though they jarred the plane like a burst of 40 mm fire below its aching belly.

He hoped they'd get the slurry loaded before the bar in the terminal closed.

Shawn left his car blocking a tarpaulined sport car, a jeep, and two mopeds chained together in the driveway of the Isla Vista duplex. Across the street he noticed a Patrol Division black-and-white.

He sidled past three cartons of empty beer bottles on the porch. Each was marked: "For People's Reclamation Center Pick-up." The smell of pot was heavy, doing battle with smoke from the fire.

He pressed the doorbell and found that it was painted solidly immobile. He knocked. The duplex was probably less than ten years old, but it looked as if it had been through World War II and a hurricane. The whole street was standard, collegiate ghetto: landlords simply gave up, and the kids, gouged dry with the rent, couldn't care less.

The door opened. He stared.

The girl was tawny brown, dressed in yellow running shorts. A UCSB T-shirt clung to the loveliest breasts he'd seen in years. The legs were long and slim, the face a perfect oval, and the black eyes almost level with his own.

He showed her the badge in his wallet and asked if he could come in. She led him into a dark and shadowed living room. A blond young man with a beard sat slouched in an easy chair, and Calvin Trumbell, sour and hostile, sat opposite him taking notes. The deputy nodded. "Our friend's a little wasted."

Shawn looked down at the bearded young man. The man Lopes had seen in the VW on San Marcos Pass? Light blond hair and beard, rather than black, but the trucker could have been wrong. "You read him his rights?" he asked Trumbell.

The girl looked startled and Trumbell, puzzled, shook his head. Shawn gave the kid the Miranda and asked him for the missing woman's name.

"Lynn, but it isn't her."

"Lynn who?"

"Holmsted," muttered the young man. He was spaced to the eyeballs; Shawn wondered if he'd be any good to him for hours.

"What's your relationship?" he asked. "To the deceased?"

The kid looked blank.

"He's her friend," answered the black girl. She'd heard the VW described on TV, she said; they'd called right away.

"Yeah, a friend," Trumbell sighed. "Everybody's very friendly here." He arose, beckoned Shawn to the kitchen, and leaned against a sink full of greasy dishes. The place smelled of garbage, grass, and lovemaking. Trumbell wrinkled his nose, poked at twisted marijuana ashes in a cup. "She forgot some, here, and there's joints out there, too, enough for a bust. What do you think?"

Shawn shook his head. "What for?" He asked Trumbell if he'd determined the next of kin. "Not really." He'd worked on it, he said, for five minutes: "First he's high, then crashes . . . Got to catch him in between." He poked at the toke in the cup. "Wish *I* could find stuff like that." He leered. "Or stuff like that, out there."

Trumbell gave Shawn the information he had: John, or Jack, Holmsted, for the father's name; Denver address unknown, phone unknown. Trumbell couldn't believe the offhandedness of it all: the kid had been shacking for a whole semester with the missing woman and didn't even know her parents' names? "He says it can't be his girl, *his* wasn't pregnant."

"He might not have known."

"Wish I'd gone to college. *She* heads home for Christmas, *he* takes up with the jig."

"Who wouldn't? I'll take it from here," Shawn said, and Trumbell left.

To show the blackened, unrecognizable corpse to the bearded young man, whose name was Rick Davis, would be cruel and futile. The only way they'd identify her was from dental records. Shawn stepped back into the living room.

Davis was out of it again, laying back, eyes closed, leading Neil Diamond in "Sweet Caroline." "Shut that off," Shawn ordered the girl. "Rick?"

His eyes fluttered open. He smiled, alighting gracefully back on earth. "Um?"

"Rick? Your girl. Lynn! She carry highway flares in that bug?"

The young man looked puzzled. "Doesn't sound like her . . ."

"Use a safety belt when she drives?"

"No way."

"How come you didn't report her missing?"

"She told me she was going home to Denver. She told me on Wednesday night. And Thursday she was gone."

"Without saying good-by?"

Davis shrugged. "We're not that much into Romeo and Juliet."

"You bother to check her clothes?" Shawn muttered. "Luggage?"

No. Why would he? He'd known—he *knew*—she'd be back after Christmas. But he'd check it now, just to be sure, and he led Shawn up the stairs with him.

The bedroom looked as if it had been sacked by Attila the Hun. "We kind of got off on each other," mumbled Davis, of the chocolate dream downstairs. He picked up an overturned bedside table and pulled out its drawer.

His face suddenly sagged. He drew out a charm bracelet, apparently one the girl would have taken if she'd intended to leave for Christmas. Moving faster, he yanked open a closet door. Inside was woman's clothing. A fur parka hung on a hook, and a pair of skis leaned in the back corner. He suddenly crumpled to sit on the tossed bedclothes.

"She wouldn't leave her skis." He looked dead into Shawn's eyes. It was impossible to believe that a few moments before he'd been stoned. "Look, I got to see this girl you got, you've *got* to let me see her."

Shawn shook his head. "Why? You couldn't tell, one way or the other."

That stopped him; he looked stunned. "If it's Lynn," Davis choked finally, "who tells her folks?"

If the kid was acting, he was worthy of Broadway.

"I'll see it's done," Shawn promised.

He was glad he'd taken over from Trumbell, who'd have had the young man booked on suspicion of murder by now, just to keep the record straight.

But this kid, in his judgment, was clean.

So his own list of suspects was back down to zero.

Seven

Jake Klinger, nee Eric Zimmer, drifted away in the moonlight from the crowds around the wrecked truck and Pinto on Gaviota Pass. He knew of one more undiscovered victim, a Mexican draped over a bush near the rim of the canyon, not far from where he'd parked his bike. Just after the crash, while the Shrink's car was still burning, he'd seen the fucker moving.

Now he spotted the man's yellow hard hat on the edge of the shoulder, kicked it slyly, sent it flying into the canyon. The bracero moaned, watching with stunned eyes. No beans for the *niños* tomorrow.

Zimmer looked back down the line of rubberneckers, ambulances, tow trucks, and CHP vehicles. Near the smoldering Pinto crouched a fire truck, its beacon painting the faces of squatting paramedics and lounging firemen. Eight, no, nine bodies lay waiting for more ambulances. He could hear a siren wailing up the Solvang side of the grade, and another, distantly, shrieking from Gaviota State Park by the beach.

He felt drained after the excitement. The National Guard truck had damn near wasted *him*, before it hit the Pinto. But he'd escaped by inches, braked, and returned, every nerve singing with exhilaration. He'd quickly tossed a match under the Shrink's car, thrilling as it caught in a *vroom* that very nearly lit off the wreck of the personnel truck too. But the truck had escaped the flames, and he couldn't get close enough to light it.

After the cars of horrified tourists had come, and truckers, and finally, CHP, he'd drifted among them, listening to the fuzz, keeping his visor down, helping to light flares, speaking to a moaning campesino laborer lying draped over a culvert on the road.

Adiós muchachos, compañeros, caballeros . . .

Something he'd heard on late TV, in some honor camp, or doing time at 'Tasky, or Lompoc, he couldn't remember. He was always hearing songs he couldn't get out of his head.

Though I must leave ya, don't let it grieve ya . . .

A woman, left in the car behind his bike while her husband walked forward to gawk, was watching him. Safe behind the visor, he could probably have kicked in her fender and scared hell out of the old bag, but she might hit her horn, there were too many cops up ahead. He dropped the idea and climbed onto his bike.

He jabbed the engine into life and rocked the throttle for a moment, blasting the night. The woman looked as if she'd shit.

Adiós, muchachos . . .

He hung a U, lay back, attacked the curves, and headed toward the sea.

So long, Fink . . .

So long, Shrink . . .

Soaring down the coast, he diverted long enough to start a minor brush fire at Stow Grove County Park, and another behind the county fire station, in Los Carneros Canyon.

The last set amused him but made him jumpy, too, so close to the firehouse, as if the Shrink might find out if he got caught.

But hey, the Shrink was dead!

He sailed the bike back to his trailer, stretched on the bare mattress, and slept better than he had for years.

Shawn Ortega parked between the Kentucky Fried Chicken kitchen and the gas station, avoiding the parking lot. Here he hoped to find whoever had last seen the girl alive, and so intended to do only the unexpected from here on in. It was a habit learned on patrol, from good cops like ex-Sheriff McCrae: you drove innocently down a street, stopped suddenly, backed into a driveway, and reversed. Bad cops, like Sleepy Doyle or Cal Trumbell, never made an unexpected move, not wanting to rock the boat. But half Shawn's busts in the field had been prowlers and Peeping Toms who thought he'd already passed.

He waited, reluctant to begin. He was very tired. He picked up the microphone, called in, and gave the watch officer the missing girl's name, asking him to check on her VW with the Colorado DMV.

A fat young Mexican, dressed *cholo* in a T-shirt and cuffed khaki pants, was hosing down the pump area by the filling station, wasting water which could better be saved for the homes in the hills. The wind whipped spray back on his cuffs, making him dance, and the blowing sheets of mist spread a haze under a streetlamp, painting a rainbow. Shawn supposed he should chastise the kid for extravagance: there was a city ordinance against hosing down during a drought, and another against splurging water during a fire.

He gave up the whole badge-heavy notion. It was not duty tempting him, simply the Santa Ana trying to drive him into a silly confrontation. Devil-wind: no wonder arrest sheets piled up.

He hesitated, drumming his fingers on the wheel. The light in the Colonel's bucket went out. It was 9 P.M. His eyes were dry and heavy and his blue suit hot and restrictive. He felt grimy. He had shaved before the TV program, but already his cheeks were rough. He longed for a shower and bed.

But he knew he wouldn't sleep anyway. He strolled to the KFC stand, ignored the customer entrance, and went to the kitchen, faithful to his principle of random appearance. He knocked. In a moment a sad-faced, obese gentleman in a chef's hat cracked the door. Shawn showed his badge, and was let in.

The man was the manager, standing in on the fry cook's day off. His counter girl had indeed failed to show up for two days, he was holding a paycheck for her, and he seemed genuinely concerned. The last persons to have seen her, so far as he knew, were the fry cook and the other fulltime girl.

Shawn took all the information he had and asked to see the girl.

She was a beautiful blonde, and she flashed him a speculative grin. My sweet, he thought, my daughter's not much younger than you. When she had decided that for herself, and simmered down a little, he asked when she'd last seen Lynn.

"Well, the last night she was here," she said, addressing the manager.

"Thursday," prompted the man.

"Well, Thursday, then, remember, I told you. The fat kid in the gas station, you know, the Chicano? He and she were rapping, you know, by her car?"

He led the blonde to the back door. She pointed out the Chicano, hosing down. "Lynn was parked over there, by their biffy, talking to the Chicano, he gave her something—"

"Gave her what?"

She didn't know: money, she thought. Shawn asked both the blonde and the manager not to mention his visit, went back to his car, and drove to the pump. The kid turned aside his hose and nodded at the unlighted dials.

"Sorry, out of gas, closed, mister."

Eighteen years old, nineteen, maybe. And definitely local: his English was too good for a wetback's or a green-card legal in from the fields. He was too well fed to be wet, anyway, and his accent was barrio, maybe Pueblo Viejo. So the job was probably steady and he'd still be here tomorrow, when Shawn had more to go on. He couldn't hold him, anyway, so he'd better drop it before the youth made him, and panicked. "Where can I get gas, then?"

"Try the Exxon on Cathedral Oaks." The kid was studying him. "Hey, you know this town better'n me, you puttin' me on? I seen you on TV."

"You want an autograph?" Shawn smiled, starting the car. "Go easy on the *agua*, they need it for the fires."

He drove away, cursing inwardly.

Thank you, Sheriff. Thank you, Neil Hart. Thank you, "Tonight in Santa Barbara."

Next time they put him on the air, he'd better go faceless, like Julian, the All-American torch.

Eight

Assistant Supervisor Jerry Castle of Los Padres National Forest lay on the uncomfortable leather couch in the command vehicle, staring at the corkboard ceiling. He had almost given up trying to doze.

He'd had no sleep Thursday night. Friday, at headquarters, he'd napped for an hour around midnight, in his office. Saturday he had moved himself and his fire camp to the top of the pass, and spent the rest of the day watching the combined fires chew through 70,000 acres of prime forest land. He had collapsed to the bunk less than an hour ago.

If he'd dozed this time, he had no recollection of it. And he could not sleep now. His status chief, plans chief, and air boss man, Mike Kane, had all become very quiet when he laid down, like visitors in a sickroom, but they'd gradually forgotten. Now the garbled radios from the air service trailer, the roar of equipment arriving, the ceaseless chomp of choppers staging at the heliport outside the permanent ranger station, were all blasting at his rest.

He sat up. The room spun around him. He waited until it stabilized. Then he arose. His plans chief was staring at him.

"That wasn't very long, Jerry."

"I slept," he lied. He moved to the map on the fire status board. The 10:30 P.M. fire line, a crimson curve arching through the mountains, looked familiar: the fire was consuming Paradise County Park, where had he seen that? He remembered. He had seen it predicted before he lay down, on the ten-thirty model brought in by Robert

Wendell Holmes, soothsayer of doom, whom he had called in from Boise and was beginning to hate for his accuracy. Los Prietos Ranger Station must be going up in flames—

"Jesus!" he barked. "Luke get his family out?"

"By chopper," said someone. "About half an hour ago. And we almost lost the bird."

OK. The next danger point was a Baptist camp on the inland side of the range. They told him that that had been evacuated, too, except for a CDF task force, which was trying to save the buildings. Trout Club Canyon had been cleared when? Last night? Yes, except for one old codger who didn't care if he lived or died, and had miraculously saved his shack when a tanker had missed its target and deluged the place with slurry, permanently dying the cabin pink, but making the old man an instant legend and a bad example for the next fire.

The next community was Sky Crest, and the local day camp next to it, run by hippies for their kids.

He asked for a status report on the residents from his fire status officer, who had winged in from Bangor, Maine. He was a classic Down Easter, and didn't understand at all the breed of cat he was dealing with in the fire hills of California.

"They're *stayin'*, y'know?" he announced incredulously.

There was technically nothing you could do, if a landowner insisted on sticking to private property, to move him off. In Los Angeles County, fire authorities took the easy way, and let people stay to fight the fire.

Everybody stupid enough to live in the box canyons and on the ridges had his own stories, of previous fires and neighbors who had stayed, and won. Never mentioning those, over the years, who'd died trying to save wooden shacks that could have been replaced in weeks.

It was safer for Jerry, legally, simply to stay out of the argument.

But kids? "Send an evac chopper in there, if he can land. And an armed special agent. Roust 'em out."

"That's private property, according to the map."

"Do it!" He was damned if he'd let the way-out counselors fry a bunch of children to prove a point. He studied the map intensely. "And that CDF rig that was at Maria Ygnacia, it's at the Baptist spike camp, according to this. That gal did pretty good. Send her up there too."

All that stood between the fire and the day school was the Los Robles inmate crew. Prisoners were unpredictable, but between inmates and wonder-women, braceros and college kids, Navajos and Modocs, hotshot and helijump crews, and various other airborne heroes in choppers and tankers, they should be able to save the camp long enough to get the kids away.

He was through worrying about federal funds. He had another Marble Cone disaster on his hands, if Holmes's models continued right, and a city of 70,000 to protect which didn't yet know it was in trouble, and probably couldn't yet be warned lest it panic and clog the freeways.

He'd called in another 800 supervisory personnel and another 2,000 "overhead." There were 6,000 men on the line now, or waiting to go in. The rest was up to God and the weather.

"Call Holmes," he said tiredly. "Let's see the next Firemod." He might as well look at it and get the midnight shock over with: it had been almost two hours since he'd suffered the last mortal blow. He was pouring himself a cup of coffee when he saw his air boss, Mike Kane, towering in the doorway.

"The 146th can't fly!" Kane collapsed to the leather couch. "Some contract outfit bitched. Pentagon won't authorize one gallon of gas until every private tanker in the West is full of slurry and flying."

"Well, fill 'em!"

"Everybody's working but Haley Air Service. And I think Snaproll Suzy is the one that blew the whistle."

"Well, use them! That's simple! They got a contract, like everybody else."

They had used Haley at Marble Cone. Steamboat was great, Snaproll impossible, and their equipment execrable.

"They're down on our ramp to load. But no way. Leaky tank," Kane said.

"Again?"

"Not gasoline. This time it's their slurry tank. They'll slop up the runway and spill on the city. If the FAA doesn't cream us, some citizen would sue. I won't let the mixmaster touch 'em."

Castle felt the pressure building. He hadn't smoked since the Marble Cone fire, but he held out his hand, and Kane, sadly, offered

him a pack. It tasted as good as if he'd never quit. "Look, if Haley
has a leaky tank, he can't *expect* to fly. So tell the Pentagon *that!*"

"It isn't him, it's *her*. She knows some Air Force general, called
him at home—"

"She probably *screwed* every Air Force general there is," grated
Jerry. His cigarette was out. He ground it into his coffee cup, lit another. "OK, OK! What's she want?"

"Money," growled Kane. "Flying time, while they look for their
own leak, on the *ground!*"

Flying time for the B-17 was a thousand dollars an hour. Jerry no-
ticed the man from Maine: his eyes were wide with Yankee horror.
Jerry knew that if he gave in, the blackmailing of Jerry Castle
would become Forest Service legend. He turned away. "Where's
Holmes?" he demanded, stalling. "I told you guys to get me
Holmes."

"I'm here," the young meteorologist said.

Castle looked at the new Firemod map and groaned. In an hour
the fire would be threatening Camino Cielo Road, climbing the
northern slope of La Cumbre Peak, and worrying at the mountain
shacks which were the first suburbs of the city by the sea. By tomorrow they'd be sweating out Foothill, and the next day the munici-
pality itself. There was no other way to slow the monster: he needed
the 146th.

"Two new fire sets in town," called someone from the liaison
board. "Los Carneros Canyon and Stow Grove County Park. Class
B, county responding."

Jesus, they'd light off the county fire station next!

He'd let blind respect for the rule of law sway him before, on another pass, in another land, and it had cost the battalion half a company of infantrymen. Not this time, not again, if it cost him his career. Besides, he had an idea for Steamboat and Suzy which might
justify his keeping them standing by, if it didn't kill them both.

"Pay her anyway," he murmured.

"Jerry?" Kane breathed. "If we pay her, they'll *never* find that
leak!"

"Then leave her on the ground, but pay her," demanded Castle,
"and get us the 146th!"

"Yes, sir," Mike Kane said, and left the trailer.

The man from Maine was staring at him as if he'd sold the Russians a warehouse full of Forest Service gear. "Mac," Jerry asked grimly, "you need something to do?"

The Yankee shook his head and turned back quickly to his desk.

The Down Easter might be an expert on economical fire suppression, but he didn't know the problem of suppressing Snaproll Suzy.

If he stayed on this fire, he'd damn well soon find out.

Bull Durham, California Department of Forestry, supervisor of Inmate Crew ⅔3, La Mirada, squatted in darkness on a knoll which rose like a displaced vertebra on the spine of Camuesa Peak. His attention, as always, was on the fire cresting the hills to the west. But he was very conscious, too, of his crew, working toward him from below.

He'd had Cubehead, his bus driver, dump him and the crew before dusk and return to the Lower Oso Ranger Station spike camp. There, the other La Mirada crews were resting, along with the California Department of Corrections officer, who was unarmed like Bull, but was nominally responsible for their security.

Bull had been reading disaster in the rosy glow of fires ringing the Redrock Basin, knowing that if they didn't complete their firebreak by dawn the whole spike camp would go up when the winds shifted. He'd rather be fighting than waiting for it to happen.

So he had suited them up again and pushed out far ahead. He knew only roughly where he was. His crew was still cutting forty yards of trail an hour, down from the eighty they had slashed when fresh, but still better than the other crews, thanks to his wisdom in setting Booster, as number two hook, on the heels of Mother, his lead.

Now, far below, he could hear the clang of Mother's brush hook, see the flash of the lantern mounted miner-fashion on his hard hat. And occasionally, listening keenly, he heard Dumptruck, his drag shovel, bitching in the rear. As always, it gave him a fix on the tail of the column.

It was unbearably hot even on the ridge, wearing Nomex; below, where the brush hooks sliced and the Pulaskis tugged, it must be 120 degrees. Ominously, he could hear his big black lead hook growling when Booster got too close. "Off my back! Keep the fuckin' dime, honkey, you be singin' soprano, hear?"

And, making Bull wince: "Just you *move*, Mother. OK?"

He'd underestimated Booster's suicidal mouth and his drive for status. Booster was a nebbesh, a simple second-story man who stole to feed his habit; Bull had no doubt that Mother, with bare fists or brush hook, could do a final number on him anytime he cared.

He didn't want Booster sliced in half. He'd better drop him back to drag shovel, to keep him away from the black.

He was about to make the change, when suddenly, out of the night, an immense shape appeared, silhouetted in the glow. It was his swamper Cortez, under a pack as tall as he.

"How about a break?" the Chicano asked, for the others. He himself could go on forever, like some sort of Mexican Sherpa.

Bull cupped his ear. "Say again?" He liked even Cortez to underestimate his hearing.

"*Break,* man?" blared the foreman, pantomiming a sleeping head.

Bull arose, tested the wind against his face. He smelled salt from the ocean. The wind would shift within the hour, driving the fire upon them: he felt it in his bones. He wanted the crew safe behind their fire line when it did.

"No," he told Cortez. "All the way to the peak first, tell 'em. Then double back. *Then* the break."

Cortez oozed back into the night. In a moment, Bull heard the news hit the line below, bursting to a splatter of angry English, Spanish, and ghetto-black, prison jargon that none of them thought he could hear, or understand if he did.

Sorry, men, all for your own good. He decided not to demote Booster to the rear, not just yet. They'd lose twenty yards an hour when he did, and the flames would not wait.

He could only hope that, in the meanwhile, Mother didn't turn on the thief and carve him into chunks.

He'd keep them cutting. To lose an inmate to an escape, or murder, was merely inconvenient.

To lose one to fire would be unforgivable.

He was after all a forester, not a screw.

Shawn parked the plainclothes car in his driveway and got out, sniffing. The gale from the northeast was straining their eucalyptus again, and the faint smell of smoke disquieted him. He saw his neighbor, a boozy painting contractor, spraying his roof with water, stealing pressure from those who needed it higher in the foothills. Too early, way too early . . .

He opened his door and found Crissy wrapping her paintings in sheets. Her face was frozen and her voice dripped ice. Migraine, still. Damn!

"Well, hello, Shawnito! Where in *hell* have you been?"

"On TV, for openers, which I take it you didn't see—"

"I saw. You were very big at Casa de la Raza. *Everybody* watched you, congratulations. A little John Birchy: Lock 'em up and throw away the key?" She shrugged. "But that was, what, six o'clock? And it's one A.M. tomorrow, now. We wondered it they'd signed you on full time."

"You were super, Daddy, just super," bubbled Mary Lou, glaring at her mother. At 1 A.M. Mary Lou was finally wiping dishes in the dinette, slow-motion, like a Tai Chi devotee in a Shanghai park. "You just simply tore them apart!"

He was glad that Mary Lou was proud, and that he was loved for his moment of stardom, but he had a statement of policy to make about the Big Mac job that he knew would destroy that particular mood; and anyway, his present problem was his wife. He got a beer from the refrigerator, and a handful of crackers from the cupboard. He was starved.

"Crissy," he said, trying to dull the edge to his voice, "Sorry, but I *do* work for the county, right? Like, I'm trying to ID the woman in Trout Canyon."

She ignored the excuse. "Everybody on the block, and I mean everybody, has been wetting down. The Mission Canyon fire's all the way to Mountain Drive! I've been hosing the back yard since I got home, and your grandfather—"

"Where is he?" he asked quickly. Obviously, not in bed in the den: the door was open, and the TV on.

"On the roof, sprinkling."

He glared at her. "At eighty-*three*? In the dark? That's for the birds!"

"For the Rainbirds?" she asked pointedly. "That never got installed? Mañana, mañana . . . Well, mañana's never come."

"Jesus!" He put down his beer and charged to the patio. There he found a ladder braced against the eaves. He climbed it. Don Miguel was silhouetted against the rosy northern sky, balanced on the soggy slope of the roof. He was dribbling the shingles with a trickle from a hose limp as a dead snake. "Come on, Don Miguel," Shawn muttered, scrambling up the shakes. He twisted the nozzle, shutting off the water. "You know better than that! That fire's three miles away!"

"It makes them feel more secure," Don Miguel said. He was shivering, though the wind was warm, for he had managed to soak himself through.

Shawn got a firm grip on his arm and guided him to the ladder. "My g.d. *daughter* ought to be up here instead of you."

"She tried," coughed the old man, as Shawn eased him down the rungs. "She talked as if I were Quixote at the windmill. But suppose she had fallen?"

Shawn sat him in a patio chair, got him a beer, and came back. "You *are* Quixote." He grinned. "You know that, don't you?"

"Your grandmother told you that, I think," Don Miguel murmured, sipping his bottle. "¿No es *verdad?*"

"Maybe. I forget."

"Por favor, do not forget." In the light from the living room window, Shawn saw his green Irish eyes grow distant. The old man was sliding back a half century to the fire at the ranch in the hills to the north. "Your father, he was still very small, I made Rosa leave with him, she was frightened, you know, like Cristina now . . ."

A distant fire engine, trumpeting like an anxious elephant, wound up the canyon roads. Inside the house, Gene Forsell spoke urgently on Channel 3 of flames, ridges threatened, plummeting water pressure, rubberneckers on the streets. TV would be this way for days, if the fire lasted, bulletins piled on bulletins. And left in the ashes when finally it was done, ready for fire seasons to come, would be more stories of those who had lost everything, like Don Miguel.

But people like himself would still mortgage their lives to live in the treacherous hills.

The old man droned on, and Shawn, who had heard it so many times, let his mind drift. He had seen the ruins of Rancho Rojo only once, hunting ground squirrels high in the hills with his father, who had stood for a long while looking at a cobbled fireplace and a chimney stark against the bright blue sky. His dad had said he recalled nothing much but an old balloon tire to swing on, hung from an oak by Don Miguel. They'd searched for the tree, but it was gone.

The hell with it. Shawn came from a line so impractical that he had forgotten to put sprinklers on his own shingled roof in fire country; if the ranch had survived, what difference would it have made? How could he have run a thousand-acre spread?

El Viejo was right. The Anglos would have got it in the end.

The sound of the fire engine faded. Don Miguel drifted back to Eucalyptus Road, over half a century of fire and flood and fiscal grief, from Rancho Rojo high above. "I think I could have saved it, but I thought of Rosa worrying below, and I drove down that road finally with my vaqueros, who wanted to stay and fight, no longer a ranchero, you see, no longer *el patrón* . . . To become a professor . . . No, more a character actor than professor . . . Teaching Anglos about *our* land, which they thought was theirs . . . A thin Leo Carrillo, I was . . ."

He shrugged. "No matter. It *was* theirs, of course, the bank's. And cattle prices dropped: they would have got it anyway in the Crash."

Shawn squeezed the old man's shoulder and went in to Crissy. All the paintings were wrapped and piled near the front door, and she was quietly watching TV, but her face was crinkled in anguish, triggered by something she saw on the screen.

He paused for a moment. The usual Saturday night head-on: a car on Gaviota Pass had just creamed a National Guard truck full of bracero fire fighters from Salinas, bound for the great Trout Canyon fire. He wondered which of the drivers had been drunk, GI or civilian. This time of night, possibly, both.

In the background he saw Curt Blossom's unmarked, anonymous coroner's van. Thank God his Ghoul Squad days were done.

If he ever got off the shit list himself, he'd rescue Curt before it was too late.

He massaged Crissy's neck for a moment, then headed up to bed.

His fingers had felt good on her shoulders, but he was gone before she could truly relax. So she stayed at the tube. She saw sheeted bodies on the highway, covered litters borne away. There were campesinos everywhere, most of them dead, but of course the GI driver had survived.

Standard. Trucks were forever spilling flesh onto the highways and lettuce fields of Santa Barbara County. It was always the poor damn Mexicans riding in back who paid.

She sat staring at the TV screen, reluctant to test her headache on the stairs. Why hadn't he stayed a moment longer? He spent more time nowadays talking with his grandfather and his daughter than with her.

Tears welled up. She'd sold one of her watercolors today at the bazaar: wildfowl thrashing aloft on a steely morning from the Clark Bird Refuge. It was a painting that no one but she and Shawn had really liked, and now it was gone, and she had only the seventy-five dollars, and nobody knew about it because Shawn hadn't asked and she was too proud to bring it up herself.

Her art classes were making her a stranger to her own family, and she didn't know why. She was becoming ignorant of the currents at home. The football Shawn had given Mary Lou was a mystery to her. She'd never seen it around the house. So where had he got it, and why hadn't he offered it to her, first? She wouldn't have kept it, but it would be nice to say: "Very sweet, but let's give it to Mary Lou, she'll wear it more than me." I? Me? She could never remember.

Where had he *found* the dumb thing, anyway?

Nicole? Something there, from their past together?

Impossible. He was too loyal to Brink. And to herself, she was sure.

But he'd said they went to her bank together, to get some papers.

If she'd found the football in her vault, a lost memento, and returned it, as a symbol that all that was past, he'd have taken it, she guessed.

Phony, Anglo bitch. Always acting, always on . . .

Now the migraine was truly roaring up the tracks, a locomotive rushing from the night. She got up and tiptoed to the TV, stiff-necked, cushioning her gait to protect her head. Don Miguel wandered in from the patio. She hadn't made up his couch, and now she did it, in a sea of throbbing pain. He thanked her, graciously, but made no move to help.

She climbed the stairs carefully. Shawn was already asleep. She looked down at his broad tanned face, sunlines at the corners of his eyes. If she'd wanted to paint pure, uncomplicated honesty, it lay on the pillow before her.

She went warm inside. He was safe from Nicole. She began to get undressed. She still had, essentially, her Fiesta queen build, curved where Nicole's was angular, but still not yet fleshy. She had nothing to fear but fear, which could drive him off.

She thought that tonight, despite migraine and fire, she just might sleep.

She had been teaching perspective all day.

She had better keep her own.

Nine

Hash Ono sat with the door of his scout car open, parked high in the foothills on Stanwood Drive. The orange sun, faint with haze from the Mission Valley fire, squinted over Montecito Peak.

He was commanding officer and 50 per cent of the personnel of Santa Barbara County's first combined air–ground arson investigation, and he had not the slightest hope of its success.

Friday, miraculously, his phantom firebug had jogged his way past an Operation Torchy team not far from here, unsuspected until a fire had been spotted afterward, but then remembered and turned into flesh and blood.

Now Hash tightened the laces on his new Etonic running shoes. They seemed fine on his feet. The kid in the running shop had begged him to break them in gently, but there was no time for that. He'd invested in yellow nylon running shorts, too, but drawn the line at a $37.95 warm-up suit. The county would never reimburse him for any of it, so he'd worn his Ventura College football parka, tight over his belly, provoking giggles from Riko, his wife.

His radio howled and growled on the Operation Torchy channel, and through the static he recognized Shawn Ortega's voice. "Mary Two from Mary One. You positioned, friendo?"

"Affirmative, Mary One. Just suiting up."

Shawn, on time and on station, was presumably circling Sheffield Reservoir in what he'd described as a "Yellow Peril" biplane, a World War II trainer. Hash peered in the general direction. He could see nothing through the brassy haze, but he thought he could hear the drone of an engine.

He was surprised. He'd never really expected the lieutenant to show for the crazy operation, at least this early on a Sunday morning, and, since he was part Latino, certainly not on time.

Last night he'd seen Shawn on TV. Until then, Hash had almost forgotten that he had a police colleague. Reminded, he'd phoned Shawn late, probably waking him up, and told him of his plans for this morning, feeling like an amateur detective. Shawn being a runner, would he care to pull on a pair of jogging shoes and take to the trails?

Ortega agreed to help, if they started early enough. He was busy trying to pin down the movements of the woman in the Trout Canyon fire. He'd hinted that she might be a victim of something more unpleasant than her own carelessness, like, confidentially, Murder One.

Maybe, but Hash reserved judgment. Cops and firemen were different breeds. Firemen saw themselves as Galahads, rescuing maidens and thumping cardiac arrests. They seldom mistrusted their fellow man. Cops were always looking for foul play and finding it where there was none.

This he hadn't mentioned. He wanted help, not dialectics, and when Shawn suggested that there was a better plan than for both of them to thrash along the trails looking for his Jolly Jogger at ground level, Hash listened.

Shawn apparently had the use of an airplane belonging to a wealthy friend. It would, he said, be perfect for surveillance: no firebug would suspect a wide-open, garish Stearman that looked as if it belonged in a World War I movie. It was slow but maneuverable, and he'd even tow an advertising banner to complete his camouflage.

Hash thought the scheme idiotic, and said so; on the other hand, Shawn swore that the bush would be so jammed with early morning joggers that the only chance of spotting the shadow runner was from the air. And if they got lucky, the only way to run him down along the hiking trails would be afoot.

There had to be a catch. "What would it cost, Rickenbacker?"

"Plane and gas is Brink Southerland Corporation, on the house. Maybe they can write it off for Community Relations. Me, I'm courtesy of the Sheriff's Department. Not one skoshi yen, Tojo."

"How would we communicate?" He still hadn't liked it.

"Torchy Channel Orange. Open cockpit plane, my walkie-talkie ought to do it."

And so Hash had agreed. His suspect had been identified only as a well-built Caucasian with a moustache, wearing a white T-shirt and green shorts with red shoes. He'd been logged by the Operation Torchy team on Sycamore Canyon only minutes before the Friday morning fire.

According to Shawn, the area Hash was parked in now should be alive with early morning runners. As he tied his shoes, the first of them pounded past the scout car, up a trail that looked very long, and all uphill. Hash peered after him. He was looking for red shoes, an athletic build, green pants, white shirt. This one had green shoes and skinny shoulders. No soap.

Another jogger slapped past, moving fast, and he could hear him gasping fifty feet away. Idiot . . .

He picked up the microphone. "Mary One, from Mary Two. I'm all suited up. Start your sweep."

"Roger. Departing the reservoir, heading east over Stanwood, one thousand feet."

Nothing to do but wait.

The jogger's last blaze, contained and put out by dark, had been set not far from here, exactly where the Sycamore fire had started four years before. It was thus a proven tinderbox, now that the brush had regenerated, and one still without roads or water.

Hash had gone to work on the fire site yesterday, early. Studying char heights and twisted stalks of grass, alligatored twigs and scorched rocks, he'd pinned the source by noon, to an area one foot square.

There, after a quarter hour with a magnifying glass, he'd discerned the burned and fragile outline of a standard, unimaginative device, a piece of evidence rookies were taught to look for in every fire academy in the world. It was simply a full matchbook wrapped around a glowing cigarette; you took a few puffs, tossed it, and were gone.

He'd carefully photographed what was left of the matchbook with his Nikon, from half a dozen angles. Squatting in the warm ashes, squinting in the hot sun, eyes stinging with smoke from Mission Canyon—which was another set, he suspected—he had dusted the device carefully, time after time, with a fine mist of acrylic lacquer from a spray can. Finally he'd lifted it, safe in its shell of varnish, and slipped it into an evidence box labeled with time, date, and location.

All of which would come to nothing if he couldn't find the idiot who'd deliberately tossed it there, into a jumble of bone-dry brush.

But he'd developed, under yesterday's blazing sun, a faint mental profile of the firebug. Whether actually a jogger or not, he was quite distinct from the pyro working the Goleta side of town, who had used gasoline in Ygnacia Canyon and who, he suspected, was insane. The phantom jogger was rational—if you didn't like fire departments.

His fires were always far from firebreaks and hydrants, as if he'd studied the fire maps. Hash had plotted them out, and found them spaced in distance and time so as to cause the maximum strain on city and county forces. The firebug seemed to know something of fire suppression, and to be playing on his knowledge.

He was quite possibly a fireman, ex-fireman, would-be-fireman, or even a fireman's son who heard too much fire talk at home. The fascination of fighting fires could turn easily to the urge to set them. The history of non-commercial arson was heavy with fire fighters who had flipped, angry small-town firemen making sets while they struck for higher wages, sons, even daughters, of firemen, and fire-season crewmen trying to stretch employment through the year.

It was the best-kept secret of the profession, but you always looked first at your own.

"Over Stanwood and El Celito," crackled the mike. There was a note of urgency. "Hey, man, you got me in sight?"

Hash slid from the seat, craned to the west. From the distant haze appeared a gleaming yellow biplane, nose high, crawling toward him out of a sky tinged with brown. It banked ponderously to the left, and now Hash could see a banner streaming behind it: "BOY SCOUT XMAS TREE SALE: At the Fairgrounds Now!"

"Gotcha."

"Try the north El Celito equestrian trail. I got a suspect northbound approaching Stanwood."

Hash dove back into his scout car, started the engine, and peeled out for the intersection. By the time he had reached it, Shawn had made a closer pass at the jogger, discovered him to be running with a little boy. A father-son combination seemed unlikely, but by this time Shawn had spotted another suspect, on a fire trail to the south.

Dutifully, Hash hung up his mike, tore off his parka, left the car and started off at the good solid pace of a collegiate linebacker. In five minutes, with less than half a mile under his Etonics, he had slowed the pace by half. One pallid youth in green shoes had passed him, and a potbellied man in blue ones. He'd been left by red shorts and white, gray striped with red, a ten-year-old kid in yellow, and a broad with a beautiful ass wrapped in orange.

At three quarters of a mile, he was shocked to find Shawn's banner hanging from a tall pine tree: apparently his colleague had got overeager in the chase. There being no debris from an airplane in sight, he'd apparently escaped unscathed. He wondered if he knew he'd lost his camouflage. There was no way to contact him to ask, without returning to the car, so he continued on.

At a mile, a runner overtook him on the grade past Flores Road. Red shoes, green shorts, the T-shirt white as snow.

Clothes-wise, the jogger fit the Phantom's description exactly. But she was a little old lady of fifty or so, and she hoped he'd have a nice day.

If she'd set the hills ablaze in front of his bleeding eyes, there was no way in the world he could have caught her.

The yellow Stearman was somewhere lost in the haze. He could no longer even hear it. He quit and walked back to his scout car.

Shawn Ortega entered the headquarters lobby. He was loose and glowing after the morning's flight, though obviously it had failed and whatever he'd snagged had almost pulled the tail off the plane. He hoped he hadn't got Hash lost in the hills of home.

He grinned at Sergeant Curt Blossom, who was reading a teletype message behind the counter.

"Morning, Curt, your house burn yet?"

Curt shook his head. He seemed exhausted. Shawn frowned into his bloodshot eyes. "You're old before your time. Exercise, will you, or something?"

"When I make lieutenant, *I* can sleep all night," muttered Curt. "Here, this'll bring you down."

He handed Shawn the teletype. It was from the Colorado DMV:

NO RECORD LYNN HOLMSTED REGISTERED OWNER ANY COLORADO VE-
HICLE BUT JOHN HOLMSTED 265 TETON DRIVE DENVER REGISTERED
OWNER RED 68 VW SEDAN LAST SIX DIGITS MATCH YOUR VIN LICENSE
TP4238 NO WARRANTS NO WANTS.

So, that was it. "Shit," breathed Shawn. The girl had died Thursday night. Her father was about to learn of it Sunday morning.
Shawn felt guilty: he should have done better than that, or Curt
should have.

Anyway, it was Curt's job now: the Coroner's Unit handled
notification of next of kin. Shawn handed the message back. "You
going to call him?"

"Hell, no, I'll teletype Denver PD, that's SOP."

"No way," Shawn objected. "Too long already."

"Bullshit!" Curt answered heatedly. He'd been cutting back brush
from his house, high on Mountain Drive, all day yesterday, then
he'd been up all night on the Gaviota Pass mess, and his deputy
Phelps was still at the morgue with the bodies. He didn't have time
to track down a Denver phone number, or the funds to call long distance; it was Denver PD, or nothing. "Or let him find out in the
newspapers."

"OK," Shawn snapped. "I'll phone him myself."

"Good," said Curt quietly. "And all I want out here is her dental
records, *not* her old man. So tell him she's kind of, you know? Well-
done?"

"Beautifully expressed, compadre," murmured Shawn. "You hug
your kid today?"

"Screw you, Shawn." Blossom started toward his office, turned.
"Look, you're up there on *Eucalyptus,* that's pretty high, what makes
you so happy?"

"'Cause we weren't stupid enough to buy on Mountain Drive, I
guess."

He watched the sergeant stalk to his office. Shawn had once seen
him wet-eyed over the body of a lacerated child. No more: too long
in his job, and now Curt had fire nerves, as well. A few days of hot
roaring wind and drifting smoke could shake anyone.

Shawn was sitting at his desk in the Detective Bureau, girding
himself to call Denver, when the light on his phone began to blink.
It was the young man in Isla Vista, begging for hope, so he had to
break the news twice, once to him and again, finally, to her father,

without mentioning his suspicion that the daughter had been murdered. The father didn't believe the call at all, and would doubtless be in Curt's hair all day long, calling again and again for confirmation, instructions, details; he sounded as if he might even fly in, in the flesh, despite Shawn's admonitions.

That would be Curt's problem, not his. He left for the Kentucky Fried Chicken stand to check out the blonde's story with the cook, and perhaps to question the Chicano he'd seen at the pumps.

The fry cook stirred the morning batch of chicken legs. He was sure that the blonde and the manager knew now that the girl was gone forever. He had first sensed it when the blonde arrived at the kitchen late for work. Her face was closed, and though she opened the reefer automatically for something to eat, she shut it without taking anything. She wandered vaguely to the register in front, dragging her pretty ass.

The manager, when he arrived, was very quiet. He sat slumped at his little desk, hiding it with his bulk. He finally sighed and started calling a list of numbers he'd accumulated, of high school kids wanting jobs.

Zimmer guessed that the police had identified the body, had talked to him and told him that the girl wasn't coming back. The blonde confirmed his suspicion when she asked him out of a clear sky whether the two of them hadn't been wrong about which night they'd seen the Chicano pass the girl the money outside the service station john.

He lied and told her no, they hadn't been wrong: it was Thursday, the night she'd disappeared. But it meant that someone—sheriff or Santa Barbara PD—had already ID'd the body in the canyon.

That was too bad. He hadn't given it all that much thought, but he'd somehow hoped that with no plates, and the body burned too badly to trace, it would be weeks before they made her. They'd done it from her engine number, probably.

So the old fart and the blonde, he decided, had been questioned yesterday, on his day off. Some pig had warned them not to mention it. He decided not to bring the subject up. The stupid blonde, reassured about the day of the week, would back him: he wanted to stick around to finger the Chicano, just for laughs.

He wished suddenly that he'd buried the VW license plates some-where, instead of tossing them into the garbage. He carried out the GI can, spilled it into the dumpster in back, sneaked a look inside.

Empty: they'd picked up yesterday, on schedule. Her plates were probably resting in the city dump. Feeling better, he lit a cigarette and walked back to the kitchen door. The morning wind was awakening. Already the sun was hidden by smoke; he imagined his fires swirling through the canyons as they awakened to the breeze. On a morning news flash he'd watched a fireman panting after a close escape—he'd lost an LA county engine in a blowback. He imagined, later today, women and children trapped in their hillside homes. He wished he had another day off.

The bedsheet covering his Harley was flapping. He stooped and tucked it under the rear sprocket. He'd have to cruise around and find another tarp.

Rising, he noticed a Chevy parked between the kitchen and the 76 station. Plainclothes car, he knew instinctively. The driver was watching him. The man got out, tall, broad-shouldered, bouncy. He looked familiar. Jesus, it was the same cop he'd seen last night on TV, with the Shrink and Julian.

Zimmer flicked the cigarette away. Small world, as they said. OK. If they made him, at least the Shrink would never know. He went inside to get ready for the heat.

Ten

Still in his running shoes, but with Levis over his green shorts, the young man with the cavalryman's moustache sauntered across the porch at Derf's. It was jammed with off-shift firemen, most of them in their filthy yellow jackets. Fire gear and hard hats were lying everywhere, and the bar was lined with haggard faces streaked with grime.

Inside, he took his usual barstool. There was a new girl on, and he wondered if she'd buy his put-it-on-my-tab routine, or check with the manager, which would be fatal: he was forty-three bucks into the place already.

"Hi," said the girl brightly.

He rested his elbows on the bar, which raised his shoulders, and pumped his biceps just a shade. He looked deeply into her eyes. "Man, am I glad to be *here*."

"You been on the line?" she asked. She was studying him, smiling.

"Yeah," he lied. "Coors, draft?" She drew him one. "On my tab," he said hurriedly. "It's under Ned Roberts. You new here?"

She nodded, but instead of simply writing a ticket, went to the file. Shit . . . He turned quickly to the man beside him, a Navajo or Modoc or whatever, anyway, obviously brought in from somewhere for the fire. "You working Mission Canyon?"

The man nodded, unenthusiastically. "Yeah. You?"

He shook his head. "Trout. I'm CDF, Riverside. Engineer. Fucking firebugs," he muttered.

"Agh." The Indian shrugged. "Where'd we be without 'em?"

The girl was approaching, apologetically. "Look, Ned, you got cash? I checked your tab, the manager's out, and—"

He dug in his pocket, snapped his fingers. "Damn! Left my wallet in the rig."

"I got it," said the Indian.

The bar phone rang, and the girl picked it up. She looked startled and began to make notes on a paper napkin. "Anyone from C platoon, Hollister Avenue?" she called out. "And A platoon, Storke Road! Plus the Tucson hotshot crew! They want you all at Fire Camp Three!"

There were groans from the bar and the tables began to empty.

The Indian drained his glass and left and the young man sipped his beer. Why should he have to cadge beers from frigging Indians? He'd be as good a fireman as the stupid totem-head, whatever he was.

They'd found the Cold Spring Canyon blaze. He began to wonder what they'd do for troops if they had still another fire. Like, on Juanita Springs Road?

He'd take another jog this afternoon.

Eric Zimmer relaxed in the Colonel's kitchen, sitting on the sink counter, swinging his feet. He'd decided that the lieutenant, compared to the pigs up north, was a piece of cake. "The blonde," said Zimmer easily, "*she* saw it too."

"And you're sure this was *Thursday*, Jake? It's important."

"Yeah, Thursday. Ask her!"

"Oh, I believe you, all right." The lieutenant wrote it down in his notebook, slow and easy, like he didn't spell too good. Last night, on TV, he'd looked pretty sharp, and hard-nosed, too, with all his shit about mandatories for setting fires. In the flesh, he wasn't all that bright.

"So," he said, "the Chicano handed her *what*?"

"Like I said, bread. You know, a bill."

"But, hey, Jake, it must have been dark out there. You could see all this at night?"

"She saw it too," he said, nodding toward the blonde, who was showing the new broad how to stuff the buckets to make them look fuller. "When they light up that big orange seventy-six, you can see."

"All the way across the parking lot . . ." murmured the lieutenant. Not calling him a liar, just thinking.

Zimmer nodded. "I was taking the tarp off my bike, you know. And I—"

"Where's the tarp now? There's a sheet over the bike."

Watch it! "Ripped off. Last night. Goddamn Chicanos."

"OK," said the lieutenant. He seemed to accept it. "Go ahead."

"I was taking the tarp off my bike, and I look over toward the station, she's coming outa the crapper. And then he hands her this bread."

"Why do you suppose he did that?"

He hadn't expected to be asked *why*. He fished his mind for answers.

Because she maybe just sold him head, in the john? Tried to sell me some, once. The lieutenant would think the Chicano wanted more, couldn't pay, killed her in the canyon. Fantastic!

No. The lieutenant was stupid, but he wouldn't believe that.

OK, then, she was dealing! Tried to sell me a bag once. She sold the beanbag a balloon, ripped him, so he wasted her?

Suppose the beanbag didn't shoot and tested clean? Even *this* cop would check that out.

"Why, Jake?" asked the lieutenant again, like he really respected him, and would respect his answer. It was hard not to give one, for kicks, just to head him the right way.

"I'm sorry, sir. I got no idea."

The Shrink would have liked that: *Yes, sir, no, sir, I'll try, sir. Social-adaptive behavior . . .*

"Thanks," said the lieutenant, putting away his book. He asked for an address. Zimmer gave him the phony one on his license, and he left.

Zimmer waited, then wandered to the kitchen door. The lieutenant had pulled up to the gas pumps. He was talking to the fat young Mexican, who began to argue and wave his arms. The old Mexican joined them, after a while, seeming very sad.

Finally the lieutenant patted them both down, the young Chicano got in the car, and the two drove away.

So long, beaner. Lots of luck.

He began to cook up the noon batch of Crispy. He noticed that the new girl, a puffy redhead with a face like a dirt-tire and an ass like a touring Honda, was overfilling a box of Family Thrift. "Watch you don't put in too many thighs."

The Shrink would have told him to split, by now. Well, he'd split when he fucking felt like it. When he did, he'd hit the register, and he just might take the blonde.

Eleven

Shawn sat back in his chair in the barren little interrogation room opposite the Detective Bureau office. The fat Chicano, now over his initial fear and anger, seemed to be calming down. Up to now Shawn had stuck to investigative questions: Where were you born? Heatedly, Oxnard, California, a U.S. citizen. Where'd you go to school, you like your job? Oxnard High, his uncle leased the station, yeah, he liked it, why?

Now it was time to turn accusative, and to advise him of his rights. He flicked on the hidden tape and told the kid that he was entitled to counsel, counsel would be provided if he couldn't afford it—

"Public Defender? No way, man! I didn't do nothing, what do I want—?"

"OK. And any answers here can and will be used against you, and you need not answer any question which will incriminate you . . ."

"I don't think I even got to *stay* here."

He was right. Shawn wouldn't dare arrest him, and without arresting him, he couldn't hold him against his will. "No, you don't. But if you do, you'll save us both a lot of trouble."

"Save *you* trouble, not me." The Chicano sighed, studied his fingers, looked up, resigned but watchful. "Shit, go ahead. What do you want to know?"

Shawn asked him if he knew Lynn Holmsted: no. He described

her, and her job: yes. He asked him if he'd ever talked to her: yes. Where?

"Colonel Sanders. I buy that chicken two, three times a week."

"You bought it last, when?"

He thought back. "Wednesday. Wednesday night, the night the Santa Ana got bad, I spilled it all over the counter."

"And when'd you see her last?"

"That night. No, the *next* night. Thursday. Hey, what's comin' down?"

"She's . . . missing." He watched the Chicano, saw nothing in his eyes but shock. "Where'd you see her *Thursday?*" he continued.

"Heading for her car."

"You speak to her?"

"No. Not Thursday."

"When?"

"Well, like I say, *Wednesday*. I spilled my chicken. We picked it up. I didn't have enough cash, dollar short. She said, OK, pay them later. I paid her back when they closed."

"Where?"

"Outside our john. She used our crapper. Come in for the key, I said it wasn't locked. I tapped our register, paid her back the dollar when she come out. And she drove away."

"Anybody *see* you pay her?"

"My uncle, maybe. It's, like I say, his station. And maybe that blond chick, too, waiting for her ride."

"She saw you, all right. But she says that was Thursday. The night she disappeared."

The Chicano shook his head. "She's full of it! Wednesday."

"The fry cook? He see you?"

"Ask him." He shrugged.

"I did. And *he* says it was Thursday."

"He's full of shit, too."

"Your uncle see her leaving Thursday, too?"

"He don't come down Thursday. I was all alone."

"Anybody in her car Thursday? Anybody standing around? Any commotion?"

"Didn't see nobody, didn't hear nothing."

Truth rang from every word. Hands steady, eyes steady too: you could often tell when a person lied by his eyes: right-handed men looked left. He'd check it out with the uncle, but he was damned if he'd try to hold the kid. The blonde was stupid and the fry cook he didn't trust anyway. They simply had the day wrong: mutual hypnosis, or something. Every day was the same, probably, if you worked in a KFC stand. He flicked off the tape and called for a patrol car to take the kid back to his station. "Sorry. Had to check, you know?" He stepped with the kid to the corridor. "That Harley the fry cook rides?" Shawn asked. "Was it parked there Thursday night?"

"Nothing but her car and a pickup."

"You ever see the pickup before?"

The kid shook his head. He thought it was black, couldn't remember the year or make: "Dodge, maybe, Ford . . . That all?"

Shawn nodded. The Chicano said quietly: "Now, *I* got a question, man."

"Sí, señor." Shawn smiled.

"'Sí,'" repeated the Chicano, coldly. "That's 'yes'? That means I can *ask* it?"

The fat face was frozen. The eyes, which had been cheerful and amused in the gas station, were icy now. Shawn hated this part of his job, but he had found no way to shake down a man, take him from his work, and interrogate him without earning his dislike for life. There was nothing you could do but take it.

"Go on," Shawn said impassively. "Ask."

"OK. You know, I never been picked up, for nothing, before. Oh, maybe boostin' a pack cigarettes, when I was small. Tell me, you *got* to pat a guy down before you put him in your car?"

"Only if I want to keep going home to my wife and kid."

"Yeah. Suppose I'm one of them *Anglos* pumpin' at the Exxon? You gonna shake me then?"

"Sure." Their eyes locked, and Shawn found it impossible to hold his gaze. "Well, it depends," muttered Shawn. "How can I answer *that*?"

"Hey, your name's Ortega, man," murmured the Chicano. "Try answerin' it in Spanish."

Shawn watched the kid waddle down the corridor and went back to his desk. He was writing a report on the morning's work when

Curt Blossom came in, bearing two cups of coffee from the Silex in the Ghoul Squad's office. He apologized to Shawn for being jumpy earlier: the wind, and no sleep. He sipped his cup, regarding Shawn speculatively. "Look, I got a piece of news might shake you a little. I just this minute figured something out."

"That shakes me, all by itself." Unfunny. No day for fun and games.

"That crash last night, on Gaviota Pass?"

Shawn told him that he'd seen the coroner's van responding, on late news. Curt described the scene: half the private ambulances in Santa Barbara County, nine bodies. Curt had found enough in the Pinto passenger's wallet to ID him. The driver held a twelve-hour pass out of Atascadero State Hospital for the Criminally Insane. Shawn chilled, sensing what was coming.

"Oh, *no*," he groaned softly.

"Oh, *yes*. I heard about your show. Well, not too many of your fellow entertainers made it home."

Shawn couldn't believe it. His hand began to tremble. He put down his cup. He'd been sitting in front of the cameras with them and now they were dead. Upstaged the shrink, then watched him driven from the parking lot into oblivion? Cursed the bug—Julian somebody—for marring the hood of his car, as he'd pulled away into eternity?

"What happened?" he asked hoarsely.

Curt had had it figured as a straight highway accident until just now, when Phelps had brought something in. "Are you ready for this?" He tossed the twisted, dimpled slug from a .45 onto the desk.

Shawn picked it up. His hand was still shaking. "Where was this?"

"In the kid's left temporal lobe," announced Curt. "Blew his fucking head apart. We thought his skull hit the wheel. This changes my thinking."

"I *guess*," agreed Shawn.

Curt was smiling mirthlessly. "You're the senior officer around here today. My question is this—"

"My question is," Shawn interrupted, "who's handling the 'accident'? Us?"

"Highway Patrol." Curt took back the slug, scratched a tiny X on it for courtroom identification, finally slipped it into a cardboard box labeled with the date and filled with cotton. "Who takes homicides now?"

Shawn thought for a moment. He'd gone as far as he could on the Trout Canyon murder, would have to give it up anyway, so there was no justification for taking on another one, without even arson involved.

"Well, Perkapek, I guess. Crimes Against Persons: there's no more Homicide."

"It's Sunday," Curt pointed out.

Shawn knew what he meant. Perkapek crewed on the sheriff's sailboat every weekend, either to brown-nose the boss or from genuine love of the sea. Unless the fires had kept Castillo in town, the two of them were swilling beer in some cove on Santa Cruz Island, probably plotting how best to rid the department of Shawn Ortega.

Well, Gaviota Pass wouldn't be solved in a day or a week. Or ever, possibly.

"I guess you can wait until tomorrow," he said reluctantly.

"Car *burned*," Curt informed him innocently.

Shawn sat up. "That's not arson," he pointed out. "Pinto, right? Pintos always burn."

"*Truck* didn't burn," Curt said thoughtfully.

"Truck was lucky, maybe. It was probably just your normal, heavy-duty highway fire, there's no use crapping ourselves. Look, when two hypotheses conflict, you choose the *simpler*."

"That's from Don Miguel," muttered Curt. "Without him, you'd be just another cholo pickin' lettuce. Anyway, this doesn't interest you at all?"

"No."

Blossom moved to the bulletin board, and studied the notices for a moment. Shawn could practically hear the turning of his cogs and wheels. "What?" Shawn said finally. "What's on your mind, asshole?"

Curt returned to the desk. "I saw the GI driver up there. He was still in shock. He thinks he saw a rubbernecker standing around, just watching."

"They always crawl out of the woodwork," Shawn shrugged. "You know that!"

Curt's eyes met his. "Sure."

"But *this* guy," Shawn murmured, "didn't try to pull him out?"

"Didn't make a move."

Shawn contemplated him. "You're pushing me. Why?"

Curt shrugged. "Like to see somebody find the son of a bitch that'd light off a wreck on the highway. Or maybe just bored, I don't know." He colored. "Shit," he said finally. "You're the only asshole from sergeant up with a brain cell working, maybe I like to watch you. Aw, skip it."

"Where's the GI now?"

"Base hospital, Vandenberg."

Shawn's heart began to race. "On second thought . . ."

"Bring the reports to you?"

Shawn nodded. "Just for curiosity."

Curt left. Shawn called the watch officer and asked him to get a rap sheet from the California Bureau of Investigation, on one Eric Zimmer, arsonist, ex-con, paroled patient of Atascadero State Hospital for the Criminally Insane.

A long shot, but the first obvious move: If Zimmer, whoever he was, had been in the area and seen the TV show, he might have struck, out of anger, like a bushwhacking rattler. The second move? He thought for a moment. He called County Fire, got a number for Hashimoto Ono, in Carpinteria. Hash was in bed after the morning's jog. His wife went to get him. When he came on the phone, his voice seemed wrenched from some private well of agony. "Hello?"

"How's the bod, Paavo Nurmi?"

"Hey, you woke me up to ask? I thought you crashed that airplane. I was tired, or I woulda reported it."

"You ever hear of a guy named Zimmer? Arsonist? Psycho?"

There was a long and pregnant silence. "Is *that* the 'Eric' they meant? On TV?"

"So you've heard of him, I take it?"

"Every fire marshal in California's heard of him." His voice rose incredulously. "They let *Zimmer* out?"

"Apparently."

"They ought to be shot!"

Shawn told him about the "accident" on Gaviota Pass.

"My *God!*"

Shawn spoke of the mysterious figure watching the blazing Pinto. "Sound like *Zimmer?* Assuming he caught that show?"

"Well, his MO used to be gasoline— Oh, Jesus!"

"What?"

"Ygnacia Creek *was* gas, I think."

"You ever met this dude?" Shawn asked him.

"Hell no. I've only met three convicted pyros in fifteen years!"

So Hash would be no help for a description. Shawn hoped aloud that he hadn't ruined his nap, and asked him if they were jogging again tomorrow morning.

"Screw you, buster," growled Hash, and hung up.

Twelve

Robert Wendell Holmes sat in the weather van on San Marcos Pass, hypnotized by the computer terminal's screen. He was trying to read the mind of the giant Wallops Island computer before its mind was made up.

He felt all at once alone and very young. There were only three or four drainage wind specialists throughout the world who would comprehend the danger he saw unfolding: Hans Grossman, a kind of meteorological Freud under whom he'd studied at Berne, an Algerian professor named Messali Abbas, and Petar Pavelić, director of Yugoslavian bora-wind research in Belgrade.

He was eavesdropping on inputs speeding from electronic fingers probing soils he had never seen, on data from lonely weathercocks sniffing tundra winds and desert breezes, on bits of information flung from satellites locked in space flight high above the earth. He felt like an Athenian emissary sent to the Delphic oracle, urging her to hurry.

What he saw, he processed in his own mind, painfully, reluctantly, but in a kind of horror-stricken fascination. He read of arctic temperatures and upper-air flow, dew-point spreads on mountain peaks that had seen no men in months, pressures dropping and soaring again, maritime masses and polar intrusions, isobars and gradients.

And all of the symbols dancing across the screen before him were evil. The cathode ray tube shrieked with a silent message: another lake of chilled, heavy air was forming this moment over the Great Basin, squeezed dry of moisture by the last northern front, implacable, destined to escape through the bottom of the great mountain womb, over the passes of Southern California.

There would be hot, searing gales tomorrow and the next day: the weight of the air gathering now would make all that they had suffered so far look like a balmy desert breeze.

The LA fire-weather forecaster entered the van, chewing at a huge Dagwood sandwich. "Take a break, Bobby-boy, you *glued* to that thing?"

"Take a look," begged Holmes. Everybody thought he was crazy, in his preoccupation with raw data, when all you really had to do was wait for the mapped fire-weather forecast from Wallops. "Because," he said slowly, "we are going to have winds through these canyons the likes of which, in living memory, mortal man has never seen. I will guarantee it."

The LA man wandered over and stood behind him, chewing meditatively. "I don't see it that way, I don't know how you integrate all that, anyway," he said finally. The implication being, thought Holmes, that I don't—I'm faking it.

"Just unlucky, I guess," he muttered. If a *meteorologist* was skeptical of his fears, how would the fire boss react? He had better wait a few more moments before panicking everyone, until the model for tomorrow spewed from the printer, giving him more authority.

He left his seat and pushed the door open against the wind. Smoke was pouring over the pass. He knew that the fire was still eight miles away, but he could feel the heat. The fire camp was almost deserted: most fire-fighting equipment had been sent down to the other side of the ridge, and the field kitchen was in hiatus. He saw a fire fighter led from a jeep to the aid trailer: there seemed nothing wrong physically with the man, though his face was black with grime, but he was weeping. Combat fatigue—probably not the first case on this fire, certainly not the last. The winds were still merely toying with them. Tomorrow would be different, and the day after, indescribable.

His sinuses ached, and he was very jumpy, though he'd cut himself off from coffee at 10 A.M. That had not helped. Somewhere, he knew, deep in man's ancient brainstem, lay a sensor which reacted to ionized air, setting him squirming to be free of it. It was working full time now, more sensitive to the Santa Ana than the computer was.

He was very tired, finding it difficult to concentrate, and he knew that everyone else was too. If it affected Jerry Castle, in the next van, it could be serious. There were decisions that Castle would have to make in the next few minutes that were staggering.

For Holmes was no longer worried primarily about the five thousand men on the northern slopes of the Santa Ynez Range, or even, specifically, about the girl he had met in the field kitchen. They would lose, lose big, lose tonight, but they were pros, and would simply retreat and gather to fight again.

Now his fears were for the city. He wondered what kind of civil disaster program it had. It had tried, after decades of loss, to *prevent* brush fires, as in the last few days, though that was of course impossible. He had read its publications and knew its codes and acronyms: Operation Torchy, Red Flag Alert, "Firescope," a scheme hatched in Riverside which was supposed to co-ordinate everything in Southern California and eradicate the chaos of previous fires.

But it would take more than names piled on names, more than helijumpers, hotshot crews, planes which could carry fire engines but never did, tankers, and infrared eyes in the sky, to stem the fires he envisioned pouring over the mountain passes in the next few days.

A cheerful electronic beep told him that tomorrow's 9 A.M. Firemod map was through the print-out, ready and waiting. He returned, drew it forth with dread.

"Oh, God," he murmured. Dumbly, he passed the map to the LA man, who stared at it unbelievingly.

"Get a confirmation," the man from LA murmured. "There's something wrong."

But Robert Wendell Holmes had grabbed the sheet, swept through the door, and was stumbling through the smoke to the command van.

For the third time in three days Shawn Ortega walked down Old Trout Canyon Road. The crews cold-trailing Thursday's fire were long gone, presumably on the other side of the range, fighting for land to the northeast on the borders of suburban Santa Barbara.

But the smoke was still there, and the ashes, and the twisted, heat-wizened oaks, their agonized limbs upthrust. He wondered how long it would take before the arroyo grew green again. A hawk wheeled above him, riding the Santa Ana, and slowly dissolved into the yellow sky. The sun was a brown blob hanging above the western rim of the gulch. He was depressed and very tired.

He wished he had brought water. The dry, smoky air made his mouth taste sour. He began to sneeze. His head ached. He thought of Crissy, alone in her shell of agony; her migraines seemed to last forever.

Frustration, maybe? Hell, he hadn't touched her in a week, longer than that. Ever since Brink had laid the burden on him, he'd been too shaken for sex.

He forced his attention back to the blackened ditch on the right of the cluttered road. He was looking for the heavy military-type green tarpaulin that he'd seen while he and the highway patrolmen were returning from their search for the missing plates. Friday? Only two days ago. It seemed like a week, or a month . . .

He reached the scene of the so-called accident, which he recognized from the hillock and the earthy gray slash where the car had hit. There was shattered glass strewn at the point of impact, and the twisted carcass of the right door, left when the chopper had plucked away the rest of the car. A bright Pepsi can shone in the sun, left by the search and rescue team, and that was all.

He started back down the road. The wind at his back arose, and the smoke became thicker. He was sorry he'd come; the whole walk up the road had depressed him, as if he were returning to a battlefield. He remembered the voice of the girl's father on the phone, querulous, argumentative, on the verge of tears.

He thought of Mary Lou's plea to work, like Holmsted's daughter, in a fast-food chain, serving pushers and nuts, deviates and flashers, murderers, psychos, hotshot young wetbacks, braceros, high school jocks trying to score. No way, ML . . . No way.

Which was something he'd have to get across to her shortly, and hadn't found the time to, yet. Or the guts.

Suddenly he spotted something in the ditch. He stopped, moved over, inspected it.

It was the tarp, hauled back off the road by someone, probably the coldspotting crew, and left. It was badly scorched in spots, even burned in places, but protected in other areas by its own folds, so that much of it was hardly charred at all.

He left it where it was and traced its path from where the crew had dragged it. He found the spot, on a level plot a few feet from the ditch.

Level enough to have parked a bike . . . And three days ago, doubtless heavy with cover.

He looked for tracks but found none. He returned to the tarp and picked it up, handling it away from his body, to save his clothes from the cinders and grease and oil he found everywhere on it. There were grommets along its edges, to tie it down, and a few scraps of line left threaded through it. There were creases along one end. The marks of handlebars? He couldn't be sure.

Very carefully he dug a hole in the ashes and planted a charred oak limb in it. Then he wrote the date and the time on a slip of paper, signed it, and buried it, safe from wind, adjacent to the stake.

Finally, he folded the tarp and started the long trek up to San Marcos Pass Highway, and his car.

Shawn sat at his desk facing the dough-faced manager of the Kentucky Fried Chicken stand, shuffling the time cards the manager had brought. He'd called him to headquarters and the man had arrived within minutes, flushed and scared. Shawn told him that he believed the Chicano when the young man said he'd returned a dollar to the victim on Wednesday, not Thursday: why would both his employees be wrong?

"Well, the blonde doesn't know what *month* it is, Lieutenant. She just knows Christmas is coming."

Shawn pointed out that between the two of them, they practically hung the Chicano.

"Well, that cook, maybe he just doesn't like Mexicans."

Well, Shawn didn't like Klinger, either.

Shawn had a lot to do. He thanked the manager, kept the time cards and personnel records, and warned him to say nothing of his visit. The manager left, and Shawn went to the watch officer to see if the rap sheet on Zimmer had arrived. He wanted to take Zimmer's picture to Vandenberg Air Force Base, where the truck driver of the Gaviota Pass vehicle was in the base hospital.

The rap sheet hadn't come in. All right, he'd check out the home address that the fry cook had given him.

He was leaving his desk when the phone rang. It was the dispatcher, with an incoming call from Operation Torchy. "Can't take it," said Shawn. "Just left."

"It's the DA!"

Shawn groaned but took the call. He'd never met George Kelso, but he sounded on the phone like a tense and unhappy man. He'd been unable to reach the sheriff, who he therefore assumed was out sailing, *literally* at sea today, rather than *figuratively*, as on weekdays. He let that sink in for a moment and said he needed a Sheriff's Department representative at Operation Torchy headquarters for a meeting, and he needed him now.

"Meeting? Yes, sir. Can I ask what it's about?"

He knew at once that he'd erred. There was a moment of pregnant silence, and when Kelso spoke again, his voice was vibrating with anger. "Chief *Dubbs* didn't ask that. Of course, he may not be as busy Sundays as you."

Shawn winced. "Rubadub" Dubbs was the Santa Barbara Chief of Police, and he probably *wasn't* as busy, but that was beside the point. The DA pointed out that he'd managed to get the mayor downtown, and the head of the civil defense program. He sounded as if he'd been tuned an octave too high and was ready to break a string. "Now, I obviously can't get the sheriff unless I alert the Coast Guard. But do I maybe get the liaison officer from the Sheriff's Department? Or do I have to promise overtime?"

"No, sir. I'm on my way."

He hung up. The sheriff had predicted that as Operation Torchy liaison, he'd get to know the DA.

Better than he wanted to, no doubt.

Thirteen

Eric Zimmer prodded at the cage full of unsold, simmering legs. The drumstick he had chosen to be the blonde was deep in the basket: he tonged it up. Seared. Too bad, but at least he'd given her a fighting chance.

"OK?" he asked the Shrink. "Like, fate? OK?"

No answer. The Shrink would never answer again. He knew momentary panic, then got hold of himself. Screw him.

He'd conned the new girl into leaving by promising to punch out for her. He'd noticed through the serving window that the blonde had already wiped down the counter, wanting to close the place early, which meant that her mother would be picking her up outside.

He shut down the stove. He selected a five-inch knife from the array in the block above his cutting board. He whetted it meditatively. He heard the blonde, who'd finally learned the register, ring up their last sale, and heard the front door close. He moved to the pass-through window.

She was beginning to count the receipts. This would probably take her ten minutes, and she'd have it wrong, and have to repeat, but tonight it wouldn't matter what they grossed: he was getting it anyway.

He slipped the knife into his apron pocket and drifted through the door to the counter. She glanced up. "Four sixty-four, sixty-five . . ." she mumbled. "Hi."

He smiled, studied the switch box, found the switch labeled "Bucket," and flicked it off. The groaning of the Colonel's bucket on the roof stopped, and the parking lot outside turned dark as its light went out.

She had begun counting again, but she stopped. "Hey, you're early, you know? Four ninety-seven, eight, nine, five hundred."

He moved from the back of the counter to the entrance, locking it. She looked at the clock. "Look," she protested, "it's OK with me, but it's only—"

"We're *closin'* early." He smiled.

"Who says?" she asked nervously. He felt the warmth rise in his loins. He returned swiftly to the swinging door. Now he had her blocked, from kitchen and entrance. He relaxed and began to clean his nails with the knife. "Keep countin'. Then give it to me."

Her mouth sagged and her pink tongue darted to her lower lip, making it glisten. "Are you kidding? Now, look!" she whimpered. "*Please,* OK?"

He jabbed his finger toward the cash drawer. "I want to know! Count the fuckin' money!"

"OK, OK. Five, ten, twenty, thirty—oh, God, please—OK, twenty? Five twenty, twenty-five—"

"Shit!" He slapped her hard, across the face. She went spinning into a heap, like a blond rag doll, and looked up at him, her eyes glazed with shock. A trickle of blood ran down her chin. He stacked the bills, jammed them into his pockets, scooped the silver from the drawer, and motioned her up.

"No!" she whined. "What do you want?"

He smiled down at her, stooped, and whipped the knife past her cheek. She recoiled, moaning. "Please, please, Jake, *please* . . ."

"Jake the Flake. Say it *right.* Jake the *Flake!*"

"I never—"

"You *both* said it. Say it again!"

"Jake . . . the Flake?"

"Get up!" He kicked her ass. It was firm and bouncy. She scrambled to her feet, crying.

"What are you going to *do?*"

"Goin' to put you on that hog, and goin' to ride, ride, ride . . ."

"Where? My mom—"

"Ride, ride, ride," he sang. He shoved her through the kitchen, whipped off his apron, let it fall. He lit a book of matches, tossed them into the big pan on the counter, watched it flare and spread to the greasy towels hanging on the rack above. Knife out, he crowded her to the door, paused at the time clock. He ripped it from the wall, hurled it at the stove.

"Ride, ride, ride," he murmured, darting the knife like a silver tongue by her forehead. He whipped off his chef's cap and sent it sailing toward the stove. "Ride, ride, ride . . ."

She was whimpering again. He opened the door, ceremoniously, waved her through with the knife, jabbed at her left buttock when she hung back. She screamed, and in an instant he had her back inside, arm around her throat, blood-tipped knife to her jugular. "Shut up!"

"What are you going to *do?*" she whispered.

Holding her in the doorway, he looked out across the lot. The Santa Ana was rattling the orange 76 in the gas station: the Chicano was inside; in this wind, he couldn't have heard.

Relax, beanbag, at least *you're* off the hook.

He yanked her out to the Harley, ripped the sheet off the bike, dropped it to thrash its way across the lot. He forced her astride the tank, wrapped his massive arms around her, and poked the engine into life. He saw orange flames inside the kitchen window.

Rocketing down Fairview, he grinned. She felt good there, firm but soft, brown legs and flying hair. She was yelling. He flicked open the manifold cutout and the pipes began to roar, real good sound, drowning out her voice.

She'd be screaming to screw when she knew, begging to fuck him, crying she'd blow his mind if only he'd let her go.

All be wasted on the wind.

Because, baby, tonight or tomorrow, I'm going to fry your pretty ass.

Shawn had absorbed the shock of the model fire-projection map on the conference table. Now he began to study the face of Santa Barbara's Anglo establishment.

Police Chief Dubbs, comfortable belly stretching the youth out of a tennis shirt, had obviously been called off the court, probably from the Santa Barbara Tennis Club. He was complacent, apparently un-worried by the bombshell that had burst before them all.

At the head of the table, the mayor's lined face seemed relaxed, al-though his eyes were alert enough and Shawn had found them assessing him, trying to evaluate the unknown quantity at the meet-ing. OK. The mayor was neither friend nor foe of the Sheriff's De-partment. He was a figurehead, above it all. And he certainly didn't believe that the town would burn.

Alfred Maxson, a retired contractor appointed to head the volun-teer civil defense committee during the bomb shelter days of the six-ties, had already pled lack of funds, denying responsibility if worse came to worst.

The DA's face was tense. Kelso was a handsome man with an acrid smile, a fine conviction record on all but arson, and a mind like a whip. Having run on a promise to bring firebugs to justice, and not having seen the first one apprehended yet, his image was at stake. If the set fires, combined with the Trout Canyon fire, turned the conflagration into urban disaster, he faced ruin. Brink knew him and didn't trust him. Kelso was probably looking for a scapegoat, past and future, and Shawn must be careful what he said.

Shawn glanced at the map again. He'd come in during the middle of a discussion. The DA had spun the map across the table and con-tinued the conversation while Shawn scanned it.

His heart had dropped at the first glance. If the future fire lines, as projected on the map, were right, nothing north of Foothill Road would be safe by tomorrow noon. By tomorrow night his own home would be consumed, along with everything landward of Alameda Padre Serra—APS—and by the following morning the fire would be tearing at downtown Santa Barbara.

He saw instantly why the meeting had been called here at Opera-tion Torchy, rather than at City Hall. If the press got wind of this projection and handled it badly, it could ignite an exodus which would jam the freeway with vehicles trying to escape.

To accept the prediction seemed unthinkable: they would be writ-ing off a thousand, five thousand structures; sentencing forty, fifty thousand Santa Barbareños to homelessness. Ridiculous . . .

"What do *you* think, Lieutenant?" Kelso asked now.

"I'm no expert on fire—"

"We understand that. How about *evacuation?*"

"Jesus, sir, I just *got* here. Could I have a minute?"

Kelso weighed his answer for a moment, nodded, and the discussion swirled around Shawn again. He tried to assess in his mind the department's capabilities to handle catastrophe. It was largely untested. The department had been involved in minor evacuations from the foothills almost every fire season: Coyote Canyon, the Sycamore fire, Box Canyon, all the rest. Bullhorns would squawk from squad cars, LA County choppers would plead from the sky, deputies would lie to homeowners. You had to threaten without authority and bend the truth to save their lives. Horses would neigh, dogs bark, cars crash in the smoke, women curse you. Half the peeps would demand to stay while the others screamed to go.

Bad enough if you lost two hundred homes, as at Sycamore. Multiplied five, ten, twenty-fold, there was no way the Sheriff's Department, on two days' notice, was going to do anything more than open the floodgates with bullhorns and cower in its black-and-white cars.

"Lieutenant?" Kelso prodded. "We have to have an answer."

"If this thing's *right*—" began Shawn.

"It *isn't* right." The mayor smiled. "It can't be right. Hell, Lieutenant, you're an Ortega—Your grandfather's Don Miguel?"

"Yes, sir."

"Taught me California history," recalled the mayor. "So *you* ought to know. We've had the mountains burning behind us for two hundred years. We're still here." He sat back, clasped his hands behind his head, and smiled into Shawn's eyes. "Your great-great-grandfather lit off Mission Canyon himself, a few years back, and damn near won his war. Right?"

Shawn sighed inwardly. The last thing they needed now was an historical anecdote. He imagined that he was supposed to be overwhelmed by the mayor's interest in his family, impressed by his erudition, lulled and softened by friendliness into promising results the department couldn't give. And the mayor, like most Santa Barbara historians, had the facts skewed anyway.

In 1846, during the Mexican War, a 200-man force of Mexican irregulars from Los Angeles had moved against the ten-man U. S. Army detail occupying Santa Barbara. They had chased the Anglos up La Cumbre Peak. Tiring of pursuit as siesta time approached, the *Californianos* had decided simply to torch Mission Canyon, hoping to incinerate the Yankee presence once and for all.

The U.S. troops, under command of a strutting little lieutenant named Talbot, had escaped the flames. Guided by a Tulare Indian, Talbot had climbed, crawled, and slithered over the Santa Ynez Range, later to return from Monterey with Major Frémont, for revenge.

Shawn's great-great-grandfather, José Vicente, wealthiest and most truculent of the local dons, had always taken public credit in Pueblo Viejo for temporarily running Talbot out of town. But family legend knew that the old hidalgo, busy protecting his hacienda from the fire, had avoided the "battle": and even proved his innocence to Frémont's satisfaction, to keep his lands intact.

Shawn pointed out that *that* fire was 135 years ago, when the population was 900, and that if the whole damn village had burned they'd have simply watched it from the beach, slapped together some more adobe, and rebuilt it in a month. "But seventy thousand people trying to get away on U.S. 101? Chaos!"

"We can't *ignore* the fire map, obviously," murmured the mayor. "But we can't panic, either."

"It's crap," scoffed Dubbs. "Soil 'experts,' erosion freaks, weathermen with crystal balls! They all got to justify their cost. Plus, the Santa Ana's got to everybody's head."

"It's a *computer* readout," Shawn reminded him. "They aren't *guessing.*"

"Garbage in, garbage out." Dubbs shrugged. "There's a computer somewhere claimed I owe Master Charge $18,560. Turned out it was $18.56."

"Well," suggested Shawn, "if that's your consensus, there's no evacuation problem."

"Hang on!" said the DA sharply. "I want an input from the Sheriff's Department. What happens, county-wise, if they're *right?*"

"Bullhorns," said Shawn simply. "From our cars. It's all we got. We don't even have our own choppers! And we can't *make* people leave, it's against the law. They'll sue our ass if we force them out and they lose their homes. If there's looting, we've had it, and, Chief, you have too. Just don't count on *us* for anything but bullhorns."

"That doesn't sound very co-operative," muttered the mayor. "Who *do* we count on?"

"Call for the National Guard."

He meant it, seriously, but the mayor chose to treat it as sarcasm. The old man flushed and stood up. "I guess there's nothing more to say. My best to your grandfather, Ortega. Good afternoon, gentlemen."

Dubbs and Maxson followed him out. The DA searched Shawn's face, stood up, moved to the fire index map on the wall, red from one end of the county to the other. "Stupid old bastard. You're right, he ought to call the governor and get off the hook." He turned back. When he smiled, he looked like his campaign poster. "I didn't know you were Don Miguel's grandson."

How did you answer that? "There are a million Ortegas."

The DA sat down, offered a cigarette. Shawn shook his head, folding his copy of the fire map to show to the sheriff, if he ever sailed home again.

"Don't let that map get out," warned the DA.

Shawn shook his head. "No way."

The DA seemed to have all day. Shawn suspected that he'd simply decided to use Castillo as a lazy *cholo* punching bag, accuse him of dereliction of his duty, if the fire took off. Kelso flicked an ash. "Saw you on TV. You're good."

"Thanks." He wanted out: he was hungry, tired, and he had to check out the fry cook's address.

"I liked your ideas on arson sentencing," said Kelso. "I wish you could find us an arsonist."

"The ideas aren't original."

"Last thing you want in politics, originality." The DA stood up, gathering notes. "You going to run for sheriff some day?"

"I haven't even made captain. My political base is zero."

"You don't have to make captain, and it sure as hell isn't zero." He stuck out his hand. "You decide to file, let me know."

Meaning, *run*, estúpido, and split the Spanish vote. Shawn smiled and shook hands. Kelso wanted McCrae back in as sheriff, and that was all right with Shawn, but Shawn didn't like people trying to use him.

He was glad he hadn't torpedoed poor old Castillo with a bunch of airy promises.

"See you, sir." He nodded at the recorder he'd noticed on entering, grinding away on a bookshelf. "Don't forget to turn that off, Mr. Kelso, you'll run it out of tape."

Fourteen

From an altitude of sixty feet, chomping by moonlight up the bed of the Santa Ynez River, Jerry Castle peered from the chopper's right-hand window. The pilot had skirted a sea of orange flames from Los Prietos, where Luke Tallman's ranger station had been swallowed hours ago. He had threaded and sidestepped along the northern slopes of the Santa Ynez Range, dipping into hellish valleys bright with new fire, skimming blackened hillsides where the fire had been.

Castle had seen faces upturned in the moonlight, and lights, here and there along the lines, but the thousands of fire fighters below were mostly lost in an immense void, and even a trained eye would miss them. It was as if the flames had eaten the whole vast army alive, or chased them away, as if the fire had already won.

As it would, inevitably, unless nature or he tricked it back on itself.

He jerked his thumb upward. The pilot caught the motion, and the chopper reared like a startled horse. In a few seconds they were high above La Cumbre Peak on the skirts of the flames. They were feeling for a change of wind direction, using the helicopter as a probe. If a fire storm was starting naturally below, the pilot should feel its drift as the chopper was sucked into the smoke.

The pilot was concentrating on his controls, shaking his head. And the Santa Ana was easily overcoming whatever reverse effect the rising hot air was having on winds aloft. No backwind, then, all pure Santa Ana, still flowing toward the city and the sea. His options were narrowing to one: to set a backfire between city and flames, causing a fire storm which would suck the Santa Ana away from the city and into itself.

A backfire could conceivably save the city.

Or destroy it.

The chopper bucked suddenly, dipped, then soared as a thermal caught it. The pilot cursed.

He was the best helicopter jockey on the fire line. If *he* was having problems staying aloft, Jerry would have to scrub the mission he'd been planning. His hope had been to set a backfire with a "helitorch," a Bell 206B chopper which dangled a tank dripping burning, jellied gasoline. But in winds like these, he couldn't order helitorch pilots into the cauldron below.

Jerry raised a forefinger and made a circular gesture toward the ocean. The pilot climbed above the ridges separating the city from the inferno to the north.

From 8,000 feet, Jerry could see the lights of Santa Barbara, Montecito, and Goleta, tumbling like spilled diamonds from the dark mountains down to the moonlit sea. The inland slopes were aflame as far as the eye could reach. The Mission Canyon and Rock Spring fires, great orange sores, had metastasized and spread like cancers during the day and were marching toward the fire mass to the north. The picture was clear, clearer than the computerized print-out, or any fire map Holmes could draw.

"Let's go home," he called across the gulf of noise between him and the pilot. He pointed toward San Marcos Pass. "Home!" he yelled again.

He sat scowling in his bouncing seat. So the helitorch was out, a toy too fragile for the flaming facts of life below, piddling tiny dabs of fire on endless hills.

His last hope?

But a fixed-wing, war-tested B-17?

Marvin's Mistress?

Napalm?

In ten minutes he was on the ground, stooping under the thrashing vanes. He trotted from the helipad to the little city of trailers and kitchens and tents that he had caused to grow on the crest. Behind him he heard the chopper take wing again, heading for safety at Santa Barbara Municipal.

He paused at the door of Mike Kane's air control van. He foresaw a battle with his air boss, and decided that it should be held outside, away from eastern and midwest strangers, who might, when they found what he had in mind, actually go over his head to Washington.

He opened the door. "Hey, Mike?"

Mike was standing over one of his controllers. He turned. His cheeks were stubbled and the lines in his face had grown deeper. He unfolded like a long, hinged scarecrow as he ducked from the door into the night.

"Mike, find me some napalm."

Mike stared at him. *"Napalm?"*

"That's what I said."

"No way." He seemed to get even taller in the night. Unauthorized burning agents were forbidden by Forest Service regulations.

"Get it, Mike," Jerry said softly. His eyes rested on the distant glow at the base of the smoke clouds across the valley.

"From where?"

"The military."

"They won't give it to us!"

"Ask!"

"Who? Not the Air Force. Or the Navy. They'd call Boise for authorization. Or even Washington. You know that."

"Find it," Jerry murmured.

"Who'd drop it?"

"I'll think of somebody," Castle said grimly.

Their eyes met. "Oh," murmured Kane. "I see what you mean."

"First, cut 'em off. No more ground pay. Their slurry tank leaks: not a cent more."

"We *can't—*"

"Let 'em hurt, for tonight, while you get the napalm. Give her one day with no flight pay. She'll get him to drop it, or toss him out the bomb bay."

Mike looked down on him. "You play pretty rough."

Well, he'd learned the game in North Africa, before Mike was even born. And he'd never lose another life by betting for the rules.

"Get the napalm," he told Kane. "I'll take it from there."

Bull Durham, marching stolidly along the crest of Camuesa Canyon, peered into the gorge where his men were cutting. He tried to penetrate the darkness and establish their position between Mother's guttural bitching at Booster up front and Dumptruck's grumbling in the rear. An orange glow on the opposite face of the canyon seemed to be growing brighter. He sniffed the wind, letting the hairs on his nose tell him its direction and speed. He did not like what he felt.

"Juan!" he shouted.

His swamper, trudging ahead, materialized silently. Ten minutes ago the Mexican had left the crew below and climbed the ridge, which meant he mistrusted the fire behind the other canyon wall. Bull hadn't sent him back. Juan's fire sense was good, and his eyes younger and better than his own. It was comforting to have him nearby.

He peered at Juan's silhouette. His pack seemed to have grown. "Who you carrying for?"

"Dumptruck."

The alcoholic drag shovel, malingering as usual, must have pled exhaustion. Well, that was Juan's problem, not his. He nodded toward the opposite ridge. "What you think, swamper?"

"No es bueno."

Bull left Juan and climbed to a knoll. Along the opposite ridge, clumps of brush were spontaneously busting into flame as if the ridge were under artillery barrage. A huge fireball charged over the ridgeline on a gust of wind and bounced into the canyon, leaving a swath of flame. Trees on the horizon began to blaze from the tops down. Crown fire!

"Spillover!" he yelled down to Juan. "It's crowning! Tell 'em to split for up here!"

He raced back to the swamper. Juan was already shouting into the radio. Below, Mother would be getting the word, hopefully passing it down the line. Bull glanced at the canyon again. Too late . . .

He grabbed the radio from his swamper. "Mother! Cancel that! *Hit the tents!*"

Too steep, uphill, to outrace the flames. They'd have to weather the fire storm, if they could, below, under their fire shelters, pup tents carried in each pack, made of fiberglass and aluminum foil, with straps and ropes attached to keep them over their prone bodies if flames made a typhoon above.

Flimsy protection, and men had died trusting to them, but better than nothing at all.

Shelter tents? Jesus, *Dumptruck's* shelter must be in his pack!

Suddenly Bull was tearing at the gear Juan had dropped to the ground. He ripped it apart, found Dumptruck's tent, and charged blindly downhill to the tail of his column. He passed Mother, struggling on the ground to cover himself, and Booster, already down and quiet, and a shrouded line of prone men cursing in Spanish.

The heat, when he met it, was like a wall. His Nomex suit was good for ten seconds, no more, but he penetrated the barrier screaming for Dumptruck. His own shelter was still stuffed into his pack; OK, they'd share Dumptruck's, huddle together . . .

"Dumptruck! Dumptruck!"

He heard thrashing in the brush on the slope. The damn fool was trying to outrun the flashfire.

"Come back! *I got it!*"

The heat manhandled him to the ground. He clutched the folds of the shelter to himself, no time to find the straps, and all at once he was groveling into the earth like an infantryman caught in cross fire, breath sucked from his lungs, no air, no air at all, a hurricane trying to overturn him like a cockroach in a gale.

Fighting to stay belly-down, he hung onto the flapping fabric, winding it around himself. The sound rose. A locomotive was racing toward him. The gale whipped free a corner of the shelter; air, air, he needed air . . .

He was sobbing and gulping and crying, now. No more time to fool with the straps, the eye of the storm was coming, he heard it bellow from the canyon bottom. A flaming bush slammed his back, hurtled onward. He hung on, and finally it was past.

Smoke, then, blinding smoke, but he was used to smoke and only pressed his cheek closer to the calming earth, and breathed slowly . . .

For a long while he lay gasping. Finally he shed the shelter and crawled to his knees. The fire storm had passed, and he was in a moonscape of blackened limbs and torn bushes. He could hear his crew above, arising from the dead.

All but Dumptruck. Painfully, with blistered ankles and a singed calf, Bull hobbled up the side of the canyon to where he'd heard the crashing brush.

The smell told him more than his eyes in the orange light. The body was twisted and blackened, huddled into the fetal position and very, very small. He heard someone coming and turned. Mother, a towering shape in the darkness, stared down at his mate.

"Dumb fuck," said Mother.

"Yeah. Your radio work?"

"Plastic melted."

"Didn't hear you," said Bull, cupping his ear.

"Fuckin' *plastic* melted!" shouted Mother.

"Climb up and tell Swamper to call base camp. Stay in the black, this blowup maybe ain't dead yet. I'll wait for a chopper, jeep, whatever."

He moved a few feet upwind of Dumptruck's body and squatted. He lit a cigarette and studied the twisted corpse.

Chalk up one for the fire.

Not much of a man, Dumptruck, but the first he'd ever lost.

Zimmer, chewing a Hostess Twinkie, scowled across the house trailer at the blonde.

She crouched at the head of his bed on the torn mattress, where she'd hurtled when he slammed her through the door. She'd hardly moved since, and it irritated him, as if one of the cats he'd tail-torched when he was a kid had simply sat down on its flaming ass and let it burn.

Cata . . . Cata-something, she was. Hey, Shrink?

No more Shrink. He found himself studying her.

Catatonic!

"Hey," he told her, "you're fucking catatonic. You know?"

She didn't answer, only sat there, blue eyes wide and glistening. Stupid cunt. Screw her. He had things to do. If the fire in the Colonel's kitchen had caught, and they'd already knocked it down, they'd have discovered the money was missing. The blonde's old lady would be screaming fit to tie, and he had to be gone, trailer, truck, and bike, by the time the heat came down.

He took his .45 from the cupboard, checked it, pointed it at her. "Blam!" he muttered. "You know?"

She didn't seem to understand, so he slapped her once across the face, which anyway made her blink and cover her eyes. He hurled her to the floor, lashed her wrists to the sink drainpipe with a motorcycle bungee.

"One squawk," he warned. "Just one, you know?"

He stepped outside, leaving her huddled on the floor, yanked out the electric cord that connected his trailer to the fuse box on the Mexican's house, checked the trailer's tires in the light of the streetlamp, which was snapping and buzzing from electricity in the hot, dry wind. He climbed to the roof, yanked his TV antenna down and threw it onto a heap of hubcaps he'd ripped off. Let the greaser's kids sell them . . .

He started the Harley, keeping the throttle low, and gentled it up the ramp to the bed of the pickup truck. He turned the fuel cutoff valve and laid the bike down gently, so it wouldn't show, quietly closed the pickup's tailgate.

He siphoned some gasoline from the low-rider Chevy owned by his landlord's eldest son, into a five-gallon can, which he placed next to the rear wheel of his Harley in the bed of the truck. That should light off half Gibraltar Canyon, and if this wind kept up, set everything afire from Gibraltar Reservoir to Westmont College campus. Plus the trailer and the blonde . . .

He backed the pickup truck over the trailer hitch, heaved mightily at the tow bar, and connected truck to trailer. He climbed into the pickup, eased through the junk in the back yard and onto the driveway. He left the headlights off until he was well onto the street: he owed the Mexican five months' rent for trailer space and didn't want to wake him up.

Once on the street, he poured on the coal, peeling rubber to wake the greasers up and, if the blonde was fighting her bonds, to spill her on her ass.

Swaying onto the freeway, heading east toward gold plate canyon country, he tried to steady the fishtailing trailer against the wind. He switched on his radio.

> "You picked a fine time to leave me, Lucille . . .
> Four hungry children and . . ."

Three LA city fire rigs went screaming west, honking and blaring, a whole frigging light show by itself. Two King City pumpers, heading the *other* way passed him, bleating like ruptured steers.

The fires had them going north, east, and west already, and in circles, probably, in the hills. He began to chuckle. When he lit off

Gibraltar Canyon, the rigs would be meeting each other on one-way roads.

> "You picked a fine time to leave me, Lucille . . .
> Four hungry children and a crop in the field . . ."

They'd get him, this time, for sure.
But in the meantime, he and the blonde were on their way.

Fifteen

Checking the address the fry cook had given him, Shawn Ortega stopped his plainclothes car at the termination of a dead end on Palermo Drive. He took his flashlight from the holder under the dash and shone it on the house number at the end of the block.

The fry cook's address didn't exist. If it had, it would be somewhere out in a dark and empty field between Hillside House Cerebral Palsy School and Arroyo Burro Creek.

Sonofabitch . . .

He backed into a driveway, spun the wheel, and shot up Las Positas Road toward Highway 101. He had a very bad feeling, growing worse with every block, a long-shot intuition, unsupported by facts, but spreading like chills through his whole being, that Klinger was in fact Zimmer. Passing within a few blocks of headquarters, he called in on impulse, to see if Zimmer's rap sheet had come in. Not yet, according to the desk man; he'd send Sacramento a TWX to speed things up.

He rocketed west toward the Kentucky Fried Chicken stand. Ahead he could see the orange underbelly of the newly combined brush fires at Stow Grove County Park and Los Carneros Canyon. An Oxnard city fire engine, hooting its way from the sister city to the east, passed him, then cut him off as it swerved to take the Fairview exit. Shawn followed it, heading north toward the glow over the mountains. He stared. A nearer, more brilliant flare told him that on top of all the others, there was a structural fire ahead.

He followed the truck over fire hoses snaking along the street, weaving past two more rigs parked nearby, ignoring a reserve deputy in uniform who tried to wave him away.

The Colonel Sanders kitchen was roaring skyward. He jammed the car into a slot between two fire trucks, turned up the volume on his radio, and trotted to the parking lot.

The manager was wringing his hands like Oliver Hardy in an old comedy. A newspaper photographer was climbing back into a press car. Hash Ono was talking to the young Chicano from the service station. There were firemen everywhere, and a fire captain was trying to calm a fat blonde of forty wearing high heels, an orange mumu, and hair curlers. She was the young blonde's mother, wailing that her daughter was nowhere to be found; she must be inside.

"*Nobody* inside, ma'am," yelled the fire captain, above the garbled radios, throbbing Diesels, and hiss of water on the flames. Warily, he watched the blaze. "I got a guy in, earlier, they use gas to cook, and I'm not going to push my luck."

"Your daughter *left*, lady," called the Chicano, suddenly.

The fat blonde waddled over, stumbling on a hose. She was close to tears: the girl *never* left early, her *boyfriend* picked her up, when she couldn't come herself.

"*Saw* her leave," insisted the Chicano, "on the cook's motorcycle. She's maybe home now."

"She wouldn't ride a motorcycle!"

Shawn drew the Chicano aside. "Riding in back? Or in front?"

"In front. Like a little kid."

"What time?" His heart was hammering.

"Just before the fire. Maybe quarter to ten?"

"Which way?"

"South on Fairview."

"Oh, God," muttered Shawn. Above the cacophony he heard his dispatcher calling him on the radio. For privacy and silence, he moved to the service station pay booth, invested a dime, and called the station. "Ortega here!"

The rap sheet on Zimmer had arrived. "Read it," Shawn ordered.

There was a shocked silence. "It's eight yards long!"

"*Go,* man, OK?"

As the deputy began, in a fast monotone, Shawn closed his eyes, painting a picture on his mind. "Age, twenty-four, now. Five-eleven, a hundred and eighty pounds, hazel eyes, black hair . . ." Close enough to Klinger. No beard, but . . .

"Acne scars? Right cheek, forehead?"

"Yep."

Right on! Jesus . . .

But lots of men had black, frizzly hair, hazel eyes, acne scars.

"Now read his priors. Any ADWs?"

"Just three. Two with guns, one with a knife."

"MOs?"

"Well, arson, mostly. Hey, he torches zoos. And dog pounds. Neat, he assaulted a woman in Central Point, Oregon. With a motorcycle! This is one bad dude!"

Motorcycle . . . Zimmer was Klinger. There was not the slightest doubt in his mind that they'd find Zimmer's prints, when they beat down the fire, on every pot and pan in the place.

And not the slightest doubt in his mind, either, that if he'd ignored the call from the DA, the girl would have been home by now with Mama.

"Send out an APB," he said swiftly. "Eric Zimmer alias Jake Klinger. And now he's got a full black beard. OK?"

"Yes, sir."

"Last seen Fairview and Calle Real, Goleta—"

"*Goleta?*" The deputy sounded shocked.

"Goleta fucking California, about three minutes from your own dead ass, you want to lock the door? Riding a chopped black Harley," continued Shawn. "Blond female, around twenty, riding with him. In front. Approach with caution, she'll be a hostage. License number not observed." Which was his own G.D. fault, he thought, for not noting it when he talked to the fry cook. He dug for his notebook, found Klinger's page. "He also drives a black pickup, make unknown. Check for both vehicles with DMV, under Klinger, but I'll bet they're hot."

"Ten-four," said the dispatcher. "Hey, he shows 'undesirable discharge, USMC.'"

Shawn's mind whirled: worse and worse. "'Consider armed and dangerous—'" He suddenly realized that he had his suspect for the Gaviota Pass murders, too. "Armed with a .45." Now, what had he forgotten for the APB?

"So what's the 'want'?"

"Murder, arson," said Shawn. "And kidnapping. *And* ADW, he must have the weapon now. And parole violation. That's enough for openers . . ."

He heard the clacking of a Teletype. "OK, he's opened," said the deputy. "Good luck."

Slowly, Shawn hung up. He guided the woman back to her car. Her place was at home, in case the girl turned up. And they had a good description out, in case, just in case, her daughter was in danger.

Not to worry, though, OK?

He moved back to Hash Ono, nodded toward the blaze. "That fry cook's Zimmer, Hash."

Hash's eyes filled with pain. "I was afraid you'd say that."

Shawn started for his car. "Where you going?" asked Hash.

"Cruising," said Shawn. "You carry a gun?"

"What for? I couldn't hit my ass with both hands."

"Go home to bed." He walked to his car, got in. The dispatcher was broadcasting Zimmer's description. Hash Ono, at the wheel of his scout car, suddenly pulled up beside him.

"I'll go east," called Hash. "Just stay on Channel Orange."

"Hey!" protested Shawn. He needed Hash unarmed like Hash needed *him* in the ashes.

But the Kamikaze Kid had already pulled away, so Shawn eased past the fire trucks, turned west, and began to scan Goleta's smoky, winding roads.

It looked like a long and lonely night.

For himself and the blonde that he might have saved.

If she was still alive.

THREE

Fire Storm

One

Jerry Castle had spent the night in the command van, napping between crises. It was six now, and he had been up since 3:30 A.M.

He had okayed the retreat of two thousand fire fighters from a line battling to save the Painted Cave Community near San Marcos Pass, dooming the structures. He had sent them to a position on La Cumbre Peak, where they tried to save the FAA repeater station, and failed there too. He had adjudicated an argument between Luke Tallman, anchoring the western end of the line, and a choleric line boss from Oregon, who had somehow found his way with ninety Lummi Indians from Washington to a dead end on Camuesa Peak, well into the Wilderness Area, where no fire lines should be at all. Extricating the lost patrol, he had turned to other things: Caterpillar tractors to clear the Santa Ynez River banks; a decision to set, by hand, a backfire to save White Oaks Camp on Arroyo Burro; an evaluation by Holmes of the effect of the Santa Ana wind on a new series of fire-sets apparently starting along Gibraltar Canyon Road, far to the east of town.

All the while, despite the airdrops, Caterpillars, hotshot crews, Firescope plans and suggestions from Riverside, the predictions on Holmes's Firemod maps continued implacably true: nowhere along the whole vast range of mountains was the fire more than a thousand yards off schedule. He grew to hate the updates, and the sight of Holmes's shaggy face and anxious eyes.

By 4 A.M., infrared aerial photos showed that Los Padres National

Forest had lost 80,000 acres in the last three days and that the fronts of the five major fire heads marching seaward totaled twelve miles long. Still only half of what they'd lost at Marble Cone, but, according to the fire forecasts, only a fifth of what they'd ultimately lose if the winds kept up.

They had dropped just less than a million gallons of slurry on 180 aerial sorties. California Department of Forestry inmate portable-kitchen crews had fed 30,000 meals to 6,000 men and women. Miraculously, they had lost no aircraft, and suffered only one death so far, from an inmate crew on the Camuesa Canyon fire.

But walking wounded were said to be everywhere, with broken bones, snakebites, exhaustion, heat prostration, burns. Smoke from poison oak was already putting sensitives out of commission. The volunteer mountain-medical crews from Arizona and New Mexico were swamped in their aid stations.

At 5 A.M. the national press had arrived, with two tired UP-INS photographers from Los Angeles, sent groping up San Marcos Pass. The weekend had blunted the interest of the wire services, but someone on the East Coast had all at once realized, on coming to work Monday morning, that the fire in Los Padres National Forest, combined with Sycamore, Mission, Stow Grove, and Los Carneros, was more than a local story: it might well be the fire of the century, and destroy a living city.

Jerry remembered the onslaught of the media at Marble Cone. And Marble Cone had threatened nothing but the little village of Carmel: Trout Canyon-Ygnacia was burning at the hilly gates of the oldest metropolis in Southern California. He contacted his minuscule press room at Goleta headquarters and authorized them to yell for public information help from Washington: a good press now, if the city survived, meant easier funding next fiscal year.

He knew that today, after dawn, the skies would be plagued with photo planes—no light planes, thank God, in these winds—darting through the firebombers, and that all had to be co-ordinated. Mike Kane was on his secret errand after napalm, so he had to stand in for him until he returned, having no trust in Mike's assistants.

Santa Barbareños, by reports that reached him, had gone to bed unworried last night and presumably slept well. They seemed as immune to the normal fear of fire as Londoners to bombs.

He wondered, once the media really began, if the citizenry would sleep as well tonight. And whether, if Holmes and his maps were right, they'd get to bed the following night at all.

By 6 A.M. the tiny windows of the command van were gray with dawn, and Jerry Castle could stand his cell-on-wheels no longer. The air was stale with the stench of cigarettes, bitter coffee, sweat, fear, and half-eaten sandwiches abandoned in the night.

He turned to the youngest man in the van, an assistant operations officer from Alaska Region whose name he could never remember. "Get this trailer cleaned up, OK?" he demanded. "It's a pigpen!"

The young man's eyes widened. He probably hadn't been spoken to that way, Jerry realized, since he was a child. Jerry retreated from the startled gaze, opened the door, and stepped into gray swirling smoke outside.

Immediately, he wished he'd stayed in the van. A few feet away a gangly youth in an orange hard hat, face blackened and arms bandaged from wrists to armpits, was limping from a Forest Service scout car to a police ambulance. Behind him stumbled a fire-shocked youngster, shirt torn and bare back bleeding from some fight with clinging brush. His face was sculptured in horror and his eyes were blank. His skin was unburned, but Jerry knew that he would suffer more and longer than his companion up ahead.

God knew how many more like them, men and women, too, lay in clearings in the spike camps beyond the crests, or continued to battle the brush with hoe and rake and axe, ignoring pain and exhaustion in the blazing hills. Or how many *more* there'd be if the fire, as Holmes predicted, backed them off the mountains onto the foothills near the sea.

He should this time have stayed at Regional Headquarters, to isolate himself, keep his mind clear of the hurts of the frontline troops.

A green contract chopper loomed suddenly out of the smoke. It skimmed the mess tent, reared at a gust, and sandblasted a crew of fire fighters sleeping in the open. Jerry clamped his eyelids against the stinging ash.

Mike Kane scrambled from under the thrashing vanes. His seat was taken instantly by a burned smoke eater, and the chopper rose into the murk. Mike moved from the helipad, with a long forester's gait that, Jerry had learned, was impossible to match on the trail.

He had been all the way to El Toro Marine Air Station, in Orange County, south of LA. And he had been successful, to a point.

"Last chopper we'll get up here *today!*" he predicted. "But your napalm is still in the Halls of Montezuma. The Corps won't deliver it themselves." They started back to the little circle of vans. "Listen, Jerry, I made my living dropping that crap in Nam. On babies and little fucking kids, right? Ask anybody! Anyway, I know what it'll do. How many smoke eaters did we paint pink in the last twenty-four hours? Slurry's one thing. You going to drop napalm on 'em instead? These idiots I got can't hit the right *county*, let alone the right goddamn ridge!"

He'd heard more profanity from Mike in the last thirty seconds than in the last five years.

"Steamboat—" he began.

"Steamboat's a goddamn alcoholic," flared Mike, "and that woman's wall-to-wall insane!"

Jerry Castle retreated to his van. He'd have to write off further help from Mike, he guessed, if the fire backed him up against the wall.

Two

Shawn Ortega arose to a buzzing alarm clock. He stumbled to the window to shut it against the rising morning wind. The fire-weather predictions were right. He looked north, toward the nearest fire: Cold Spring Canyon. At 3 A.M., when he'd got home, city firemen and a company from down the coast in Malibu had been controlling it. Now, from its cherry glow on the base of a rising yellow cloud, it seemed to have got out of hand again.

He explored his mouth with his tongue. He was thirsty and his eyeballs stung. He looked down at Crissy in bed. They'd had a stupid fight when he'd come home, and he wondered if she was playing possum until he left. It might be better if she was.

He'd stumbled in half dead, after hours cruising the western suburbs on the minuscule chance he'd spot the fry cook. He'd checked out the plates on the motorcycles that passed on U.S. 101, then run DMVs on three black pickups he'd found parked on residential streets, in the dim hope that Zimmer had the girl in some house nearby. Only, when headlights were dancing in front of his eyes, and he'd very nearly entered a freeway exit ramp, had he finally headed for home.

To find, instantly, that he should have slept in the car.

She'd been awake, propped on a pillow, blazing mad. Why hadn't he called and where'd he been? How could he leave her in the path of a brush fire with a senile relic she couldn't keep tabs on and a teen-ager bitching because she was missing a tennis date, while the mountains were in flames? And dry brush still scraping the back door and no Rainbirds on the roof and only a trickle of water and the lights on and off all night long?

And the rest: when did he intend to buy the Christmas tree, and when would they have time to talk about paying the Sears account? And how about a decision on the Big Mac job, before their daughter drove her up the wall?

"Anyway," she'd finished, "where in hell were you?"

He'd tried to call, and told her so, but the lines were busy, as always in a fire. She'd flopped to her stomach, buried her head in her pillow, and lay tense and angry while he crawled into bed. For a long while he stretched, taut with fatigue, staring at the ceiling. Then he'd reached over and begun to rub her neck, and finally she'd dropped off to sleep.

Now he began to gather his clothes to dress in the bathroom. If he woke her it might start again.

He winced as a siren screamed, somewhere up in the hills. Ambulance, he guessed. Fire casualty?

Or had someone found the blonde murdered, incinerated in the pickup, in the bottom of some canyon?

He was entitled to FBI help today, after twenty-four hours: he'd better get moving on that.

Crissy's eyes flicked open. She smiled. He had a surge of hope. Her migraines were always better in the morning.

"Buenos días . . ." she murmured.

"Buenos días, querida," he said carefully.

She held up her arms, and he kissed her. "I'm *sorry* . . ." she murmured.

He stayed sitting on the side of the bed, still bushed. "My fault. I should have kept trying to get through."

"I must have sounded like the policeman's wife on a TV show!"

"You're scared of the brush." He pulled on a sock and grinned at her wearily. "It's all right, *mijita*, if we lose the house, we don't have to worry about the Christmas tree."

She produced a smile, brave but artificial: "True. And we can pay Sears with the insurance money, because it sure won't buy another house. And if my paintings burn, we still have the brochure from the exhibit."

"And if Don Miguel goes up with the house," he added cheerfully, "he wasn't going to live forever, and we don't have to worry about a nursing home!"

"And Mary Lou can always get on the Avon Pro Circuit and live in motels," she pointed out. Her eyes darkened, and she looked away. He sighed. Whatever was bugging her, he might as well coax it out: otherwise she could nurse it for weeks.

"What?" he asked softly. "Lay it on me."

She nibbled her thumbnail for a moment, another symptom of the Santa Ana wind. "All right," she said briefly. "It's that gold *cojon* ML's wearing on her wrist. Where'd it come from?"

"I gave it to her," he said carefully.

"I *know* that. Where'd *you* get it?"

"City College, after the All-Star—"

"I know where you *won* it! And I'm pretty sure who won it from *you*, and how. My question is, how'd you win it *back*?"

"Come on, for Christ's sake! Nicks found it with some stuff in her vault . . ." Now, why in hell had he said *Nicks*? Too tired to think straight. "So she *gave* it back."

"How sweet of 'Nicks.'" She was smiling sweetly. "Why? After seventeen years?"

"She thought Mary Lou might want it."

"Not me?" She beamed more widely, her eyes glittering. "Well, I can't have everything. I got the ring."

"Crissy, gold footballs went out with crew haircuts!"

"Hey, I'm flattered. She assumed I knew that? I mean, a Chicana housewife, primitive painter? She could at least have sent beads. Or maize?" Her eyes filled. "What your people call 'corn'?"

He reached for her, to massage her neck. She shook her head, shrugged off his hand. "At least she could wait," she choked, "until the poor bastard's dead!"

He stared at her for a long moment. He heard the thump of Mary Lou's stereo, and outside the sound of a fire truck grumbling up Eucalyptus.

"It's the migraine talking," he decided, squeezing her shoulder. "Not you."

"Migraine?" she shrilled. Her face shrunk, clenched like an angry child's. "What the hell do you mean, *migraine*? Don't you think you, and Brink, and 'Nicks' are enough, all by yourselves?"

"Crissy," he insisted, "you don't mean that."

Eyes brimming, she held his stare. "I know what I mean! Do *you?*"

He dressed and left. Going down the stairs, he realized that for the first time in years he was leaving without kissing her good-by.

She found herself standing in shock in the kitchen, full of shame and still unable to believe herself.

She filled a bowl full of Granola for Mary Lou: two weeks ago it had been yogurt or nothing, laced with nuts and raisins. She poured milk over it and started water boiling for Don Miguel's oatmeal: that, at least, hadn't changed in four long and tiresome years.

"I wanted to talk to Daddy about the Big Mac job," Mary Lou said, from the dinette. She was wearing the goddamn football. "Hey, didn't he—you know—come home last night?"

So at least she hadn't heard the fight: *two* fights, back to back, last night and this morning. Well, the Big Mac job was dead, for sure, with the kidnapped Colonel Sanders girl. It wasn't fair that Momma always had to break the heavy news. "He got home for an hour or two. Are we eating sugar this week? I forget."

"Brown, Mother," Mary Lou explained, as to a child. "Unrefined."

Don Miguel shambled into the dinette, morning papers in hand: the Spanish *La Opinión* and the *News-Press*. Even at 7 A.M., he was wearing a tie. He had apparently fallen into a reverie, shaving; the left half of his face was still silvery stubble; also, his fly was open. She herself couldn't mention the zipper without offending him. As she served Mary Lou, who stood somewhere in his mind between the Virgin Mary and Jeanne d'Arc, she murmured quietly to her daughter, "speaking of unrefined . . ."

"Fly's open, Pops," Mary Lou said, digging into her cereal.

He zipped it up, stony-faced. " 'A sweet disorder in the dress, kindles in clothes a wantonness . . .' "

"Yeah. Let me see the funnies, OK?"

"That's Robert Herrick," he said, handing them over, "1591 to 1674, English."

" 'At least avoid all citations from the poets, for to quote them argues feeble industry,' " mumbled Mary Lou, finding *Doonesbury*. "Hippocrates."

He sat down, spilling the coffee Crissy had poured in his cup. "'Quotations from the great old authors are a blessing to a public grown superficial and external . . .' Louise Guiney, American poetess."

They could keep it up for hours. They were bringing back her headache. If the fire came close, she'd feed it his Bartlett's.

"If BS were music, you two could start a brass band," Crissy interrupted. "*That's* Cristina Ortega, revolutionary artist."

"¿Qué?" asked the old man. "What was that?"

"Never mind, Don Miguel. What's in the paper?"

He scanned the front page. "My God!"

She glanced over his shoulder. Under "WINDS, FIRES THREATEN," was "Kidnap Victim Sought," the lead story, on Shawn's case. Well, she might as well get it over with. "A seventeen-year-old blond employee," she read to Mary Lou significantly, "of a Goleta fast-food restaurant—"

"Oh no," groaned Mary Lou, putting down the funnies. "Not *now!*"

"—thought kidnapped last night by another employee, was sought today by local deputies . . ."

"Animals," snarled Don Miguel. "I hope he burns in hell!"

"Your father's on that," she told Mary Lou, looking her dead in the eye. "In fact, he just missed breaking it, *before* it happened."

Mary Lou's face flushed and her eyes went full of tears. "And now," she squeaked, "I suppose he won't let me—"

"The Big Mac thing? You're damn right he won't let you," said Crissy. "Are you *kidding?*"

"The Big Mac isn't in Goleta," she whined, "and I'd be on the same hours as Rodge, he'd be driving me home—"

Crissy felt her head begin to throb. She tried to simmer down: Mary Lou's height fooled you, she was still a little girl, no more self-centered than any other, no more pitiless than she herself had been at fifteen. Maybe it was irritation over the stupid football dangling from her wrist. But she found she couldn't keep the edge out of her voice, or keep silent, either.

"I don't suppose," she asked, "you could spare a little of that self-pity for the girl herself—"

Mary Lou's eyes widened. "I *feel* sorry for her, but—"

"Or your dad, how *he* feels, I told you, he almost got there first."

Mary Lou shoved back her chair, got up from the table, and stalked from the room. Don Miguel glared silently at Crissy.

"I'm sorry, Viejito, you don't understand." Her head was aching worse than ever, and she was deep in the aura of another attack.

"I understand. And I agree, that 'job' is impossible. But there are good ways to tell her, and bad!"

"Then maybe," she grated, "you better explain them to your grandson." She got up, slammed the paper savagely onto the table, and marched to the kitchen. "If you can find him!"

"¿Qué?" he called after her. "What did you say?"

"Nothing!" she yelled, from the depths of her soul. "Nada, god-damnit! Nada, nada, nada!"

He shot her a look of outraged scorn, and strode from the room himself. She heard him open the closet door, to get his coat, and slam the front entrance. She heard a fire truck bleating in the distance, and the howl of the wind up the canyon.

"Damn," she whimpered. "Damn, damn, damn . . ."

Button Berger stopped her rig in the middle of Arroyo Burro road. She heard the air hiss from its master cylinder, then glanced at Cieneguitas Ridge across the brush-filled ravine of Arroyo Burro. The base of the yellow clouds throbbed with a rosy pulse: the fire was just over the crest, and coming fast. As she watched, a twin-engined DC3 firebomber, appearing from nowhere, skimmed the ridge at treetop level, banked, sank into the canyon, and reared in shock at finding the opposite slope so close. It passed over with a roar, close enough so that she could see crimson slurry dripping like blood from its ventral slit.

She was nearly exhausted. The past forty-eight hours were a blur of battles lost: her own private fire at Maria Ygnacia Creek had overcome her Friday, and joined Trout Canyon fire, which they had fought at Los Prietos until the ranger station had burned, then at the Baptist Camp until it had disappeared in a blaze whipped up by a single gust.

They had rested and fed at San Marcos Pass Camp—when? Yesterday? Where she'd met a fire-weather forecaster, heavy with vibes, and gone to sleep in his face.

Then they had battled the flames on every mountain road along the Santa Ynez ridges, covered the evacuation of a day-camp full of hippy children, replenishing from a well at Lower Oso and a swimming pool at a deserted boy scout camp on San Antonio Creek. Sometime yesterday Mac, on the nozzle, had been hit by a blazing limb, airborne and hurtling down a canyon throat in the arms of a thirty-knot gust. It had burned his wrist and forearm, and he had refused to be evacuated, so she had bound it as best she could with the aid kit in the truck, but he still moved painfully, his gritted teeth a slash across his blackened face.

Now, dozing beside her as she stopped the rig, he awakened when she reached for the mike: "Goleta Dispatch, this is CDF 8411. Ten-ninety-seven at Arroyo Burro near Cieneguitas Road, four hundred and fifty gallons remaining. What now, Joe?"

"Can you hold Arroyo Burro Road?" asked the dispatcher. From the cab, she looked over the topography. The canyon, like all of them, was full of brush. She checked the road ahead and behind. It was rough, but fairly wide, and with the 450 gallons and a little help from the air, she could squat here and fight for the peak to the east. Getting out might be another problem, but she hadn't buckled to fear so far, and she wouldn't show it now.

"Ten-four," she told the dispatcher. "We'll try."

As she climbed from the cab, she caught a glimpse of herself in the side-view mirror. She looked like a clown in blackface— smudged from chin to forehead. She thought of smoke-borne poison oak and began instantly to itch.

What was a nice girl like her doing in a place like this? She remembered the meteorologist, on San Marcos Pass. Cute, with the beard, nervous in the smoke from the canyons. She wondered how old he was.

Sweet, professorial, intense, and undoubtedly very bright. Probably no good in a firefight.

But he looked at you as a person, not a piece of tail, which was more than you could say for most of the men she met lately. Even Mac . . .

The firebomber made another run, this time from east to west, still very close overhead. It waved its wings as it hurtled over, just feet above the truck. Then it was shaving the opposite ridge, dumping a scarlet shower of slurry, instantly disappearing into dirty yellow smoke.

From the floor of the canyon a dog began to bark. She peered down. In a glen above a wooden bridge, an old wooden shack nestled on the opposite face. Next to it sat a red jeep. Above the dwelling was a cultivated plot, a truck farm, perhaps. Well, the shack was a write-off, there was no way to get the rig down the cowpath which led to it, and she doubted that she had the hose to get there either.

Someone was still there. No sane flatlander, with the cherry glow licking at the hilltop behind him, would be stupid enough to wait for the fire to crest the hill. But the hill people were a special breed, and though she saw no one, the dog and the jeep meant that whoever lived there remained. There was no telling what heroics they might have in mind.

She called to Mac to set up a progressive hose-lay along the road and began to scramble down the jeep trail to the floor of the canyon. By the time she was halfway down, orange tongues of flame were darting above the skyline.

A dumpy old lady in Levis appeared, hauling a ladder from a toolshed which leaned on one side of the house. As Button approached, the old lady propped the ladder, dragged out a garden hose, climbed to the roof, and began to sprinkle it down. Button noted that the jeep was empty of all the household goods she would have expected to see with the fire so close. The woman was obviously senile, or suicidal.

A tree at the top of the ridge began to burn, torched from a blowing ember. Button drew nearer, staring up at the woman on the roof. Her skin was the color of weathered teak, and now she was scowling down. The dog's barking peaked in an ear-jarring crescendo. Button shifted uncomfortably. She should have sent Mac, and told him to carry a stick.

"Look at the ridge!" Button piped. "You got to get out of here!"

The woman glared at her, continuing to water. Button stepped to the hose, kinked it to stop the flow. The woman glared and pointed back up the path. "No comprendo inglés! Vete, por favor!"

She had a gap in her teeth that Button could have driven the fire truck through.

Button yelled: "Too close! Too big! You would die here!" She groped for the words, from high school Spanish. "Fuego, muy caliente! Morir! Get out!"

The woman climbed down, yanked the hose from Button's hand, draped it out of reach over the pommel of a saddle on the porch railing. God, if they had to get horses out too . . .

The woman outweighed her by a hundred pounds, but Button grabbed her arm. It was firm as a shoulder of lamb and as big around as her own leg. The ancient shook off her grip, marched to the porch, broke the arm off a rocker as if it were a toothpick, and faced her. The dog reached a new peak of hysteria.

Button glanced up at the ridge behind the house. Now three trees were blazing, and as she watched, a clump of greasewood exploded in flame. Her eyes narrowed. All the way up the canyon spread six-foot-high plants, in disciplined rows, of whatever crop she grew.

Button took a deep breath and braved the steps. The dog glared at her, collapsed, and lay brooding on her trespass. The old lady looked into her face. Her eyes held the wispy film of the very old, but something more, besides.

"You *do* speak English, don't you?" Button said harshly. "What *is* this? You *can't* save the place!"

"No? I've been through two of these, and the house has too."

"You won't get through *this* one."

"You won't get me out." The old lady tossed the chair arm aside, brushed past Button, and returned to the foot of the ladder. She stooped, got the nozzle, and climbed up a step. "Clear that hose."

Automatically, Button straightened it. The old lady began to water again, pitifully. Twenty pounds pressure, max, through a half-inch hose. No way . . .

"I can't get my rig down here," Button explained. "You ought to know that!"

"My! *Your* rig?" She grinned down, sprinkling the roof. "I know you can't, *chiquita*. I didn't ask you to."

"We don't probably even have enough *hose!*"

"Probably not."

"Or water!"

"Way it goes. Good pressure, though, if you *could* make it."

"God *damn* you!" She whirled and started back across the bridge.

"Drive up in the jeep," called the woman. "Key's in the lock. And there's homemade wine for your guys, and plenty of grass in the house."

Button hopped into the jeep, started it, and drove furiously up the trail to see what they could do.

Grass? Oh, *grass!*

The old lady, whoever she was, was really something else.

Three

Shawn watched Sheriff Armando Castillo shove aside the Zimmer file. The sheriff glared at him across the desk. Castillo did not like the file at all, or Shawn's involvement in the case. The sheriff shifted, and the swivel chair complained. The strap of his shoulder holster made his fat bulge, and he eased a finger under it. He moved restlessly, agitating the chair even more.

"What else?" Castillo demanded. "Since you been running the county?"

Shawn handed him the Firemod map. Castillo barely glanced at it. "I know." He shrugged. "Kelso called me last night. Whole city's going to go up in flames, right? You promise them anything?"

"Just to bullhorn the peeps out of the foothills, if it jumps the crests."

"Computer crap." Castillo shrugged. "Won't happen. Never has. Might burn you people out along Eucalyptus and Alameda Padre Serra, again—"

"That's nice, thanks. Now, about Zimmer—"

"Never get below Milpas Street, too much concrete."

"Whatever you say. Don't count on it, though, you just might *need* your boat."

Castillo leaned back in the wailing chair. "Kelso says you're thinking of running for my job."

If I ever got it, Shawn thought, I wouldn't leave town in a brush fire. "Kelso said that? The son of a bitch! *He* brought it up, and I said no!"

To his surprise, Castillo seemed to accept the denial: "Well, he wants to split the Chicano vote."

"No shit." He took another stab at the kidnapping. "About Zimmer—"

"Which," Castillo murmured, ignoring him, "doesn't mean you *won't* run. To help McCrae."

"No, it doesn't," he agreed. He might as well keep him off balance. "But I don't like being used."

"You run, I'll beat you," warned Castillo. "*And* McCrae. I'm heavy-duty Chicano: you're not fish *or* fowl. *Ni el uno ni el otro.*"

"I'd split my *own* vote?" Shawn smiled mirthlessly. "Hell of a thing."

"I'm not kidding." Castillo seemed uncomfortable. Kelso must have eaten him out on the phone, for sailing away on the weekend. Good.

"Hey, I meant to ask, you have a good trip?" Shawn smiled. "Nice crossing? Fair winds, following seas, all crap like that there? Perkapek get seasick again?"

"Knock off the BS!" Castillo barked. "Look . . . The mayor? Or Kelso? You hear them *say* anything?"

"Gosh, sir," smiled Shawn, "you know me. Apolitical as a lamb. Good man in the field, but when they start talking about things like, you know, *recall* petitions, I—"

"*Recall—*" bleated Castillo with a howl from the chair. He was learning to orchestrate it like a concert organist. "Recall?" He studied Shawn's face, relaxed, and growled: "Knock off the Bob Hope. I asked you: nothing got said at the meeting?"

Shawn shook his head. "Nothing got *done!*" He nodded toward the Zimmer file. "Except a seventeen-year-old kid gets kidnapped by a maniac because I had to go!"

"Don't sweat it, hombre. That case, you're off."

"No!" protested Shawn. "Look—"

"You shouldn't have taken it as far as you did. It's Perkapek's."

"Wait a minute! You made me Arson! Zimmer's an *arsonist!*"

"When he lit off a woman and maybe blew away two men on Gaviota Pass, it wasn't arson anymore, as you knew damn well. It was homicide. And you *aren't* Homicide. You got that straight, or do I have to have them read it at roll call?"

Shawn stared at the Zimmer file: arson reports, rap sheet, descriptions, fingerprints on the trunk of the VW, matching Zimmer's. The file was an inch thick already, and Perkapek would double it in size by tonight, without leaving his desk, while the poor blonde died, if she wasn't dead already.

He saw her now, with vacuous eyes and simple grin, frank as Mary Lou's, but, unlike his daughter's, unclouded by thought.

If only he'd ignored the DA's idiotic meeting . . .

"Sheriff?" he pleaded.

"No."

The light began to flash on the phone. Castillo picked it up. It was the mayor's office: yes, Castillo said, he'd called in Sheriff's Reserve, they had five cars to roll if needed, there'd be more, if necessary; county foothill residents would be alerted.

No, even if worse came to worst, *city* cops would have to evacuate Alameda Padre Serra and every other street inside the city limits, no matter how loud Chief Dubbs cried for help: sheriff's authority stopped at the county line. "And our responsibility stops there, too, tell the mayor."

He hung up. He leveled a forefinger at Shawn. "From you, I want an evacuation plan."

"We got three-month rookies in Patrol that can do that!"

"No, I want your name on it."

"I *know* Zimmer! I've met him, questioned him, questioned the victim, I know the case! I know who I'm looking for!"

"What you're *looking* for is a Board of Rights hearing, if you don't drop it!" Castillo barked.

For a long while, Shawn stared into the sheriff's eyes. Castillo did not blink, or look away. "If I *help* Perkapek?" murmured Shawn. "If it's *his* bust when we get him? OK?"

Castillo shoved the file to the side. Zimmer, Castillo assured him, was in Nevada now, or Arizona, and the girl was dead, and some poor damn highway patrolman would pull him over a year from now for a busted tail light and end up on a slab. "You *blew* it, man! You'll never bust him, and Perkapek won't either."

"He's still here!" protested Shawn. "Fire country, fire season, Santa Ana wind? Read his file! He's within fifty miles! Let me try!"

"No!" The sheriff hoisted his bulk and the chair groaned in relief. He moved to the window. "I heard you lived in Pueblo Viejo as a kid," he said suddenly. "Family like yours? Why?"

Surprised, Shawn answered: "My grandfather had to. Burned out and busted."

"I lived in East LA," murmured Castillo. "Then Eagle Rock, shit, hombre, that's worse." He seemed to drift away, staring out the window. "Damn smoke . . . If anybody'd told me at fifteen, sixteen, I'd be here . . . As sheriff? *There,* maybe." He nodded across the parking lot at the jail. "But here? Have my own *boat?* I didn't know those fucking islands were *out* there until I was thirty! And I'm going to lose it back to McCrae? Or you? No way!"

"I *said* I wouldn't run," Shawn repeated. The sheriff stared at him balefully. Something was coming, and Shawn couldn't pin it down. He decided that the sheriff's hand was out, for something. He sagged. "OK. What do I have to do to get turned loose on Zimmer?"

Castillo studied him. "Support," Castillo said softly. "I'll need support, at election."

The case was important to him, but he wouldn't sell his soul for it. "No." Shawn rubbed his eyes. They were tired, stinging with sleeplessness and smoke and the Santa Ana dryness that had seemed to last for weeks. "Look, I'm just a frigging lieutenant on the Sheriff's Department," he protested. "I supported McCrae before, and he lost. What good's support from me?"

Castillo regarded him coldly. "Things change."

Now he was honestly confused. "What things?"

"Come on! *Kelso* asked you if you were going to run. Why would *he* care?"

"Like we said. To split the Spanish vote."

"Gomez or Rojas or Arguello could do that. Arguello's a captain! You're too young! So why'd he ask *you?*"

"I figured"—he shrugged—"he fell in love with my charm? On TV? And he found out I'm Don Miguel's grandson: there are viejos sitting around Sunflower Park that would vote me for Pope, and he knows it. Plus, I don't look that Mexican."

Castillo was smiling at him. "You serious? You really don't know why?"

"All right, *why?*"

The sheriff turned back to the window. "Man, that wind!" He faced Shawn. "Money."

"Say again?" Shawn blurted, startled. "What money?"

"*Southerland's* money." The sheriff's eyes were probing, though the smile remained. "Your friend's estate."

"*Brink?*" Shawn felt his face go red. "It's none of your goddamn business, but he's leaving me one Honda motorcycle and a forty-year-old biplane I can't afford to keep!" *For which, he added silently, I'm supposed to commit Murder One, on request, there being no free lunches in his circles any more than ours.* "That satisfy your goddamn curiosity?"

Castillo continued to smile. "Can we cut the bullshit?" He returned to his desk. He opened a cigar box, selected a cigar, suddenly offered the box to Shawn. Shawn shook his head.

The sheriff licked the cigar, bit off the end, and spat it into his wastebasket. He lit it, watching Shawn impassively. "He's leaving you more than a bike and a plane. Maybe he don't know it, but everybody else does."

"What's he leaving me?" grated Shawn.

Castillo spread his hands. "His widow! Well, wife! What's her name?"

Shawn felt his hands go cold. It had happened before, the only time he had ever hit a suspect, a pervert who'd taken them to the brutalized body of a five-year-old girl in an abandoned icebox. His knees were shaking and his lips felt frozen. "Nicole?" he whispered.

"Nobody *blames* you . . ."

His legs began to tremble. "For what?" he murmured.

"Moving in." Castillo shrugged. "I heard you knew her from way back, so it isn't like you weren't there *first*. And he probably don't care. Up there on the hill, everybody's bangin' everybody, so—"

The light in the room seemed to dim. Through the open door he could hear a dispatcher's radio: *"Unit eight, Code seven for doughnuts at Winchell's on Fairview. Unit three, cancel the ambulance on the fender-bender . . ."*

He found himself rounding the desk, fist cocked, knowing that this was what Castillo had wanted, from the first, but unable to stop, no way to stop; he was halfway to the sheriff when he saw the snub-nosed Smith & Wesson in the sheriff's hand, drawn so swiftly he'd hardly sensed the motion.

"Hold it!"

Shawn froze. "You son of a bitch," he intoned. "You fat cock-sucker—"

"On the desk," Castillo barked. "The gun, first."

"No way!"

"Do I have to call in the morning watch?" Castillo moved toward his phone. "You want this in tomorrow's *News-Press?*"

Shawn pulled his gun from his holster, and slammed it on the hardwood desk, marring the varnish. "If you weren't so old and fat, Castillo, I'd jam this up your ass."

"Madre de Dios," breathed Castillo. "I wish you'd try." He holstered his own weapon, emptied Shawn's, spun the cylinder, and tossed it into his "incoming" basket. "Pick it up when you get a permit. Now, the badge."

Shawn tore the badge from his wallet and slapped it on the desk. Castillo sat down. The chair moaned. He moved in it comfortably, rocking from side to side. "Love that sound more all the time." He looked up at Shawn. "You going to want to bother with a Board of Rights?"

Shawn licked his lips. "I want nothing from you, Castillo, *nada!*"

"You know, I feel the same way about you. Finally." The sheriff picked up the badge, regarded it happily, and dropped it into his drawer. He flashed the famous campaign smile. "Now, Mr. Ortega, the county's on fire, and I'll be busy. Was there anything else?"

Shawn whirled and left for home. He was halfway there when the red, raging shock hit him, and again he began to tremble. He pulled over, counted to fifty to calm himself, and continued on his way.

Whatever happened to him, Crissy, Nicole, the blonde, or the fire, the sheriff had won, hands down.

Four

Steamboat Haley sat waiting with Snaproll in his scaly goatskin flight jacket at a mess table at San Marcos Pass Fire Camp. He was still jumpy from the heaving, bucking chopper ride up the canyon from Santa Barbara Municipal. If God had intended man to hover like a bumblebee, there wouldn't be fixed-wing aircraft.

He swirled the coffee in his styrofoam cup. An ash from the fire fell into it and he teased it out with his finger.

The camp was a smoky madhouse, and evoked something he couldn't instantly pin down. Clean fire trucks from the Santa Barbara side of the mountains, manned by rested, confident men, were meeting battered, filthy rigs from the other side, their fire fighters exhausted, collapsing onto cots and bare ground, too tired even to eat.

He was suddenly back in time and space, to an airstrip newly taken on Biak Island off New Guinea. The Japs were counterattacking, fresh troops from a transport on the beach were mingling with casualties from the jungle fighting. In the chaos, the squadron had discovered in the arriving supplies an unguarded case of beer, cold from the reefers on the transport, beaded in the tropic heat, Bud, it was, in the wartime cans . . . Jesus, he could use a can of it right now . . .

"Steamboat," Snaproll instructed swiftly, "remember what I'm telling you. *Whatever* they want us to do, at first it's suicide! We wouldn't touch it with a ten-foot pole. You got that *straight?*"

"It may *be* suicide," he said irritably. Christ, she was talking to him like a stupid drunk, and he wasn't drunk, just tired. She'd found him in the terminal bar last night and dragged him back to *Marvin's Mistress,* where she'd forced him to try to track down the leak in the slurry tank. He'd had only one small belt of booze this morning, before she'd spotted his bottle in the engine nacelle. His tongue felt like a pitot tube cover left too long out in the wind. "Just getting that fucker airborne's suicide, all by itself."

She fastened her eyes on him, eyes clear as youth. How this could be, he never knew: how she could drink almost as much as he during the night and come up freshfaced in the morning.

"You know," she said thoughtfully, "you're probably right? They got a kamikaze mission, that's why they cut us off, to soften us up. Lover, we got 'em over a barrel!"

He thought of the pile of bills on her desk in the hangar at Cachuma, of the old mechanic who hadn't been paid, of the overdue overhaul on all four engines. Some barrel, and who was over it?

"Here he comes," said Snaproll.

Jerry Castle had aged ten years since the Marble Cone fire. Join the club, Castle, Steamboat told him silently: alcoholics, workaholics, we all end up at the same place. While the eyes of the Snaproll Suzies stayed young forever.

Castle greeted him coolly and Snaproll not at all. "We got a little problem over the hill."

"I noticed that," said Snaproll. "There's all this smoke. Fire?"

Castle ignored her. "I want a bid on picking up something at Marine El Toro," said Castle, to Steamboat. "And flying it to the Santa Barbara mixmaster ramp. And leaving it there, in case we need it. And then dropping it, if we do."

"What is it?" asked Snaproll.

Castle glanced at Snaproll, looked away, sat down, drummed his fingers on the table. Someone with a bullhorn began to page him from the command van. He ignored it. "Well . . . Napalm."

A tired fire fighter set down his plate, dragged his feet over the bench, and sat staring at the food, apparently too fatigued to eat. A siren whirred to a stop from the San Marcos Pass highway and someone called on a radio for a paramedic for spike camp ⋇ 5.

"Napalm?" breathed Suzy. "You starting a war?"

"Backfire, maybe," murmured Castle softly, glancing uncomfortably at the fire fighter. But the man had decided he was too tired and was already shambling off to a sleeping area. "Since we can't use you for slurry—"

"You got any *nukes* you want hauled around?" she asked. "Steamboat, let's go."

Steamboat glanced at her, and felt sorry for Castle. Even knowing she was bluffing, he found it impossible to read her hostile eyes. She stood up. "Steamboat!" she demanded again.

"Wait," Steamboat said. "Jerry, why are you asking us first?"

Snaproll cut in before Castle could answer: "Because *Marvin's Mistress* has the only racks that can handle napalm, probably. And he wouldn't trust any of these other yoyos dropping it within ten miles of the city. And the answer is no!"

"Two grand a flying hour," Castle said suddenly.

Steamboat felt his guts contract. "Three thousand," Suzy said. "Five if we drop. Fifteen grand guarantee. Half on acceptance, half on performance, within twenty-four hours."

"You *know* I can't pay that."

She shrugged. "Steamboat?"

He was sure she'd blown it. He struggled out from behind the bench, scraping his knee. They started toward the helipad. Shit . . . Now he wanted it, wanted it bad, not for the money, screw the money, just to make the drop, precisely and on time. He almost stopped. She sensed it. "Keep walking," she murmured, stiff-lipped. "Just keep walking, will you?"

"Hey," they heard Castle shout. "Come back here a minute, Suzy."

"*Me*," she said grimly. He could sense the tension in her voice. "You stay where you are." She turned and walked back to the table, feigning reluctance. He watched her approach Castle, hips loose and swinging, and was afraid of how she'd try to close the deal if Castle balked, begging her to let well enough alone: he'd turn her down flat, hurt her, she was too old, couldn't she see? Castle wasn't the type.

But when she came back she was beaming. "We got it, we're in! We pick up at El Toro Marine."

He patted her ass, put his arm around her waist, and they started toward a chopper stirring a dust storm on the helipad. She tugged at his leather jacket.

"You know," she yelled above the noise, "what the old bastard wanted besides?"

He looked into her face. "A little on the side?" he managed, knowing it wasn't true.

Her smile was dazzling. "Would you believe it?" She chuckled. "At his age? And mine? I mean, the silly old goat?"

She seemed still to be smiling, but her eyes were blurred suddenly with tears.

"You old fucker," she shouted above the nervous blades. "You don't believe that at all!" She hopped into the cabin, pulled him aboard, and grinned. "And you know," she admitted, "you're right."

He closed the hatch. A drink at Santa Barbara, and then to El Toro, if he could get *Marvin's Mistress* off the ground; then back to Santa Barbara, to wait and pray that they'd really want the drop.

Anything to keep the shine in the eyes of Snaproll, Girl of a Thousand Laughs.

Jerry Castle leaned wearily on the counter in Mike Kane's air ops van. He looked down at Mike's stubbled face. He needed a shave himself. "Well, I got them."

"Congratulations," Mike said sardonically. "How much?"

Jerry heard a garbled transmission from a South Coast Air tanker, apparently working the east slope of Cathedral Peak. He was water-bombing from 1,000 feet in extreme turbulence. The pilot reported air temperatures over the fire head of 160 degrees. Incredible, at 1,000 feet: Jerry wondered what the ground temperatures were: 300 degrees, 500, perhaps. Hell on the crust of the earth . . .

Jerry took a deep breath. "Well . . . Fifteen. Fifteen grand."

Mike flushed. "You get to keep the airplane afterward? Or take the old bat home to bed?"

That, he ignored. He moved to the huge fire map dominating the end of the air ops van. It was slashed from one side to the other by the red line of the main fire head, and splotched with the fires that the firebug, or bugs, had set.

"Now let me show you," he said, "the Castle version of the Maginot line." He smiled. "You will not like it, Michael. You may very well walk out. For what I am going to ask Steamboat and his girlfriend to do will turn your balls to stone. But . . ." He picked up a red Mark-a-Lot and began to search for Gibraltar Road. "This is the way it's going to be."

Reluctantly, Mike unfolded his frame and joined him. Jerry began to speak.

Five

Shawn Ortega turned off U.S. 101 toward Eucalyptus Hill Road and found the city darkening at noon. A brown quilt of smoke had been drawn over the streets by the northeast winds. Headlights were groping through the haze.

The Santa Ana was gusting mightily along Milpas. Empty garbage cans bounded from alleys onto the sidewalks. Cardboard Chamber of Commerce Christmas trees, tied on the lampposts, were bending double. A three-foot plastic Santa, suspended from a jeweler's sign, tore loose, sailed to the street. Instinctively, he honked as it bumped beneath his wheels.

Too late. Sorry, Santa. Hit-run.

His rage at Castillo had cooled, leaving him cold and fearful. He had no idea how Crissy would take the news, which was a measure of their lost communication, for he hadn't really known for years whether she liked his job or hated it. His mind skittered among alternatives: despite his bridge burning, he could still ask for a Board of Rights hearing, but it would inevitably go against him: you didn't threaten the sheriff with your fists and survive on the force. He might work full time towing aerial banners, but that way lay bankruptcy; he might try to start a private investigative agency: ditto.

Twelve years down the drain, in a moment of anger: incredible.

And faked out by a man he had always thought stupid. He wondered whether Castillo had simply manufactured the Nicole rumor, hoping for just the result he'd got. He doubted it: the sheriff lacked imagination. The rumor had started somewhere else.

He turned up Mason Street, passing Sunflower Park. Automatically, he glanced at Don Miguel's favorite bench. He slowed as he saw his grandfather sitting in his usual spot, smiling placidly, eyes distant, as the other oldsters talked around him. Then he continued up Mason. El Viejo was better off here, far from the danger of fire, than at the house, stumbling around in the way. Shawn could return for him when things were packed in the car.

An old wino, last relic of the famous "Jungleville" hobo city by the beach, stumbled out from the park, recognized Shawn from patrol days, and waved his bagged bottle. Shawn waved back. Nothing ever changed in Sunflower Park.

Seeing the alcoholic, he flashed on the source of Castillo's rumor.

Nicole and he had left Montecito Savings and Loan carrying briefcases. Sleepy Doyle, ex-deputy and current bank guard, had seen them. He had probably blatted it out in every bar on State Street, and in his old police haunts as well. The story had flowed upstream, through cops and those who dealt with cops, into the Winchell Donut shops where Patrol ate, or Stubby's Restaurant across from headquarters, or, for all he knew, through the VFW bar all the way to Santa Barbara Yacht Club on the quay. Somewhere, Castillo had picked it up.

A small town, despite its size, and merciless with gossip . . .

Thank you, Sleepy, you drunken old fart . . .

As he drove north along the faceless bungalows on Mason, he noticed more and more cars parked in driveways. Men were taking off from work to gather their treasures and load their automobiles. He was surprised. This, you saw in the foothills in the early stages of an onrushing fire, but he'd never seen it before in the flatland stucco belt. He switched his radio on, dialed to 1020, the Extra News Station.

". . . warned that water pressure in the area north of Foothill Road was dangerously low. Red Flag Alert has been changed to *Extreme* Red Fire Alert, with Extreme Fire Danger in all foothill canyons from Laurel to Chelham. Residents of Northridge Drain, upper Mission Canyon, and Las Canoas Road are advised to evacuate."

"Elsewhere in Santa Barbara County, high winds gusting in the lower canyons cut power lines—"

He flicked off the radio. No word on Eucalyptus Hill, anyway, or on Las Pumas Estates or Wildcat Ridge. A station wagon towing a twin-horse trailer rocked onto Alameda Padre Serra, heading for lower country. He wondered if Nicole was at Wildcat Ridge with her horses, or at St. Francis Hospital with her man.

The trailer was followed instantly by a jeep, a scout car full of vaqueros in cowboy hats, and a Cadillac Seville. Some millionaire pseudo-ranchero was scooting out early.

The wealthy seldom chose, in a fire, to stand and fight. Smarter, perhaps, or simply better insured. Which was a problem he didn't care to face now, himself, though it overhung his spirit like the smoke clouds: premiums had risen so fast that his home, reputedly worth almost a hundred grand, was still insured for thirty.

Of which he would hear more from Crissy, he imagined, today.

He followed the twists of Alameda Padre Serra to Eucalyptus Hill Road. Every block showed more signs of worry, preparation, and confusion. Everyone wanted to live in the hills, until this moment: now you wondered why you'd moved here and swore you'd sell and leave, if the house survived. Then, in a month, when all was cleaned of ash and cinders, you always decided to give it another go.

His next-door neighbor had three of his house-painting trucks half blocking the street. Chicano painters, reeling with beer, were loading them with household effects. He hoped they didn't forget the gallons of paint stored in his garage when the trucks drove away. The neighbor himself was frantically cutting back brush from his front patio, as Shawn had promised to do.

Crissy and Mary Lou were loading Crissy's little Datsun with his grandmother's silver and plates. He could tell by his wife's stiff-necked posture that the migraine was still with her. She turned, distractedly, as he got out.

"I've been trying to call you at headquarters," she said. She clutched at a wisp of hair, whipping across her face. "The line's been busy."

I don't work there anymore, he almost blurted. But there had to be a better time and place than this. "What's wrong?"

"Don Miguel's taken off!"

"Sunflower Park," he reported. "I'll get him later." He surveyed the activity on the street. "Bullhorns come through, or something?"

She shook her head. "No water pressure."

The first seeds of panic. But too early to split. After twelve years of coaxing stubborn householders from their homes, he'd changed his philosophy. When the place was your own, you stayed as long as you could.

He followed her into the house.

Now he had to tell her he'd been canned. At least, he was here to load their gear, she should be happy.

It was when she found out *how* he'd got himself fired that the crap would hit the fan.

Eric Zimmer parked his pickup in six-foot-high brush on a ridge above Rattlesnake Canyon, overlooking Mount Calvary Monastery and St. Mary's Seminary College. The Santa Ana howled outside the cab. Far to the west, he could hear the roar of the main fire, borne on wind funneling through the pass at North Portal. The hidden flames cast a cherry glow on the billowing clouds of smoke. The view excited him.

He had skirted a Red Flag Alert checkpoint on El Cielito Road, using an old ranch route paralleling Gibraltar Road. Twice, grinding up the canyon, he had almost lost the trailer. Once it had sunk hubcap-deep in dry crumbling dirt in an old wash. He had heard the girl screaming then, lashed her wrists more tightly to the sink drainpipe, and quieted her with a backhand slap that fattened her lip and opened a two-inch cut in her cheek.

He left her huddled between sink and stove, staring after him with the big blue baby-eyes. He had tugged out the trailer, by shoring the pickup's wheels with rocks and branches. Then, on impulse, he'd trundled the Harley back to the road and retreated half a mile by bike. Not far from El Cielito he had found a jumble of brush, siphoned gasoline in a ten-foot circle, lit it off, and roared back up the canyon to his pickup. By the time he had the bike back in the truckbed, he could see smoke mushrooming from the new fire. He began to fear the eyes of aircraft from the sky, so he'd bounced to a clump of brush on the wooded ridge to hide the trailer and the truck.

His new fire was burning good, now, he could tell from the billows of smoke. He'd seen fire trucks—LA County, probably all the way from Malibu—trying to knock it down. Now they had split back for the coast. An aerial tanker was still making passes at his blaze, disappearing, returning to bomb it again. But the fire had cut off pursuit.

He'd scouted this country during the hot, dry summer, on a dirt bike he'd stolen and later sold. He'd wanted to make some sets then, but the Voice of the Shrink had warned him not to, loud and clear. Now he was glad he'd listened. The wind was higher now, the brush thicker, the air drier, last summer hadn't been the time.

The time was now.

In a year in Santa Barbara, he'd met no one he didn't hate, or who didn't hate the Flake.

Too bad he couldn't be closer to their pretty white houses to listen and watch while they cooked.

The blonde, he could watch. And hear.

He yodeled, his body surging with energy. He jumped to the bed of the pickup truck, climbed over his bike, pounded on the roof of the trailer to tell the girl he was back.

He heard her scream, hopped to the roof of the truck and yowled in delight.

This next fire, hers, he'd planned very carefully.

He began to unhitch the trailer from the truck.

Six

Hash Ono's heart began to pound. He crawled from the jungle of smoking toyon.

The source of the new fire had been gasoline; he'd known it from the moment he'd cold-trailed the brush. It was a set. Fifty feet had gone up in a whoosh, instantaneously, in this second blaze near Gibraltar Road: he could sense this from the scar signs and the alligatored limbs.

He could even catch the smell of fuel, for it was a very fresh fire indeed.

Now he stood on El Cielito Road, brushing himself off in the hot, dry gale. To his surprise, he saw that while he'd been scrambling around in the brush, the firemen had left and his scout car was standing alone. Strangely, it made him nervous. He jumped at a sound in the burned-out brush. Nothing—a hot branch splitting as it cooled.

A crew from the Malibu substation, a hundred miles down the coast, had knocked down the source long enough for him to get at it. They were veterans of the Malibu-Agoura fire of '79, and, though they were only LA County firemen, every bit as good in the brush as a Santa Barbara crew. They had wrestled with the head of the fire, but it had shaken them off like a raging bull and charged eastward toward Stanwood Drive.

And now, apparently, they had retreated to the coast. From what he could see in that direction, Gibraltar Road was sealed by flames.

To the north, he could hear the roar of the holocaust beyond Cathedral Peak.

Flames south, and flames north. He could see an aerial tanker making passes over Rattlesnake Canyon, so there was something burning there. The brush-choked walls of Rattlesnake would be explosive. No exit there.

He'd spent too long sniffing like a bloodhound in the toyon bush, had isolated himself on the landward side by a ring of fire around the city. He was sure that the wild, howling gusts would prevent helicopter rescue, even if he called for one.

He'd violated the rule of firemen and burglars: never close a door behind you.

He had a sinking sensation in his belly. It was not fear of the encircling fire. He knew back-country topography, roads, and fire trails crisscrossing the Santa Ynez and San Rafael mountains as well as any man alive, and had lived all his life in Santa Ana winds. It was from fear of the firebug trapped somewhere with him, in the brush-covered hills to the north.

He had never got close to a pyromaniac at work, but he was very much afraid that he was closing on this one now.

He climbed into the scout car and called Shawn Ortega on Channel Orange, then tried to raise Dispatch on Yellow and Red. Nothing . . . The relay transmitter on La Cumbre Peak must have perished. He drove north along Gibraltar Road toward the main blaze, heading for the first building he could find, Mount Calvary Monastery.

The Brothers, he noted, had fled, perhaps lacking faith in God. He parked the scout car outside the stuccoed walls and tried the front door. Locked. No faith in mankind either.

His bowels rumbled, as they did in any lonely place. The monastery was Spanish, beautiful, flowered, spooky, and deserted. A mural of St. John the Baptist with his serpent guarded the entrance. He tried several doors. The wind howled, banging a shutter somewhere. The windows were barred in ornate iron. He returned to the main building, tried to slip the bolt by inserting his ID card into the lock, and failed.

Finally, impatiently, he simply braced himself and yanked. The doorjamb split. He walked in. In an office to one side, he found a phone. He picked it up.

The Sheriff's Department line was busy. He called the Santa Barbara Police Department. Busy too.

Jesus . . .

Well, there was no way he was going further up Gibraltar Road, until he got help, by chopper or otherwise, even if the nut burned half the state.

He thought of the kidnapped girl and tried again.

Still busy.

Shit!

He sat in the prior's austerely carved chair and began to dial continuously.

He was very worried about the girl, and would not split, but he had a wife to stay alive for. He'd hang in where he was, but he was not about to leave the monastery and go hunting alone and unarmed.

He only hoped the nut hadn't spotted his car, and wouldn't come hunting for him.

Cristina Ortega had left the TV on in the den. Now, wrapping one of her paintings in a dishtowel, she turned down the volume.

"Crissy!" Shawn said softly. "You haven't answered. I'm *fired!*"

She found herself studying the paintbrush she'd been using when the last news bulletin had prompted her to start the bailout drill. She'd forgotten to clean it. Now the paint had hardened. She carefully dropped it into the wastebasket. She might as well have tossed it onto the floor: the house was going to burn anyway.

"Honey?" Shawn prompted her. "So what's the answer?"

Oh, God, she'd forgotten the question.

"You asked . . ." she began tentatively. "I'm sorry . . ." She rubbed her eyes.

"I asked," he repeated patiently, "how you really felt? About Castillo . . . and me getting canned. About the goddamn job in the first place . . ."

She faced him. His eyes were bloodshot, from smoke or lack of sleep. His hair was tousled, and there were pouches of dark above his high cheekbones. He would do this, often, exhaust himself on a case, forgetting everything else: the Solvang Slasher thing had dropped him eight pounds in a week.

Now, no more cases?

"You always *have* been wasted, down there," she said tentatively. "Everybody knows that. Now you can—" Her voice trailed off. She couldn't seem to keep her mind on anything, with the wind howling outside and the sirens wailing and the smoke eating its way into her brain. "Well, you could . . ."

"What? Shuffle papers? Teach flying again? Look, I *like* this frigging job! I just didn't *know* I liked it!" He collapsed in Don Miguel's old chair, legs outstretched, staring dead ahead. "I should have shut up and taken his shit."

"But *what* shit?" She was still puzzled. He'd told her why he *hadn't* hit Castillo, not why he almost had.

He rose, moved to the window. Behind him, framed in the huge oak tree, in a billow of smoke racing seaward, she saw a male head take shape, high above the canyon. It became the face of an angry, bronze god, long hair tousled like Shawn's, swirling behind. It dissolved in the northeast wind. Shawn turned.

"He picked up a rumor I didn't like," he said. "And he repeated it."

Her heart clenched. "What rumor?"

"That Nicole and I—"

"'Nicks'?" she asked, immediately sorry.

His face hardened. "Whatever . . ."

"Nicole and you . . . what?"

"That I planned to move in, I guess, when Brink died—and—"

"Planned to move *in?*" she repeated incredulously. "You mean, *marry* her?"

"Christ, Crissy, I don't know!" he exploded. "What difference does it make?"

"It made a difference to *you*, didn't it?" she demanded. "Just what exactly triggered you?" She tried to stop herself, and could not. Her voice rose. "That he forgot you were already kind of married, like? With a fifteen-year-old daughter? To a used housewife?"

"Crissy, my God! Hold it down!"

"Or," she finished viciously, "was it because you couldn't stand to hear that paddy bitch's name pass his greasy cholo lips?"

He turned dead white, his eyes narrowing. "'Paddy bitch,'" he murmured. "*Muy interesante* . . . Hey, girl, I din' hear talkin' like that before, from Cristina Gonzales, even in the barrio . . ."

She felt the tears welling up and her throat was tight but she could not stop. "She *is* a fucking bitch, and she's never quit trying, and if you and Brink weren't so goddamn stupid, you'd know it—"

He was staring at the door. She turned. Mary Lou, who had probably never heard her mouth anything more damning than "damn," was standing wide-eyed, searching her father's face, avoiding her eyes. Oh, God, what had she done?

"Daddy? Telephone," gasped Mary Lou. "Nickie Southerland . . ."

Mary Lou turned and ran from the doorway. Shawn glanced angrily at Crissy, moved to the kitchen phone. In a moment he was back.

"Brink needs me," he said coldly.

"*Brink* needs you?" He mustn't go. Not this instant. "What about—?"

"I'm taking the Yamaha. Load the paintings in my car. Mary Lou can drive it. Don't wait for the bullhorns. Split. Pick up el Viejo at Sunflower Park. Go to Casa de la Raza or Stearn's Wharf."

Her migraine shifted gears, became a locomotive drumming down the tracks. "Shawn, you can't!"

His eyes were shadowed with some secret fear that she didn't understand, but which cut her off. His fright was so palpable that she forgot her own anger and grasped his arm.

"What *is* it?" she demanded.

"They want to get him out of there. He's fighting them. I have to go."

"Fighting them?" she exclaimed, but he was on his way out of the room.

In an aura of dancing pain, she watched through the door of the den as he called Mary Lou, spoke to her. She nodded, came in, glanced at her mother, and instantly began to help with the paintings. Crissy heard the motorcycle start in the garage, and roar off down the street. By the time they had packed Shawn's car a sheriff's cruiser was passing, the deputy chanting on a bullhorn: "Please lock your homes and leave the area *immediately*. This is the Santa Barbara Sheriff's Department. Please lock your homes—"

She looked around the house. She could think of nothing on the bailout drill they'd forgotten. The telephone rang. It was the county arson man—the Nisei—looking for Shawn. Bitterly, she referred him to Brink's hospital room, and hung up. Anything else? No . . .

Outside, she got Mary Lou, still silent in shock from the scene in the den, settled at the wheel of Shawn's car, watched her jerk and buck it into the crawling traffic.

She turned back and locked the house. For a moment she stood under the lone eucalyptus tree, staring at the silly heart Shawn had carved the day escrow had closed. It was inscribed in barrio Spanish, "*Crissy por Shawn por vida.*" Scar tissue had almost overgrown the carving, and it was very hard to read.

For an instant the hot wind died. It was 1 P.M. and dark as dusk. The smoke was searing her nose. The traffic from the hills had jammed, and the squad car bullhorn was far below, toward the city. In a sudden silence, she could hear a roar, from somewhere beyond the crests above, like the moan of a passing jet.

Or a huge and distant furnace . . .

She climbed into her own car and inched into the stream.

Seven

Shawn had promised to meet Nicole in the fifth-floor waiting room of St. Francis Hospital.

He threaded the Yamaha past a line of city, county, and private ambulances lined up to load at the emergency entrance. Everywhere were nursing Sisters, fighting to manage frantic skirts in the winds. The smoke from the hills was thickening; he saw patients breathing through handkerchiefs. His eyes stung.

He parked the bike. In the lobby patients lay on gurneys, waiting. Nuns, interns, nurses, and attendants were everywhere, too calm and cheerful—their panic covered with efficiency, thinly stretched. Every blinker on the paging system screens was flashing: chimes bonged continually; the muted PA system chanted for doctors on the staff.

He sidled into an elevator full of relatives who'd come to take ambulatory patients home. On the fifth floor, he squeezed through a queue of wheelchair patients, stepped into the waiting room.

The place was jammed. A Mexican woman wept silently in a corner; an old gentleman in a bathrobe sat glowering, waiting for someone to take him; a woman with a tiny girl argued with an attendant that her home in the hills was more dangerous than the hospital itself.

Nicole strode toward him from across the room, head high. Built-in theater: no cure.

"It's been bad, Shawn," she reported. They'd tried to move him twice, and he'd flailed out at them, finally threatening to pull his tubes loose, and they'd given up temporarily and called his doctor. "Now he's got Val blocking the door."

She said nothing else, except that Brink wanted her and Val to leave. She was going to Wildcat Ridge for the horses. She gave no hint that she knew why he was here.

Well, Brink was right to send them away: she should be nowhere near when it happened. And she was right, even if she knew what Brink planned for him to do, not to show it in any way.

Still . . .

The hell with it.

There was nothing else to say. He left the waiting room and started down the corridor. He heard her sandals slapping behind him, turned. Oblivious to the corridor traffic, she was all at once in his arms.

He had seen her crying on TV once, in an excruciating western soap, at the bedside of a sick child. He had even seen tears in her eyes when Brink had dumped her into the Colorado, for goosing their guide. She could cry exquisitely, on command, without deranging a lash.

But now her face was ugly as a heartbroken child's and tears were smearing her cheeks. "Shawn, I *know*. I've kissed him good-by. If *he* hadn't asked you . . . *I* would have asked you myself."

For a moment, her eyes seemed honest as the sea. He tried the door. It resisted. He called softly to Val, and it opened.

"No hero crap up there, OK?" said Shawn. "Just get the horses out and go."

Val nodded and left with his mother. As the door closed, the TV came to life with a roar. A shout of agony, bottled probably for hours, filled the room, chilling his guts.

Shawn turned to the scarecrow on the bed.

Hash Ono hung up the phone. He arose from the prior's desk and moved to the leaded window with the banging shutter. It opened onto a tiled courtyard. Dust devils whisked in and out of the entrance gate. The day was lemon-yellow, gloomy as an eclipse. He was becoming very nervous.

His forefinger was sore with dialing. He had finally given up on the Sheriff's Department, on the County Fire Department, and even on city fire and police. The lines were constantly busy. The city must be in chaos.

He had finally got through to Shawn Ortega's home and spoken to Shawn's wife. She'd seemed distraught and angry, but had found a hospital number where she thought he might be reached.

And now, of course, the hospital lines were busy.

At the window, he stared as a rabbit hopped into the courtyard. It crouched stage-center, with only a wiggling ear to show that it had not died of fright or exertion. Hash sensed that the fire had spilled over the ridge. He left the office, found a staircase, and mounted to the second floor. The corridor was lined with cells for brothers on retreat. He found one, entered, and peered out the tiny window.

Cathedral Peak, three miles away, stood like a rock in a fiery surf. Orange-black clouds were pouring over its flanks, and he could only intermittently see the summit, for the wind was hurling huge brown billows to eddy in the lee of the crests, rising and curling and seeking out the canyons on its shoulders. La Cumbre Peak, behind it, had disappeared.

He tried to estimate how long he had to escape. Deer were already leaping across the open fields. Animals knew best.

On a ridge between him and Cathedral, he saw for the first time a silver-gray trailer parked. Abandoned, he thought, and then glimpsed motion in the brush beside it. A deer, probably, distraught and panicky.

But he was sure that the firebug was somewhere in the rolling brush between him and the blaze, and the trailer made him uncomfortable.

He went downstairs to dial the hospital again. He'd give it ten minutes, and then try to split for safety on a firebreak he knew over Montecito Peak.

Eight

Shawn held the tiny brown bottle to the light from the hospital window. Half full. He hoped that Mamá Lola knew what she was doing. He picked up the syringe. Sterile? Jesus, what a stupid thought.

He had expected his hand to shake, but it did not. He was steadied by the staring blue eyes, which, for all he knew, were playing to him, as *he* was playing to them, as always it had been, since they'd met in the canyon: testing, probing . . .

Brink was watching his hands. "Pretty good . . . Looks like I bought a piece of the rock . . ."

"The whole farm," murmured Shawn.

Brink grimaced suddenly, shut his eyes, and arched his back as some hidden spasm ripped him. But when he opened his eyes again they were unclouded. "Make you feel better," he asked, "if *I* do this one?"

It was a private joke. They'd been flying the biplane over Lake Cachuma. Shawn, in the front cockpit, had been teaching Brink the split S: half a slowroll, followed by the last half of a loop. They'd been alternating: Shawn would fly one, shake the stick, and Brink would fly the next.

It was his student's turn. Shawn remembered his pride in Brink's steady roll, precise heading, remembered hanging head down from the seat belt, then the nose dropping below the horizon, feeling the slow return of G-forces on his haunches as the aircraft plummeted into a vertical dive. Still solid, controlled. Brink, with less than three hundred hours, was becoming as good as his intructor. But suddenly the dive was holding too long, much too long, they were screaming down, down, down, toward the precise center of the lake, air speed building, struts howling . . . Jesus!

"¿Qué pasa?" he'd screamed on the intercom. "Brink!"

And Brink's voice had come back, over the crackling cacophony, softly and calmly as if asking for the time: "Oh? You want *me* to do this one?"

Shawn had grabbed his own stick, horsed back, almost torn the wings off the airplane, and pulled out over the dancing waters of the lake with only feet to spare.

"You asshole," Shawn murmured now, the syringe slippery in his hand, "I think you set that up, that day!"

Brink was grinning. The face was more skull-like than ever. The past twenty-four hours must have been brutal. "'¿Qué pasa?' you hollered. Hey, Bean?"

"Yeah?" His voice trembled. Steady . . .

"You were one . . . scared . . . half-breed."

"Yeah. You?"

His knees began to tremble. He had to sit on the edge of the bed. Brink took a long, shuddering sigh. "No way."

"Come on, you turkey," Shawn insisted. His throat was tight and his voice sounded squeaky. "Around four, five hundred feet?"

Brink shook his head. "Not then . . . Not now . . ." His grin dissolved into a mask of agony. He suddenly poked at a button and the TV roared louder. Shawn heard a groan, realized that it was his own.

"Shawn!" Brink yelled suddenly. *"Now!"*

Shawn felt Brink clamp his wrist, the grip immensely powerful, crushing, tightening. Brink arched again, curving his belly high, and let go of Shawn's wrist, as a last thin wail drowned itself in the TV.

Shawn grabbed an arm, plunged the needle, and squeezed.

In a while, the wasted body relaxed.

A smiling pharmacist on the screen bellowed of Preparation H.

He was sitting by the bed, staring into nothing, when he heard the door open. The owl-faced nurse gaped at him. She rustled quickly to the bedside. She felt Brink's pulse, at the throat. She glanced at the syringe, still in Shawn's hand. "Mother of God, what *was* that?" She reached for the emergency cord. "I'll have to call Father Gomez . . ."

"It's too late."

She moved to the window. "You have a telephone call," she said faintly, "at the night desk."

He slipped the syringe into his shirt pocket. "OK." He felt nothing.

She swung back. Her eyes were enormous. "I *have* to report what I saw."

He shrugged and moved to the door.

"Lieutenant?"

He turned. "Yes?"

"*Don't* I?"

"Whatever . . ." he murmured. He suddenly didn't care.

Looking him dead in the eye, she removed her glasses, began to wipe them on the edge of her cowl. Her plain Irish face shone in the afternoon glow. "But with eyes like mine, I *could* have seen . . . What? *Nada?*"

He moved across the room and took her hand. It seemed rough and calloused, and he squeezed it for just an instant.

"Nada." He nodded. "And gracias."

"Vaya con Dios," she said.

He left to take the call.

Nine

Button Berger, groggy with fatigue, struggled to hold the rising hose against the pressure from her battered truck. Mac's enormous bulk towered before her; he'd been on the nozzle a full twenty minutes without relief, drowning the old woman's shack nestled under Cieneguitas Ridge.

The old lady—she called herself only "Mamá Lola"—had been incredible. She had to be seventy-five, maybe eighty. Until a few minutes ago, she'd been clawing at a stack of firewood banked against her cabin, hurling it clear; then she'd hacked her outhouse clear of a jungle of dried manzanita; finally, Button had noticed, she'd harvested a last-minute bundle of the marijuana leaves growing up the hillside behind.

Now she was braving the spray, running in and out for the last of her kitchen utensils, piling them into her old red jeep, which waited, like an overburdened pack mule, at the wooden bridge Button had been afraid to trust with the weight of her truck. Atop the pile in the jeep, sitting on a sag-bottomed rocking chair, was the dog she called Perro, barking at the truck, Button, her crew, and the holocaust on the other side of the mountains.

They'd laid hose across the bridge, hose they might have to abandon if the fire jumped the crest. The truck? She'd die before she left it.

She found herself dozing on her feet. She clutched at the pulsing hose like a lifeline. She heard Hal behind her, chanting: "Flashover! Flashover! Flashover!"

She swung her eyes to the top of the ridge. He was right. The first flames were only tongues, licking at clumps of brush on the distant skyline. Then, instantly, the crest itself was afire and the yellow bushes were dissolving, as if a giant were chomping at an ear of corn on the ridgeline. Finally, in a wave of bright orange flame, the fire began to spill down the slopes toward them, like water breaching the walls of a dam.

This was it, then, for Mamá Lola's house. Button glanced back at the stubby old lady. She was lifting a jug of white wine from her jeep, toasting the end. Good: fire-wise, the old gal realized that all was gone. She flashed Button a smile through her gaping teeth. Then she cinched a rope tightly across the mess in the back of the jeep, patted Perro on the skull to quiet him, and climbed behind the wheel.

The heat became a living thing. Now the rivers of fire were halfway down the slope. A furnace blast of wind slammed up the canyon behind them, stopped the flames short, drove the fire partway back up the hill, and changed direction, sucking them onward.

"Last chance!" yelled Button, jabbing Mac in the back. "Let's *go*."

He nodded, without looking back, and she raced along the hose line, over the bridge, to the master panel on the truck. She cranked off the valve, saw the hose go limp, and beckoned Mamá Lola. The old lady bounced the jeep over the bridge. By the time she was there the heat was so fierce that Button was yanking the shelter blankets out of their rack, in case they had to dive under the truck.

She waved the old lady past the truck. "Get out!" she screamed above the roar of the flames. Then she hoisted herself into the cab, started the engine. A nearby bush burst into flame, triggered spontaneously, from heat. The door opened and Mac dove in.

"You take it!" she yelled, knowing she couldn't wrestle the truck up the hill. He nodded, slid under her and beneath the wheel.

Perro leaped out of the moving jeep and headed wailing back across the bridge. Mamá Lola scrambled back to the ground, and stumbled after him.

Button hurled open the door. She saw Mac, as in a dream, face distorted in anger, grabbing after her, but she squirmed loose. Outside the cab she heard the thundering, now like a jet taking off, resounding from the canyon walls. A gust of wind knocked her to her knees. She brushed a hot clinker from her forehead, raced back across the bridge.

She caught the old lady at the porch. Inside, she could hear the dog yelping. A flaming eave fell to the deck in a shower of sparks. She grabbed Mamá Lola's shoulder.

"Let me *go!*" yelled the old lady, swinging her arm. She caught Button backhanded, by surprise, on the side of the cheek. Button hung on, but the woman was twice her weight. "I got a little girl!" Button screamed, into the old woman's clear eyes.

The old lady reached out, touched Button's cheek, and quit. Button hustled her back to the jeep, slid behind its wheel, and followed the truck up the hairpin turns. At the top, she looked down.

The cabin was ablaze from top to bottom.

Mamá Lola stared straight ahead, refusing to look back. "Too old," she sighed. "Too old and dried up for the hills . . ."

"No," muttered Button. "You're not."

"Hey," Mamá Lola murmured. "Not *me!* Perro! And the house."

The old lady lit a joint, leaned her head back, closed her eyes, and smoked quietly all the way back to the fire blockade on Gibraltar Road.

Shawn Ortega eased the Yamaha up Alameda Padre Serra, weaving through a double line of traffic coming down. Dazed with fatigue, he tried to erase from his mind Brink, Nicole, the nun, Val . . .

Hash Ono had said he was in the hills and thought the firebug was there too. He had sounded scared on the scratchy phone and ready to split if he didn't get help, and soon.

Shawn swerved to avoid a ponytailed girl leading a horse down the drain gutter. He could feel on his cheeks the heat of the fire, still miles away over the mountains. Immense dead cinders were falling everywhere. Some of the faces he saw in the cars bore the look of battle refugees, but others wore devil-may-care grins, like schoolchildren freed from class. Everywhere, on roofs above the street, homeowners with hoses, ignoring orders, were dribbling water onto their shingles.

He heard a bullhorn cruising the streets above. He needed help for Ono, so he followed the sound up Camino Alto.

He found Cal Trumbell, driving his unit sourly through deserted streets. A reserve deputy manned the bullhorn beside him. Shawn waved them down and spoke through Cal's window. He told him that County Fire Arson had a lead on the kidnapping, and told Trumbell to get himself cleared and follow him to Mount Calvary Monastery. It was no time to mention that he'd lost his badge.

"No, *sir!* Ain't nobody going to get *up* to Mount Calvary: everything's coming down, and it's all burning past Foothill. Chrissakes, they're pulling out *fire trucks!* You want to hear?"

Trumbell turned up his radio. The frequencies, normally punctuated only by sporadic bursts of dispatcher or patrolman, were jammed with cross talk: reports, inquiries, demands for assistance. He heard a paramedic yelling for plasma and a city cop for a fire truck.

Instant chaos. He had never heard anything like it.

He watched Trumbell glide down the street and around the corner. He sat for a moment astride the idling bike, trying to collect his thoughts in the smoke and the gusting wind.

His instinct was to stay in the foothills and fight for his home, only four blocks away. He didn't know what good he could do unarmed in the mountains with Ono, anyway. But it was he who had put Ono on Zimmer's trail, he'd sounded nervous on the phone, and he wasn't going to leave him there alone.

He had better get a gun. He kicked the bike into gear and rocketed through barren, smoky streets toward home and Don Miguel's old horse pistol.

If he ever had to pull the trigger, it would probably blow up.

But anything was better than nothing at all.

Ten

Jerry Castle, sitting on the edge of the bunk in the command van, gathered himself to stand. If he rose too suddenly to his feet, he knew he'd get dizzy and topple. All through the interminable day he'd had this problem: he had no idea what caused it, probably the gallon or so of cardboard-tasting coffee he'd poured down in the last —how many days? Three, four? He couldn't remember.

Robert Wendell Holmes was standing at the huge situation map, mumbling of low pressure systems off the coast of Oregon, and a lessening of the Rocky Mountain high . . . A song? Jerry wasn't even hearing right.

"Rocky Mountain High?" he called from the bunk. Everybody at the map turned, slow motion. Their faces seemed blurred. He grinned, to show that he was kidding. "Neil Diamond?"

"John Denver, boss," said Mike Kane tolerantly. He was looking at him oddly. Jerry took a deep breath, stood up, clung for a moment to the radio console, and moved to the map.

"Did I hear you say the wind would break?" he asked Holmes.

"I think it will," Holmes said. "Tonight. Midnight, maybe. Of course, we'll lose half the town by six."

Holmes pointed out his new low off Oregon. He claimed that this one, at last, was a warm front that would shatter the cold sea of air still giving them hell. Instead of feeling grateful to whatever weather gods Holmes worshiped, Jerry was angry. Why couldn't it have happened yesterday, while there was hope? Why not now? If the Santa Ana died with the last ember of the last foothill home, what good was that?

He felt rage at the gales that had scarred, for the next fifty years, his forests, and would destroy half the lovely city by the sea.

"Well"—Holmes shrugged—"we came close, but no cigar."

Close. But no cigar . . .

"If we'd held the west flanks of Cathedral Peak and La Cumbre . . ." Mike Kane was saying. Jerry fought to concentrate, he must concentrate on the fire . . .

Close . . . But no cigar . . .

Not Wadi Akarit, not *today . . .*

"Close, Lieutenant, but no cigar . . ."

He could escape North Africa no longer. Everything here was too much the same: desert wind, smell of tension, young faces stubbled and scribed with strain.

And stupid orders, written by men too far from the scene . . .

He was in a sandbagged OP high on a bouldered crest, peering down at the wadi and brown-baked valley below. Invisible panzers sent dust devils curling up the rock-strewn hills. Rommel, they said, had left for Berlin and General Arnim was gathering his forces for a last counterattack, but the names and numbers had not really changed since El Alamein.

Warble, warble, warble . . . Crunch! Incoming mail, a 105 mm searching for 2nd Platoon, Dog Company, nested not far behind him. He had, long before dawn, spotted the Kraut battery from its flash across the valley. He had its co-ordinates ready for Regiment, he had everything but the guts to lie again to Regiment on the air.

For he had, by the rules, to wait until someone was hit.

His radioman was studying the reverse slope behind him, waiting for a casualty. No casualty, no return fire. Such was the colonel's edict. An ammo shortage, Regiment claimed, or maybe they didn't want to give away their own genius-generated artillery positions before the German attack.

"Short," the corporal sighed. He sounded as if he were rooting for a Kraut hit. "Close, but no cigar."

Bait, Dog Company was bait, and probably knew it. So why didn't they *fake* a casualty, so he could save them. Shit!

Another shell yodeled overhead. *Warble, warble, warble . . . Crunch.* Come on, Dog. Anything will do: A purple-heart ping in the ass? A broken finger diving for cover? He listened, begging for the familiar yell, on the radio or on the howling desert wind. *Medic, medic, medic?*

Nothing.

"Still short, sir."

Warble, warble, warble . . . Crunch!

"Over! About fifty! Lieutenant, they're straddled!"

Damn! If he called for return fire, Regiment would check, for sure, afterward. He'd cheated before, and the colonel knew it. If he didn't have a casualty to prove his case, he'd be bait himself, back in a spotter plane, or worse, jammed in a Sherman tank for the next fish fry . . .

He didn't care. He knew Dog Company well, had bivouacked with them at Fondouk Pass, fuck the colonel, fuck the Army . . .

"Corporal?"

"Yes, sir?"

"Call it in! Grid three-five-niner, four-two-six—"

Warble, warble, warble . . .

Too late, he knew instantly. Christ, why'd he waited?

"Bravo, two rounds—" he shouted, anyway, praying for a miracle.

Crunch! And then the boom of a secondary explosion, Dog Company must have had ammo cached, or gasoline, and even *then* no call for medics, because there was no one to make the call . . . Shit, shit, shit!

He rushed to the back of the OP, peered down at a plume of smoke, which was all there was left. He slammed his helmet to the ground and pressed his head into the topmost sandbag.

"Lieutenant?"

He turned. The corporal was offering him a cigarette from a khaki pack of Luckies. *Lucky Strike green has gone to war . . .*

"We'll call it in nice and easy, sir, huh? 'Cause they ain't no hurry now."

He felt a hand on his forearm. He was back in the van, and Mike Kane was gripping his wrist. He must have been wobbling again. He shook off the hand and moved to the map.

"When'll it ease?" he asked Holmes. "The wind?"

"Well, we show a positive gradient at thirty-five thousand feet, but the high pressure—"

"Goddamn it, *when?*" He glared into the young man's eyes.

Holmes looked startled, and his beard jerked up defiantly. "I . . . Should start to slack off after dusk. Six, seven hours."

Jerry Castle placed his hand on the map, covering the east flanks of Cathedral Peak, La Cumbre Peak, and the valley between. He knew what he had to do, but he might as well check with the expert. "What would happen if we backfired this? At, say, five P.M.?"

Holmes stared at him. "You can't get a crew in there!"

"From the air, then. What would happen?"

Holmes looked at the map, glanced at his watch. "I can run it through Wallops—"

"Screw that! What'll *happen?*"

The young man frowned. "Fire storm," he said uncertainly. "It'd suck the winds back to the west. And it just might save the show. But how you going to set it? You can't *helitorch* it, you'd just lose the chopper, these winds. And even if you didn't, *their* payload, you'd be trying to turn an elephant with a gnat!"

"Jerry," said his air boss gently, "you tried. You can't beat City Hall. *Or* Washington."

Close, but no cigar . . .

He looked up at Kane. "Get 'em. Steamboat and Snaproll."

Mike was silent for a long moment. "Only if *I* run it. Airborne. On site."

Jerry studied his air boss. To direct this operation personally would put Mike's neck on the guillotine, precisely next to his own. To start even a *legal* fire storm would be risky enough and could conceivably destroy the city they were trying to save, if the winds had tricked Holmes.

To do it with napalm would finish the career of any airborne director within miles of the scene of the crime.

"No," Jerry murmured. "Me."

Mike stared at him. "You're out of your mind!"

Jerry glanced at his watch. "Seventeen hundred hours, tell 'em, on site. Or the mission's scrubbed. I'll be riding the Beechcraft at angels eight."

"Look, you aren't qualified to—"

"I got more time," Jerry said stiffly, "over fire lines than most of you got in the sack."

That the last of it was over a fire line near Salerno, calling in artillery for a battalion of ass-dragging infantrymen, he saw no need to mention.

His job here in the fire camp was done, win, lose, or draw.

No chopper could fly in such winds, so he headed for a staff car, and Santa Barbara Municipal Airport miles below.

Shawn idled the Yamaha slowly up Eucalyptus Hill Road, coughing as the yellow smoke poured from the mountains above. Vehicular traffic had been bottled off by fire equipment fighting the flames. Drivers had abandoned their cars and become pedestrian refugees. A stream of last-minute escapees trickled down the street and sidewalks, tripping over hoses laid like pulsing veins across the road.

Someone waved him back. He ignored him. A block below his house he passed his next-door neighbor's wife, hysterical at the wheel of an empty U-Haul truck, screaming at a city fire captain who wouldn't let her return for another load. As Shawn drifted by, the fireman reached into the truck, plucked out her keys, and hurled them into the bushes.

On his own block his uphill neighbor and a teen-age son were trundling an antique surrey, complete with fringe on top, from their front lawn. It was creaking under mattresses and chairs, like something out of a Viet Nam movie.

His home seemed forlorn and accusing. From somewhere in the canyon behind it he heard a whinny. Out of the smoke, across his sunburned lawn, loped a huge black gelding, mane flying. Its neck was flecked green, saliva dangled from its lips, its ears were back and its eyes glittered in fear. It clattered onto the sidewalk and disappeared into the smoke below, scattering the house owners.

For an instant he sat astride the bike outside his home. The dwellings sat shoulder to shoulder along the canyon rim. When the first one caught fire, in the circling wind, there'd be no hope for any of them. He could hear a roar from the north, as if someone had built a steel mill on the block above. The cackle of radios from fire trucks told him that somewhere his battle was being fought for him, but he could see nothing through the smoke.

The heat was crushing. It burst on him in waves. He expected the eucalyptus tree to explode above him. None of his neighbors had stayed to fight.

An ember sailed downwind, end over end, and landed, in a shower of sparks, on a shingled roof across the street. A ring of fire began to gnaw at the shakes. There was not a fireman in sight.

Climbing off his bike, he stiffened. His front door was open. He'd told Crissy to lock it. A looter? Or had she simply forgotten? Swinging in the gusts, it spoke to him of abandonment, angering him. She should have shut the house up, properly, to live or die in peace.

He jammed his handkerchief over his mouth and sprinted up the walk. He paused outside, incredulous. He could hear the sound of his TV. He burst into the living room in a cloud of swirling cinders, rushed into the den. He stopped short, staring.

Don Miguel sat in his favorite chair. On TV, volume full-up, unfolded the eternal agonies of "As the World Turns."

"What in the name of Christ—?"

"Do not swear," his grandfather warned him.

"Where'd you *come* from?"

"The park. It was time for lunch."

"Suppose I hadn't come *back*?" He dove into the hall closet, found the ancient .44, jammed it under his belt. Ammo, where'd he hidden the ammo? Kitchen. He strode to the kitchen, found the six rounds, glanced out the back window in time to see the fallen oak in the yard burst into flame. Closer than he'd thought.

He returned to the den, yanked Don Miguel from his chair. "Come on!"

The old man hung back. "I haven't eaten."

Shawn looked down at him. Ash dusted his hair. He seemed somehow shrunken. His eyes were clouded with hurt. He was hungry.

"Later, Pops." He pointed out the window.

The flaming oak seemed to bring Don Miguel back to reality. "¡Dios mío!" He spotted Crissy's sketchbook, apparently forgotten in her rush. The Madonna and child, destined for the Montecito overpass, were smeared with dust and grime. Don Miguel grabbed it, hugged it to his chest.

"Come *on*," yelled Shawn.

They left the house. Engines were retreating down the hill. Shawn was trying to flag one to take the old man when a red jeep bounced out of the smoke above.

It was Mamá Lola's, loaded with everything she had. A worn but pretty woman in a CDF hard hat was driving. She squeaked to a stop and deserted the wheel, which Mamá Lola took over. The fire-woman signaled the next truck to stop. It was apparently her own: she began to issue orders and in a moment the street was ribbed with hose.

Shawn installed his grandfather in the jeep, looked into Mamá Lola's face. "With Brink," he said, "it's done. And . . . He thanks you."

She nodded slowly, patted his hand, and drove off with Don Miguel.

Shawn crisscrossed fire trails and jogging paths he had used for years, like a rat in a maze, high on his foot pegs, looking for a passage through the fire lines.

Finally, not sure in the thick smoke exactly how he had got there, he found himself on Gibraltar Road on the way to Mount Calvary Monastery.

Eleven

Eric Zimmer looked for the last time around his trailer. He'd stolen it a year ago at Leo Carrillo State Beach, north of Malibu, while the owners were surfing. He'd towed it right past the state forester, who was busy at the ticket window on the entrance road, and so far as he knew, nobody'd ever come close to finding it, or the pickup ripped off with it.

He hated to torch the trailer. It was the only home he'd ever owned himself. He'd always been crowded in with a million people: his own brothers, first, in Santa Ana, running from the Chicanos who ruled the streets, then juvie hall, foster homes, halfway houses; finally, barracks at Camp Pendleton, the brig, Lompoc, Chino, 'Tasky.

Too bad to lose the trailer, but he'd rip another just like it, somewhere, or maybe a motor home.

Now he lounged on the bed, watching the blonde. He'd untied her arms, and she sat staring at nothing with the big blue eyes, sitting on the floor. He could stir her up with a match or two, probably, but he wouldn't have time; there was lots to do.

"Who's down in that monastery?" the Shrink's voice asked suddenly. "Who came in the scout car?" The Shrink had come back, somehow, very confusing, maybe they'd saved his life at Gaviota Pass, hard to believe, but there was his voice, loud and clear.

"Fuck off," Zimmer told him. The blonde swung her blank blue eyes to him, blinking.

"You know what I'm gonna do?" Zimmer asked her. He got up, prodded her in the stomach with his boot, bent down and yelled into her ear. "I'm gonna deep-fry you! Like a fucking chicken, you hear? Hey, Crispy? Or Regular?"

She only stared into space. He moved to the door, ripped the handle off from the inside. "Gets warm in here, you holler, hear? Holler for Jake the Flake!"

He stepped out of the trailer, slammed the door, mounted to the cab roof of his truck, hidden in the brush. He felt the hot wind ruffling his beard; the Santa Ana was as strong as ever, though becoming more erratic. A tumbleweed bounced up the side of the hill beneath him, lodged against the trailer door, and clung there.

Jesus, he hadn't realized that the fire on Cathedral Peak was moving so fast: it was charging across the ridgeline already. He looked south for an exit through the coastal ranges. But everything in the Santa Barbara foothills seemed afire, from Montecito Peak to East Mountain Drive.

He had already unhitched the pickup and moved it a safe distance from the trailer. Now, seeing the two converging tides of flame, he decided that when it came time to leave, he had better abandon the pickup too and take the Harley. He opened the tailgate and ramped the bike down.

He got his can of gasoline and was twisting off the cap when he heard the whine of a bike below. He hopped back on the bed of the truck to see above the brush.

He could see nothing past the monastery, because of the brown haze in the valley. But the whine was unmistakable: Kawasaki two-stroke, or a Yamaha, and coming fast. At least, not a cop.

He didn't know what kind of asshole would be riding dirt in a fire like this one, but for some reason it irritated him. He checked the clip in his .45 automatic and slammed a round into the chamber, in case the idiot continued up the hill.

He began to circle the trailer, sloshing gas on its sides, from the five-gallon tank.

The blonde began to scream. He could see her beating at the window over his bunk, nose pressed to the glass.

She must have smelled the gas.

He slopped some onto the pane.

She flinched and he smiled.

Shawn Ortega, parked on his bike next to Hash's scout car outside the monastery, listened to Ono's briefing. Together, on Hash's radio, they tried to raise county Emergency Services, Goleta, San Marcos Pass Fire Camp, anyone. No soap.

His stomach felt fluttery. If Zimmer, presumably driving his pickup, had trapped himself on the inland side of the coastal fire, he was still here. No four-wheel vehicle was going to penetrate the wilderness fire trails: he'd found it rough enough on the Yamaha. And the Harley street bike wasn't, either, unless Zimmer was the world's greatest dirt-rider.

Presumably, the pyro was still carrying his .45.

He didn't like the prospect. He'd been on the department twelve years, had never had to fire his weapon, had never even heard a gun fired in anger. Now, he was a civilian, legally speaking, and *practically* speaking, unarmed.

He pulled Don Miguel's old horse pistol from his belt. Hash was watching him. "Jesus," he mumbled, "what *is* that? You going to rob a stage?"

Shawn flicked open the cylinder, peered into the barrel, and winced. He hadn't really inspected the relic since childhood. From the looks of the tired barrel, it must have dispatched injured horses by the dozen, and rattlesnakes by the score. And apparently no one had cleaned it for years. The rifling was shot, lands worn smooth, grooves edgeless. He slipped in the six rounds of ammunition, wondering if they'd misfire from age or simply tumble wildly in the air like passes from a tired quarterback.

Shawn told him tersely where his own service revolver was, and how it had got there. "Ortega," growled the Nisei, "I knew you were stupid twenty years ago, first play of that game."

The hell with it, thought Shawn. "Where do we start?"

Hash swept his eyes along the ridge. Shawn followed his gaze. No sign of life: only an abandoned trailer half hidden behind thick yellow brush on the crest above them. As he watched, smoke drifted down from far-off Cathedral Peak and obscured the trailer.

"Earlier," muttered Hash, "I thought I saw movement up there." He started the scout car's engine. "Follow me."

"You're a fireman," Shawn said, kicking the bike into gear. "*You* follow *me*."

"*You're* a civilian," Hash yelled over the roar of the wind.

"I got the gun."

Shawn took the lead up the sweeping hillside through the smoke and rising heat.

Shawn and Brink had torn through this country together, raced Yamaha against Moto Guzzi up this same sunburned hill, traded bikes at the top to speed down again. First he had crashed, then Brink. Now, groping through smoke, it was even harder to keep his seat.

Cresting a hummock, he rose on his pegs to snatch a glance behind. The scout car was bouncing along behind him. Ono, grinning, face blackened with grime, raised a hand over the windshield and wiggled his fingers daintily.

Under the fat of twenty years, the Kamikaze Kid seemed screaming to get out.

Twelve

Far below the lumbering Fortress, the amber sun was plummeting into an apricot haze. Steamboat Haley flung up a wing and banked left, scanning the terrain.

Toward the ocean, the enormous column of smoke trailed as far as he could see. The city itself was hidden. Fire rimmed the mountains which cupped it. Bouncing along at 12,000 feet, he could smell the burning brush.

He was looking for Flores Flat, nestled in Rattlesnake Canyon near Mount Calvary Monastery. He couldn't find it in the murk, though he'd seen it a hundred times.

He leveled his wings and banked right, to give Snaproll a chance to search from her seat.

He needed a drink.

An odd twitch had begun to pluck at his right arm. He'd first noticed it as they'd taxied from the Forest Service Staging Area at Santa Barbara Municipal. If he could sneak one blast from the Old Taylor stuffed into the map case by his left knee, he knew that the twitch would disappear. But there was no way to get the bottle uncapped, swigged, capped, and back without Snaproll noticing: if he let go of the yoke, turbulence would stand the plane on its tail.

"Look west of Cathedral Peak," he urged her, above the beat of his engines. Uselessly, he worked his number three prop-pitch, trying to synchronize it with the rest. He only made it worse. A tooth began to ache, from vibration or altitude.

"I *know* where the fucking flat is," flared Suzy. "It's—Hold it!"

He felt control torn from his hands as she grabbed her yoke and steepened their bank to see better. He winced. They had four pods, eight feet long and pregnant with napalm, fused and ready, quivering out of his sight below, hanging from creaking wings. They weighed 500 pounds each; she was pulling two Gs; he had no idea whether the bomb-release shackles, installed on *Marvin's Mistress's* wings for some arcane World War II experiment, could sustain their weight in so steep a bank. He envisioned the pods tumbling end over end into Santa Barbara, wiping out City Hall in a sheet of flame.

Now he really needed a drink. He was reaching for the bottle, stealthily, when she leveled the wings again. "I see the flat," she announced triumphantly. "And the air boss!" She banged the mike against the panel to scare it into life, and bawled: "Air Attack One, Air Tanker Niner-Seven reporting in, ten-ninety-seven, southeast flank of the fire at twelve thousand above Flores Flat . . . And I got you in sight, in the cute little Beechcraft Baron."

Too late for the drink. He should have made his move while she was distracted. He took back the controls, spotted Air Attack One, a tiny red-and-white twin Beechcraft bouncing along the flank of the fire at 8,000 feet.

Air Attack One rogered. Shocked, Steamboat recognized Jerry Castle's voice. He felt irritated: apparently Castle didn't trust him to lay his eggs alone. On the other hand, the fire boss didn't trust even his air boss Kane to direct the attack either: a measure of its importance.

OK, he'd hatch the damnedest fire the county had ever seen, precisely where they wanted it.

Castle was talking now, cutting in and out. "Got you in sight . . . Want you to . . . left-hand orbit about six thousand . . . Mount Calvary Monastery . . ."

Steamboat struck his earphone with his palm, decided that Snaproll could explain it all to him later, and began his descent. His heart was pounding strangely. Everything was wrong and sour. The turbulence was awful. Air this hot could rob your engines of oxygen, and you lost your lift above such flames: superheated air was thin, like taking off from Denver on a hot and windless day . . . Six thousand feet, he'd said? He was there. He leveled off.

"Safeties off," he chanted, touching his bomb release switches. "Armed . . . Green light . . ." He'd reverted to World War II without effort or thought. After Biak, he'd flown from Port Lyautey, in North Africa, in B-24s, in just such hot and searing weather . . . Ashes were pitting his windshield now, flak from the fire below.

"Report six thousand," he told Snaproll. "Where's he want the run?"

"Ridgeline above Calvary Monastery," she yelled. "He wants to lead us in himself. When the wind shifts south. Fifteen hundred feet. And it's *two* runs, not one."

"Bull*shit!*" he howled. "A *second* pass? Through a fire we're gonna set ourselves? *One* salvo, tell him!"

"Split load, he wants," she insisted. "Two pods at a time."

"No!"

"Air Attack One," he heard her transmit placidly. "Roger on your splits. Say when."

He glared at her speechlessly. She grinned back, patted his hand on the yoke. She leaned across, lifted his earphone. Her lips were warm on his ear, sending shivers up his back. "Fifteen grand, baby: splits, salvos. Or I'd even screw him in the cockpit, upside down at thirty thousand feet, OK?"

"OK," he muttered. Twenty years of bullshit, and a ring right through his nose.

He reached at last for the bottle, and took a long, long slug. To his surprise, she was smiling when he finished. He wiped his mouth and offered it to her, though she never drank in the air.

She hoisted it daintily, little finger crooked, and finished it off.

"You can buy an awful lotta booze"—she smiled—"with fifteen thousand bucks."

Shawn Ortega lay trembling in a shallow declivity on the crest of the ridge above the monastery. Don Miguel's horse pistol smoked in his hand. He was trying to whip up courage to peer along the ridgeline, before the firebug, or whoever had shot at him, simply charged down and killed him where he lay.

The Yamaha sprawled ten feet away, creaking as it cooled. A ground squirrel cheeped from somewhere past the ridge.

He'd heard the whisper of a bullet even before he heard the

gunshot. He'd heard it through his helmet and over the howl of the Yamaha, instinctively hit the kill switch on the handlebar, and laid the bike down in a cloud of dust. As he hit the dirt, he rolled into the closest clump of brush. It was cactus and he never even felt the spines.

Instantly, he'd craned downhill. Ono, a quarter of a mile below him, had been bouncing innocently up the slope. Shawn had yanked the old weapon from his belt, aimed it high over the scout car, and jerked off a warning blast.

His shot had sounded like a 20 mm wing-gun and the kick almost tore the pistol from his grip. He saw the scout car skid to a stop and nose into a toyon bush. Hash had dived for the dirt. Only then had Shawn realized the mess he'd got them into.

His hard hat was white, very noticeable against the brush. Now he eased it off. It tumbled to the bottom of the depression, sounding like a kettledrum.

Cautiously, he peered around the trunk of the largest cactus. He could see the gray trailer, fifty feet away, and a black pickup truck hidden in the brush behind it. At least, now he was sure: Zimmer.

He glanced at the weapon in his hand. Enormous, imposing, but probably, in a gunfight, useless as tits on a bull. His temptation was to remain where he was, quietly, and hope that Zimmer, knowing he was armed, would climb into the pickup and flee.

But there was the blonde, and from what he knew of the pyro, Zimmer would murder her first, if he hadn't already, and then kill him where he lay and Hash Ono too, if he could find him.

When in doubt, go to the net . . .

"Police officer!" he suddenly bellowed. "You're surrounded, Zimmer! Come out! No weapons, hands—"

A gun roared from the brush. There was a *splat* above him. Cactus juice sprayed down on his head. It felt sticky. He groveled in the dirt. *Shit, shit, shit . . .*

He couldn't stay. No matter what happened, he had to abandon the bike and move. He eased to the back of the shallow dish, found a cracked rain-fissure a foot deep leading down the ridge, and slithered along it. Every five or ten feet he would ease his head out of the dried grass, take a bearing on Ono's scout car, and rest. He was afraid to look back up the ridge.

But when he heard the truck door slam far above him, he stopped and risked a glance from the ditch.

The black pickup was crawling toward the cactus clump. He could see the driver silhouetted on the ridge against the glow to the north. If he'd had his own gun instead of the relic, he might have chanced a shot. He saw Zimmer peer into the cactus from out of the window. Zimmer pointed an automatic into the clump, fired three times. The shots echoed from the slopes of Cathedral Peak, enveloping the valley.

Shawn calculated quickly. One shot first, and then a second, into the cactus. Then three from the pickup truck. Three left in the eight-round clip. And no telling how many clips.

For a moment Zimmer studied the clump of cactus. Then the truck backed, turned in a cloud of dust, and bumped back to the trailer. Shawn snaked down to the scout car. The Kamikaze Kid appeared instantly, from behind a bush. His face was impassive, but his eyes were shifting nervously. "Jesus, I thought he got you. What now?"

Shawn thought swiftly. Ono, unarmed, was useless, but if he could drive the scout car back into radio range, or penetrate the coastal fire fronts when the gales subsided, he could send a chopper back with help.

"You go back—" Shawn began.

Ono was not listening. He sniffed the wind. "Smell that?"

Shawn caught a whiff of gasoline, strong on the smoky sage.

And faintly, from the trailer, he heard a woman wail in terror.

"Oh, shit," he grunted. Hash was hoisting himself behind the wheel of the scout car. Shawn dove into the passenger seat, and in a moment they were grinding up the hill.

Shawn glanced at his gun. One round gone in warning, five left, and a gun that might well have gone up San Juan Hill with Teddy Roosevelt. "*Weave* a little," he demanded. "We're sitting ducks."

Ono began to zigzag. Shawn glimpsed a moving shadow by the trailer ahead. Suddenly, with a *whoosh,* the trailer was engulfed in flames. A thin shriek drilled his ears. They skidded to a stop outside the circle of fire.

Ono yanked an axe from the rear, grabbed his fireman's jacket, and raced for the door. Shawn stayed outside the flames, ostensibly to cover him, actually because he was unable to force himself through the ring of fire. He heard a shot from near the pickup, ducked as a slug, intended for Ono, slammed into the trailer. He heard Ono swiping at the lock with his axe, saw him vanish, reappear in silhouette, yanking the girl from the trailer, dash back through the fire.

Shawn heard the deep-throated sound of a street Harley, swung the gun to waste a shot at Zimmer roaring up into the smoke sluicing from Cathedral Peak. The pistol almost kicked from his hand. Two rounds gone, four to go . . .

"Get her!" yelled Hash. The girl, rolling eyes like a frightened fawn's, had broken away. Her tiny skirt was flaming. Shawn dropped the gun and tackled her, banging his bad knee on a rock. He pressed her close and rolled with her in the dirt. Hash flailed at them with his jacket and finally tore off her smoldering skirt as Shawn struggled to his feet.

"Get her back," he ordered Ono. "And get me help." He jammed the gun in his belt and sprinted for his Yamaha by the cactus clump. In an instant he was howling past the blazing trailer, up the flank of Cathedral Peak, eating up ground, glimpsing Zimmer finally, losing him again as a billow of smoke whisked down the slope.

His front tire hit a fist-sized rock. The shock jolted his forks, shivered up his arms, slammed him down on the seat. He wobbled, almost went down, hung in. Zimmer, apparently heading for a fire trail through the flames, was one hell of a dirt-rider, but the Harley was no match for the light, knobby-wheeled Yamaha. What Shawn would do when he caught up, with four rounds left in the ancient gun, he had no idea.

He rose on his pegs, peering into the murk as the cycle bucked under him. His wrists, seared by the girl's dress, burned with pain, and she had kneed him in the groin.

He hoped that her face was unscarred: she wasn't much older than Mary Lou.

Whom he'd forgotten to hug when he left at noon . . .

Have you hugged your kid today?

He hadn't kissed Crissy, either . . .

Another ditch . . . Watch it . . . Too late.

He was sailing skyward. Going down, he glimpsed Zimmer,

stopped astride his bike and watching through drifting smoke from a hundred yards above.

For an instant, the world went black. Then he was on his back in the brush, staring at a Forest Service twin Beech, dipping low along the ridge, wiggling its wings and climbing.

Far behind it, he heard the roar of a tanker plane.

So if Zimmer didn't drill him, they'd half drown him with slurry from above.

He rolled to his belly, cocking the gun, rose to one knee, snapped off a two-handed shot. Fifteen feet left of Zimmer, a puff of dust flew from an oak tree. The .44 slug ricocheted wailing up the slope.

Three rounds left. And Zimmer, off the bike and stalking him now, was laughing.

Terror clawed at Shawn. He scrambled into a combat crouch, took a deep breath, exhaled half, squeezed another round. High: Zimmer barely flinched. He fired again. Five yards in front of Zimmer, a rock disintegrated, showering the pyro with flakes. Zimmer chuckled and continued down the slope. A gust of wind howled from Cathedral Peak. Shawn fired his last round. The bullet rang from a boulder and whined away over the valley.

Slowly, the .45 came up, its muzzle a tiny black hole not thirty feet away, pointed at his chest.

"*Six* for you, man," Zimmer chortled. "All she wrote! Pig, *you* are going to die!"

Steamboat Haley craned to see through his ash-smeared windshield, trying to line up the bucking nose with the murky ridgeline three hundred feet below. The fire boss, leading him in with the Beech Baron, had already disappeared into the smoke from the flank of Cathedral, having made his pass too low. Steamboat wished him no harm and hoped he'd emerge safely, but Castle's heroics had carried him and his pilot so deeply into the haze that it was hard to see where they'd rocked their wings to signal the drop.

Snaproll was tense beside him, transfixed by the darkening smoke mass hurtling toward them. "Here?" she yelled, above the engines.

"No," he muttered, thumb on the bomb release on his yoke. From the corner of his eye he glimpsed the monastery: when it disappeared under his left wing, he'd drop. It was gone. "*Here!*"

He jabbed his thumb, felt the plane lighten as it shed his first two pods, and was all at once fighting for control in a heaving, flame-tinged hell.

Shawn dropped his gun, raised his hands, and began an entreaty: "Zimmer, look—"

Zimmer only beamed. "On your knees, greaser!"

Useless. But damned if he'd go out whining, any more than Brink. *Sorry, Crissy, sorry, Mary Lou . . .*

He charged uphill, braced for the slug in his chest. He heard a roar above the crest. The tanker passed suddenly overhead, squeezing his gut and shaking the mountainside. Zimmer stared up and flopped to the ground. Shawn dropped as he glimpsed two huge cylindrical shapes tumbling over his head, glinting in the orange sun.

The canisters struck twenty feet beyond him, together. One bounced over Zimmer, exploded in a dull boom. The other caromed up the hill, spreading a lake of dirty orange fire along the crest. Shawn pressed his forehead into the dirt, too weak to rise.

For a moment there was silence. The sound of the bomber receded. He raised his head. The heat from the fire uphill struck him like a blow. For a moment he could hear nothing, see nothing. He struggled to his feet, began to run downhill.

Then he heard it, a rising howl of agony from the inferno above. He turned and stood, transfixed, as it grew closer. An apparition took form, charging out of the flames. Its clothes were afire, its hair a golden halo. It sprinted past Shawn, stumbling blindly, downhill, arms flailing, as the flames consumed its clothes and skin.

"Drop!" Shawn yelled after him. "Roll!"

The apparition screamed, white eyes rolling at him as it passed, and continued to race downhill. Far below, it fell to its knees, rolled to its back. Shawn, running, ripped off his own shirt to beat at the flames, but by the time he reached him, the flames had turned to smoke.

The smell of burning hair was sickening. Shawn kneeled by the smoking body. Zimmer was staring blindly at the sky. What had once been his mouth was a blackened hole moving in a charcoal mask. Shawn held his breath and bent his head close, listening.

"The Shrink . . . Tell him . . . I made it . . . on the street."

The body quivered, once and again, and silently, Zimmer was gone. Now there was only the roar of flames higher up, the aircraft circling somewhere beyond the smoke. Shawn dragged himself back to his bike.

The backfire the Fortress had started was sucking the wind up the slope, robbing the valley of fuel for the fire on the crest. The brush fire near the trailer would join it.

Zimmer's body was already safe beyond a scar of burned and burning brush.

Still, if planes were dropping napalm—incredible—he didn't want to be anywhere around. Wearily, he tugged the bike erect.

Only then did he see that his right fork was bent almost double, the handlebars twisted and jammed. He heard a rising beat of mismatched engines, stared up.

The Fortress emerged again from the pillar of smoke, so close he could see the pilot's white face.

Shawn screamed and began to wave his arms.

Thirteen

Steamboat Haley had been orbiting at three thousand feet over the eastern flank of Cathedral Peak, ready for his final pass. Snaproll was jiggling beside him, craning over the lowered wing, for a glimpse of the backfire they had already set.

He wished she'd quiet down. He was listening with his better ear for the fire boss, who was still cutting out sporadically on the radio. For he'd thought he'd seen something, pulling up after the drop, that disturbed him.

"Try 'em again," he urged Snaproll.

The twitch in his right arm returned. He hid it by fiddling with the radio.

He steepened the bank, praying nevertheless that Castle would abandon the second salvo. The backfire was burning well. It was a sure-enough fire storm, now, turning the wind on itself, reversing the gale and drawing it toward the west. It was already bending the base of the smoke column away from Santa Barbara and back toward uninhabited hills.

He'd flicked his remaining bomb switches to "ready." To forget, and to fail to release, would be fatal. Air over a forest fire was hot and exhausted, drained of the lift the wings needed, too thin for the props to bite, empty of oxygen for the engines. Rising thermals didn't make up for thin air. If the next half ton of napalm hung on the racks too long, and surprised *Marvin's Mistress* with extra weight as she flew over the flames, they'd sink into Cathedral Peak in a ball of fire that would go down in history.

Snaproll dipped her hand down, pantomiming a bombing run. "He says go!" she shouted.

He heaved the old Fortress into a wingover that nearly blacked him out. He cut back his power, spotted the monastery, lined up with the ridgeline.

Marvin's Mistress settled into her run as if on tracks, bouncing gently. He cleared the monastery by five hundred feet and banked to follow the spine of the ridge.

Snaproll began to chant the height above the terrain, squinting at the ancient radio altimeter. "Five hundred . . . Four hundred . . . Three-fifty . . . Three . . . Lookin' good . . . Mixture rich?"

"Mixture rich," he confirmed, searching the terrain. Ten seconds more, nine, eight, seven . . .

"Two hundred feet . . . One-fifty . . . Trim tabs set?"

He brushed his hand across the elevator tab, holding nose-down trim against the sudden rise she'd make when she dumped her load, but ready for the sickening drop they'd know afterward when he entered the fire zone. "Tabs set," he affirmed.

His drop zone was a half mile ahead. He had a tailwind, twenty knots or more, sucking him into his own fire storm. The plane lurched, settled; he eased back on the yoke. All clear ahead . . .

"Five seconds," he yelled, above the engines. "Four, three, two . . ."

"One hundred feet," he heard Snaproll bark. "Drop, baby, *drop!*"

All at once he stiffened, craning ahead. A tiny figure on the ridgeline, glimpsed through the murk in the dying light, was waving frantically. It dropped to the ground.

"Shit!" he screamed. "Full flaps, gimme high rpm!"

"No! *Drop*, goddamn it!" She was jabbing at his bomb release button on the yoke. He slapped her hand away, dropped the flaps, slammed props and throttle to the fire wall. *Marvin's Mistress* coughed in surprise, shuddered, strained for altitude in the gutless air, engines bellowing and nose high, like a heifer swept toward a waterfall.

She was into it now, sinking under weight she'd not anticipated, tugged toward the blazing mountainside. He groaned. She'd never make it, not over this furnace, with engines gasping for breath and wings flapping in thin, hot thermals . . .

But now she was well past the figure below. He jabbed the bomb release, felt the napalm leave, sensed a great lightening and surge aloft, then a mighty shove upward as the pods exploded in the fire below, heaving them free.

Suddenly he was climbing, banking toward the torch of Cathedral Peak, climbing, climbing, climbing . . .

"Jesus!" he shouted. "She *did* it! She—"

The pain started dead center in his chest, gripping it in a tightening vise. He turned rigid, squeezing the yoke against the agony, no breath, no air . . . He tore at his collar . . .

"Take it!" he grunted.

"Steamboat!" screamed Snaproll.

He felt her take the controls. He caught the smell of burning brush, and passed out.

He awakened once, to the drumming of engines, and the pounding of his heart. He floated downward, a cadet in a bright blue trainer, doing a falling leaf, and, finally, the pain released his chest.

Later, he sensed runway lights flashing by. Snaproll was bringing her in too hot and too high, he wanted to tell her, but it was too late . . .

He was swept again into a sea of black, and could not speak or move, and for a long while that was all.

Fourteen

Shawn Ortega looked down from the jouncing helicopter. Gibraltar Road writhed below. He was enveloped in clammy sweat, now that help had come on the dying wind.

He had thought he'd been drained of fear by the sight of Zimmer's muzzle, pointed squarely at his chest, but the second run of the B-17 had terrified him more; when it had passed without dropping, he'd still been panicky, terrified that it would return. He'd scrambled to his feet, raced downhill for the sanctuary of the monastery, hurtling clumps of cactus on the hillside, jamming his ankle on a rock, slamming the injured knee on a twisted limb in the gathering darkness.

He'd finally got through on the phone to the Sheriff's Department from the monastery, reported Zimmer's death to Perkapek, and demanded a helicopter out of the combat zone. At last a Forest Service chopper had flailed up the canyon and picked him up. The bearded, taciturn pilot was hurried, distracted with a dozen more assignments stacked up, now that the wind had died.

Over Las Pumas Canyon, the pilot pointed down. Las Pumas Estates were smoldering. There was literally nothing left. On the crest above, Wildcat Ridge was dark. Shawn squinted into the murk. It was too black to be certain, but where the main house and stables stood, all seemed finished. He saw a last tongue of flame lick sky-

ward from the dwelling area. It subsided quickly, but he knew
Brink's home had turned to ashes with the rest.

Bull Durham leaned back in his seat on the forestry bus. He kept
his eyes closed as Cubehead bounced down the twisting dirt road toward Wildcat Ridge. To his crew, Bull seemed asleep, and the mur-
murs in which they'd been discussing Booster's "escape" grew louder
and more careless.

Everyone knew where he was: what they didn't know was that
Bull knew too.

At dusk, they'd been hacking bush against the dying fire, while
Bull, like a sentry buffalo, watched the blaze creeping up on the
magnificent estate far below. It was doomed: a damn shame. If
there'd been engines available, or if the estate's swimming pool
pump hadn't, apparently, failed, it could have been saved, for the
winds were slackening fast.

If the crew had been closer, Bull would have given it a shot himself. He might have run a scratchline around it wide enough to frus-
trate the flames. But the place was more than a mile away, and his
crew, cold-trailing the flank of the peak, was exhausted.

He'd nevertheless held binoculars on the ranch for a few minutes.
A long-limbed woman and a broad-shouldered kid coaxed two horses
into a trailer, and a gardener worked uselessly at a water pump by
the swimming pool. Finally, a Mexican maid began to dash from the
main building to the pool, dumping silver trays and serving dishes
into the water.

So, finally, he'd watched the whole millionaire circus below load
into cars and trucks and bolt down the road, between walls of fire.
In ten minutes the flames had jumped the road and the estate was
an inferno. He had put down the glasses, to find that Juan Cortez
was watching, too. It was Juan, probably, who'd spread the word
about the silver in the pool. Waiting for the bus, Bull had heard,
sotto-voce, the soft Chicano phrases: "Plata . . . en agua . . ." and,
scornfully, "Tío Taco . . . estúpido . . ." for the apparently faithful
servants who'd done what they could to save what they could against
their return.

Still, only Booster had split to loot. He'd get picked up, too, probably fencing the silver he dragged from the pool. And everyone in the crew knew it.

"Well," chortled Mother, from somewhere in the rear, "Booster be ridin' the heat when the Man get home. Next fire he don't be havin' that brush hook up *this* mother's ass!"

Don't be so sure, Mother, thought Bull. He'd already lost Dumptruck, who was almost useless. He wasn't about to lose Booster, who was trained, strong, fire-wise, ambitious, and stupidly confident, which was just what you wanted on the line. Allowed to escape, he'd be caught and returned to La Mirada only to be stuck in Upholstery Training, or Automotive Skills, no matter how hard Bull pled for his body. Bull intended to solve the problem now.

He opened his eyes. The bus was at the gate of the estate, almost the only portion of it left above ground level. "Stop here," he told Cubehead.

Cubehead glanced at him, startled, in the light of the dash panels. "*Here?*"

Bull nodded. A silence fell over the bus as he arose, moved to the rear, selected a brush hook. He dropped to the ground, flashlight off. He picked his way around the rubble of the house, to the pool. He could hear sloshing. He waited in the darkness until it stopped, then crept silently to the edge of the patio. He could see Booster sitting in the moonlight silhouetted on a brick barbecue, fingering a chafing dish. He turned on the flashlight.

The blond, bearded face tightened in anger and the green eyes blazed. "Who finked? Mother?"

"What's that?" asked Bull. "Say again?"

"Mother!" spat Booster. "That black sonofabitch! I'll *waste* that motherfucker!"

"No, I just figured you got lost, Booster," said Bull mildly. "And was looking for a phone to report in. And, hey, you talk like that about Mother, I'll make *you* drag shovel." The silver that Booster had salvaged lay on the brick grill, but Bull noticed in the flashlight's beam a crested silver ladle which had dropped under the oven. He stooped to pick it up. The blackened iron door of the oven had twisted in the heat of the fire and was half open. As the beam swept past it, he noticed a safe inside, imbedded in concrete. He flicked off the light quickly, before Booster noticed it.

He wondered what people who trusted their silver to a swimming pool would keep in a safe, but he guessed he'd never know.

"Throw it back in, and let's go."

"Suppose I stay lost?" asked Booster peevishly. He measured Bull speculatively. "Maybe I ain't goin' back?"

"What'd you say?" Bull asked. Idly, he ran his finger along the razor inner surface of the brush hook. He'd demonstrated his skill in training sessions. For ten yards, before age caught up with him, he could outcut even Mother in deep brush. "I didn't catch that, Booster."

"Never mind," Booster said. He began to toss the silver back into the pool.

When it was all returned, and Bull had patted Booster down, he led him to the bus. There was something tickling at his memory. Suddenly he knew what it was.

He remembered Booster's rap sheet. He was not only a second-story burglar, but a tumbler artist as well: he'd done safe-cracking time at Norco, before he'd ever come to La Mirada. He thought of him sitting unwittingly on top of the safe.

Some men were born to lose.

When Bull climbed onto the bus he was laughing, which troubled the crew no end.

But soon they were all asleep. He closed his eyes and pretended to sleep himself.

Jerry Castle hung up the landline phone from the fire status cubicle at Goleta Headquarters to the fire camp on San Marcos Pass.

According to Robert Wendell Holmes—Jesus, that *name*—the dying Santa Ana would not return.

He moved to the enormous map on the wall.

Steamboat Haley had broken the back of the western fire; the eastern front was almost contained. There were thousands of men still knocking down hot spots on the slopes of the Santa Ynez Mountains, but threat to the forest and city was gone.

Statistics would come later, but the taciturn Down Easter from Bangor had estimated that suppression had cost ten million dollars and would reach twelve million before all the vouchers were in.

There were weeks of fiscal and physical mopping-up to do, and it would be months before the Service returned to normal.

Miraculously—if Steamboat Haley survived what was said to be a heart attack—they would have lost only one fire fighter, the inmate from La Mirada. But thirty-three had been injured in a flare-up on Day Two, another two hundred after that during the course of the battle. There were hundreds of civilian casualties, besides: he'd heard a report that three citizens had perished in the hills, fighting for their homes or fighting to get out.

A hundred and seventy thousand acres of Los Padres National Forest watershed had perished, and 30,000 of Santa Barbara County, and 10,000 in the city limits itself.

A contract helitorch chopper had been lost, trying to set another backfire not far from Fire Camp One, before the winds had eased enough. The forester and pilot were OK, already in the emergency room at St. Francis Hospital, which was taking patients again.

Mike Kane stumbled in, unshaven and gaunt. "He'll make it, Jerry. He's out of ICU."

Steamboat Haley, hero of the day, had been in intensive care since Snaproll had landed their monster at Santa Barbara, with no more problem than burned-out brakes on roll-out.

"Thank Christ for *that*," he muttered to Mike. He'd almost had a heart attack himself after landing, when he'd heard there'd been a casualty from the napalm, and again, in relief, when he'd learned that the victim was probably the murderer who'd caused Trout Canyon in the first place.

But the hostage had been rescued and the pyro was dead, and that particular stroke of luck he didn't want to go into now; he could only thank God that the cop hadn't been burned too, and hope that Washington would apprecaite the forest they'd saved and the city they'd rescued and ignore the policies he'd shattered to do it.

The dispatch room was suddenly sickening with smoke and the taste of bad coffee. He moved down the hall to his office and slammed open a window.

Distantly, a siren was warbling. Flare-up, somewhere, nothing to fret over since the wind had died.

According to Holmes, there'd be rain in forty-eight hours.

Warble, warble, warble . . . The sound of the fire truck receded.

When the mess was cleaned up, he was going to Houston, to see his ex-wife.

He had thirty years in federal service, counting the Army.

He just might retire and stay in Houston with her.

The hell with fires, and wars, and the rules men made for fighting them.

Hash Ono slumped, exhausted, at the bar at Derf's. He'd turned the blonde over to her mother and a female deputy at the Santa Barbara Community Hospital, where the deputy had tried to interrogate her, without success.

She had first-degree burns on her fine slim legs and a chipped tooth where the son of a bitch had slammed her, but otherwise seemed physically OK. Psychologically, she was shot. She hadn't said word one all the way down from the hills, along the fire trails, hadn't even flinched when they'd had to speed cross-country to traverse a flaming ridge—and barely made it before a last flare-up set the mountain behind them afire.

Driving home from the hospital, he'd seen the crowd of fire fighters on the patio at Derf's, and he'd stopped in on impulse, knowing he wouldn't sleep anyway, without a beer.

He yawned as he finished it. A huge Navajo Indian he'd known for years slipped onto the stool beside him. The Indian asked if he was still County Arson. Hash nodded. "Well," the Indian said, "that young guy at the end of the bar, moustache? He's a phony. You want another beer?"

Hash shook his head. "Home. Bushed."

"Said once he was CDF Riverside, name's Ned, I heard him tell the girl. But *before,* he said he was Mission Canyon Station, county."

Hash squinted through the smoke. The place was hysterical with tension released and strain too long endured. There were people here who had been in the brush for four solid days, who had seen friends collapse and mates carried out on litters. There were men here who had watched, according to rumor, a homeowner perish screaming on the roof of his house. Now that the fire was beaten, alcohol was wasting the winners.

He studied the young man across the room.

"He's not Mission Canyon," said Hash.

He met the Indian's eyes. They had gone through fire school to-gether, fifteen years ago. Both had heard of impostor firemen, setting fires. "Thanks, Chief," he said. He glanced down the bar, memoriz-ing the young man's face. Well built, weight lifter, perhaps, or surfer . . . Caucasian . . .

Hash went to the john, this time returned to crowd in beside the young man. He glanced down.

Red jogging shoes . . .

Suddenly the man got up. Hash followed him to the door, inter-ested in his vehicle. But he headed on foot for the beach. No car?

The temptation was to catch up, learn his name, talk to him.

But to sniff around now would tear the net before it was woven.

If the impostor hung out at Derf's, it was because he was fas-cinated with fire and fire people; he'd be back. Hash would some-time sneak a picture with the Nikon, somehow, coming or going, in-side or out, for next season's Torchy teams to study.

Tomorrow, or the next day, they said, it would rain. Next summer would come another dry season. If the impostor was the Phantom Jogger, he'd be back with the next desert wind.

For now, he belonged in the file, under N for "Ned" and J for "Jogger."

Whatever he was, and whatever he'd done during *this* Santa Ana, there wasn't a thing you could prove, not now.

Hash left and went home to bed.

They were breaking camp on San Marcos Pass. Button Berger, in the last chow line, observed that the big black cook who had tried to shock her with the fireman story was drained by fatigue into silence. The fire-weather forecaster, who'd homed in on her as if by instinct the moment she arrived, sat next to her at the mess table.

While she played with her sandwich, he talked nonstop about Boise and skiing and cold fronts and winds and the joys of mountain sunsets: John Denver with a Ph.D. Tired as she was, she listened.

Mac was watching her from across the table. She handed him the rest of the sandwich. He was ordinarily a walking garbage can—incredible how he could keep his build—but now he shook his head. His eyes were steady on hers. For almost a year when he had looked at her thus, something inside had slipped, and she had lost her self-image as a rational, trained being and become a stuttering adolescent. Damn!

"Linda staying with your Mom tomorrow?" he asked.

Linda was, and the rest of the week, too, and ordinarily that meant Mac would be with her day and night, if he could lie his way out of hearth and home. She braced herself. She was impelled to hide behind her daughter, but damned if *she'd* lie, for the easy way out.

"Yes, all week."

"You want me to come over? Go over the loss inventory?"

Hal, her youngest fireman, smirked, then looked delicately at the clearing sky. She could have tossed her coffee in his face. "No, Mac."

"We lost fifty feet of hose," he reminded her.

Why *now*, you idiot? she asked him silently. In front of the crew? He had all the way home to screw up her head in private. Did he have to make it a public occasion?

Bragging, to impress Hal and Mitch? But that was unlike him. Besides, they already knew, *everybody* knew, probably, outside of Mac's wife.

No. Staking out a claim, he was, in front of Robert Wendell Holmes.

"I'm going to *sleep*," she said, eyeing him steadily. "For four solid, uninterrupted days."

She could not have said "alone" more clearly if she'd yelled it aloud. That ought to hold the son of a bitch. She left the table and dragged herself back to her truck. Holmes followed, and then he was saying good-by, over a rumble of Diesels starting, backup bells ringing, and bosses yelling directions.

The circus tents were coming down fast.

She sidled to the cabman's side of the seat, to let Mac take the wheel for the long journey home. Holmes's face appeared at her window.

"I didn't ask, do *you* ski, Button?"

She nodded. "But not tonight, OK?"

"I got a reservation at Sun Valley, week after Christmas?" He talked in questions; Mac never did; Mac, on the other hand, had the normal fireman's allotment of one wife and two small sons.

"Good." She yawned. "Ski heil . . ."

"And I wondered?"

Holmes looked tired, too. His eyes were red, but there was a vacant glint of loneliness speaking to her loudly.

She'd bet he'd read *The Ring*.

Mac had read *Jaws* 2, halfway.

Mac climbed in to take the wheel. "This is a fire engine, friend," he told Holmes. "Not a goddamn singles bar." He peered into the rearview mirror to back the rig around. "We're rollin'."

Mac had been her lover, but he wasn't her daddy or her bodyguard, and she was still in charge of the rig. "Hold it!"

She turned to Holmes. "Do you have a number up in Boise, or something?"

His face lit. "BIFSY, weather section. And it's Robert Wendell Holmes? The poet, only Robert?"

"Got room at Sun Valley for a five-year-old daughter?" The crucial question, not that she'd bring her, but it was nice to know how dishonorable his intentions were. "No problem, Robert," she added. "She bunks with me."

The brown eyes dropped. "Love to have her," he lied gamely. "Bring her, sure."

"If I go," she said softly, "I just may."

She rolled up the window and leaned back. Mac cranked the wheel viciously and headed for the road. "Or," he muttered, "you may not."

"Screw you, Mac." She smiled sweetly, and then dropped off to sleep.

Fifteen

Shawn faced the sheriff from across his desk. A KEYT-TV crew was waiting outside the office, and Castillo was anxious to let it in. The sheriff was rednecked-angry, but strangely confident, and his chair seemed amused by it all. It jeered every time he shifted his weight, which was more and more frequently as he fought to keep his voice down.

"Legally, I was off the force," Shawn insisted. He looked at his watch. "That all, Sheriff?"

"No! I know what I had in mind! *You* don't! That suspension was unofficial. It wasn't put in your record, and it lasted—what, three hours? When you apprehended Zimmer, you were a sworn officer!"

Despite his disgust, Shawn felt a tug of joy. He could come back if he wanted. But he couldn't bring himself to agree, not yet.

"I was a civilian, trying to make a citizen's arrest."

"Then that cannon you got in your belt's illegal. Where's your permit?"

"OK, book me. On the air. That'll pull in the ratings."

The light was flashing on the sheriff's intercom. Castillo's chair chortled as he leaned forward to answer. "Yeah?"

Perkapek's voice crackled nervously, insisting that KEYT-TV wanted the interview for its eleven o'clock news. Could he bring them in to the office?

"Tell them yes," grated Shawn. "I got to get home."

If there is a home, he added silently. Castillo studied him. He pressed down the intercom. "No." He got up, moved to the window, yanked up the venetian blinds. The smoke had cleared. He let them drop again.

He swung suddenly back. "Why are you doing this?"

"That 'fat Jap,' as you call him, tracked down the suspect. *He* rescued the victim. All *I* did was back Zimmer in a corner and luck out. And, thanks to you, man, I wasn't even a cop when I did it. So that's what I'm telling them!"

The sheriff's eyes narrowed. "You wouldn't be after that five-grand reward, would you?"

Shawn hadn't even thought of it. As a police officer, he was ineligible; as a citizen, he was a shoo-in. "No. Point that TV crew toward Ono, not me."

"Ono," said the sheriff, "won't want his cover blown. Don't worry about Ono."

He was probably right. They couldn't drag Hash before a camera with a Caterpillar tractor.

The sheriff sighed, looked at him thoughtfully for a moment, and seemed to make a decision. "There's something you don't know, Lieutenant—"

"Mister," insisted Shawn.

"No. 'Lieutenant.' " Castillo was smiling. "Let me tell you something. In two minutes we are going to have a press conference. Now, you can give the Jap all the credit you want. And you can be as modest as you want yourself. But KEYT assumes you were head of the Arson and Explosives Squad when this case was cleared. And you won't tell them anything different."

Shawn looked at him curiously. The son of a bitch had something up his sleeve. "What makes you think you can still jerk me around?" he asked cautiously.

Castillo grinned. "I had a call from St. Francis Hospital."

Shawn felt his fingers go icy. He had been tired enough to drop, but now his mind was racing. "Who from?"

"A doctor. Stewart."

The son of a bitch, in the middle of the worst fire the state had known since 1906, had followed through. "Yeah?" he asked hoarsely.

"Your friend Brink died." The sheriff looked sharply into his eyes. "Did you know that?"

He wouldn't be asking, if the nun hadn't kept her silence. Good. Shawn shook his head.

"Stewart thinks," Castillo rumbled, "somebody put him away. Well, Southerland's *wife* was in there today, and his son. Stewart wants an autopsy."

Shawn shrugged. Careful . . . His mouth was dry and his heart was pounding. Castillo's eyes hadn't left his face; he felt like a mouse in a snake pit. "So what?"

"For forensic purposes."

"He's got to have a reason."

"That's what I told him. And then, all of a sudden, I heard from the widow . . . What's her name?"

"Nicole . . ." He envisioned Stewart's fat face splitting under his fists. He took a deep breath to quiet his pulse.

"Your friend Nicole, she's raising hell. She just got burned out on the ridge, but that doesn't bother her at all. *Autopsy?* Hell, if we try to autopsy, she'll sue the doctor, the hospital, the county, me. *Cremation*, she wants, tomorrow. Says you're going to drop his ashes from his plane— *That* news to you?"

He kept his face blank. "Go on."

"She's overdoing it, shit, she just lost a five-million-dollar estate, and *this* is all that's on her mind? Very dramatic woman, on the phone: wasn't she an actress, or something? Anyway, she's hanging herself by the minute. Hanging herself, or her son, or *somebody*. As your granddaddy would say, she doth protest too much. And threatening! Well nobody's threatening *me!*"

Nicks, Nicks, couldn't you have cooled it, just once?

Castillo sat down again at his desk. "Puts me in a funny spot, coroner-wise," he continued happily. "I don't *have* to order an autopsy: no evidence. On the other hand, why's she trying to scare me off? Suppose that doctor's right?"

Shawn's head was throbbing and his knees were shaking. The anger was welling up, he could not stop: "Suppose he *is?* Jesus Christ, Castillo, he had terminal cancer, it was ripping the poor sonofabitch apart, and he wasn't going to last—"

"*Hold it!*" Castillo barked. "Not another fucking word!"

Shawn turned away, sick to his stomach.

"Holy shit," murmured Castillo, "euthanasia's *still* murder! You're worse than her!"

Shawn heard a drawer open. He turned. His badge and gun were on the edge of the desk. Castillo was looking dead into his eyes. He pressed on the intercom switch: "Send 'em in, Perk." To Shawn, he said: "So, what's *your* advice? Autopsy?" He glanced at the badge. "I mean, if you were *Homicide* again?"

"You prick," Shawn murmured. He fought down laughter. Hysteria, perhaps, from fatigue. He picked up the badge and holstered the gun. Castillo motioned him to join him behind the desk.

"Good man," said the sheriff companionably, "but don't feel you can't resign next week, OK? Quietly? Now, let *me* do the talking. You got a tendency to hog the stage."

He told Shawn to pull over a straight-back typist's seat and leaned back comfortably in the swivel chair, which shrieked for a moment in insane glee and became stone silent when the TV crew entered.

"Sorry, gentlemen," apologized Castillo. "He had to make a full report. Right, Lieutenant?"

"Yes, sir," said Shawn.

Shawn was becomingly silent, the sheriff was modest and spoke of all-out departmental effort, and the half minute on minicam hurt hardly at all.

In five minutes the crew was packing its camera and Shawn was free to look for his home. He conned Transportation into twelve-hour use of a plainclothes car, on the strength of his new departmental image and the loss of his Yamaha on official business. He was pulling from the parking compound when a silver Porsche wheeled into the slot reserved for the department's jeep. It could only be Nicole. He tensed and braked.

She slid from behind the wheel and started for the building. He hopped from the car and cut her off. "Jesus, what are you doing *here?*"

She looked into his face. Her own was expressionless. She inclined her head toward headquarters. "That fat bastard, do you know what he's going to do?"

"I know *you* had him ready to order an autopsy."

Her eyes seemed vacant. "We lost Wildcat Ridge."

"I know. I'm sorry. You said you wouldn't care."

"He loved it, is all, and now it's gone. Val got the horses out."

Hysterical? Too calm. In shock? Maybe, but maybe not. Whatever her state, she was very, very dangerous.

"Good."

She shrugged. "So Wildcat Ridge went down the drain, and Brink loved it, and if they autopsy him you're going down the drain too, and I won't let them, because he loved you, too. Shawn?"

"Yeah?" he asked tightly.

"Brink told me if anything went wrong to see that you didn't get burned."

He doubted that; Brink's whole point had been to keep her clean of it.

"OK," he said. He just wanted her gone: if Castillo wandered out and saw them together, it was rubbing his nose in the dirt. He didn't even want her seen by the boys from KEYT. "I *won't* get burned if you'll get *out* of it. Nicks, I already had to damn near sell him my ass. Why'd you come down here, anyway?"

"To see him. Maybe, for that. Or this, whatever it takes." She shrugged and opened her handbag. It was stuffed with hundred-dollar bills.

His heart began to pound. He slammed her bag shut explosively. "Get in that car and get out of here and don't you get *near* that son of a bitch, or phone him, or answer a single fucking question without your lawyer. You understand? You're *looking* for trouble! This isn't a goddamn TV show! Quit writing the script!"

She flinched as if he'd hit her. Her pupils widened, her mouth went slack, and her eyes filled up with tears. "How can you *say* that, you bastard? When I'm trying to—trying to—"

"Get us in trouble," he said brutally. "Together. And start it up again."

She was suddenly beating his chest, and then she was in his arms and he smelled mesquite in her hair, and her body swayed soft and willowy against his own, and for a moment it was as if sixteen years had never happened.

"It never stopped," she whispered. "Oh, goddamn you, Shawn! Damn you, damn you, *damn* you!"

He fought it, and won, and it was over, and she sensed it. She pulled back and looked into his eyes.

"Until now," she said softly. "Right, Shawnito? Until right this second? Now?"

He nodded. She caught him with a stinging backhand slap, turned, and climbed into the Porsche. He watched her drive from the lot, got in his car, and headed for Eucalyptus Hill Road.

Cristina Ortega noticed suddenly that the wind howling past the cracked window in Casa de la Raza was silent. Almost simultaneously, her migraine left without a trace.

The PA system announced in Spanish that foothill areas north of Salinas Street were opening to traffic, residents only, but that bedding and bunks remained available here for those who had lost their homes.

She gave up her position behind the Red Cross steam table. She drifted through the crowds of children, oldsters, and women. Men were leaving, to look over the situation before returning home with their families. The Christmas tree committee was decorating the huge pine that the Santa Barbara Fiesta Board had donated; it towered over a group of adolescents filling piñatas for the Santa Claus party.

Don Miguel was sipping coffee in a corner, making pronouncements. He was surrounded by the sycophantic crowd of viejos which gathered wherever he lit. Her sketch for the overpass was safely by his side, though turned face-inward so that no one could see it. To think that he had saved it still tightened her throat.

Mamá Lola touched her arm. "¡Shawnito! ¡Fabuloso en la TV!"

"Gracias," she said absently. He *had* been, too, though he'd looked exhausted, and subdued somehow by the sheriff.

She'd waited for him here long enough. She found Mary Lou at a table in the back patio, chomping on a hamburger and fending off a leering cousin from another branch of the Ortega family. The damn fool football swung from her wrist. On impulse, she asked for it. Mary Lou, strangely, unclipped it without protest.

"Keep an eye on el Viejito," Crissy said. "I'm going to see what's left."

Mary Lou stood up. "Hey! It's my house, too!"

"Please," begged Crissy. "Stay?"

Mary Lou seemed all at once five years older, and to understand very well. Crissy weaved through the crowd, crossed the street to the parking lot, joined the traffic heading back to the foothills.

She showed her driver's license to a deputy at a roadblock to prove she wasn't a looter, and started up Eucalyptus Hill Road.

Sixteen

He stood in orange moonlight, one foot on the charred and twisted carcass of the great oak tree, under which they'd always had their Sunday barbecues. To its upper branches, Mary Lou had fled one day when she'd spilled a pack of cigarettes from her school bag, as if he'd ever have laid a hand on her. And, refusing to come down, she had turned his wrath into comedy, which could have been her purpose all along.

The air tonight was pungent with burnt sage, and absolutely still. From further down the canyon a dog howled, at the end of his world.

If any of his neighbors had yet returned, they were as silent with grief as he. The whole of Eucalyptus Hill Road had burned, as if fire, after allowing all the close escapes, had grown tired of the game.

He could never afford to rebuild, even if Crissy agreed.

He wandered through the ashes to the chimney, surrounded by blackened rubble, which was all that remained of the house itself. He found, where the den had been, the skeleton of el Viejito's easy chair, blackened springs hanging out, survivor of Rancho Rojo, now a twisted corpse.

Gone, all gone, with the flowers and the plants, the bougainvillea and the eucalyptus on the lawn.

But the growing things would sprout again from the fire-baked earth, stronger than before.

He looked seaward. The normal ocean breeze had cleared smoke from the Santa Barbara Channel, and he could see the pinpoint light on Anacapa Island winking on the southwestern horizon.

He had loved to watch it from the bedroom window. He would have to sell the land, or the bank would; he wondered who would be watching the light a year from now, for the hills would work their magic and men would forget and the homes, like the brush, would grow again.

Swept by headlights, he turned. Someone had crunched into the ash-strewn driveway. At least he would never have to fix the garage door opener, or clear the brush, or put up Rainbirds.

"Shawn? Shawnito?"

She moved gracefully along their fence line, skirting the creaking mound that had been her home. And suddenly she was in his arms, oval face golden in moonlight. Her eyes were enormous and glistened with tears.

"Shawnito . . . I'm *so* sorry."

He knew instinctively that her headache was over, because her back, under his fingers, was supple and warm. "*I'm* sorry, Crissy." He looked down at the city, sprinkled with moving lights. "We'll live in El Encanto, lower down, or maybe Goleta, closer to work."

"No!"

"Down in the flat, no brush, no hills—"

"We're not *living* anywhere else!" she said fiercely. "We're building again, if I have to hammer nails myself! We're building *here*, and we're building just like it was. *¿Comprendes?*"

Her fingers were tracing the line of his jaw, and he caught a glitter on her wrist. He grabbed her arm. She wore the gold football.

"It's *mine*," she murmured. "I'll leave it to Mary Lou in my will, OK?"

He squeezed her close, looked over her head at the rubble. Maybe, just maybe, they *could* . . .

"Let's find a motel," he said softly. He winced. He'd forgotten. "Damn! Don Miguel! Mary Lou . . ."

"The Casa's a refugee center," she reminded him. "They're refugees. *¿No es verdad?*"

She was right. Tonight, they needed each other, and they needed their sleep.

Tomorrow, he knew suddenly, there'd be cleaning up to do.

He led her through the ashes to her car.

The dog down-canyon quit yelping in fear and began to bay at the rocking-chair moon.

To Shawn it sounded like laughter on the ocean breeze.

Master storyteller **Hank Searls** is the author of the best-selling novels *Jaws 2, Overboard, The Crowded Sky,* and *The Big X.* Born in San Francisco, Mr. Searls still lives in California with his wife.